Praise for *Light to the Hills*

"A bright and vibrant debut. *Light to the Hills* is a touching meditation on motherhood and the importance of community, especially during difficult times. Bonnie Blaylock will be one to watch in the realm of historical fiction."

—Olivia Hawker, bestselling author of *One for the Blackbird,
One for the Crow*

"The packhorse librarians of the 1930s opened up entirely new worlds to people through the power of literature, a power no better showcased than within these pages: the vibrant Appalachians, courageous women, and a moving tale of compassion, justice, and forgiveness. Lush and rich with detail in a setting like no other, Bonnie Blaylock's *Light to the Hills* will transport readers, capturing not only the resilience of those living among the Appalachians but of the lasting and binding magic of stories."

—Gabriella Saab, author of *The Last Checkmate*

"Bonnie Blaylock is a gifted author, and her *Light to the Hills* is an impressive debut. Set in the eastern Kentucky mountains during the Great Depression, Blaylock takes the reader into the lives of an Appalachian rural coal-mining family hit hard by hard times. Blaylock skillfully weaves a grand story of moonshiners, coal miners, tough people, regional language, a beautiful setting, danger, romance, and more than a little humor. The compelling characters in *Light to the Hills* will live with you long after you finish the last page. This is a beautiful novel, and I recommend it heartily!"

—John Carenen, award-winning author of the Thomas O'Shea series
and *Keeping to Himself*

"Bonnie Blaylock's *Light to the Hills* paints a loving, vivid portrait of the families, communities, and landscape of 1930s Appalachia. Its characters endeared themselves to me in their pluck and spirit, their attunement to the natural world, and their fierce love for one another. I wanted to stay immersed in their world."

—Susannah Felts, author of *This Will Go Down on Your Permanent Record* and cofounder of Porch Writers' Collective

Light to the Hills

A NOVEL

BONNIE BLAYLOCK

LAKE UNION
PUBLISHING

Published by Lake Union Publishing, Seattle

www.apub.com

Amazon, the Amazon logo, and Lake Union Publishing are trademarks of Amazon.com, Inc., or its affiliates.

ISBN-13: 9781542039925
ISBN-10: 1542039924

Cover design by Kathleen Lynch/Black Kat Design

Printed in the United States of America

For Sally and Bob, who always believed.

Chapter 1

At dusk, the far stretch of shifting blues and greens where the mist over the mountains met the sky reminded Sass of an ocean or, rather, how she imagined it. People say an ocean never stops moving, that it changes colors depending on the clouds passing by, and that you can get lost just staring at the endless reach of it. It sounded downright lonesome. The eastern Kentucky mountains stretched and reached far off like that, too, as far off as you looked, but to Sass, they also folded you close inside the trees and streams and old, grown-over trails from deer, loggers, and footsteps of the Cherokee who'd lived there first. Sometimes, when she idled long enough to stare, long enough to hear the breeze whisper through the tall hickories like the sigh of a ghost, Sass imagined that the rounded forest ridges of the Appalachian hills moved. Not by some miracle of faith that some people believed could do such a thing but by sheer force of their own will. She swore if she looked just right, she could see those hills push upward, like great shoulders shrugging with a *so it be*, or maybe the kind of give-out sigh her daddy breathed when he crawled up out of those hills of a morning, teeth shining bright in his coal-blackened face.

Today the far-off ridges seemed to lie still, but Sass knew all the busy critters that rustled underneath the trees—deer, turkey, foxes, and bears, even painters, though these she'd never seen, only ever heard them scream like a woman scared to death. *Panthers*, she corrected. The schoolteacher had once pronounced the word, and Sass turned it over in her mouth, whispering it out loud and biting the tip of her tongue on the middle sound—*thuh*. Funny how folks outside the hills said different words but meant the same thing.

Sass didn't have time to lollygag and watch the mountains move today. She was hunting sang so that she could get a birthday present. It was 1936; Sass had just turned twelve, and her mama warranted she had enough sense to keep clear of the snakes in the woods, or if she didn't by now, some fangs might serve her right. A full satchel of ginseng would bring a nice sum, and her mama had said she could pick a piece of birthday candy from the mine store if she found enough. Twelve was a mite big for candy, but she wasn't about to refuse the offer once it came her way. Sweet is sweet, anyhow.

Sass trailed along by herself in Gingko Holler, where the roots of the poplar trees clung for dear life to the steep, rocky slopes. September was schooltime, but there weren't many days she could be spared to walk the miles to school and back, the way her daddy saw it. Tending her little sister and the weeds in the garden were her jobs, the main ones. She hummed along through the undergrowth, snippets of familiar hymns or reels, keeping her eyes peeled for the flashes of red berries beneath five leaves.

Hunting ginseng wasn't the easiest chore. Besides keeping shy of poison ivy and poison oak, it took gentle hands to get the roots out, lifting them free just so or risking leaving some of the treasure behind in the soil. Then, just when the root was safe in the bag and it was time to move on, the berries had to be replanted so that new shoots would come back after a couple of winters.

The warm autumn air hung thick and close as a cloak around her shoulders as Sass knelt at the base of the plants. Her older brother, Finn, had taught her to find and dig the roots when she was just five. It was easy to talk him into a walk in the woods back then, even if he had to hoist her onto his back and tote her most of the way, her small fingers gripping the collar of his shirt. The clear mountain air is good for what ails you, he'd told her, and she'd known even then he was thinking of having to forsake it for the dark, dusty mines the following year, when he'd turn thirteen. More than anything, Sass wished Finn could be free of that burden. Sass dropped the root into her satchel, her fingers smudged with dirt, and cinched the neck of the bag with a satisfied jerk of the twine. That was another thing Finn had shown her: how to make a slipknot that could snug up a bag as quick as a long-eared hare.

Usually lit by shafts of sunlight reaching down through the swaying treetops, the woods dimmed, and Sass squinted to see under the thicker brush. She stopped humming, and without the lilting notes filling her ears, the full quiet of the woods settled like a last breath before sleep came. The noisy black crows that had announced her appearance earlier had shushed their black beaks. Heavy drops of rain splashed against the leaves underfoot, and the wind started to mean business. A brief flash dazzled her eyes, and she caught the movement of a pair of panicked squirrels leaping across the treetops.

"One, two, thr—" Sass counted automatically and quit when the bass crack of thunder shuddered deep inside her. The brewing storm was closer than she'd thought. With one hand, she brushed a strand of sweaty brown hair out of her eyes, and she quickened her steps. She scouted for an oak tree and, finding one nearby, used her sturdy cane pole to stir the leaves at its base. Lucky she spied one in the storm. She stooped to gather a handful of acorns, slipping them into the limp pocket on the front of her thin cotton dress, an assurance, she believed, to ward off being zapped by lightning.

Sass smelled the rain now, the moist tang of the earth as it opened its anxious, thirsty throat. The rain, and something else. The spray of light freckles danced on her nose as it picked up the spicy scent.

"Knew it," she said, marching toward the telltale leaves. "Mitten, oak, and hickory," she recited, already digging out the root of the familiar plant. Her mama would be pleased. She could make some spiced tea or keep it on hand for a salve. It was sassafras, the curious sapling that grew three different-shaped leaves on one tree. She held the unearthed plant in her hand, shifted the strap of her sang bag on her shoulder, and turned toward home, the patter of raindrops faster now.

Sass used larger saplings as handholds to steady herself as she made her way across the slope above the holler. Thunder roared again, and it didn't matter how long since the lightning; the storm was already upon her. The leaves she'd crunched through on the way to the sang patch turned soft and slippery with rain, and more than once, Sass struggled to keep her footing. Home was still a mile or more off. Sass sighed, wishing she could hitch a ride on Finn's back and save herself the trouble of scraping her hands raw. She could hear his voice in her head. *"Whadd'ya think the good Lord gave you legs for?"* he'd tease her if he were here. Sass fixed her eyes on the far end of the slope. Once she got there, the land would level off into a clearing beyond, and she could make a run for it, rain or no.

A sound, and Sass knew before she saw it that she'd come upon a rattler. It sounded like the gourd full of dried beans they gave her sister, Hiccup, to play with when she was a baby. Sass froze midstep, her head swiveling as her eyes swept the leafy ground to find the cunning rascal. Just there to her left, it lay coiled, downslope from where she walked. She clapped and stomped her feet, issuing her own warning she hoped the snake would heed. Its tongue darted in and out of its smiley snake mouth, and she narrowed her eyes at its smug insistence that she step aside.

Sass took two careful steps uphill, trying to give it a wide berth and get back on her way. Her too-tight boots had grown muddy, and the wet leaves gave little traction. She scrabbled, trying to hold on to a branch, a rock, or anything that would let her gain purchase and stay put instead of tumbling downhill into the rocky creek bed below. One more step and she'd be far enough past the snake that she could continue on. Her slipping shoes rained a small avalanche of pebbles and leaves onto the serpent. Hateful thing. It coiled tighter, the rattles whirring like Mama's tambourine by the fire after supper. Sass stretched her right foot forward in slow motion. One more step. Lightning flashed and glinted against the black eyes of the rattler. She raised her cane pole, ready to bring it down upon the serpent's head if it struck.

The crack of a gunshot split the heavy air in the woods, louder than any thunder, and Sass ducked into a crouch, grabbing at the cane pole as it tumbled out of her reach and caught in the brush below. The snake flew backward into the air, the rope of its body a cracked whip uncoiling. Sass jerked her head around, searching uphill for the shooter. She clutched the sang bag to her side. Moonshiners or vagrants from the train would consider her harvest a nice surprise, but she wasn't about to give up on that birthday present just yet.

At the top of the hill stood a tall gray mule the color of the storm clouds that roiled above. Its pale muzzle fairly glowed in the dim light of the woods. Sass squinted as the rider holstered the pistol and held up two empty hands. No moonshiner, then. She drew a breath, and when she glanced down at her feet, her eyes lit on the fresh-dug sassafras sapling lying across her boots. Snatching it up, she hustled the remaining distance across the slope and reached the level path toward home, breathing hard. The rain beat down steady, and her wet dress clung to her chest and skinny legs.

The mule and rider waited above the rise where the path emerged from the woods. It was a woman, but she wore no skirt to ride. She sat astride like a man, with trousers like Sass's daddy. An oil-coated rain slicker draped the woman's back, covering most of the saddle and the bags that fell on either side of the mule's flanks. The mule regarded Sass with a blithe glance, unperturbed by the rain, the shot, and the breathless, wet girl who stared at it with wide eyes the color of winter wheat.

"You all right?" asked the woman. She had a soft, easy voice, almost hard to hear in the downpour. It wasn't the voice Sass expected to come out of the mouth of a lady snake killer.

She nodded, wiping the rainwater out of her eyes. "I coulda managed him," Sass said, brandishing the dripping sassafras sapling.

"That's a fact. But I didn't fancy having to collect you from the bottom of that creek. And Junebug, he would've had something to say about it, too." The woman slapped the mule twice on his neck and peered through the rain-dark woods. "You want to look sharp out here all by yourself. There's some who'd take advantage." Her voice suggested she may have had some experience with such. Sass reckoned that explained the woman's deadeye with the pistol. "You live close? I can give you a ride if you've a mind."

Sass shook her head. What would her daddy say if she were to come riding up the path on the back of a strange mule with an even stranger woman? One gunshot today was a good plenty. "I can manage," she said again. "It ain't far, and I'm already wet." She started down the path and had only trotted several feet before she stopped and whipped around with an audible sigh. The woman had turned the mule—what was his name? Junebug?—after her and followed along behind.

She planted her feet and stood with her hands on her hips. "You need something?" It was queer to see a stranger in these parts, especially riding a mule in a rainstorm. Since the Depression had hit hard, folks poking their noses in this area generally turned out to be revenue dogs hunting stills or vagrants wanting something from the nothing folks had to give. Junebug stopped and snorted, shaking the rain from his eyes and jawing his bit in a patient circle.

"I'm calling on folks in the hills," she said, and Sass had to strain to hear her. "Was hoping I could pay a visit to your house if it's not far. I have some books to share."

"Books?" Sass wasn't sure she'd heard right. "What for?" A sudden memory popped into her head: a rare day sitting by the woodstove in the schoolhouse while the teacher read the class a story. It had been about some old clock and a girl who solved puzzles. Nancy something. The teacher had stopped after a few chapters and promised to finish the story the following week, but Sass hadn't gone back. She'd never found out how the Nancy girl figured out the mystery.

"How 'bout we get along to a nice dry place, and I'll show you? I can help your mama get supper. I brought along some sugar and apples, enough for a pie."

Sass's brows lifted. A birthday pie did sound nice, and Mama was always on about needing an extra pair of hands. Maybe her daddy wouldn't mind so much if this lady had something real to bring instead of a list of I'm-a-needings.

She shrugged. "It's a free country."

Sass quickened her feet, eager to be out of the wet, and the mile home down the creek bed slipped by beneath her in two shakes of a lamb's tail. She kept glancing behind her, and sure enough, the woman and mule trailed, stepping over the ruts and roots in the road without trouble or stumbling. Now and then, the mule snorted, spraying the dripping rain off his muzzle with the force of his breath.

Shaded by the hardwoods surrounding it, Sass's house appeared in the distance, the tentative reach of its crooked split-rail fence marking the yard's perimeter. Woodsmoke wisped from the stacked-stone chimney and hung in a blue fog just under the damp trees, smelling of welcome and warmth. The house was made of mostly hand-hewn logs and a simple plank porch that ringed the square dwelling like starched crinoline. The yard was tidy and sparse, with no adornment besides volunteer wildflowers, yellow ironweed, and witch hazel. In a few places, worn pathways snaked between house and road, house and privy, house and garden. Out back stood a smattering of smaller outbuildings—smokehouse, corncrib, small chicken pen. Two skinny hounds with mottled gray hides and lolling tongues lay draped on the porch beneath one of the small front windows. Immediately, the dogs leaped to their feet, the hair bristling down their backs, baying and hollering a warning to the cabin's inmates. Now that Sass was soaked to the bone, the rain had let off to a sprinkle.

Like twinkling stars in a night sky, a trio of faces appeared at the windows, which were nothing more than shuttered cutouts in the logs to let in air and light. Strips of overused muslin hung on either side and passed for curtains. Sass counted her older sister, fourteen-year-old Fern; her younger brother, ten-year-old Cricket; and the youngest sister, four-year-old Hiccup, her head bobbing up and down as she tried to see over the sill. No sign of Finn or Daddy.

"Hush your racket," Sass yelled to the hounds. "Go on, shush now." At her voice, they stopped baying, and their long tails thumped the porch railings, their hind ends wriggling with delight. Sass glanced back at the woman, still astride her mule. Sass had tried to sound mean, but she couldn't resist the way they nosed her palms while their paws danced all over the tops of her boots.

"This 'un's Digger," she said, pointing to the larger of the two, his gray head broken by a streak of black that ran from the tip of his nose to either ear, like he'd gone snout-first into a mudhole. "And that 'un's Tuck." The smaller dog, gray with four brown-freckled feet, stood with his eyes half-closed in pleasure while Sass absently rubbed his ears. "Once they know you, they ain't mean. Don't pay 'em no nevermind. They might slobber you to death is all."

Sass's mama stepped out onto the porch, and a towheaded wisp of a girl squealed at the sight of Sass and pushed out the door and down the steps. Sass handed her mama the sassafras sapling and absorbed the blow of her sister's embrace.

"This here's Hiccup," she said, laughing. "And now you're wet as I am, silly." Sass busied herself with unsticking her dress from her skin. "And Mama."

The other two children poked their heads around the doorframe and stared, but Sass didn't bother introducing them. The woman stood up in her stirrups, cocked her weight to her left foot, and swung out of the saddle, landing lightly on the muddy ground and shaking out her oil-slicker cloak. Junebug crooked his neck around to her, his ears swiveling. Mama stood with her thin lips pressed together, her hands fingering the root of the plant Sass had given her. She cut her eyes at Sass. Mama could say more with her side-eye in a quick minute than a whole passel of ladies at a quilting bee.

Sass swallowed, and the words tumbled out. "Mama, this here's a lady I met with on the trail. She says she's come visiting and could help you with supper and maybe a pie."

"Pleased to meet you," the woman said, holding out her hand. "Name's Amanda Rye. I don't mean to put you to any trouble, ma'am. I ran into your daughter on my route, and then the rain hit."

Sass tidied Hiccup's damp dress and whispered to her, to avoid her mama's pointed glances.

Mama stepped down to the second porch step, and Sass measured the two of them, now eye to eye. The woman was unusually tall, old as Finn or thereabouts.

"Rai MacInteer," Mama said, offering her hand, her chin tilted up. "Short for Rainelle, but only my mama ever called me that, God rest her. We don't get many visitors up here. Not unless you're kin or coming for tax money."

The book woman shook her head as she drew the reins over Junebug's long ears. "I'm neither. Got a job takin' books to folks in the hills. If you've a mind, I've brought the makings of a pie I can share, and you and your children can look through what I have."

Rai drew herself up tall and brushed the front of her dress with her hand. "You can just turn right around back the way you came. We don't take charity. Lotta folks a lot worse off." Her dark eyes fixed Amanda with a hard stare. Sass didn't envy the woman this attention. They could go without dinner for a week, and her mama would still give a few extra eggs to a neighbor who was going on eight days of hungry. Some days, Sass admitted, she would rather have a bite of pone than an empty stomach full of pride. She held her breath. She'd already been tasting that apple pie in her head, imagining the sweet dissolving on her tongue.

The book woman shook her head. "No," she said, then laughed, likely knowing the absurdity of even offering such a thing. "Of course. This is a new idea from FDR, for folks who live too far out to get to schools. He means to bring books to *them*. A delivery service for news and such, no charge or barter."

Sass had sidled up the front steps with Hiccup. Fern and Cricket made faces from beyond the doorframe, but Sass ignored them. She would answer their questions later. Hiccup's shriek interrupted the conversation. She'd stuck her hand in Sass's pocket and felt something poky.

"Mama," Sass remembered, "during the storm, I found an oak tree and got a mess of akerns." She dug into her pocket and scooped out the handful, sprinkling a few into Hiccup's palms. She moved to the front windowsill and placed the acorns on it in a neat row.

Rai nodded her approval. "That's lucky. Next storm, we won't worry about lightning strikes, then. That's one less thing." She seemed to remember something and turned back to the woman and her mule. "You say you got the innards of a pie with you?"

"I do." The woman nodded. "Apple, with some extra sugar."

Sass caught Fern and Cricket exchanging a glance. With times as lean as they'd been, a surprise like an apple pie—with sugar—was an unexpected delight.

"Cricket, take Miz Amanda's mule to the back and tether him by the barn. Fern, you and Sass wash up and give me a hand. Your daddy and Finn'll be home 'fore too long and will be needing some supper."

Amanda nodded her thanks to the boy and gave a reassuring squeeze to the mule's nose. She removed the saddlebags before Cricket took Junebug around back. She draped them over her arm and followed Rai into the house. Rai tossed the sapling back to Sass before she left the porch. "Strip the root and leaves like I showed you," she said. "I'll put some water on for the tea. Take Hiccup with you to tend the hens 'fore you come in."

Sass breathed a sigh of relief. Maybe the promise of apple pie had saved her from a tongue-lashing for bringing a stranger right to their doorstep. Her daddy was partial to apples. Finn would sure enjoy a slice, too, she thought, her heart dancing at the prospect of bringing a bit of happy into his dark days.

As Amanda passed by Sass, she winked and patted her side. where Sass knew the holstered pistol hung under her loose shawl. She gave Sass the barest shake of her head. *One less worry again,* thought Sass. The book woman wouldn't tell about the snake, and Mama wouldn't have to know Sass had been careless. Miz Amanda, the book woman, had been there less than twenty minutes, and already the load was lifting.

Sass headed for the chicken pen, with Hiccup jabbering away in her ear. Across the path, she spotted Cricket, hands in his pockets, walking back from where he'd tied the mule. Hiccup clamored for Sass to hoist her onto her back, but Sass was tired from her walk through the woods.

"You're too big to tote around. You can walk on your own two feet," Sass said. They scattered a few handfuls of corn for the small flock, and the hens cocked their combed heads and pecked up the grains as Hiccup counted them and stomped her feet.

"Tick! Ticky!" she called, still using her baby word for them, as the hens ignored her. "Tickens!"

Only six eggs. The days were getting shorter. Sass wondered why the sun going down early meant fewer eggs in her pocket when the darkness coming sooner didn't shorten *her* workday any. She gave a half-hearted kick at the hens as she closed the gate to the pen. They scattered with indignant squawks and flying feathers, intent on their corn.

As she turned to make sure her little sister followed her back to the house, the strap of the ginseng bag shifted on Sass's shoulder. She'd forgotten all about the sang, the reason she'd been out in Gingko Holler in the first place. This birthday was shaping up fine. Now she had the promise of a piece of penny candy, maybe a book to look through, and a taste of apple pie, all in the space of a day. If her luck held, maybe the book woman might have brought the story about an old clock and a girl named Nancy.

Chapter 2

Rai's husband wasn't a hard man. Years of toil and lean living marked him on the outside, weathered his face into deep lines and stole the tip of the little finger on his right hand from a worn-out saw at a lumberyard, but the knocks and know-hows of the world hadn't burrowed down inside him like they had in some others. His blue eyes still crinkled at the corners when he played the mandolin, and while he didn't abide shirking chores, he'd still reach out a big paw and jerk Sass's braid every now and then with a wink, or cuff Finn or Cricket on the shoulder for a good day's labor.

Harley MacInteer only set foot outside the eastern Kentucky mountains for one brief turn near Lexington, lured by tales of rich landowners with sleek horses that could run like the devil had them by their tails. There wasn't a horse born that Harley couldn't ride, and his finished colts would no sooner run from a rifle shot than a bag of corn, they were that steady.

Lexington horses, he'd found, were something else altogether. Nervous and hot-tempered, they were bred to run in a circle, fast and long, until their legs gave out. Harley couldn't see the use in that, and the men who lined up to lay their money down for a chance at the spectacle of the race were born fools, in his opinion. All folks wanted from a horse in the hill country was some sense between their ears and the ability to pull a straight furrow when asked. Many of those fancy horse outfits folded after the stock-market crash, scattering the light-footed Thoroughbreds over the state, and their highfalutin owners were in the same fix. So much for the racetrack leading to easy street. In the hills of Kentucky, there wasn't any such address.

Rai poked her head out the door when Harley and Finn stomped up the porch steps. She picked up their lunch pails while they stopped to remove their boots, caked with mud and creased with several years' wear.

"Got a visitor, mind. Supper's ready when y'all are. I 'spect you're hungry doin' hay in between mine shifts."

"What smells so good, Mama? Is that spiced apples?" Finn dropped his boot on the porch with a *thunk*. The two hounds nosed him up and down while he slipped out of the second one, and he nudged and patted their heads good-naturedly.

"Get cleaned up and you can come find out."

Harley ran a hand through his thick hair, standing it on end. Not so many years ago, it had been a shade or two darker, but now, a few years past forty, wiry gray framed his temples. He splashed his hands in a bucket that had been set out on the porch for this purpose and palmed a cake of lye soap to scrub his hands and arms up to his elbows. While he was at it, he splashed cold water on his face and neck, rubbing the salty sheen from his skin. Finished, he tossed the soap to Finn, who caught it in both hands and stepped up to the bucket for his turn. A younger version of his father, at nineteen, Finn was tall and thin, his worn trousers hanging low on the bones of his hips. He was in peak physical shape, muscled and full of beans. His hair was pepper where his daddy's was salt, and he dunked his whole head into the bucket and came up dripping. His eyes squeezed shut, Finn shook his head, standing his hair up in all directions and sending water all over the porch. Digger and Tuck beat a hasty retreat, their nosy enthusiasm doused, and trotted off to flop beneath the chestnut tree near the road.

"Dad-gummit, boy, I just got dried off good." Harley yanked the towel from its nail and went at his face and neck again. "You're no better'n those hounds, the way you shake after a bath."

"It's faster'n a towel, and cleans the porch off, too." Finn caught the towel his daddy tossed to him, gave a cursory pass over his head with it, and threw it against the wall, where it caught on its nail. "Putting up hay is hot and scratchy."

"You got that right." Harley pushed Finn ahead of him into the house. "Least we can get a share of it for the stock come winter. We'll be glad to have it then."

Rai came inside with the men and began bustling around the table, laying plates and pots with Amanda and Fern, while Sass occupied Hiccup off in a corner to keep her out from underfoot. Rai smiled at the spectacle of Finn, with his spiky, dripping hair and the playful way he winked at Sass and poked Hiccup in the ribs. To her, he'd always be half-boy, half-man. He filled his broad chest with a big breath of air.

"Apple pie? How'd you manage that, Mama?" Finn stuck out a still-damp finger to poke the crust and received a swat across the back of his hand. The scrubbing on the front porch had removed the top layer of dirt, but coal work stained Finn's nails a permanent purplish black.

"Supper comes first, and we have a visitor." Rai cut her eyes at the woman, who finished laying plates and smoothed her hair back from her face. "This here's Miz Amanda Rye. She's a book woman workin' for the president. She's the one done brung us this pie."

Finn seemed to notice the young woman for the first time, and he stood taller, his antics forgotten. He wiped his hand across the front of his pants and flashed a shy grin at her. Rai watched his eyes snatch a glance at the woman's hand, where a thin gold band circled her finger. It occurred to her that Amanda was right pretty, wearing pants and a loose blouse and sweater, hair pinned up in a loose knot, and her cheeks all flushed from the heat of the stove. Amanda drew herself up and stuck out her hand.

"Mighty fine to meet you," she said, her voice small but clear. Her reserved smile flashed quick across her lips as Finn clasped her fingers with his right hand and rubbed his scruffy whiskers with his left. In turn, Harley's big paw closed over Amanda's small one and gave it a brief tug. He nodded at her and took a seat at the table, his lips curving into a tentative grin.

"Reckon I'll take apple pie often as I can get it. For the president, now? Long as it ain't that great humanitarian, Mr. Herbert Hoover. Where're you from, Miz Rye?"

Rai hovered over the table, gripping a pot she held with the edge of her apron. She spooned potatoes and onions onto each plate as Harley, Finn, and Cricket sat around the rough, wood-planked table. She motioned for the book woman to sit as a guest, and the remaining chair she would take for herself. Fern and Sass sat cross-legged on the chestnut puncheon floor by the hearth, where they took turns picking over bits of potato with their sister Hiccup, who licked the salt from her fingers after each bite.

Rai waved her hand at them. "Y'all go ahead. Don't wait for me." Fern had drawn water from the well earlier, and Rai set a tin pitcher of it on the table.

"My folks are from up in Big Leatherwood originally," Amanda said. "After they married, they settled in Putney on the Cumberland." Rai lifted a cast-iron skillet from the woodstove and spooned greens seasoned with a little bacon grease alongside the potatoes. Far from her folks, the young woman must have taken up delivering books to make do. Rai hoped Amanda's husband was sharing the load.

By the time the sun went down, Harley was usually so tuckered out he'd fall right to sleep at the supper table. Rai would let him sit there snoring like a snugged-up winter bear while she tidied up and got the children settled. He'd only get in a blessed few hours before she roused him to head back out to the mines for the night shift. Even so, they scraped to keep shoes on little feet and a bit of sugar and coffee in the larder.

Harley wiped a stray bit of greens from his beard. "So, up north of Harlan. Got a cousin or two that direction. You know any MacInteers over thataway?"

Amanda sat with her hands in her lap, and Rai finally got to study her without being rude. She figured Amanda Rye must be some sort of lady, with her dark lashes against her pale-white skin and the way she held her back straight against the cane chair. The same way she rode that big gray mule. Her nose turned up just the slightest bit at the end, and loose strands of brown hair hung in a sweep around her face. She chewed slow, careful bites, like she knew she'd be having another meal in the morning. "We weren't there long, moved around wherever work took my daddy. After I married, we lived in the mine town for a bit before I left for the free town on the far side of Grant's Knob. My boy and I are renting a place with my friend Mooney and her daughter right now."

Harley looked down at his plate, pushing the onions around in the bacon grease. He glanced at Rai before asking the young woman, "Why's that?"

Amanda cleared her throat. "At present, I'm obliged to take what work I can find for my boy and me. My folks—that'd be Jack and Beady Wick—have all they can handle with their church work." Here she paused, casting her eyes on Rai, who'd finally settled at the table and had a mouthful of potatoes. "Lost my husband, Frank, a few years back. He—" She paused, doling out her words in careful measure. Her spine lengthened farther, pressing against the chairback. In her lap, she clearly fidgeted with her hands. "Was out looking for work and got swept away in a flash flood."

"Why, I met Beady Wick at a shucking across the mountain." Rai smiled, hoping to fill the space with her warmth, while her mind tugged at the mention of the name. "Hard worker! She had almost two bushels

done before I's halfway through my one. So you're the Wicks' girl?"
She'd heard whispers about Jack and Beady Wick's daughter, noted the
glances between some of the women at the shucking that afternoon
when talk turned to folks' children. She'd seen one or two sharp nudges,
and the subject had switched to tomatoes. Rai hadn't heard the full
story and wasn't one to pry. It was curious, though, to finally lay eyes
on the girl.

A person's name carried everything. In closed rural communities
like those in the Appalachian hills, a name was a placard identifying
your people and your past and, more often than not, charting your
future. If a person were on this side or that of old Civil War feuds, their
name might toss them into a lifelong brawl that would dog them until
the grave, through no blame of their own. Blood might paint a person
in a line of healers or miners or bootleggers, and good luck breaking
that mold. However carefully parents bestowed a child's given name, it
could be dropped or twisted into all manner of nicknames based on her
personality or looks. But the family name was the thing that clung, the
thing that dragged behind a body on a string of tin cans, announcing
who she was to those who knew—or knew of—her people, no matter
how far she moved or how many times she took another name in marriage. Tenacious as a hound on a treed raccoon, mountain people picked
and dug until they got to the root of a person.

"I should have noticed. You do favor your mama some, now that I
know to look. We been to the Pickins church a time or two and know
a few of the families that live thataway. News did trickle down some
about your misfortune. I was right sorry to hear of it. You know how
folks is to talk. Can't think when we were up there last, but it's been a
good while."

Amanda nodded, and a flush crept up her neck. She appeared to
have trouble swallowing her bite of food. "I don't see my folks much.
My mama's family was hard hit in Paducah after the big flood. Wasn't
much worth saving, but she gets up there now and again. Between the

trips and church work, time is scarce." The clink of forks and plates hushed. Everyone had a tale or two of kin who'd lost everything when the Ohio flooded, as it was prone to do in some areas. Land stayed submerged for weeks, horses and cows tumbling head over hoof in the sweep of water before they succumbed. Even when the waters receded, the silt and scrabble that washed over the already-hardened soil in the west made it almost impossible to grow even a family vegetable garden, never mind produce anything extra to sell or trade. So many people lost life and land that a number of folks in the eastern mountains had long-lost kin showing up on their porches, needing bed and board that were already in short supply.

"It don't matter if you're down to eating possum tail, it does a mama's heart good to see her children." Rai rested a hand over her heart. "My own mama and daddy loved it when we could all get together. Hard times scattered us kids all over creation, and they've since passed on. Sure do wish we could have got together more'n we did."

"Yes ma'am, close families can be a balm, that's certain." Amanda sighed, staring at her hands for a beat too long before she drew a quick breath and spoke, her voice bright. "Long story short, I picked up this route with the WPA, and it brought me to you kind folks this evening."

Finn cleared his throat—he'd developed a raspy cough recently—and Rai cut a sharp glance at her son. If he and Harley were going to get any rest, supper needed finishing. "Slice of pie, Finn? Harley?" Their plates had long since been scraped clean.

Sass hopped up to help, leaving the greasy-faced Hiccup to Fern's minding. "I already put the tea on to boil, Mama. Reckon it's ready to pour." To her daddy, she said, "Found some sassafras this afternoon, so we get both pie and tea to go with it."

When Rai poured Finn's, she added an extra bit from a pot she had steeping on the stove top. "Here's a dose of horehound right quick for that cough while I'm at it."

"Angel of mercy." Finn swigged a mouthful of tea. "And Sass, ain't you Miss Handy-Dandy?" he teased. "Did you find any sang while's you was gally-vantin' all over the mountain?"

Rai and Sass placed thick slices of pie before the boys and Miz Amanda. Fern took hers by the hearth and shared bites with Hiccup, who rubbed her eyes with sticky fists, smearing her face with bits of apple.

"Sure did. Enough to trade for birthday candy if you can stop by the mine store." Sass retrieved her sack from where she'd hung it near the doorway, and she presented it to Finn. "Maybe that pie greased your wheel?"

He took it from her and hefted it up and down. "I declare you might'a found enough for a piece or two, Sassy." Finn paused and scraped the plate clean with a finger. "This right here is a fine piece of pie, Miz Rye." He fixed a steady gaze on the book woman as if to emphasize the compliment.

Rai thought she detected a sudden dip in Finn's voice, a deeper timbre. Must be the cough trying to take hold. Good thing she was keeping on him with that horehound. Harley licked a finger and tapped up the remainder of crumbs on his plate before pushing it back. "That's so. We thank you for sharing it with us. You'll want to be careful riding out alone now, the way folks are drifting in and out nowadays, don't hurt to keep your wits."

"I appreciate that. Thank you for the meal, Miz MacInteer," Amanda said as she rose from her chair. "I know you've more work coming. I'll get out of y'all's hair, but I did want you to pick something from the pack."

"Cricket, run out and untether Miz Rye's mule," Rai directed.

"Yes'm," he chirped. He jumped up and skipped out the door, taking the steps two at a time. His given name was Emmett, but by the time he was two, Cricket seemed to suit him better.

Harley rubbed his beard. "The pie's aplenty, Miz Rye. We won't be needing nothing else now."

"No, no. This is a loan," she said. She rummaged in the saddlebags and laid out a few newspapers and books on the table. "It's the library program, the reason for my visit out this way. Y'all choose something, and next time I'm through here, in two weeks' time, I'll trade it for something different."

"I done told you we don't take no loans." Rai narrowed her eyes.

"No cost, truly. These are hard times for the whole country, with the mining areas 'specially hard hit, but that's no news to you. FDR wants to send books and news to them that can't get to it easy."

"Does he now?" asked Harley. He shook his head and pointed to the spread on the table. "These books he's sending have greenbacks sewn to the pages? That'd be a far sight more helpful if he's going to all the trouble." He shook his head and chuckled low in his throat. "Well, I reckon you girls can pick something to look at if you think you'll have time between your chores."

Amanda picked up each of her offerings in turn. "There's newspapers only about two weeks old. A *Publishers Weekly* from May and June." She stopped to consider, rifling through to find something with pictures that told the story along with the words. What good were words if they didn't speak to you? "How about this one?" She picked up a worn copy of a thin book with rich illustrations. On the front was a young boy and a toy bunny. "It's called *The Velveteen Rabbit*. I think you'll like the story."

Amanda held it out to Fern, who reached out a thin hand to take it, mouthing a soft *thank you* with her eyes on the floor. She smoothed her hand over its cover.

"You gone be all right getting back this evening?" Finn asked.

"I'll be fine. My mule's steady and knows the way home, and now the rain's stopped, we'll make good time. Prob'ly get back not too much after dark."

"You best get started, then." Harley lit the bowl of his pipe and pulled on the stem, small clouds of blue smoke escaping his lips. He lifted a hand in a wave and shuffled to the back corner of the cabin, toward the corded bed with its simple tick mattress filled with rye and feathers.

Outside, at the foot of the steps, Cricket danced in place as he held the book woman's mule by its bridle. Amanda draped her saddlebags behind the saddle and threw her rain slicker once more over her shoulders. Taking the reins from Cricket, she turned the mule's nose so that they were facing back the way they'd come.

"Enjoyed the company," she said, and placing her left boot in the stirrup, she swung up into the saddle in one sweeping motion. "I'll aim to come back thisaway in a couple of weeks, Lord willing and the creeks don't rise."

"I'll put in a good word for the rains to hold off, then," said Finn with a lopsided grin and a wink. "So them creeks won't be a hindrance."

Sass came out and watched Miz Rye go, the mule's ropy tail swishing side to side. Mama also stood on the front porch, a sleepy, too-big Hiccup on one hip, her little sister's head nestling into its accustomed spot just beneath her mama's chin. Sass was already thinking ahead to the next time the book woman came through, what she might have in her library satchel. She hadn't got to ask about the book with the clock. Still, an uneasiness had curled up in Sass's stomach when she'd seen Fern clasp the book to her chest, an unwelcome sourness of being not quite up to snuff, which Sass didn't like one bit.

Amanda pulled up Junebug and turned in her saddle. "Oh, and happy birthday, Sass!" she called with a wave and a smile. The mule tossed his head, impatient to be on his way. Sass leaned into her mama with a sigh as they watched Amanda disappear into the dusky forest. Rai placed a tender hand on Sass's head.

"You're gettin' nigh about as tall as me," she marveled. "Maybe we need to stop havin' birthdays." She rubbed circles on Sass's back. Her hand warmed Sass's still-damp dress.

"What happens when she comes back?" asked Sass.

"I wouldn't be expecting a pie ever' two weeks, if I's you," Rai said with a chuckle.

"No, I mean when she figures out we can't read the books she got." Rai's hand stilled.

"Ain't no shame in that. Lotta folks can't read. It's all fine when you got a full belly, plenty of firewood, and no holes in your roof. Then you got time to figure and study on things. You see any of those things 'round here?"

"I know, Mama."

"Everybody's got their something, Sass. You reading is the same as Miz Rye's husband."

"Could her husband not read either?"

"That's not what I meant. Mind your business, and keep today's worries for today. No need to stockpile 'em for two weeks from now. Get on in and help with the washing up, but be quiet about it. Your daddy's snoring loud enough to wake the dead."

As Sass turned to go in, she scooped a sticky bit of apple from Hiccup's cheek with her finger. She rolled it around gently on her tongue as she headed back into the cabin, savoring the unfamiliar sweetness.

Sass and Fern had dried and stacked the last of the plates and sat side by side on the hearth, their heads bent together over the pages of the book. Cricket sprawled on the floor, one leg splayed in front, the other bent at the knee. He whistled softly as he chipped away at a soft piece of basswood with a sharp pocketknife, turning it over in his hands this way and that. Hiccup snuggled against Mama's chest as she rocked near the window and watched her brood, absently stroking the child's curls. The rocker chirped a steady squeak in a mesmerizing rhythm that drew Hiccup's heavy eyes closed. Over on the corner bed frame, Harley and Finn lay motionless in a deep and mindless sleep.

The two sisters whispered to each other over the pictures as they turned the pages.

"Lookit, Fern, this 'un here is the boy's toy rabbit."

"He's got a whole room full of toys by the looks. Maybe he's a prince and this is his castle."

"Sure enough, but he looks to be sick."

The pictures told the story pretty well but Sass knew there was more to it than what they showed. She glanced at the letters strung together in lines, ran her finger down the page as she'd seen preachers do in the worn Bibles they waved from the pulpit on Sundays. She knew bits of the Bible from memory, and plenty of songs, but could not for the life of her puzzle out how to make the words in her head translate to what lay on these pages. Sass frowned. Books held secrets she wasn't allowed to know. It wasn't fair. She knew other girls her age who could read, had seen them in town as they read the signs in the mine store, and she felt their scoffing eyes land on her like live hot pokers.

Sass rubbed the edge of a page between her fingers. She folded it back and forth in a little triangle and creased it with her thumb while Fern chattered on about the pictures. Her face burned hot. It was suddenly too warm by the hearth. The words on the page swam for a brief minute before she blinked hard. She wouldn't look at the words anymore if they were just going to shame her. It was silly, thinking the book was being deliberately hateful toward her. She knew this couldn't be true—a book couldn't have intentions, but Sass felt it turn spiteful and mean in her lap. Well, Sass could be spiteful, too. She looked Fern in the eye and mumbled something about how soft the rabbit's fur looked while bit by bit, she soundlessly tore the tiny creased corner from the page.

Mama leaned over her husband and shook his shoulder. "Harley," she whispered. "Time to rise." His eyes opened and focused on her face.

"Ayup. Them five miles to the mine ain't gonna get no shorter." He sat up and coughed. Turned around and patted Finn on the leg.

"I've got your dinner pails by the door. And don't forget Sass's bag of sang for the store."

Sass's head popped up from the book at the sound of her name. She smiled. "Find some big diamonds, Daddy."

This was their joke. Nothing but lines of coal streaked the mine walls down deep in the mountains, but Sass had heard them talk about mining for black diamonds when she was younger, and she'd thought they meant for real. Since then, they pretended to count up the diamonds they found on each shift and imagine what they would buy with them when they traded them in. Sass thought they should save for one of the red tractors with a crank handle on the front. She'd seen one in town once, perched on a trailer slated for some other place, another family. It would make plowing and cutting hay go a sight quicker. Finn wanted a fishing pole with a reel and something called a telescope that let you look far off into the sky and study the stars. Cricket and Fern just imagined food, tables of gravy, biscuits, and pork chops, with bread pudding and sweet cake for dessert. Harley voted for a full pantry, a new dress for Rai, and a blood bay horse at least seventeen hands high. As long as they were imagining, why not shoot for the moon?

Cricket sprang up and skipped over to where Finn sat on the bed, pulling on his socks. He held his hand out, palm up, and Cricket deposited a lump of wood, which Finn studied, his brows knitted together.

"Nice job," he said, handing it back. "Next you gotta figure how to make some legs. Crickets got six legs. You gotta make it in your head 'fore you make it in your hands." He thought a minute. "How 'bout using some old chicken wire from the coop? Bend it like legs."

Cricket turned his creation over, nodding. From the way he scrunched his face, he pictured what Finn meant and knew just where to get the wire. He shifted from his left to right foot and grinned at his brother. The wood disappeared into his pocket, and he plopped onto a floor pallet near the hearth. The girls had promised to tell him the rabbit story once they'd puzzled it out.

"Night, Finn," Sass whispered to her brother, mindful of Hiccup breathing heavily on the pallet. "Night, Daddy."

Harley nodded to her as he slipped out the cabin door. The tin dinner pails clanked on the porch as he settled them to pull on his boots. Finn smiled at Sass as he followed his father out.

Sass jumped up and caught Finn by the sleeve before he was not quite out the door. "Sunflowers tonight, Finn," she told him. "A whole acre of 'em."

He winked at her as he let the door close behind him. Since he'd gone to work in the mines, she'd think of the happiest, airiest places she could imagine, someplace filled with sunlight and color, and as she fell asleep, she'd let her mind settle on that picture. If she could bear down and think hard enough, wish it for him strong enough, maybe the image would will itself into Finn's head, too, while he worked in the dark.

Sass opened her palm and stared at the sweaty paper triangle in her hand. The sweet apple pie had begun to sour in her stomach. Pie or no pie, she was beginning to wish she'd never met Miz Amanda Rye on her big gray mule. It would be hard to concentrate on sunflowers when all that danced through Sass's head were rabbits made of velvet.

Chapter 3

At the end of a day's route, Amanda arrived home spent, weary from the ride, the weather, and the images of the poor families that met her at the doorway of each cabin in the hills. Junebug expertly picked his way through the creek beds that served as roads between communities, and he took his job seriously, minding to lift his feet over loose rock so as not to stumble and toss his rider. Amanda shared the mule's diligence, determined to do her best to earn a living for herself and her boy.

By the time she paid for corn for Junebug, small tokens of groceries for those she visited, and necessities for herself and her dear friend and roommate, Mooney, who looked after their children while she was away, not much remained to save for the future. It'd been seven years since the crash on Wall Street, but despite FDR's efforts, the country's Great Depression slogged on in a steady march. Amanda felt a good deal older than her twenty-one years.

Amanda slipped the saddlebags from the mule's back and left them in a heap on the porch. She led the mule behind the cabin to the picket line, where she gave him a firm pat on the neck and tied him with a snug knot. Loosening his saddle, she slid it off onto the crook of her left arm and, with a smooth motion, pulled the bridle off over his ears with her right hand.

"Night, buddy. Tomorrow's a day off. I'll come give you a good brushing in the morning."

In response, the mule lowered his big head and rubbed it against her, up and down, almost knocking her off-balance. Amanda laughed and pushed him away with an elbow. "Enough of that. I'll be covered in mule hair." From her pocket, she pulled a bruised quarter of an apple and offered it to him on her flattened palm, smiling as his nimble lips plucked it up, a reward for bearing her steadily in the rain.

She set the tack on the porch, collected her saddlebags, and opened the front door of the cabin. One long creak of the door's hinges announced her entrance, and Mooney's round face peeped from behind the corner of the stove, where she knelt feeding kindling into the door on its front.

"Look what the cat drug in." Mooney shut the stove's door with a metal clang and stood to wipe her hands on her apron. Though Mooney fancied her nickname came from being a night owl and having to be roused repeatedly in the mornings, Amanda suspected it had more to do with her build. Everything about Mooney was round. Her face, made even rounder by her short, bobbed hair, danced with a ready smile and wide blue eyes. What she lacked in height, the top of her head only reaching Amanda's shoulder, she made up for in girth, her crossed arms resting on the natural shelf between her bosom and hips.

"I *feel* like something the cat drug in," Amanda admitted. "A drowned rat." She hung her oil slicker on a peg by the door and unpacked the saddlebags, making neat stacks of periodicals and books on the table near the stove. She hoped the dampness they'd absorbed on her route would dry out. She turned and started to speak, but Mooney held up a finger.

"'Fore you even ask, Miles is right as rain. S'posed to a' been asleep for an hour, but I bet he's still holding out to see you." Mooney nodded toward the curtain they'd hung between the kitchen and far wall of the cabin, and Amanda reached out to pull it aside. There, on a straw tick pallet on the floor, lay two small curled children, one—a girl—sound asleep, and the other—her Miles—peeking his nose out from beneath the patchwork quilt, his eyes shining in the lantern light. Amanda knelt by his side of the pallet and bent over his small figure.

"You sneaky little mouse," she teased, "what're you doing still awake?"

He reached up for her neck, his arms warm from the bed. "I wanted to wait for you, Mama, to tell you my word for today."

She nodded and whispered, "All right, then, what word did you learn? And then you must close your eyes."

"Misfortunate." Miles pronounced it carefully and beamed at her, proud of remembering such a long one. Amanda's brows rose in surprise.

"My! As many syllables as all your years. And where'd you hear that?" She touched the tip of his nose.

"Them ladies came by bringing baskets for the misfortunate, they said. That's us."

Amanda frowned. He meant the Peepers, as she and Mooney called the local busybodies. "*Those* ladies," she corrected. "Miles, do you know what your word means?" He shook his head against the pillow. "It means miserable, wretched, someone you should pity. Do you feel like any of those things?"

"No, Mama." He sat up and stuck out his chest. "I'm not miserable."

"That's right, Miles. Neither am I. Didn't you have a full tummy before bed tonight? Doesn't Mama have a job? We are not misfortunate, no matter what *those ladies* might say."

"Is it a bad word?"

"No, baby, it's not bad. They just didn't use it right because maybe they don't know all the things we know or live the way we do." Amanda dismissed the ladies with a wave of her hand. "I am *very* fortunate to have you, Miles."

"They said it's 'cause of Daddy." Her son's small brow creased.

Amanda drew a sharp breath. "Did they, now. Well, those ladies can't help who they were born to no more'n you can."

She smiled and kissed his forehead. "Now, go to sleep, and I'll tell you about my travels in the morning."

He nestled down under the quilt once more, his light curls framing his head like a halo. "No snoring or you'll wake up Maisie." She winked at her small son, who giggled and closed his eyes.

As the curtain fell behind Amanda, Mooney held up two hands in the kitchen. "Now 'fore you go saying anything, I was out in the garden when the Peepers came knocking. Maisie'd done let 'em in here 'fore I could hightail it back to the house."

"Maybe we could use a dog," Amanda said, remembering the two hounds that barked and howled on the MacInteers' front porch.

"Need something fiercer than that to turn back the Temperance League. Anyhow, they did leave a basket of biscuits with a slice of honeycomb, so maybe it was worth the price of admission."

Amanda shook her head. "Mooney, you'd open the door to the devil himself for a teaspoon of sorghum."

"And send him off with a kick in the rear after I'd licked my fingers clean." Mooney stood with her hands on her hips and such a look of indignation on her face that Amanda couldn't stifle her laughter. She helped herself to a biscuit smeared with honey before slipping into her nightdress and blowing out the lantern.

As she lay dozing beneath the quilt, the muscles in her legs at last easing, the day replayed itself in Amanda's head. She heard the pistol report as she shot the snake and recalled the easy laughter of Sass's brother Finn, who had kind eyes. If wishing were enough to erase her time with Frank, her life might've played out differently. Miles's soft snores carried across the room, and gratitude welled in her heart. She wouldn't trade the boy. No matter what Frank might've cost her—her safety, her reputation, her family. Frank and that barnacle Gripp Jessup who'd been attached to his side every living minute. Bile rose in her throat at the thought of him, even after so much time had passed.

Her father's words echoed in her head as her eyes grew heavy. "Your mama and I made a good life together," he'd told her. "Beady is more than a man deserves in this lifetime, and I hoped for as much for you."

Amanda laughed bitterly to herself and turned over in the bed. She fell asleep finally, bone-tired. She dreamed of the MacInteers paging through *The Velveteen Rabbit* and, in a confluence of her subconscious, of Hiccup and Miles chasing chickens through the yard.

Chapter 4

Riding the rails made for an easy transfer if a feller wanted a quick jump on an opportunity. Gripp Jessup had availed himself of the L&N boxcars more than once when opportunity came knocking. Usually, after he'd milked a place dry, he didn't bother stopping by a second time, but something about the mining town at the base of Pickins drew him like a bee to honeysuckle. Mainly, he knew for a fact prime spots for stills lay untapped up the mountain, and he was itching to get there and get to work.

Gripp's looks had changed since he'd been there last. He'd chipped a front tooth (never mind how), grown his beard out, and gained a scar over one eye. He was like an old tomcat who took his beatings and kept on the prowl. Then there was the matter of his hand, which had taken some time but he'd finally gotten used to. All he had to do was keep an eye out, and sooner or later, the right feller would come along to set up an enterprise. If he was lucky, he might find a willing woman somewhere in the mountains who'd lend him a bed, although mostly he'd found they were more trouble than they warranted. All except his mama, who was only a ghost and hardly counted.

Gripp Jessup did know his mama, they told him, at least that first year after he was born, though he had no memory of it and certainly no picture. He imagined he'd heard her sing and felt her cool hand smooth the cowlick on the crown of his head like a reflex. She'd probably bent down to hold his raised hands as he teetered his first wobbly steps across the cabin floor. He'd walked early, his pa had told him, because the world knew he was meant to make his own way sooner than most.

When Gripp's mama took ill, his daddy started beating the bushes for some help. Nola was the first woman who'd shown up on the doorstep before the pine box had had time to settle in the earth. She carried over poke sallet and a stewed rabbit, and that was possum on the stump as far as Jay Jessup was concerned. It wasn't long before Gripp shared a bed, head to toe, with two other littl'uns, who kicked and shoved him to where the quilt didn't quite reach.

Folks jawed about Nola being a good woman and how his daddy was lucky to have chanced on her. She was certainly good to her boys, but apparently, Nola didn't consider Gripp a bud on her particular family tree. He was the oldest, she preached, so he should learn to share, shoulder more of the work, and give his brothers a break. If any of these things had earned him favor, that might have been one thing, but all Gripp ever garnered was scorn and sharp words. Children were women's concern, and Gripp reckoned his daddy'd rather have curves and warmth in bed with him on a cold night than a coddled son who couldn't take some briars.

Gripp kept out of Nola's way. As he saw it, she was colder than a witch's tit and twice as sour. The only things she loved were her two boys and a flea-bitten hound dog that lived under the porch and followed her everywhere. Many a time he'd be fixing fences or chopping wood and glance at the house to see her kicked back in a chair, cooing and petting on that hound.

Gripp learned two things from his time in that house: that jealousy could cling like ivy and that he had a knack for storytelling. When his brothers were small and left in his care, the only way to stop their constant torment was to tell tales. Gripp could weave a web. He could make those boys sit stiller than a church mouse while he concocted stories, and he had no idea where they came from, just bubbling up from some word factory that pumped them out on demand. A gift, maybe, from his long-dead mama, trying to send him some comfort in the world.

Gripp's fairy tales turned to exaggerations, untruths, and straight-out whoppers just because he could. And why not? A lie was a gamble that could land him a gain, and Gripp had about as strong a taste for gambling as for biscuits and gravy. It was all in how you told it, just enough truth to sink the hook and reel them in. But he couldn't fool Nola; she had his number.

"Boy, don't piss on my leg and tell me it's raining," she'd scold, clamping her fingers on his shoulder till he thought his bones might break.

Gripp sat back from the edge of the boxcar as the rhythmic clack-clack-clack of the wheels against iron track lulled him into a half doze. The landscape had changed since Memphis, flat fields finally rising into hills. Gripp had been restless to get a move on. He'd taken up with a young blonde thing, who'd put him in mind of a girl he'd been sweet on once. He scratched his beard as he thought about it.

Gripp had wheedled his way into the Sutton family and started courting Rebecca. He was this close to asking Rebecca's daddy for permission to get married when he'd run up on Jay and Nola Jessup talking to Mr. Sutton and his daughter near the schoolhouse. Gripp had watched as Rebecca blinked hard, her long, dark lashes trying their darndest to hold back tears, the tip of her lightly freckled nose turning pink. Jay and Nola seemed not to notice. They'd been too focused on Rebecca's daddy, his hands thrust deep in his trouser pockets. His mouth was clamped tight beneath his bushy mustache, cheeks blotched with spots of red.

Nola laughed gaily as she lobbed stone after stone, her hand resting lightly on Gripp's daddy's arm. "Gripp? *My* Gripp?" His stomach had twisted at the hint of ownership. When had she ever treated him as hers? "Why, he's so poor he can hardly pay attention!"

"Racehorse?" his daddy had said. "If the Jessups had links to any racehorse people, I reckon I'd know of it. That boy's so dumb he could throw hisself on the ground and miss." The joke, Gripp saw, was him.

A cold fog of loneliness had lowered itself into Gripp's gut, one Gripp reckoned had never quite burned off. He was meant for bigger things, better things than a country lawyer's daughter and being the butt of his own family's joke. A foul, sour taste rose in his mouth and he spit into the dust. His own daddy had made a fool of him without missing a beat. Gripp didn't need to be told twice.

Before he hopped a train for the first time that afternoon, Gripp headed back to the only home he'd ever known. He could still picture the scene in his mind's eye, clear as a bell. The last of the morning's fire smoldered in the hearth, unraveling in a thin ribbon of smoke up the stone chimney, and the cast-iron skillet hung on a hook over the stove. By the door, his daddy's empty work boots flopped open, and Nola's extra dress hung on a row of pegs alongside a pair of chambray shirts she'd recently stitched for his brothers. Gripp found nothing that belonged to him alone; it was as if he were already gone.

He mashed a hat down on his head and knotted up a sheet bundled with one of the chambray shirts, the little bit of money he had, and his daddy's filled lunch pail. He caught sight of his daddy's pistol where it rested on its shelf near the door. Might as well take his inheritance now. Not much chance of any leavings on down the road. A leather pouch of hand-filled bullets hung beside it, and he tossed that inside the sheet, too.

"Don't mind if I do," Gripp mumbled. "Since you're offering." Nola's sneering words echoed through Gripp's head: *"If that boy had an idea, it'd die of loneliness."* He snugged up a rope around Nola's hound's neck and decided he'd bring him along. Might be worth trading for a meal along the way. The whistle of the distant train drifted across the mountain ridge like the call of a lonely owl.

Gripp still took grim satisfaction in imagining Nola's face when she came home to find the dog gone. He'd waited far too long to light out from that place. Now, here he was again, back on the rails, riding to the next adventure. Smug pride painted the semblance of a smile on his lips.

The train slowed, and sure enough, Gripp recognized the station in the distance from when he'd been here last. It apparently hadn't changed as much as he had. Gripp shook his head, thinking of his partner and how the whole business had gone south.

He'd met Frank Rye riding the L&N, same as him. Right off, he'd figured Frank for a decent partner—he was strong, kept his nose out of people's business, wasn't too straitlaced. The man was clearly putting distance between him and some matter he'd rather forget, so they had that, at least, in common. Together they'd worked a beauty of a scheme that ended with Frank losing their take on a horse race. After that, Frank wouldn't go within a mile of a track, and Gripp kept a ledger to make sure Frank paid him every penny he'd wagered.

But wouldn't you know, on the road into the next town, Frank'd fallen for a preacher's daughter, and Gripp's plans for debt payment and a ready-made business partner threatened to crumble like cornbread. Briefly, it crossed his mind that Frank's wife might still be around, but what trouble could she cause? Nothing a man's hand couldn't fix.

He bargained on needing some help in setting up an operation again. If he kept his eyes peeled, he'd likely find a feller down on his luck enough to cast in with him. He hiked up his pants and got ready to jump.

Chapter 5

Sass woke to the clang of the cast-iron skillet against the stove top. That'd be Mama, up with the birds, tinkering with breakfast. She rubbed her eyes and turned her head to the right, where Hiccup, two fingers tangled in her hair, lay between her and Fern. Cricket was somewhere on Fern's other side, likely twisted in the quilt to gain purchase for a few more inches of its warmth. With Sass and Cricket being on the ends, Fern said they tugged back and forth on the quilt so much that she and Hiccup might just go up in flames like sticks of kindling.

This morning, Sass let the covers go and slipped out of bed to the kitchen. She made a quick trip to the privy outside and stopped to pick a handful of Queen Anne's lace on her way back, with a sprig of yarrow for a touch of yellow. A fat red-tailed hawk perched on a far hickory limb, and Sass caught its movement as it preened its speckled breast in the morning sun. Since they'd cut hay, there'd be more than a few hawks about, chasing field mice and rabbits now that their cover was laid bare. She glanced at the chicken pen, where, for now, the hens seemed safe from the big bird.

"That pretties the place up right nice," said Rai when she saw Sass's fistful of wildflowers. "I set a jar on the table already. Saw you picking 'em through the window." The smell of fried potatoes and onions already filled the small cabin, and Sass scooted into a chair at the table to wait for her share. The book woman's book lay on the table in front of her, and she stole the chance to study it without the others' chatter and interruptions.

She looked at the pictures for clues. There was a boy, his toy rabbit, and a big toy horse that looked old and worn. Her eyes trailed aimlessly over the words, some short, some long, all a puzzle she couldn't solve. Only one letter Sass recognized—it was curved like a snake, and she remembered her mama drawing it in the dirt once in the garden.

"That there's an *s*, Sass," Mama had told her. "It looks like a snake and sounds like one. *Ssss.* You say your name thataway." But that was all she could remember and, as far as she knew, all her mama could tell her. Keeping a cabin in the mountains didn't much call for book knowledge. As long as you could cipher a few numbers to know your wages at the mine or the lumberyard, as long as you could make change at the store for supplies and maybe trade folks what you grew or made with your own hands, people got along all right.

Stories came from corn shuckings or hog killings, from setting up at a neighbor's wake or helping a new mama with the young'uns. Side-splitting tall tales and sobering remembrances of hardship and loss were spun 'round the fire of an evening, sometimes with a guitar or mandolin chiming in. Now and then, on a special occasion or a particularly fine day, you might make it to the church on the slope over in Pickins to hear a tale or two from the Good Book. All the rest was memory. Recipes, songs, nursery rhymes, family history, and knowledge of signs or tokens. It all came from words told over and over until they stuck fast in the head and heart and became easy as breathing.

Sass spotted one *s*, then another, and another. She practiced looking for them like they were real snakes, like the one that hid in the leaves near the sang patch. Each time she saw one, she whispered its sound, *sss*, under her breath, until it sounded like a whole nest of serpents hid beneath the kitchen table.

"What're you up to, girl?" asked Rai. She placed a steaming bowl before her daughter. "Sounds like you done sprung a slow leak."

"Nothing, Mama. Just playing. These taters smell good."

As if on cue, three tousled children tumbled out from behind the curtain partition and scooted into chairs at the table. Sass slapped the cover of the book closed and cleared her place to make room for the others. Mama bent down and lifted Hiccup to settle her in her lap. Plenty of years from being a baby, Hiccup still managed to get coddled like one.

"Good morning, Glory!" Rai said. "Did you have sweet dreams?" Hiccup nodded sleepily while Cricket and Fern dug into their breakfast. "Tell Mama all about them. Cricket, when you finish up, the goats need milking."

"Yes'm." Cricket yawned with a mouthful of potatoes, then slumped in his chair. Mornings were the only time he wasn't bright-eyed and bushy-tailed.

"Fern, you and Sass can go find me a poke or two of berries if there's any left the birds ain't got. Hawk's been scouting outside this morning, so we should put some limbs atop the chicken pen just in case he gets tired o' mice and takes a mind for some easy supper."

The girls nodded. It was a good thing Sass had nabbed a chance to sit a minute before the day got started. Once Rai's gumption got going, the chores were endless. The sun was already full in the kitchen window.

"Where's Finn and Daddy?" asked Sass.

"They must have had some holdup in the mine. Lord willing, they'll be here 'fore long."

Sass studied her mama's face, and despite her calm, a current of worry tugged at Sass's insides. A holdup could mean lots of things, many of them unthinkable. Likely, a horse went lame or they lingered to talk to one or another of the men on the next crew going in. Sass couldn't remember if she'd dreamed of sunflowers last night or not. She'd meant to. She screwed up her face and thought of a whole field of them, their black faces with yellow petals swaying in the bright sun.

She hoped her breaking a promise didn't cause something dire to happen. Thinking of the biggest, brightest flowers now surely would make up for it.

The morning wore on, with no sign of the men. Cricket milked the goats and gave them a handful of corn, Sass tended the hens, and Fern drew water and collected some dandelion greens to soak and boil for supper. The girls headed out into the woods where a patch of wild gooseberries grew to gather a poke or two, as Mama had asked. The birds and other creatures had picked the bushes nearly clean, and it took almost an hour of picking carefully underneath leaves and back into the thickest patches of brambles to fill their empty mason jar with the small green fruit.

They dillydallied on the way back, knowing once they were within range of Rai's sight, she'd dream up other chores for them to do. It was a fine day, and Sass dreaded the thought of sitting bent over inside, piecing a quilt or mending someone's overalls. Fern was much more of a homebody, but Sass preferred the outdoors, wading in creeks and climbing the rocks and ridges behind their cabin. She chanced upon lots of treasures this way—buckeyes for her daddy to keep in his pocket for his rheumatism, black walnuts and hedge apples, flat stones perfect for skipping on the creek, or wildflower seeds she'd wrap in a kerchief and save for planting later around the front yard.

She and Fern chatted and sang on the way home, trading opinions on which kind of pie each liked best and what kind of boy they expected to marry someday. Fern had many more ideas about this than Sass had.

"Boys just give you more work to do once you get growed," said Sass. "Mama hardly ever sits down to rest."

"Don't you want someone to be sweet on you? Someone who thinks you're pretty?"

"Daddy and Finn think I'm pretty." Sass made a face. "'Sides, sounds like a lot of bother and fuss. I'd rather go fishing."

Fern laughed in that superior way she had that made Sass yearn to yank her sister's braid backward. She ignored her and marched on toward home.

"I think Finn might like to be sweet on Miz Amanda Rye," Fern offered.

Sass stopped walking. "The book woman? You're crazier'n a starved squirrel. She's too old for him anyhow. Got a young'un."

"That don't make her old," Fern teased. "I heard her tell Mama she was only twenty-one. That's just two years on Finn. Plus, didn't you see the way he was stealing looks at her at dinner?"

Sass rolled her eyes. "Jus' 'cause *you* want to act like a heifer in heat don't mean everybody else sees things the same. Finn don't even know her."

Fern smirked at Sass and flounced down the hill. Their cabin was just ahead through the trees. "Don't have to know her to fancy her. We can just ask him, I guess."

They both stopped short and looked at each other when the cabin came into view. A wagon sat out front with a thin chestnut horse in its traces. Several men stood around it, their faces and arms still black from their shift in the coal mine. Even from this distance away, the whites of their eyes jumped out of their faces like they'd been painted on.

Sass and Fern ran, not caring if the thorns along the path tore at their arms and legs, leaving bloodied scratches. They felt none of the sting. Sass could hardly breathe. A great fist had a hold of her heart as she ran. Was it even still beating? Was it Finn? Or Daddy? Or no, Lord, no, both of them?

As they entered the clearing where the cabin stood, they slowed, taking in the grim faces of the miners. Digger and Tuck turned in circles near the steps, tails tucked and eyes wary, prophets of bad things to come. Sass's heart sunk further and she gasped for breath, gripping Fern's hand as they climbed the porch steps. It was too dim to see inside the cabin after they'd been outside in the sun. She looked around frantically, willing her wide eyes to adjust, tears streaking her sweaty, flushed cheeks. Their chests heaved beneath their cotton dresses.

Mama put a hand on each of their shoulders. "Girls," she said, her voice steady and calm. "I'm gonna need you to mind Hiccup for a while. Seems there was a cave-in, and your brother's gonna need some doctoring."

Finn. Fern took Hiccup and sat with her by the hearth while Sass walked her leaden feet to the pallet in the corner. Harley crouched in a chair by the bedside, his arm in a sling and his face as smudged as the others' outside. Finn lay on the bed. His eyes were closed, and his left leg was bandaged from the knee down. The dressing was thick, but blood still seeped through, darkening the bandages, which bore black smudges of fingerprints from the hands that had carried him into the house.

"He'll be all right," Harley said. His voice sounded scratched and hoarse from coal dust and, Sass imagined, plenty of hollering. "Doctor said he's seen a lot worse, and Finn's strong. He's a tough 'un—you should have seen him in there. Doc done give him something to sleep."

Sass nodded at her daddy, wanting to believe him. "Your arm?" she started. Harley waved her off.

"This ain't nothing. Just a little banged up is all."

Sass knelt beside the pallet and held Finn's filthy hand, limp and cold in hers, though his hair was plastered to his head by the sweat beading on his brows. He labored to breathe, unaware of her or anyone else in the close room. Sass shook. She knew it, knew when they weren't home by morning, that something bad had happened. She'd been so distracted by the book woman's visit that she hadn't held those sunflowers in her mind.

She got the water bucket from the kitchen and gathered a couple of clean rags. Rai saw her intention and lifted the bucket from her hands. Together they knelt beside the pallet where her brother lay, dipped the rags into the water, and little by little, scrubbed the coal from his neck, face, and arms while he lay still. It took four buckets of water to get the job done. No sooner had they dirtied one than Cricket had drawn another from the well. Once Finn was clean, his face looked starkly pale against the pillow.

Mama emptied the bucket and started heating more water on the stove.

"Harley, your turn next. I'm fixing to scrub the memory of this clean out of here. Go tell those men thank you very much for carrying y'all home. Now we're just gonna sit tight and pray for healing."

In the corner, Sass picked up Finn's filthy shirt and the sack he used for toting their lunch pails. The men must have tossed it there when they'd carried him inside. She'd get some creek water and wash the shirt tomorrow, hang it on the line so that it smelled of the outside once it dried in the sun. Something remained in the bottom of the sack. Sass reached her arm in and pulled out a small parcel wrapped in wax paper. She let the sack drop at her feet as she unwrapped the square. Four sticks of red-and-white-striped peppermint candies. Sass's throat tightened as she realized what she held. He'd traded her sang at the mercantile and remembered to bring back her birthday candy, enough for her, Fern, Cricket, and Hiccup.

Pa's good hand rested on her shoulder. "He traded for that before the shift started. Wanted to be sure we got it in case the store was closed when we got through."

"I don't want it," she said, hastily rewrapping the parcel and handing it to her father.

He frowned at her. "Now, then, if Finn here went to all the trouble to remember it and make the trade, I reckon he'd take offense if you just cast it aside."

Sass shook her head just the same. The thought of sucking on the sweet mint now made bile rise in her throat.

"I'll keep it for later," Mama said. "For a happier day." She took the crinkled paper and stuck it deep inside a jar she kept on the shelf above the stove, tightening the lid for extra measure.

Sass drifted out to the front porch, where she sank onto the top step, her legs suddenly weary. The unfamiliar bustle around the cabin—pots steaming with rags and the low murmur of voices laced with concern and worry—made her breathless, her heart beating furiously inside her chest. Immediately, Digger and Tuck sidled up to her, whining and thumping their tails. They pushed their noses under her hands, shameless bids for attention. Sass pulled them in close, comforted by their warmth, and laid her head on Tuck's shoulder. As she sat listening to the tree frogs' evening chorus, a memory floated into Sass's head.

Once, in the woods, she'd followed a solitary bee lighting from flower to flower, in a path only it could see, until it led her to its hive in an old hollow gum tree. She'd told her pa about it, and he made her take him there the following day. After studying the tree for a bit, he'd lit the end of a gum stob and blew it out, leaving it to smolder. He'd wrapped both their hands in kerchiefs and had given Sass a wide cotton satchel to hold open near the tree.

Pa had pulled his pipe from the front pocket on his overalls, filled it with tobacco, and lit it between his lips, pulling deeply on the pipe stem until puffs of blue smoke had circled his head. Pipe in his teeth, he'd brandished the smoldering stob and stuck it inside the hollow gum, right up the gullet of the busy entrance where the bees buzzed in and out.

He'd told Sass to stand still and sing. "Sing?"

"Keeps you and me both calm," Pa had explained. "Pick something cheery."

So she'd sung. She got through "Oh My Darling, Clementine," "Amazing Grace," and "Down in the Valley" while Pa puffed and cut chunks of comb out of the tree with his pocketknife. He'd shaken the bees from each piece and lowered them carefully into Sass's sack, and her voice had never wavered, even when the tone of the bees' buzz went up in pitch as they realized thieves lurked at their door. Only once or twice she'd heard her father curse when an angry stinger found its mark.

The louder they buzzed, the more Pa had puffed, the sweet-smelling tobacco crackling as it burned.

He didn't rob them dry. Better to leave them some to winter on so that they'd stay put for another visit. When he'd judged they'd taken enough, he'd snugged the mouth of the sack shut, rubbed the smoldering stob out in the dirt, and gave Sass the signal to back away slowly.

"I went down in the valley to pray," she'd sung, *"studying 'bout that good ol' way. Oh, who shall wear the starry crown? Good Lord, show me the way."* Her small voice had mingled with the bees' music like they'd made their own choir in the middle of a secret woodland church.

When she and Pa had gotten far enough away that the bees left off chasing, he'd knocked the tobacco out of his pipe bowl and, for several seconds, pressed a pinch of it against the angry red spots where he'd been stung. He laid his big hand on top of Sass's head.

"I declare, Sassy, I think you done bewitched them bees with your singing. They prob'ly thought there was a' angel come to visit their little tree house."

The thought struck her now that Finn's injury was much worse than an upset beehive, and they could all use a means to keep calm. She cleared her throat, trying to ease the lump that stuck there, and opened her mouth to sing for Finn.

Chapter 6

In the past week since the cave-in, Rai had taken to sitting in the rocker on the front porch after supper. The rhythmic to-and-fro motion calmed her nerves, and the sounds of the forest at dusk brought to mind happier times, when the children were younger and her biggest worry about Finn was getting him to wash behind his ears. Now, Rai smoothed the corner of her apron, damp from her hastily dried tears over thinking of her oldest boy being crippled from mine work. Since he'd been big enough to walk, Finn had loved the outside, even at nighttime. She'd made Harley put a lock on the cabin door way up high where the boy couldn't reach, for fear he'd wake in the night and toddle into the woods alone. Somehow he'd known, even as a young'un, that outside dark was different than cave dark, something he wanted no part of.

Up in the thickets and caverns of the mountains, night falls as a thick wool blanket over everything. Mountain dark is sweet. Breezes blow with a clean smell, especially when there's rain on the way. The forests release an organic smell of life, new sprouts of sassafras and privet, flowering laurel, and the damp layers of leaves and fallen logs, mushrooms sprinkled across their tops like freckles on a young girl's nose. The trees sway above, their leaves rustling and dancing in the summer, pine needles and the evergreen cedars swishing when it's cold.

Under those mountains, there's another dark altogether. In the coal mines, chipped and hacked and blown apart until their passages reach down into the heart of the mountains, the darkness is a cruel, live thing. At first it sidles up like a sly cat, and no matter how sternly you cast it off, it brushes around your legs and shoulders. Past a certain depth, it starts to mean business. It closes around a person like climbing inside a grave hole. That kind of dark has no sweet smells, no breezes. The reliable sun never reaches its rays into the hidey-holes and corners under all that rock.

By the time Rai's oldest son had turned thirteen, the Depression had dug in its heels and decided to stay awhile. The operation near Pickins, Kentucky, managed to stay afloat, with eager laborers a dime a dozen. A ton of loaded coal earned roughly thirty-one cents, and a hard twelve hours might buy some flour, seeds, or sugar. Harley had been in and out of the mines since he was Finn's age, as had his father before him, God rest him. It was honest work if you had two good hands, a strong back, and a healthy dose of pluck. Another wage earner in the house could give them a boost, see them through another winter.

Rai had watched Finn like a hawk as the time inched closer when he would have to go with his father to do his part. The last few months before his birthday, he'd milked the daylight from the open sky each day, lingering over chores and fishing down in the creek until it was so dark Rai wondered whether he could see to bait his hook. He'd let on to Rai that if he thought about it too much, his chest tightened up, like it was practicing for the time when he wouldn't be able to draw a clear breath. She knew he was afraid, plain and simple.

"That just means you got a lick of sense 'tween your ears," Harley had told him. "It's them that ain't afraid that you want to watch out for."

Rai had hardly been able to get Finn to eat much since the cave-in, and the less he was apt to eat, the lower her spirits sank. It was bad enough Harley had to go. Four days in, he swore his arm hardly gave him any pain, but she knew that was just words to ease her worry. Every time he'd kiss her as he headed off, Rai's stomach clenched with concern. Harley was a grown man with a family to support. He could make his own choices. But Finn—her firstborn, the boy she'd carried and cared for—Rai was crushed thinking she'd almost sacrificed him for, what? Sugar and shoes?

At least Finn had submitted to her doctoring. Despite doing her best to keep his crushed leg clean and wrapped, it didn't look good. She'd tried packing the wound with spiderwebs, chimney soot and lard, and even pine resin. She made teas of sassafras and powders from lady's slipper, which she mixed with water and fed to Finn three times a day to strengthen his blood. She'd tried killing the infection by applying turpentine and sugar; nothing seemed to help. He even allowed her to bathe him, as she was accustomed to doing for Harley.

Since the day Harley first started in the mines, when he'd return home at the end of his shifts, Rai would have a tin washtub filled with warm water set up in the middle of the room and a bar of lye soap ready. Harley would strip to the waist, his overalls hanging loose over his knees as he sat in a chair and bent over the tub. Rai rubbed and scrubbed her husband's back, arms, and head, the water running black off him while he told stories of the men on his crew. Rai knew he did it to make it seem familiar, easier for the day Finn would join him.

"Hambone and Stinkbug usually work on the hauling crew; they're newer. Then there's Stove Pipe and Rooster with me on the blasting line."

'Most every miner had a nickname pinned on them if they stayed around long enough. "Why Stove Pipe, Daddy? Why Rooster?" Sass asked.

"Stove Pipe been working in the mines so long he's got a crook in his back like a pipe joint going out the roof, and Rooster's right proud of hisself. He thinks the sun comes up just to hear him crow."

"Can you see anything down there? Is it like midnight in a cave?" Sass had asked. She voiced the questions her brother left unasked.

"They give us headlights we wear on our caps and lanterns, and there's lights on the walls ever' so many feet."

"How do you find your way?"

"Well, now, there's marks along the way, air vents and such sometimes. You just get along and follow the feller in front of you. There's a heap of folks here and there, doing their own jobs. You ain't never far from a body. Or, if you're working the ponies, they know the place by heart."

One morning, Harley had come home carrying a case covered by an old piece of shirt cloth. He'd waved away Rai's bar of soap and set the curious box on the table. Harley had whipped off the cloth like a performing magician to reveal a small yellow-and-gray bird about the size of a common sparrow.

"This here's what they call a canary," Harley had explained. "Up in the main office, there's little stacked rows of these here cages, maybe ten or twelve, ever' one with a wee bird in it. Each time a crew goes in for a shift, we take one of these critters with us. Feller we call Beaker makes sure they're all good to go."

"Down into the mine?" Finn frowned. "They must not like it much."

Harley had shrugged. "Don't seem to mind it. Sometimes they even whistle and tweet a bit. They're friendly little buggers, but this one here's got a busted wing. Clumsy feller dropped the cage, and he must have got jostled. You'd be doing ol' Beaker a favor to look after him till he gets mended."

"Why do you take them in the mine, Daddy?" Fern had asked.

Harley scratched his beard. "Well, see, sometimes when you hit a vein of coal and chip away at the rock, stuff from inside the ground leaks out, what'cha call monoxide. You can't see it, and it don't smell like much, 'specially with a snoot full o' coal dust. Well, these chirpy fellers let you know right quick if there's gas floating around in the tunnels, so you can hightail it out for some fresh air."

"How do they?" Fern pressed. "Do they sing?"

Harley had backed himself into a tight spot. "Now, they might do," he allowed. "But that monoxide, well, it kindly makes 'em weak in the knees, and they might faint away real quiet-like. If you see a sight like that, you head outside. Pretty soon, the canary, he mostly gets okay again. He gets a breath of fresh air and it's like a' Easter morning resurrection."

Rai had watched Finn soak in that information. She knew common sense told him that if a bird got knocked out by monoxide, then a grown man might, too. No getting around it—if a man wanted to eat, he had to work.

The memory of Finn peering somberly inside that canary's cage tore at Rai's heart. Back and forth she rocked, the porch's floorboards bearing the brunt of her anguish, until the sounds of the girls getting ready for bed drew her back to the present. She heaved herself up and went inside.

Chapter 7

At the beginning of each week, Amanda saddled up Junebug and rode the five miles to the county seat to visit the library headquarters for her particular circuit. In good weather, it was a fine ride, but when it turned windy and cold, her feet sometimes felt iced over by the time she arrived at the snug building. To complete her route, she had to stop there first to pick up materials that the book women circulated around the communities.

"Works Progress Administration" was spelled out in careful lettering on a sign posted on the front. When she'd first applied, Amanda didn't know what the WPA was for, just that it offered jobs for women, which were scarce as hen's teeth but needed desperately. The government was finally realizing that the country was in an all-hands-on-deck situation, and women had the wits to step up. She'd walked in that day in her best cotton dress and worn shoes, her hair pinned up in what she hoped looked like some sort of style. She hadn't had a mirror in a good while, so her hands had to work from memory. She and Mooney had just found the little house to rent in the free town and moved their few belongings in the previous day, and Amanda's first task had been to look for a real job.

Amanda had almost run into the tidy woman in a knee-length skirt and a blouse with its sleeves rolled up. She'd been reading something just inside the building's door. Her friendly face and open smile made Amanda release the breath she hadn't realized she'd been holding.

"Good morning." The woman took off her wire-rimmed glasses. "Can I help you?"

"I hear the WPA has jobs?" Amanda noticed the warble in her voice and thought of Miles waiting at home with Mooney. Her next words were firmer. "I'm here to apply for whatever you have."

The woman nodded. "Of course," she'd said. "My name is Dinah Linden. We do have some openings in health services or perhaps some sewing projects over in Harlan and Leatherwood. If you're looking for something closer—"

"Yes, closer would be best."

"Then we have some packhorse librarian routes still available. Forgive me, I have to ask—are you able to read?"

"Yes," Amanda said. "I've gone all the way through the eighth grade. I'm sorry, *what kind* of librarian did you say?"

"Packhorse." Noting Amanda's surprised expression, Dinah hurried on. "It's not always a horse. In Louisiana they actually deliver through the marshes on flatboats, but here in the mountains, we find it's best to get through the creek beds and trails with horses and mules. Do you have one?"

The woman continued, "You don't have to. Some women lease one for cost plus feed. You'd just have to deduct that from your wages."

The word had jolted Amanda out of her surprised confusion. "Yes, wages. How much would that be, exactly?" Her palms were sweating. How did men talk through these things?

"Twenty-eight dollars a month. You can pick up your wages in cash at this office. We don't do script or other credit like the mines."

Twenty-eight dollars! That was more than she'd seen in the months since Frank had gone. Rent was ten dollars a month, so with the garden they intended to keep and money Mooney took in from washing and sewing, she thought they could get by. She had her mule, Junebug, that she'd had since she was a girl. She'd helped raise him from a colt, and she was a good rider. Junebug was about the only thing she'd insisted on bringing with her down the mountain when she got married. That plucky gray mule always seemed able to read her mood, and he certainly ended up being more of a steady companion than a lot of people she could name. Her heart had lifted, and for a moment, the cloud of despair that she'd felt for so long had lifted with it. Amanda had swallowed and pretended to consider for a moment rather than pouncing on the chance in breathless desperation.

"I think that would do, yes. How do I sign up?"

It had been a simple matter of registering her name and address at the office. The job was a delivery service, she'd learned. She'd start with a collection of books and magazines chosen from the few hundred that were kept there at the office. They had everything from novels to children's poems to Sunday-school bulletins and magazines like *Western Story Magazine*. These were donated by individuals or discarded by other wealthier urban libraries that considered them too worn-out.

Worn-out was just a state of mind to the folks in this part of the country. Worn-out just meant it hadn't fallen completely apart yet, so it still had some good use to it. Amanda and the other five packhorse librarians for the area met at the WPA office every week or so to mend the materials and try to keep them clean and usable. She found the other women nice enough, and it was pleasant to spend an evening now and then talking about the folks on their routes or trading news with each other.

There were Celia and Rue, sisters who lived on Straight Road and who seemed to be kin to 'most every soul on their side of the mountain or at least know them and their families as neighbors. Thalia and Esther were raising kids by themselves, like her, and tended to keep to their jobs and not linger for tea or chatter. Finally, there was Alice, the youngest of them, who could talk the ears off an elephant and saw the job as more of a social outlet than a means of delivering literature.

Most of them lived in the free town, like she did, or near enough. They'd each start at the office on Monday and head out two or three times a week, taking a different eighteen-mile route each day and repeating the process every two weeks. On the first and third Tuesdays,

Amanda delivered to three separate communities, a loose term for a handful of houses that followed the natural bend and flow of a creek bed or fence line.

On the first and third Wednesdays, she headed north toward the edge of their county, passing abandoned mines and the house of a weathered old woman named Miz Hettie, who looked to be in her eighties but could just as easily have been decades younger and work-worn. Her features favored the little corn-husk dolls many mountain children counted as toys. Sometimes Amanda's was the only face she'd seen since the last time she'd ridden through, so Amanda took extra time at her house, joining her for a cup of chicory coffee and reading passages to her from the Bible, her only request. In return, Miz Hettie would sit in her cane chair and teach Amanda about the different herbs and tinctures that lay on every open surface, musing about which ones were good for this or that ailment, which ones needed to be dosed with tea, and which parts of a plant to avoid.

"Miz Hettie, you ought to keep a record of all this," Amanda told her, sweeping her hand around the room. "I don't know how you keep it all inside your head."

"Reckon when I'm gone, folks'll find 'em another healer just as good." She spat a long stream of tobacco into the dust and worked her toothless gums around the wad in her mouth.

"I doubt that." Amanda laughed. "I'd say you're rare as a shiny new penny."

With that, Amanda persuaded Miz Hettie to agree to let her spend at least some of every visit writing down remedies and recipes. They would press dried leaves or stems and affix them to pages of a notebook, where Amanda recorded Miz Hettie's prescriptions. Amanda called it *Miz Hettie's Complete Catalog of Cures*, which made the old woman clap her hands.

"Now that's a fine title," Hettie proclaimed. "Real dignified."

The second and fourth Thursdays brought Amanda to a school-house where the teacher, Vessel McCann, taught fifteen students in the fall and spring, providing they could get there. So many were transient, dragged around by their parents to wherever they could eat and stay warm, that the students were often completely different between visits.

Amanda had become good friends with Vessel. A rare bird, Vessel had lived as far away as Louisville, stayed in school, and earned a teaching certificate. Her husband had brought her back east to his family's land, where she'd been touched by the people who lived here, poor but resourceful, determined, and proud. If idle hands were the devil's workshop, he was out of a job where Vessel was concerned. She'd managed to secure funding for the small school by writing to her people back home in the city, and with no children of her own, she labored tirelessly with the pupils who could make it to school.

Amanda and Vessel shared their lunch pails on Thursdays while the children gathered wood for the stove or swept out the schoolhouse. The two shared a love of words and learning as well, having had the luxury of finishing school and being raised in families that knew education could lift a person like a bird in flight. Coming from beyond the mountains knit them together in another way as well. They would always be "outsiders" in a sense, no matter how long they planted gardens or weathered winters in these mountains. If they hadn't already been living here since the Revolutionary War, they were newcomers and would always remain so. They'd always have to work a bit harder to prove their mettle and their trustworthiness to the people who had sprung as seeds from the mountain soil.

Fridays brought Amanda's last route for the week. Over those eighteen miles, she'd visit two farmhouses and meet one lone woman where Jag Leg crossed Muddy Road. Someone several miles down the left fork of the Jag Leg creek bed had heard tell of the woman who came through carting books and news, and every other week, Maude Harris walked six miles to meet the woman on her way, creating her own book stop. The first time Amanda came upon her alongside the dusty path, Junebug's ears swiveled forward, curious about the wiry woman who sat strumming a banjo while she waited. Now, Maude met the mule with a nibble of cane sugar and a pat on the neck. She sat on a fallen log near the path, plucking strings or whittling to pass the time until she could trade the week's books for the next batch. Amanda never met the folks down Maude's road—it would've carried her too far off her regular route—but Maude brought her stories of how this or that one had enjoyed a particular book or magazine.

It was on the second-Thursday route that she met the MacInteers because of Sass and the rattlesnake. While she always made time to visit and chat, she didn't make a habit of eating meals with the families. They already had hardship enough, and a regular extra mouth would wear out her welcome. She had received the makings for the apple pie from her friend and had been on her way home when she'd run into Sass in that downpour. They weren't that far off her regular route, close enough that she calculated she could put a visit to their house on her schedule. And Mooney hadn't known about the pie. Amanda had felt a pang of guilt sharing it without her, but Vessel was always bringing things to share; there'd be other pies.

Rai had seemed kind, and Harley, too, for that matter. Sass reminded Amanda of herself at that age, full of moxie. She had to laugh at Sass's indignant confidence, standing there in the rain with her hands on her hips. Amusing, yes, but not to be underestimated, that one! She didn't have to use her imagination to puzzle out how the girl had been labeled with her nickname.

Inside the WPA office, the others were already there, sorting through stacks of pamphlets and books. When Amanda walked in, Alice was in mid-chatter, and Thalia, her chosen audience for the day, glanced up as the door opened, perhaps hoping it would pause Alice's nonstop tumble of words.

"Oh, Amanda!" Alice turned. Amanda caught Thalia and Esther fastening their satchels while Alice was distracted. As soon as they could manage it, they'd beat a hasty retreat and be on their way. Amanda sighed and emptied her bag onto the table. She had several that needed repair. No matter how she cautioned them to take care, her readers insisted on "thummin'" the pages or turning the edges down to mark them. With so many hands on each copy, it didn't take long before the brittle pages tore.

"Nice to see you, Alice. How's the route?"

"Well, I was just coming 'round to telling Thalia and Esther 'bout a scare I had on the trail two days ago. It was pert near dark, and I was getting along home after stopping by the Martins' and Jeb Morrison's place. You know how you gotta go in that patch of woods, there, jus' before you come on out by where the railroad runs."

Amanda nodded, although she had no idea. Even after months of living here, the crooked paths and roads in and out of hollers often seemed to twist in a confusing maze. She carried a rough map with her on her travels, one she embellished with her own crudely drawn land-marks and other notes to help her keep her bearings.

"I was just coming out of those woods, riding Turnip, you see, singing to myself and not thinking a thing about it, like any other day. Course, why should I? Ever'body down there knows me and Turnip. Why, you can see his black-and-white spots from a mile off, and if he thinks he might get a snack from somewheres, he'll set up a'braying and hollering like it's the end times."

"And what happened?" asked Amanda. Alice and her mule Turnip were peas in a pod. They both had to be constantly reined in and hushed. Amanda worked steadily through the pile on the table. At least while Alice talked, her hands kept at her task.

"The train was just coming through right at that very moment, and it sent up a whistle so loud I near jumped out of my skin. At that exact minute, right outta the brush come these three fellers, a'grinning like they just won a jackpot."

Amanda stopped mending the page she'd been working on. "Land sakes, Alice."

She nodded, her eyes wide and her long red braid bobbing on her shoulder. "One of 'em grabbed at Turnip's bridle, another'n came up behind me by my saddlebag, and the other'n stood right in front o' me, like he didn't aim to let me get by." Even Thalia and Esther had paused by the door to hear more. The sisters, Celia and Rue, had stopped work long ago and sat at the end of the table, hanging on Alice's every word.

"Well, I ain't been borned yesterday, and if that train whistle hadn't blasted, I would have heard 'em sooner and had my wits about me. Guess they'd jumped from that train and seen me right off. Thought they'd pick up a good mule and who knows what all."

The women exchanged glances around the table. Of course they'd all thought about it. It was one of the things about the job Miz Dinah Linden had cautioned them all about, the long, lonely rides through the countryside, where a person might not meet another body for miles, where trains carried down-on-their-luck souls from place to place and good men bootlegged their way into territorial feuds and run-ins with the law. The mountains hid plenty of danger.

"Quick as a wink, I jerked my pistol outta my boot. That's where I keep it, case I meet up with the wrong end of a panther or bear. Them fellers don't know, but Turnip, he's not real fond of getting crowded up on, on account of he used to work with the pit ponies. He stayed down there two days 'fore they figgered he weren't nowhere near fit for that work. He'd stand in them tunnels just a'shivering and shaking—couldn't wait to get back up to the surface. Last load he hauled, the minute they got his last car hooked on good, he took off for the top, hooves flying like he been struck by lightning. He run over two fellers on his way out, put 'em out o' work for weeks, and busted up the cars along the way. That was that for ol' Turnip. He likes wide-open spaces outside."

"Alice! How did you get away?" Thalia found herself drawn back into her audience.

"Yes, what did you do?" Celia had clasped her younger sister's hand.

"Some people look at a mule and think *stubborn*, but I know better." Alice tapped a finger into her blouse. "My Turnip, he swung his rear to the left one and let go with both feet, knocked that feller clear into the underbrush, a'moaning and carrying on. That caused the other two to rush up right under Turnip's nose. Ol' Turnip, he was figgering he was fixing to get caught to go back down in the mines. Ain't no men been able to touch him since them days, but he's gentle as a lamb with me. I'm hanging on to the reins, my pistol, and my saddle horn to keep from flying off his back, and he takes a plug outta one feller's arm, just grabs him by his shoulder like a snapping turtle and won't let go.

"He's hollering for the other one to help him. Screaming like to wake the dead. Turnip's just a'shaking him like a rag doll. His shirt's all torn, and I can see where Turnip's teeth has made a nice bruise already. You ever look real careful at the way a horse bites a' apple?"

"Alice, for goodness' sake," said Amanda.

"'Bout that time I get my seat back and have my pistol cocked and aimed right at this third feller, who right about now has decided maybe it weren't such a good ideer to make a grab for this particular mule. He backs off and puts his hands up, one of 'em shy a coupl'a fingers. Yammering some nonsense about how he didn't mean nothing, the sorry sumbitch. I could see in his dirty-dog face that he for certain meant *something*, all right. He had a smile that made the hair rise up on the back o' my neck. I told them to get back on that train 'fore it got clean outta sight and make their way right back into the pit they crawled out of."

"You didn't," said Thalia.

"I did, most certainly," Alice exclaimed. "My heart was hammering so hard I thought it'd beat right outta my chest. That third feller, he had the nerve to pretend to tip his hat at me with that greasy smile on his face. Makes my cheeks burn just thinking about it. Turnip dropped the one feller finally, and he got his legs under him where he could run off. Then we lit out of there like a blue streak. I never did look back."

"You're lucky you weren't . . . hurt," breathed Amanda.

"Just goes to show, you gotta keep your eyes peeled out there, ladies. Some poor devils will even take from those who don't got much to start with. Lowest of the low, if you ask me. Might be smart to vary your routes now and again, so don't nobody get too used to you coming along the same way."

"Do you think so?" Thalia asked. "I do pass by a spot or two where there's tell of a still along the way. I haven't seen anything, and if you ain't the law, they tend to let you be."

"Wouldn't hurt none," said Alice. "And keep your gun handy. If you did happen to have to shoot one or two of these fellers, I don't reckon the world would miss much turning for it. Ain't no words in the world"— she patted her satchel—"worth the price they wanted." Her head turned toward the window. "Oh, looky, I was hoping to catch Jeremiah coming back from the lumberyard, and there he goes." She pinched her cheeks for color and flashed them a quick smile. "Y'all have a nice day, now."

Alice took her week's satchel and left. They all heard her boots clomping down the front steps, leaving an extra measure of quiet in the office.

"Well, now," Amanda said, "that was a right fair warning, I s'pose."

"Reckon some people can't bear up anymore," said Esther. "Want changes them."

Amanda wasn't as quick to offer excuses. "There's all kinds of folks on our routes who want for things. It's still a person's choice that says what they'll stoop to. Far as I can see, it's just giving in to meanness to make 'em prey on others. We ought to tell the law what happened, so they'll keep an eye out."

"That's Alice's business. Reckon if she don't report it, she's got reasons," Esther replied.

Amanda didn't want to stir the pot. She was the newest member of their crew, and jobs didn't fall out of the sky every day. She'd keep her pistol oiled for certain. Of all the things Alice had told them, it was her description of the man she'd aimed at that set Amanda on edge. *A smile that made the hair rise up on her neck.* What kind of man smiles at the business end of a pistol? She could only think of one.

Chapter 8

Among the faithful and those who remembered the Good Book (only a scattered few could actually read it), some remnant remained who considered the mountains God's country, a place set apart for plucky and hardworking servants. A faith that can move mountains is only as big as a tiny mustard seed, they said. A faith bigger than that could track a deer in the snow for miles if it meant meat through the winter. Such a faith could grant children, turn sinners, and mend what was broken.

Sass reckoned that's what Mama counted on when she hitched their mare to the buck wagon and loaded the four children into the back of it. Digger and Tuck trotted behind for a time, tails wagging, before eventually giving up and circling back to the cabin. A nap on the porch probably seemed like a better prospect than the effort of a trek through the mountains. Her daddy stayed behind with Finn so that he could keep the fire going and the lanterns lit. Finn's nightmares were worse when the cabin was too dark. It was a daylong haul to the pinewood church over in Pickins, and to get there and back before it got too dark to see their way, they had to start before daylight. Mama had wanted Finn to come, too, thought maybe a laying on of hands might convince the Lord they meant business, but he slept most of the days away, sweating and moaning in the bed.

It had been nine days since the mine accident. That meant nine days minus a wage earner. Nine days that turned Mama into a knot of worry, spending every spare second sitting near Finn as he mewled as weak as a kitten. Fern found chores to do outside, even carrying a lantern on the porch at dusk to piece a quilt rather than sit cooped up inside with Finn's misery. Cricket kept busy with nervous energy, running back and forth to the corncrib for feed, stacking wood, or jigging frogs for a supper of frog legs and greens. When it got too dark, he sat on the hearth and whittled whatever piece of wood he'd chosen that day. Within the space of a week, he had a fox, a raccoon, and a family of rabbits lined up on the stone for Hiccup to play with. Usually Finn judged Cricket's creations and made suggestions for the next ones, but lately he wouldn't rouse long enough to show interest.

Sass hunted and gathered. She'd take Hiccup on long walks with her outside the cabin, mainly to get out in the fresh air and take her mind off her mama's worried face and her brother's pale one. She chatted to keep the quiet away and pointed out things she'd learned when she'd followed Finn around this same way.

"Looky here, Hiccup, this is a sassafras tree. It's got the same name as me. See the leaves?" She made her little sister smell the root and point at the three different leaves. "My real true name—the one the midwife wrote in the Bible—is Susanna Lee. But you wouldn't never know me by that. Mama says I used to flit from one thing to the next like a firefly, couldn't make up my mind where to land, but Daddy said I'm like a sassafras tree. Too many good things to try, so why settle on just one? Sassafras has options. It can be lots of things all at once."

"Three leaves," Hiccup recited. "Sass-frass."

Sass would bring home things Finn could get a whiff of—pine or cedar, a pail of cold creek water, mint or wild thyme from the garden, a comb of honey. If only there were a way to bottle the wind as it blew through the hardwoods, or the sun that rose slow and pale in the gray sky. If she could, she would scale a pin oak and catch that breeze in her pocket if it would bring back the old merry Finn. Instead, she brought turkey feathers and smooth stones, a tortoise shell and the claw of a crawdad. She snapped cottonwood twigs to reveal the secret star hidden inside to remind him of the clear night sky. If he was asleep, she'd line up the treasures on top of the log cabin quilt he lay under so they'd be there as a comfort when he woke.

Today, though, there would be no gathering walks with Hiccup. Today they bounced and jostled together in the small wagon as it wound its way down their mountain, through the rocky creek beds, and along the narrow bridle path across the next ridge. Sass couldn't remember the last time they'd all gone to a regular church building. Likely, it would've been after a winter's thaw, when the preacher was called on to do all the saved-up winter weddings and funerals all at once. It was a far piece to travel and a day's work lost to make the trip, so they usually fashioned their own church with prayers and stories and songs around the hearth or beneath the trees.

"I see Pickins's Nose." Cricket pointed through the trees.

"Cricket," Mama chastened. "That'll do."

From a certain viewpoint on the mountain, Pickins's Ridge looked like a man's profile. The church and its simple steeple covered in vines protruded from the slope at a most uncanny spot to look like the man's nose, christening it with the unfortunate nickname. Sass idly watched the patches of sun grow between the trees as if some giant hand turned up the kerosene to light the path. A red fox watched them ford a creek, frozen with one paw lifted and water dripping from its chin. Though they couldn't see them, a flock of geese flew somewhere beyond the trees, calling and honking to each other on their way to some water hole.

About midmorning, their wagon creaked and jounced its way into a clearing, and Mama tugged Plain Jane's reins. The MacInteers sat up from where they'd been slumped in the wagon and surveyed the building before them. Pickins's Holiness Church of the Risen Savior was a square pinewood structure with two steps leading up to the front door. The planks had been whitewashed, giving the church an obvious contrived gloss that stood out from the browns and greens of the under-brush. Its shingled roof was overrun with moss, and there was a brush pile of drying ivy that had been tossed toward the back of the site. The clingy, brown climbing roots it had left behind were peppered all over one side of the building. A single square window looked out from each of its flat sides, enough to let in light and air. Along the outside, sleepy horses and mules stood tied to posts and rails set for that purpose. When the newcomers arrived in the clearing, some of the horses swiv-eled their ears and nickered a welcome.

The church was silent save for a pair of nesting crows that surveyed the spot from their vantage point high above. They sent up a racket of caws like they were sentries for the anointed, heralding the entrance of goats among sheep. Mama was unbothered. She tied Plain Jane's reins to an open space on a post while the children climbed and jumped down from the wagon. They were unusually quiet. Even Cricket stood in a line with his sisters and waited for a cue from their mama as to what came next. *Nervous as a long-tailed cat in a room full of rocking cheers.* That's how Finn would've described them had he been there.

Mama smoothed her hair, knotted at the nape of her neck, and gave them all a cursory once-over. She licked her thumb and rubbed at a smudge on Cricket's cheek while he scrunched his face in protest.

"That's it, then." Mama marched up the front steps, her shoes echo-ing off the wood. She raised a fist to knock, but just as she pulled her arm back, the door burst open.

"Oh!" she cried, stepping backward into Fern and Sass, who jostled back into Cricket, who, with only one foot on the bottom step at the time, lost his balance and landed in the dust. "Oh!" Mama cried again, whirling to face Cricket sprawled on the ground.

"Welcome, welcome!" The man smiled broadly, his teeth taking up his whole mouth like a horse's. "Didn't mean to startle you. Looks like our cup runneth over. MacInteer, ain't it, if I remember correct?" In the space of talking, he'd ushered Mama into the cool, dim indoors, and Sass and her siblings followed along behind her like ducklings. Now, all five of them stood in the back of the church, the attention of twenty or so members focused on them. Forty eyes—thirty-nine minus the patch-covered one belonging to an old man in a cane-backed chair under one of the windows.

"How do." Mama nodded at the assembly. "Y'all likely know my husband, Harley, from down at the mine." Sass's eyes adjusted to the light and skipped around the faces in the room. "Or my boy Finn. He's just lately turned nineteen."

A few heads nodded. Clearly Mama recognized lots of faces, but they weren't so familiar to Sass. She wondered if any of these were miners her father had brought home stories about. A woman rose from the front and made her way down the center of the aisle. She was a plain woman, thin and tall, with a cotton dress, blue wool shawl, and a wool hat tamped down over the crown of her head. She gathered Mama into an embrace like they were old friends, then turned and beamed at Sass and the others.

"Rai, I remember you from a shucking a while back across Pine Mountain. Beady Wick. Come on in and set down here. We'll soon settle in for a message. We'd be pleased for y'all to join." The group seemed to come to their senses then, shifting around and dragging a bench here, a chair there, to make room for the family. Beady Wick fussed over them, steering Sass to a chair with a palm flat against the back of her shoulder. Something in the woman's smile seemed familiar.

Sass watched a pair of young girls pass the time with a hand-clapping game. It was one she and Fern played at sometimes, and she tapped her foot with the rhyme they chanted. Mama and the preacher's wife chatted in low voices beside her.

"Mining sure is hard on a body," Miz Wick was saying. "It's an honest labor but a tough row to hoe."

"I imagine preaching and smithing like your husband does has its own trials," Mama allowed. "How'd you come to meet?"

Sass detected a blush under Miz Wick's curls. "Jack likes to say I'm his Cinderella, since we met from a lost shoe. My horse threw a shoe at a spring dance, and he mended it so my sister and I could ride home."

"Harley's a hand with horses, too," Mama said. "Tended the race-horses in Lexington for a time. Fact is, I watched him train a colt one afternoon, and that was all it took."

Miz Wick smiled a secret smile and nudged Mama with her shoulder. "Nothing like a man that gentles a horse." She drew out a paper fan and swiped the air with it a time or two. "When Jack told me he aimed to be a preacher and head east, I had my bag packed in two shakes of a lamb's tail. I'd play games with the children, and he'd preach the Word like the Pied Piper. You know how rough mining towns can be, though." She cast Mama a knowing look.

"I do, for certain. One of the reasons I wanted to put Finn off from getting in the mix. Least he had his daddy to look out for him."

"We had a place down there at first, but one morning I woke up and found a hole above the baby's crib where a bullet had come through from the juke joint. I asked Jack if he didn't reckon the mountain needed a good word, too. Pretty soon, he said the Lord had laid it on his heart to bring light to the hills."

Sass turned to see Mama's wry smile. "Well, I coulda told you how that story was gonna finish up," Mama said.

Miz Wick smirked. "As long as they think it's their idea." Another elbow nudge and a quick wink. She went on. "Before long, we had us a church building." She waved the fan around like it was the magic wand that had conjured the benches where they sat.

All the chatter ceased as the man who'd welcomed them made his way to the front of the church. There was no finery or fuss. A simple platform lifted him another four inches or so above the audience, and he ran his hands over a pulpit made of rough-hewn wood posts and a few sanded boards. Behind him stood a half wall of shelves stacked with latched wooden boxes. He wore eyeglasses with thin wire frames that perched somewhere between the end of his nose and his sight line, so he bobbed his head up and down to peer over the top or to see the book that lay open on the pulpit. It gave the impression that he was overly agreeable, as if nodding assent to himself as he spoke.

"Seems the Lord in His wisdom has seen fit to send us some company today," he said, nodding at the MacInteers. Mama half smiled and smoothed Hiccup's dress. "Why, that's all right because He calls us all in His time, calls us each by name to follow Him, our good shepherd. His Word is a light unto our feet and a lamp unto our path. He provides for all our needs, in times of plenty and times of want."

Several listeners began nodding at this. One or two slowly rocked to the rhythm of his speech. Sass thought he had a musical voice, with a dipping and rising melody that carried you along in its current, like sitting in a flat-bottomed boat on a gentle stream, waiting for the fish to bite, easy as you please. He spoke of desperation, how desperate times don't mark us as desperate people because we have hope. Our faith carries us, he said, carries us like a mama carries her baby, helps us bear the yokes on our shoulders, the grumbling in our children's bellies, the knocks and setbacks of this dark world.

He started softly, almost too faint at times for Sass to hear. As he warmed up, his listeners responded—with nods, raised hands with an encouraging *Amen* or *That's right*—and his volume and energy built. He paced about the front of the room, on and off the platform. The eyeglasses came off. The sweat on his face made them slide too far down his nose, and he no longer read from the book up front. The words flowed naturally, organically, like a mountain brook. He sang—or that was how it seemed, his words like notes in a song, a cadence about faith that saves, sustains, is tested, and delivers. Expertly, he dragged them down into the deep, dark coal mine of despair and fear until they were fairly shaking with the burden of it and brought them back up again into the light, a bright and shining light of freedom and fresh air that made them break out in rejoicing. One woman bent over and pulled a tambourine from under her skirts like it was the most natural place in the world to store an instrument and started shaking it in a jubilee, wiping the tears that streaked her face. Even the old man with the eye patch stood with his hands raised and his face to the ceiling, his lips moving in some silent prayer.

"Glory be," shouted a man in the corner.

"Have mercy, Lord, give us eyes to see," begged another. This one, Sass thought she recognized. She was a Gunnison—one of the Marys? She'd heard Mama talking with a neighbor woman of the husband near getting arrested for running moonshine, but he'd managed to elude the law so far. The Gunnisons lived along two fingers of Lost Creek near the base of the mountain. The parents, Ida and Dean, had been both fertile and unimaginative, or perhaps more accurately, just tired. They had had six children, all the boys named John and all the girls named Mary. It was a tangle figuring out which was which, so they went by double names or second names: Mary Jane, Mary Elizabeth, Mary Jo, John Mark, John Warren, Little John.

Sass was astonished. In the space of thirty minutes, the room had been transformed from a quiet haven in the woods to a rollicking party for Jesus. Fern sat snug against Mama, taking everything in, and Hiccup had untangled herself from Mama's neck and clapped her hands in delight. Sass craned her neck to look up where the old man had fixed his gaze. She wouldn't have been surprised to see an angel in white floating near the rafters, so filled with the Spirit was the room.

As quickly as the rush swept through them, it subsided, leaving a prickly feeling on the skin and a breathlessness, like knowing it was due to come a storm. The preacher and his wife stood together up front, heads bowed.

"If anyone has need of prayers of intercession," he hummed, "make your way up and be heard."

Mama passed Hiccup to Fern and stood up. Sass's mouth hung open as she watched her mama walk to the front, her hands in tight fists by her sides. The Wicks bent their heads near hers as she murmured to them, and every now and then, her voice cracked and warbled. Finally, they parted, and Mama sat down in front.

"One of our community has come to us today to entreat us to pray for healing. Y'all know this family's son has been struck down in the mine with a serious injury. Regular doctoring hasn't been enough, and they fear for his leg. Many of y'all have been there and know the path this soul is walking."

"Yes sir."

"That's right."

"Surely do."

"Well, we're gonna ask the good Lord to send healing to this boy, to see fit to mend the broken. Sometimes we get struck down, but we don't get discouraged. We get defeated for a turn, but not crushed. The Lord will lift us up, where we will dance on our bruises and feel nothing."

The prayer over, Mama nodded quietly and glanced back through the crowd to her offspring, lined up like birds on a roof.

Jack Wick gestured for her to return to her seat. Several of the women squeezed her hands in solidarity as she walked by. Not many families passed through the mines unscathed.

Jack Wick had turned his back to the congregation and was sliding a wooden box off the shelf at the front. As he placed it on the front bench, a low hum began in his throat, which was soon taken up by the congregation.

"Beady." He nodded to his wife, who stood and started to sing.

"On a hill far away, stood an old rugged cross . . ." Their untrained voices lifted and wavered with the notes, their voices mingling in a practiced harmony that had no need for the finery of a piano. The low rumbling bass of the men vibrated in the floorboards, and the higher lilt of the women lifted toward the rafters. Sass sang along to the familiar hymn, bobbing one foot to keep time and following the shape notes to mark the melody.

When the last notes died, Jack held up a hand. "Book of John says the Word became flesh and dwelt among them. This was no ordinary word, not something you could spell out with letters. His words have power, and we have a whole book of 'em." Jack shook the tattered Bible that lay on the wooden pulpit. "Even more than that, more than words of creation and words of scripture, God saw fit to give a Word of life—His very own son."

"Preach it, Jack."

"We ask and ask of the Lord, and He generously gives. Sometimes, He shakes His head at our foolishness and determination to have it our own way. Surely sometimes the Lord must look down with a headache and think we're dumber than a sack of hammers. Sometimes, He needs to be sure we are headed in the right direction, that our faith is sure."

"Yes sir."

"He offers a test of faith. If we are worthy, if our faith is true, He will stand in our corner." A hush fell over the room. Jack opened the wooden box he'd set on the bench, the lid hiding its contents. Sass couldn't be sure, but she thought she heard the distinct buzz of a rattle.

"The Gospel tells us the faithful will be able to take up serpents and not be harmed, that they can drink deadly poison and not fall ill. These are the tests we should pass if we think we are worthy to approach the throne."

In one swift motion, Jack's arm darted into the box and came out holding a four-foot rattler behind its head. Its body whipped and twisted as it swung in the air, trying to find solid ground.

Cricket nudged Sass with a sharp elbow. "This man's crazy as a soup sandwich," he whispered. "His roof ain't nailed tight. That bugger hits the floor, and I'm out the door. You're gonna want to be right on my tail."

He didn't have to convince Sass. She clutched Fern and was ready to run if the preacher set the snake free to roam. She remembered her encounter just a week and a half ago with the rattler in Gingko Holler, and how the book woman had sent it flying with her pistol shot. Understanding dawned on her. The book woman! She'd told Sass's father her parents' names, and now Sass suddenly remembered them—Jack and Beady Wick. The man up front with a rattlesnake wrapped around his forearm was Miz Rye's father. She studied them with new appreciation. The way she'd killed that snake, Sass never would have guessed Miz Rye was raised keeping them as pets.

Jack Wick seemed to casually handle the reptile, almost fondly, like the baby raccoon Cricket had found near its mama in a trap. He'd raised it until it was grown enough to wander off one day and make its own way in the mountains. When it was young, it would wind in and out of Cricket's arms, playful and curious.

Jack invited anyone who wished to prove their faithfulness to come forward. It was at that moment that Mama stood and took her daughters in hand. She nodded at the Wicks and at those seated around her and excused herself, whispering they had to get back home to see about Finn. At the first sign of Mama's movement, Cricket was already up and halfway to the door. The rest of them followed behind in a jumble of skirts and shawls. As they climbed up into the wagon, Mama unhitched Plain Jane and pointed her toward home.

"Reckon the Lord surely knows my heart and whether I meant every bit of prayer I prayed for Finn. We already done been tested enough," Mama said. "There's hardly call for fangs and rattles."

Mama unpacked their lunch of sliced ham and cornbread, and she passed the pail around the wagon. They'd gone at least a half mile before anyone spoke, and Cricket whistled between his teeth.

"Well, I'll be doggone. Reckon what kind of service they have on Easter?"

～

Rai already knew what Harley's opinion would be of the spectacle they'd witnessed. Her husband had his own measure of faith, but Rai knew it didn't stretch far enough to include taking up with serpents. She'd have to downplay it and pacify him with knowing Finn had been interceded for. Finn was worth anything that needed doing. Any of her young'uns were, for that matter. A wave of helpless despair rose in her throat, and she stifled it by pulling Hiccup close to her on the bench and squeezing her tight. A mama's heart is a wonder, able to hold an endless measure of love, hope, sadness, and rage all at the same time. Multiply that by the number of young'uns you had, and sometimes the torrent wore Rai down to her bones.

Rai kissed the top of Hiccup's head, her lips pressing hard against her daughter's sun-warmed hair. Riding with her sweet girl on this sunny day was some comfort. Harley said sometimes that Rai indulged their youngest daughter too much. She'd been conceived after two miscarriages, coming on close to her change in life. When the unmistakable signs of another pregnancy had come upon her, Rai had told Harley this little Hiccup would surely be their last, and she had been. Despite the extra work a baby had added to her impossibly full days and aching joints, Rai had savored the time most of all her young'uns, knowing each milestone Hiccup reached wouldn't pass her way again.

Though she was fairly certain she was past childbearing, Rai still put Harley off during certain times of the month. She'd seen plenty of miracle young'uns come later in life. Any other man might get up under a woman's skirt just the same, but Harley wouldn't push.

Rai smiled to herself as she remembered meeting behind the corn-crib recently, their fumbled kisses and grasping as a casual trio of hens scratched and pecked on the dirt path behind them. She couldn't resist Harley's lopsided smile as he followed her appreciatively with his eyes. She knew it wore on him that he couldn't provide much for the family. Bless him, he worked sunup till sundown, and still they rubbed pennies together. At least he stayed. That was more than a lot of men, who lit out for the hills when things got tough and their mettle got tested, or worse. Men like Amanda's husband, Rai reckoned. Them, she couldn't abide.

Rai let her thoughts roam to Beady Wick, the preacher's wife and—now she wondered at it—Amanda's mama. She wondered what it might feel like without the company and comfort of little ones underfoot, if she and Harley were blessed to live long enough to know such a time. Having your nest empty all in good time was one thing, but having the pleasures of grown young'uns and grandbabies yanked out from under you was another. For certain, Rai didn't envy poor Beady. Surely that mama's heart must carry a fierce ache.

Rai thought of her own mama, then, and sighed with the missing of her as her thoughts wandered. Before she was old enough to comprehend the task, Rai remembered sitting at her mama's bare feet on their front stoop, sifting through the cuttings and pouches of roots and seeds that had been collected that day. In this way, without knowing it, Rai had learned to spy what nature shyly unfurled to the keen eye. She could tell a tree by its bark or leaves, depending on the season. She knew where certain mushrooms were likely to be found and how to grind or boil the roots, berries, or stems of this plant or that. Watching her mama's hands, Rai measured the doses of teas, tinctures, or salves and discerned which part of dandelion was best for thinning the blood and which for gout or sore joints.

Rai learned much from her mother's hands—the soothing comfort of a dry palm against a fevered brow, the number of times to knead a decent biscuit dough, the careful way to make even stitches up the seam of a shirt, and how to pat a baby's back until the troublesome gas rose from his colicky belly. Rai had many brothers and sisters, some of them living and some of them passed on by now, but none close by. She'd helped look after quite a few when they were young and underfoot, keeping them from tottering into the fire on the hearth or getting too close to the hind end of their ill-tempered cow.

Her pa she'd learned from, too, but only in pieces, not like her brothers. Their labors were divided into housekeeping and farming, and although Rai remembered many times she and her sisters had to hoe the garden or tote wood or water, her brothers and Pa never mended a shirt or cooked a meal, even when her mama fell sick. Then, the house labor fell to her and her sisters, including gathering what was needed from the woods to nurse her. For weeks, at sixteen, Rai kept the house running steady for the family, her brow permanently furrowed at the sight of her mama in bed while the sun shone, her busy hands lying strangely still on the quilt tucked around her thin frame. Rai saved every bit of wisdom and healing know-how her mama had shown her. She'd pored through the stores in the lean-to, where the dried herbs hung from the rafters, and bottles of powders and salves lined the walls alongside the tomatoes and pole beans they'd put up that summer. Rai did her best, begging her mama to tell her what to do toward the end, what to try, what to grind or brew.

After, when the boys had dug the grave behind the farthest corner of the garden, where the sweet peas grew wild, Rai's habit of wandering in the woods just before sunrise stuck with her. It was then she felt her mama was still near, humming her familiar songs as she picked petals and collected the autumn webs of the orb spiders. Her pa and brothers seemed to carry on without trouble, but Rai had been untethered. Even a year later, nothing seemed to hold her to the earth; the easy surety of one day fading into the next had been rent, and try as she might, Rai couldn't piece it together as it had been. Her pa spent more time in the free town down the mountain, and no matter how she dreaded it, Rai knew it wouldn't be long before he came home with a new wife to take the reins.

Rai thought back to the deft way Amanda's hands had helped her piece together the pie, and she knew Beady Wick had passed on to her only daughter some useful skills. After hearing Amanda's daddy preach that service, she was certain Amanda must have a firm grasp of the

Good Book as well. She wondered what it must have been like growing up a single child in a preacher's house, a life so different from her own. Plain Jane half bucked to rid herself of a horsefly, and the tug of the reins in her hands brought to mind her husband's horse sense. She'd told Beady about Harley training that colt, but it wasn't the force of him she'd been drawn to. It was his patient gentleness.

Harley MacIntcer was working his way back east from Lexington when Rai's pa heard tell of a feller who could break a horse in the space of an afternoon. Before the day was out, he'd led Harley to the pen behind their barn, where their wall-eyed Appaloosa fidgeted and carried on. Rai had peered out the cabin's window at the tall, wiry figure leaning on the fence with one foot braced against the lower rung, and her abdomen fluttered like the muslin curtains in a stiff breeze. She'd been mortified when the man turned his head and caught her staring.

Pa had bet the man he couldn't ride the horse by sundown. She didn't know what he'd wagered, but this particular colt was wild by anyone's standards. The feller worked all afternoon, driving the horse around the pen until sweat streaked its sides. Rai's pa watched the sun trek westward across the sky, a smirk playing on his lips.

She found herself rooting for the man as she started supper. On her way to fetch eggs, she cast a long glance toward the pen to watch as the man stood quietly at the center with the horse facing him, its head hung low and sides heaving. As Rai stared, he placed a hand on the horse's flank and rubbed his slick withers. The horse barely flicked his tail.

"I'll be." It was her brother Clarence who'd come up behind her.

Rai watched the man's hands as he rubbed the horse down, head to toe, whispering low and soft. The rest of Rai's brothers and her pa gathered alongside the barn as the sky faded to orange and pink. Her pa's eyes skipped back and forth between the pen and the sun, and he fiddled with the buttons on his overalls.

The man planted his left hand on the horse's withers and faced his tail. He leaned against the horse and pulled down so that the colt could get the feel of him. Then, in one quick motion, the man swung up on the horse's back, his arms and legs rubbing up and down the horse's neck and sides. For a moment, the beast's ears pricked forward and his head raised up, startled.

"Ha," Rai heard her pa say under his breath. "Here we go."

The horse turned his nose to the boot that pushed against him. Then, his hooves started forward as he walked on, calm as if he were out to pasture. The sun slipped below the horizon, leaving the sky in a dusky haze of purple, and the man slid off the horse's back.

Rai's pa shook the man's hand. "Darndest thing I ever saw. I'm beat fair and square. That horse is yours."

"Naw," the man said. "You can keep the horse." The heat in Rai's abdomen rose to the roots of her hair as the man met her eyes across the yard. "How about I stay for dinner instead?" Rai couldn't hold back the smile that curved on her lips.

Three months later, she'd wrapped her arms around Harley's waist as she rode behind him on the spotted horse, heading east toward Harley's family's land. Their life together was lean but joyful. Rai allowed there were times when she'd get her dander up and act just like that spotted horse, running herself ragged and worried. Harley knew just how to tame her, though, with his low voice and slow and easy manner. He could touch her shoulders just right and lean in as he exhaled near her neck, and she'd soften with a peace that settled as lightly as snowflakes. Harley made her feel planted and sure, safe to send down roots and even blossom if she chose.

Rai thanked the Lord, not for the first time, for wild spotted horses and hoped Harley had remembered to dose Finn with the tea she'd left. She clucked to Plain Jane to pick up the pace toward home.

Chapter 9

Amanda timed her trips into town for when the post and mercantile would be less busy and she'd be less likely to run into the Peepers. If she went early enough, she could check in at the WPA office and pick up whatever items she and Mooney needed from the mercantile before most others were done with morning chores. Not that she had anything to hide, not that she was ashamed, but some nuts just wouldn't crack, and she simply didn't see the point in the effort. The Peepers were members of the Women's Temperance League, a self-organized committee from a church on the hill, but their concerns went beyond the demons of alcohol. Their mission extended to rescuing souls from most any backsliding or behavior unbecoming.

Shirley Culpepper, the sharp-eyed, tidy wife of a miner known as Boll Weevil, reigned at the top of the pecking order. Under her stood any number of good Christian women anxious to do right with an earnestness that they hoped would sweep others along in their wake. Most often, Shirley kept company with two other ladies who, within their means, organized sewing projects and collections for those less fortunate. Amanda knew them—Tilda Johnson and Angeline Bates—but before she and Mooney had learned the art of dodging the group, they had several trying encounters with the trio. While the ladies had a working understanding of tact and grace, they'd not had much practice with either. On the last occasion when they'd met, Mooney had come away thoroughly exasperated with their doggedness.

"My land, they hang in there like a hair in a peanut butter sand-wich. I'mma start calling them Goodness and Mercy."

"That's charitable of you," Amanda had said, "considering the names I'm sure they're calling *us*."

Mooney's mouth had curved into a wry smile. "It's scriptural, don'cha know."

One of Jack and Beady Wick's foremost duties had been to make certain Amanda was well versed in the Bible. She could quote entire passages by the time she was five, but she wasn't following her friend.

Mooney had feigned surprise. "Amanda Rye, I'm shocked. Why, anyone knows it says plain as day in the twenty-third psalm: Shirley, Goodness, and Mercy shall follow me all the days of my life."

The two had busted out laughing right there in front of the post office, gasping and wiping their eyes, not minding one whit about the people casting glances in their direction.

This particular day, as she closed the door of the WPA behind her, Amanda saw the Peepers heading in her direction. She couldn't go back inside the office or pretend she hadn't seen them without being outright rude, so she adjusted the books in her saddlebags and steeled herself.

"Amanda Rye, a sight for sore eyes," Shirley gushed. "Haven't seen you in a month of Sundays."

"Is that right? They keep me pretty busy with library deliveries."

"I was just talking to your sweet mama and daddy last Sunday. I bet they'd enjoy a visit from you." Goodness and Mercy stood side by side, nodding and mmm-hmming.

Amanda buckled the strap on her bag and faced Shirley. "It's no secret where I'm staying, and the path runs both ways. You can tell them, if they're wondering, that Miles is doing fine, smart as a whip."

Amanda noticed, not for the first time, that Shirley had mighty expressive eyebrows.

"Shame about the accident at Buckley."

Amanda thought it was Mercy who made the comment, though truthfully, she wasn't sure which one was which. Her hand stopped stroking Junebug's neck. "Yes. Six men lost and several more injured."

"Two of 'em church members," said one.

"I'm sure *all* the families involved are in a world of hurt right now," Amanda said.

"Of course, but I mean to say there are some who are near and dear to our hearts. One of the families came all the way up the mountain asking for prayers—the MacInteers from way over near Gingko Holler."

Amanda's head jerked up. "That so? Are they still doing poorly?" She'd heard about the accident, of course, and had been out on her route only a day before she'd pieced together the news from different stops. As it happened, the family was on her route the next day—it had been two weeks—and she meant to bring them something special. She had hoped enough time had gone by that they had started to recover.

"Please give my parents my best if you see them," Amanda said by way of dismissal. "I've got to get on my way." She swung up on Junebug, her skirt flying out behind her, and trotted off toward home. She didn't even bother checking in at the post office.

As the mule's easy stride carried her outside the boundaries of town, the landscape changed from dried mud ruts crisscrossing between buildings to a soft footing of leaves and pine needles. Autumn's slide into winter brought frequent rains, which kept the paths muddy and the creeks full. Amanda had quit cleaning her boots altogether and just let the clods of mud dry on them by the hearth. It was easier to knock off the dry mud each morning before she went out; it would only get caked on again the moment she stepped off the porch.

As she rode, Shirley's words tossed and tumbled in Amanda's head. She thought of the last time she'd seen her parents, the accusations and the way she'd clammed up, her heart so full of anger and sorrow that it overflowed with everything but words. As a child, she'd wanted for nothing. In addition to preaching, burials, and weddings, her father hired out his time as a smithy, working out of a stone forge he'd built behind their small house. Her mother, meanwhile, led a life of verbs—plant, mend, plow, sew, chop, carve, sharpen, weave, cook, knead, harvest, haul—in revolving seasons.

Despite their due diligence, her parents had only been granted one child, and consequently, Amanda had been both precious and pressured, bearing their expectations and affection in solid, stoic fashion. She learned the finer points of minding a house and garden and was required to know great sections of scripture by heart, being her father's sole heir and most important disciple. Above all, her father was adamant Amanda knew who and whose she was, and that she act befittingly. Appearances meant everything for a minister's daughter.

Junebug stepped into a rut on the trail and the saddlebag bumped against Amanda's calf. One of the families she visited had given her a few apples, and she planned to take them to the MacInteers' place. Finn sure had enjoyed that apple pie on her first visit, and she hoped another taste might lift his spirits. What a nice family, Amanda thought. Rai so kind and Sass with such spunk. If she could ease their current hardship, well of course, she should. She thought of Finn's quick grin and gentle way with his brother and sisters, and her heart warmed like she hadn't felt in a long while.

As it often did, the dark cloud of Frank Rye dimmed her sunny thoughts. What had she known about Frank back then? She'd been barely seventeen, fresh as a daisy and eager to stretch her wings. She'd stretched all right, flew clear into the blinding light like a moth to a flame.

Frank Rye and Gripp Jessup had swooped down into their small fellowship like wild and wily screech owls. They'd been heading into town to look for work when they'd passed by the Wick house one afternoon while Amanda and her mama hoed their kitchen garden. Mama liked to keep her cucumbers tidy. Frank had been whistling Dixie and could warble and trill just like a mockingbird.

"Hidy, ladies. Can you tell us if we're headed in the right direction for town?" Frank spoke first. He had a strong, deep voice, and he shielded his eyes with one hand as he leaned on the garden fence. The other man stood a head shorter than Frank and was built like a fence post. His face held a permanent squint, like either he was nearsighted or constantly wincing against the sun. Amanda thought he glanced around the place like he was taking inventory.

"Another few miles and you'll hit Flat Creek. Acrost that you'll come up on a trail that runs along a fence right into town. You hunting the mine?"

He'd nodded, a shock of his sandy hair falling forward. "Mine, lumberyard, whatever's up for grabs." His companion snickered, and Frank had thrown him a look. He leaned over the fence and extended a hand. "Name's Frank Rye. This here's Gripp Jessup." The second man withdrew a dirty paw from his pocket and held it over the fence to them. It wouldn't have been neighborly to not shake, so Amanda and Mama stepped forward and obliged. Mama didn't give their names.

"My husband's the preacher here at the church," she'd said. Jack had taken his smith wagon into town to handle some business, but as far as the strangers knew, he could walk out the door of the whitewashed church building any minute. Frank nodded and stood back from the fence. Gripp remained where he was, making himself comfortable.

"That so?" Frank said. "My mama's family back east attends reg'lar. Thank you for the directions. You ladies enjoy your gard'ning now."

He nudged Gripp, who made a show of spitting in the dirt, like he would move on when he was good and ready and not before. Gripp had studied the church building, eyeing it like he meant to make an offer. "Since we're here, could I trouble you for a bit o' light for a pipe?" He dug in his pocket and held out a carved wooden pipe, its mouthpiece worn and bearing the marks of his teeth. This sort of request was common, matches a luxury seldom known. Neighbors often borrowed shovels of coals from a hearth or took advantage of a ready light when they happened upon one on the road. Amanda took the pipe and disappeared into the cabin to drop a coal into its bowl. When she returned and handed the smoldering pipe back to Gripp, he nodded his appreciation and pulled on the stem, puffs of smoke slipping from his thin lips and settling in clouds around his head. His eyes squinted even farther against it until they were all but closed, a bullfrog blinking in the sun, waiting for the buzz of a passing black fly.

"Now Frank and me, we been on the road so long we don't get much chance to go to meeting. You got room for extra come Sunday?"

Amanda noticed Mama stand straighter. "We *are* meeting this Sunday since it's the first of the month. Can't say we're much more reg'lar than that up in these parts. You fellers are certainly welcome to join." Her voice rang brighter. "We start at ten and have lunch after. My husband, Jack, would be pleased to have you."

That Sunday, Frank Rye and Gripp Jessup had returned. A tickle of pleasure ran through Amanda when she'd watched Frank cast his eyes from pew to pew, stopping when they landed on her. His smooth skin reminded her, for some reason, of a square of sweet caramel candy. Frank's singing voice carried in the small building, and Amanda could pick out the new deep sound like a radio tuned just for her.

At the dinner on the grounds after services, they'd sat under the shade of a grand sycamore, its branches hanging low and lazy, while Mama looked on from a short distance. Frank talked of rivers and cities Amanda had never seen. He'd been to a bit of school, too. Not as far as she had, but once he'd saved up enough, he said, he wanted to head west to make a go of things. Frank had even thought about enlisting, given the talk of trouble brewing in Germany. He was a good shot with a rifle, he said, and knew how to live by his wits.

After dinner, the pluck and twang of strings stirred the already-jovial mood of the group. Perhaps her heart had fluttered to a rhythm all its own, but Amanda could still recall every note of the music they made that day.

"Now I know what I'm gonna have to start calling you," Frank had teased. "With a voice like yours and the way you make those strings hum."

"What do you mean?" Amanda had looked up at him as the sun melted slowly down the mountain. If he had a nickname for her, that meant he intended to come around to use it.

"Amanda's all right for a first name, but your middle name should be Lynn."

"Amanda Lynn?" When she said it out loud, he burst out laughing.

"That's right. You can share the name of the instrument you play so well. A-manda-lin."

She slapped his arm. "Now I'll never be able to hear it any different."

A pair of crows cawed to each other through the treetops, their ruckus pulling Amanda back to the present. She drew herself up in the saddle and glanced through the woods on either side. Except for the crows, she and Junebug were alone. She squeezed his flanks to pick up the pace, remembering Alice's tale at the WPA office.

"Amanda Lynn," she mumbled. She hadn't played since Miles had been born. She'd sold her tater-bug mandolin before finding the librarian job. Yet another thing Frank had managed to take from her.

That day after the singing, Amanda had caught Gripp leaning against the side of the church building, watching her exchange with Frank. He raised a hand, and although Amanda hadn't so much as said two words to Gripp Jessup all day, she'd had the feeling that because of her budding friendship with Frank, Gripp automatically assumed the same familiarity.

When Amanda's father learned Gripp had not yet found salvation, that fall, he took the man on as his special project. He was handy with carpenter's tools, and Jack hired him on for odd repair jobs at the church. Frank and Amanda had obviously hit it off, and when Gripp was around working, most times, Frank found reason to visit and help out as well.

Amanda and Frank carried on sparking as she came up on seventeen. Under the watchful eye of Mama, the pair sat side by side on the front porch rockers, baskets between their knees as they shucked corn, strung beans, or snapped peas. Mama warned Amanda that she knew what nonsense idle hands could get up to, and she always seemed to have plenty of tasks at the ready when Frank came calling.

When the damp spring arrived, sometimes a week or two passed before Frank could make it up to the church. Mountain runoff and spring rains filled and spilled over the creek banks, and not even the most surefooted horse could be urged across the rushing waters. Amanda couldn't keep from thinking about the last time she and Frank had been together—Frank stealing kisses when Mama went out to the corncrib to wring a rooster's neck for stew: his calloused hands, warm and rough on her arms, her shoulders, her neck; his mouth on hers, his breath hot in her ear and his growth of beard scratching her cheek as he whispered her nickname against her hair, *"Amanda Lynn, Amanda Lynn."*

If she and Frank got hitched, it would be just the two of them, without her parents watching every minute, and without Gripp springing up around every corner. Amanda's daydreams about Frank clouded with the thought of Gripp. When she'd open her eyes, flushed and breathless from Frank's embrace, she'd often catch a movement by the side of the smokehouse, of something slinking flat in the shadows. A weasel, she thought, or perhaps another egg-sucking dog from down the road. Even as she'd thought it, she'd known it wasn't a critter after the hens. How many times had she said goodbye to Frank on the doorstep and seen Gripp leaning against the fence by the roadside? She'd tried to speak to Frank about it, hoping he'd ease her mind.

"Frank," she'd said, "I don't care much for Gripp. I ain't about to keep gettin' stared at all day."

Frank had toyed with the tail of her braid, flipping it back and forth against his palm. "Pretty as you are? Feller can't hardly help it." Amanda kept her mouth in a tight line.

"Seems like every time I turn around, he's right there gettin' an eyeful." She blushed and looked up at him sideways. "Even when you're bein' sweet with me."

Frank smiled and kissed the curled end of her braid. "Aw, you don't need to pay him no mind. Likely he's jealous and pining for what you and me got. Getting spied on ain't the worst thing." He'd brushed it off as harmless. "I told you we could rustle up a more private spot."

"Pa would skin you alive if he heard you say that. 'Sides, that's not the point. I been hearing folks talk. Heard he's been finding things to do 'sides working for my daddy."

"Well, now," Frank allowed, "there might be some truth to that, but ends gotta meet some way or 'nother. Pockets ain't gonna fill their selves."

"But moonshining, Frank? Cockfights and gambling? Wide is the road that leads to destruction." She turned her head, so the braid slipped out of his fingers. How often Pa had preached that sermon.

"And the Lord helps those that helps themselves." He snorted a short laugh. "Shoot, nobody's living in high cotton 'cause of it. It's just a way to get by. Gripp ain't doing nothing folks don't want him to." Frank looked her steady in the eye. "Even folks in that little white church up there."

Everybody knew such things went on out in the lattice thickets of mountain laurel and grapevines. It was a balancing act, following the Lord but doing what needed done. Loving Jesus, but drinking a little. There was scripture truth and the truth of signs and tokens they all lived by—like planting by the moon or dowsing for water. Opposites like these somehow made sense together, like oil and vinegar could gussy up a pot of greens.

"People ain't perfect, I know that. I'm just saying he makes the hair prickle on my neck sometimes."

"You let *me* worry about your neck," he'd teased. He'd lifted her braid and nuzzled under her ear then, and she'd laughed. Charming Frank, playful Frank. Frank would take care of it, wouldn't he? It had never occurred to her to ask Frank if he, too, might be helping himself. He let on he was picking up work cutting lumber or filling in at the mine, and she believed him. He was muscled and strong and could certainly put in a good day.

Amanda shook her head, wishing she'd never run into Shirley Culpepper. She'd been having a fine day without raking over old coals. "Come on, Bug," Amanda clucked. "I'm anxious to get on home."

Chapter 10

When Amanda filled her saddlebags, she made sure to include some fried pies wrapped in wax paper and the apples she'd picked up the previous day. She gave a kiss to Miles and told him to behave, waved to Mooney, and rode out on Junebug under a pale-gray sky, the sun a faint haze of yellow bleeding through the heavy clouds. Frost on the pumpkins this morning for sure.

Over the course of a visiting day, they stopped first at one post, then the next on her eighteen-mile trek, greeting the eager families as knobby-kneed children sprang out onto the slanting wooden porches. The children's initial shyness usually wore off by Amanda's second visit; they caught on to her routine and looked forward to spotting Junebug rounding the bend. So anticipated were the books she carried, the young'uns would leave off fishing or delay the morning's chores to look through her stores. Amanda stayed awhile at each homestead, trading books and tales, often reading to the families that couldn't make out the words. Children followed along with the pictures, rapt by the stories and the way Amanda read the characters using different voices. Once she'd left, they'd mimic her as they flipped through the pages again and again, recounting the tale from memory.

More than once, she'd enter a cabin to find someone lying sick in bed, covers up to their noses to keep warm. The WPA required them to carry a book on first aid and medical treatments, and these she consulted with the adults, knowing they'd take the information with a grain of salt. Years of using what nature provided for healing and a lack of actual medical doctors made folks both largely self-sufficient and matter-of-fact about the comings and goings of life and death. She'd stopped in on the Hawthorn family once, a few months back, and Samson Hawthorn lay abed with a mysterious ailment his wife referred to in vague terms. With their three children sprawled out in a game of marbles on the hearth, Miz Hawthorn had her own share of worry. She'd waved her hand and said they'd done their best, and the Lord was taking His good time deciding which way to land with it. She was almost peeved to be bothered by the matter, and it seemed whichever way the decision ended, it was all the same to her. Amanda learned later the man had been shot during a dispute over a still. Samson had declared it to be on his property, and the other feller—unknown or unnamed—had figured otherwise and tried to settle things once and for all.

Conflict and contention were rife in the mountains, where a loose cow, a wayward hog, or a stray husband—things fences don't tame— could be the genesis of a feud that would fester for generations. With hot tempers, hot loins, and hot-burning stills, there was always some good reason to pick a fight, particularly if it meant redeeming the honor of a woman or a family name. When gunshots rang out in the hills, echoing across the rocky slopes, it was just as likely to be a violent end to a day of hard words and hard liquor as a hunter bagging a squirrel for the stewpot.

The man unfortunate enough to bear the sheriff's badge was summoned like a midwife to preside over both misfortune and misconduct, often throwing his hands up at both. The Lord gives and the Lord takes away. Tight-lipped family members weren't likely to admit any role in mischief or mayhem, and once the mountains claimed a body through foolishness or accident, there wasn't much the sheriff and his shiny badge could do at that point besides proclaim the obvious. The sheriff was mostly the frazzled parent of mountain families, preferring to let them work things out on their own, and barring that, if they wouldn't let up, he'd give them something to cry about.

The close walls of a dim cabin could seem like a prison if a sickbed was the extent of your domain, especially to a young man accustomed to prowling the open terrain with the wind rustling his hair. Amanda had rushed through her first stops to leave extra time for her visit at the MacInteers' place. The cold weather had given her an excuse to trade books through the space of an open window to save heat in the houses. Junebug stood high enough for her to reach the windows on the raised side of some cabins, but at the MacInteer house, she dismounted and tied him to the porch rail.

"Hidy!" Amanda called in her clear voice. "It's the book woman!"

A clambering sounded from inside, and Rai cracked the door to usher her in. "Come on in outta the weather," she said. "I didn't expect you with it being so cold."

Amanda set her saddlebag down and slipped out of her overcoat as her eyes adjusted to the firelit room. "It has to be howling and blowing worse than that to keep us at home. How y'all been?" She rubbed her hands together and took in the scene. It wasn't warm enough to be cozy, but it was a sight better than standing out in the wind.

Cricket and Fern sat at the oak table. Fern and her mother had been chopping root vegetables for a stew, and Cricket was boring a hole through a block of wood. Sass perched on the edge of the bed in the corner, where Finn sat propped up against the wall. Hiccup lay curled asleep next to him under the bear claw quilt, her fanned hair just visible against the thin pillow.

"I heard about the mine." Amanda turned to Finn. "I was mighty glad to hear y'all made it out."

"We're on the mend," said Rai. "Harley's done gone back already, working his shift. Won't have full use of his arm for a bit, but he can get by. Finn'll have a little ways to go."

Finn shifted in the bed to sit up straighter and ran a hand through the hair that flopped forward over his eyes. He half smiled at Amanda, but she thought it was more to encourage his mother than for any show of emotion.

Sass slid off the edge of the bed and walked over to the neat pile stacked on the hearth.

"Here's your rabbit book and the other'ns you left last time." She held them out to Amanda.

"What did you think?" she asked. "Did you like the story?"

"The pictures were real pretty," said Fern. "Sass and me figgered the boy must be some kind o' prince since he had so many play pretties."

Amanda sank into one of the ladder-backed chairs at the table and opened the book. "Would you like me to read it so you can find out?" she asked. "I don't mind a bit. I read lots of stories on my route."

"I declare, now, that would be nice," said Rai, "so I can pass the time getting these carrots chopped for supper."

Sass glanced at Rai as Fern and Cricket nodded eagerly. She slid back onto the bed with Finn, and they all listened as Amanda opened the cover of the book. "Once, there was a Velveteen Rabbit," she began, "and in the beginning he was *really* splendid."

Amanda tried not to glance at Finn as she read, tried not to notice how the twinkle she'd last admired in his eyes had gone out like a snuffed lantern light. She used different voices for the characters, a deep, quavery one for the Skin Horse and a small, timid one for the rabbit himself. Halfway through, the only sound in the cabin was the crackle and pop of the firewood as it burned and Amanda's voice as it reeled them all in to the world of the boy and his treasured toy. She kept reading, and even Rai stilled her knife, frozen in mid-chop as she listened.

Amanda showed the pictures on each page as she read, and when she did, her eyes traveled over Finn's face. He was paying attention. It wasn't like he had anything better to do. She noticed Sass did the same. Each time Amanda showed a picture, Sass would glance at her brother, gauging his reaction, searching for a stirring. Finally, toward the end of the story, Amanda turned toward the bed, and a sizzle ran through her. Finn no longer studied the pictures in the book she held; his eyes studied *her* as she read. His chest rose and fell, and he regarded her with a look of surprised interest, as he might a crimson cardinal lighting on a bare branch in the snow. The corners of Amanda's mouth turned upward the slightest bit in an unbidden smile.

Amanda closed the book, and Fern clapped her hands together. "That was better'n I imagined!" she proclaimed. "Thank you, Miz Rye."

"Certainly. Now let's look through to see what you'd like to trade for this time." She spread some of the books on the table, and Sass and her siblings fell upon them, picking up first one, then another.

"This one's got tractors and cars," said Cricket. "Daddy might like to see it."

"How about this one, with flowers and trees?"

"We've started putting bookmarks in each one," Amanda pointed out. "Thataway, you can mark your place if you need to come back to it later. Keeps the pages from wearin' out by folks notching or folding them. See? Here's one made out of a Christmas card someone donated. It's attached to a ribbon, and you just hang it like this outside the page so you know where to open up to next time."

They liked the bookmarks almost as much as the books themselves, as they'd been crafted from postcards and stationery that were rare to see. While they examined the pile, Amanda showed Rai a scrapbook.

"You might like this," she said. "It's a collection we put together at the office. We take them on our route and swap them out at different stops. It has pictures, recipes, quilt patterns, scripture quotes, and things we've cut out of magazines and papers, so you get a little of everything."

Rai was delighted. "How handy."

"You might recognize some folks' contributions. Sometimes we'll pass along a recipe from down the road, or look . . ." She flipped to the back. "This 'un here even has some little packets in the back where you can put dried seeds. Take one and give one to pass along to the next 'un."

While Rai looked through the scrapbook, Amanda ventured to Finn's bedside and perched on a cut stump they'd placed nearby as a seat.

"You're a reg'lar ray of sunshine," he said. "Who'd a' thought that a stack o' books could do that?" He shifted slightly under the quilt and leaned on an elbow, turning fully toward her.

"I've seen it happen over and over. The folks on the other end are what makes riding through the cold and wet worth it. It's funny how plain words can be so powerful. How're you getting by, if you don't mind me asking?"

He flinched. "They tell me I'm lucky. Coulda been a whole heap worse. It was a sorry mess at first. Didn't look like I was gonna make it and didn't much care to, to tell the honest truth. My one leg got mashed pretty good, and it won't never be like it was. It'll heal, but I won't be running no races."

"Well," said Amanda. "And how many races did you used to run?"

Finn chuckled, and at the unfamiliar sound, Sass and Rai turned toward him. "I can't concoct the exact total number."

"Then I expect you'll make do just fine," she said.

He glanced toward his mama and sister and lowered his voice. She had to lean in to hear him. "Maybe this here's part of my becoming real, like the hare in that book. It hurts some, but it means you've grown."

"You *were* listening," she teased.

"I was hung on ever' word," he said. "You sure know how to carry a story. Your husband must've asked you to read to him ever' night."

Heat colored Amanda's face and she bit her lip. "He wasn't around much, to tell the truth." Her voice softened, and she'd almost whispered the admission.

"Then he was both a lucky dog and a blame fool in the same skin." Finn gestured to her left hand, where she wore the ring she automatically twisted with her other hand. "Tell me to mind my business if you like, but why're you still wearing that? Hasn't he been gone a few years now?"

Amanda glanced at her hand and shrugged. "I guess it's easier. Saves folks asking questions or assuming things that ain't truth, especially since I have Miles to look after. Plus, it's about the one nice thing I have, so it keeps it from getting lost."

Finn nodded, his eyes soaking her in. Women alone with children were common enough. Men left their families to find work, not being able to bear the ache of a little one's hungry stomach, and then found it easier to just not return. Or worse, started over somewhere else, hoping for a better outcome the second time around. Amanda had heard of at least a few men at the mines rowing that exact boat.

"I didn't mean to bring up a prickly subject." He was so earnest in his concern that Amanda marveled at it. Had her sole experience made her forget what a gentleman could be like?

She shrugged and smiled reassurance. "It's all right. I'll tell you about him sometime. Maybe I should take it off. Old ways won't open new doors, my granny used to say." As Amanda held Finn's gaze for an extra beat, his eyes sparkled in the lantern light. Something about Finn made the closed doors inside of her creak open the slightest bit, letting in a stripe of light. It stirred a cautious but hopeful something, like the first warmth on a spring breeze after a spell of winter days. She liked him. Truth told, the whole MacInteer family drew her like the fragrance of sweet honeysuckle. It reminded her of days when nothing felt as secure as her mama's lap or her small hand tucked inside her daddy's big one.

"Miz Rye?" Sass stood behind her, scratching at a place on her neck. "I forgot to tell you." Her mouth was tight, and although she looked at Finn, her words were for the book woman.

Amanda turned to face the girl. "Tell me what?"

"We saw your mama and daddy last week. Went up to the church when Finn was so puny." Sass held herself tall and straight.

"Sass." Rai's voice was a willow switch.

Amanda stilled. "Is that so?" Her back went straight as a knife's edge. "Did y'all get to chat much?"

"Didn't get to stay until the end," Rai admitted. "And we don't usually travel such a piece to attend, but we had a special cause." She cut her eyes at Finn. "The Lord was merciful. Finn's doing a heap better'n he was."

She might as well come out with it. "My folks and I parted ways a few years back, but I reckon you prob'ly know that. Words travel like dandelion seeds. There's no controlling where they fly." Amanda turned to look at Sass. "I wish it weren't so, but it wasn't an easy time there for a while, after my husband was gone and I had Miles to care for. Sometimes hasty words stick in your craw, especially when they ought not have been said to begin with."

Rai nodded. "You can't choose the family tree you climb in. Harley's got an uncle or two I'm ashamed to share a name with, that's a fact. My mama's own sister was wild as the wind. Sometimes the good Lord sees fit to perch folks on the branches that require an extra measure of our grace. Sometimes those folks is us. Guess we all take turns."

Amanda laughed. "I've never heard it put quite that way, Rai."

The shadows thrown across the floor from the struggling light outside had lengthened. Amanda remembered how far she had to ride to get back to her own home, where her small son would be waiting for her to tell him about her day. She needed to finish up here. "I almost forgot," said Amanda. "I know how much y'all enjoyed that apple pie last time, and I managed to bring along some fried pies and a few apples for Harley." Before Rai could protest about taking charity, Amanda said, "Rai, if you could relay to me a recipe or two in trade, I'd be proud to include them in one of the scrapbooks we use."

"That sounds like a fine idea." Rai was happy to contribute. Trouble was, measuring and figuring were an unnecessary nuisance when it came to setting victuals on a table. Most folks put together a dish with what was available and with the muscle memory of hands that had kneaded bread and measured pinches, handfuls, and dashes for years. Seasonings were by taste, and mixing by sight. Amanda and the others in the WPA office had done enough transcribing that they had learned to translate the instructions into official-looking recipes, so Amanda scribbled as Rai began:

"Get you a hank of pork shank with some good fat on it. If it's a lean year, it won't hurt none to add lard instead. Brown it up nice in your skillet; then chop it into pieces. Put you in some water kindly like you's making gravy so as to get the nice bits from the bottom. Add a bit of sorghum and a bit of apple vinegar. How much? Oh, you know, enough so it looks right. You need to have a good bit o' paprika on hand 'cause that's the mainest thing. Let all that set and cook. Add a splash of water if it looks dry. Then, you can put in whatnot from the garden— carrot, parsnips, maybe a pepper. Salt and pepper it, you know, to make it taste right. Make you up some taters to sop it up, and that's a right nice goulash supper of an evening."

Amanda estimated the measurements based on the way Rai held her cupped hands while she described what to add and her own skills at pulling a meal together. In the space of a few minutes, she had set down recipes for cherry cobbler and goulash while Fern drew a pattern on another scrap of a magazine page.

"It's a rabbit," she explained. "You can piece it into a quilt or stitch it back-to-back and stuff it with sawdust to make a rabbit like the one in the book."

"Fern, how clever! I love the idea of having something to make that represents the books. I know the other ladies at the WPA office will think this is a grand idea." Fern beamed under the praise. "The flour mills have started making printed sacks instead of just plain white since so many folks use them for dresses and curtains. If I can get some together and bring them to you, do you think you could make some rabbits like that? Only if you have some free time, of course. Wouldn't that be a special thing to pass along to the children on the routes?"

Fern looked to Rai for her answer. When her mama nodded her assent, Fern burst out, "Yes! I think I could do that. Little'uns could have something to play with 'sides hollyhock and corn-husk dolls."

"That seems like more than a fair trade for a few fried pies." Amanda collected the books and magazines into a pile and started filling her saddlebags. "I best be on my way."

"So quick?" Finn asked. "Seems like you just walked in the door. It'd be a favor to me if you'd sit awhile."

Amanda paused as she deposited the last of the books in her bag. She was grateful for the loose fall of hair that had slipped out of its knot, hiding her face from the color she was sure he could see in the flush of her cheeks.

"I reckon I have some time to spare. Junebug wouldn't begrudge the extra breather." Amanda settled onto the stump beside Finn's bed and folded her hands in her lap, where she hoped they would leave off the unexpected tremble that had started when he had asked her to stay. The rest of the family busied themselves around the cabin, but Amanda could feel their eyes on her back as she and Finn spoke.

Despite asking her to stay, he shifted and picked at the quilt, suddenly quiet. Amanda cleared her throat and patted the covers.

"Why don't you tell me about it?" she said. "What's it like in the coal mine?"

Finn met her eyes and nodded. This, he could manage. "I been in the mine almost seven years," he began in his low, firm voice.

Amanda cocked her head and smiled. "Honest work."

He smiled back, warming up. "It is, but there's a lot to worry about. A man can get into a pocket of bad air and be knocked out cold before he knows what hit him. He can get winched between cars hauling out loads. Spend enough time down there, and the cough takes hold. All said and done, a body weren't meant to bend and crawl beneath tons of limestone."

Amanda was silent, and again she leaned forward on her stool to hear Finn better. She must have looked stricken. She imagined soft-spoken Finn coughing as he breathed in coal dust, and some part of her wanted to protect him.

He cocked his head. "Now don't look thataway," he told her. "I'm not meaning to scare you." He sat up straight against the walnut-plank headboard. "I'm what you call a mule skinner. I drive the horses, collecting tubs of coal and delivering them to where they can be hoisted to the surface."

"One of our other deliverers has a mule that used to do that. She said he didn't like tight spaces."

"Some of 'em don't, that's for certain. But the ones we got showed me the ropes. I learned which tunnels held ventilation doors by watching the sides of the mule I drove. Deeper breaths mean approaching air. A slower pace usually means narrowing tunnel walls or lower ceilings. They trace their noses along the stones, you see, their whiskers sensitive to where a turn opens up. At some point, I'd let my pony go, and it would know to bolt to its underground stable as much as three miles off, where it could get a drink and a mouthful or two of hay before its next load."

"Sounds like Junebug." Amanda laughed. "If there's a meal in it, he's ready to go. I trained him to follow me around when I was younger by keeping carrot tops in my pockets."

Rai bent to fill Finn's water cup. She placed a warm hand on Amanda's shoulder as she leaned over and squeezed. Amanda lifted her chin and smiled at Finn's mother, glad for the encouragement. She didn't want to overstay her welcome, but she was enjoying the time with him. He paused for a sip of water and nodded his thanks to Rai before clearing his throat to continue.

"I'm talking your ear plumb off," he said.

"I hope you'll go on," she replied. "Now you've made me curious how the horses get on." The way he told the tale was captivating. Amanda convinced herself it was the tale that held her attention, not the one telling it.

"They're something," he continued. "Robbie and old Joe were my favorites. Robbie's a big bay draft." Finn raised his arm to show his size. "Has a white stripe down his face, and old Joe was a flea-bitten gray. This one time, on my way out of a tight squeeze, I hopped off the cart to lead Joe on, but he wouldn't move his feet no way, no how. Right then I heard the creaking and knocking in the walls. Not two minutes later, a ceiling timber splintered and collapsed in the tunnel ahead, sending a ton of slate down onto the men there."

"Land," breathed Amanda, her eyes round.

"I was just a'shaking and holding on to Joe to keep my knees from buckling. Backed up and found another route out. Two men were crushed, and old Joe had known it was coming." Finn shook his head and shuddered. "After that, as often as I could, I'd keep a peppermint in my pockets for the ones on my shift. They're God's creatures, after all, stuck under there day after day, only seeing the sun and grass for short bits of time."

"I'm sure your small kindness eases their burden," Amanda said, her voice soft. A man who went out of his way to be kind to animals was gentle in most other ways, too.

"I hope so. To get to the deeper pits of the mine, you got to travel down an open elevator cage, with the pulleys just a'shrieking. Course they also need horses down in those pits, and no horse with sense between its ears would walk willingly into a contraption such as that."

"I don't imagine they would." Amanda thought of Alice and her tale about Turnip bolting from the mine shaft.

"My eyes bugged outta my head the first time I watched a crew bind a horse's legs, cover his eyes and ears with a length of cloth, and fit him to a harness that lifted him off the ground until he dangled from a chain above the pit shaft. They lowered him down, down, down, that chain swinging and spinning, knocking the horse into the walls as he was lowered, every flight instinct in him buzzing like a nest of hornets. Least I could do was offer a peppermint and a soft word."

Amanda let her hand lie on top of Finn's as he rested from his tale. Neither one of them seemed surprised.

"I ain't talked this much in a month of Sundays," Finn said, his cheeks coloring.

"Please," said Amanda. "I wish you'd go on. You're a fine story-teller." She smiled in encouragement.

Finn ran a hand over his mouth, and Amanda thought she detected a grin hiding beneath it.

"One time," he went on, "we showed up to work, and men were crawling all over the place like a hill of ants someone had kicked a boot into. Just before shift end, they'd blasted near a new seam, and the whole room buckled. We dug out five men and a crushed canary cage."

The sting of tears burned Amanda's eyes and she looked down at the quilt, studying its pattern and willing the drops not to fall. She didn't want to appear pitying, but it broke her heart what the miners—what Finn—had to endure. She was grateful that either he was too polite or too caught up in his story to notice its effect on her.

"I caught sight of one of the mule skinners coming out, but his cart wasn't full of coal." Now it was Finn's turn to swipe at his eyes as the tears rose. "It was good old Joe. Feller spoke up and said it must'a been the knockers, that they'd got in a good lick. I didn't know then what the knockers were."

"Oh, Finn," breathed Amanda. "Poor old Joe. I'm so sorry."

"I nicked off a lock of mane and stowed it in my pocket. I imagined Joe rolling in a field of Kentucky bluegrass like the horses my daddy used to work with, and 'fore anyone knew better, I lifted Joe's lip and palmed one last peppermint into his mouth. Felt like the whole weight of that night sky had settled on my heart. Now, I know any given day is dangerous." He patted his leg. "Obviously. But I tell you right now, losing Joe was like being filled up with wet sand. Pulling rock out of the earth just to burn it up is sometimes a bitter tonic to swallow."

Amanda's eyes shone, and it took all her strength not to lean across the distance and hug Finn close to her. "I wish I could do something to ease your sadness," she whispered. "It's more than seems right for a person to bear."

"You already did," he said. "Just by being here."

"Dinner's 'bout ready," Rai announced, her voice ringing bright.

Amanda stood in a rush. "I best be going," she said. She hadn't meant to stay this long, but it was as if she'd been caught up in a spell. "It was right nice talking to you, Finn."

"If you can make it sooner'n two more weeks, we wouldn't complain." Finn's mouth curved in an honest-to-goodness smile.

Amanda returned it, with the corners of her mouth crinkling. "I'll see what I can do," she promised. "Now, when the magazines and papers get worn out or too out-of-date, I'm allowed to give them to folks to use for wallpapering against the cold. We don't have any extra right now, but maybe directly."

"We're fine," said Rai. "Lots of folks worse off." Amanda nodded. Every family on her route said that, down to the most hangdog of them all.

"I'm gonna leave you with this reader. Each page has a picture with its name under it. See here? Dog. Cat. House. I bet if you study on it enough times, you'll be able to recognize the words without the pictures. Try it." Amanda casually placed it on the table within Sass's reach. "I'll see what I can do about making my way up here sooner. Meantime, you take care, Finn." She buttoned her coat and wrapped her woolen scarf snug around her neck. "And, Sass, if you see my folks again, be sure and tell 'em I said hello."

∿

Sass didn't meet Amanda's eyes, and the book woman turned and quickly slipped through the cabin door to prevent the cold from creeping in.

Once she'd gone, Finn patted the spot beside him in the bed. "C'mon over here, Sass, and let's have a look at that reader. Between you and me, I bet we can figger out the words."

Sass climbed under the quilt with her brother, careful not to jostle his leg or wake up her little sister on his opposite side. It had been a nice visit with the book woman, and Sass had tried to ruin it with meanness. Miz Rye had brightened up the place for certain, lifting Finn's spirits better than anything else had over the past weeks. That was just it, Sass realized. The green vine of jealousy had crept in and soured Sass's mood. She'd wanted to be the one who coaxed Finn's old spirit out. Goodness' sakes, happy was happy, she scolded herself, no matter who brung it. Sass broke one of the fried pies Amanda had brought in half and handed one piece to Finn. Together they opened to the first page as the sweet tang filled her mouth.

"Apple!" she pointed, tasting and smelling and seeing it all at once. A wonder, how letters strung together could mean all the things she sensed: the tart crunch, the sweet juices, the red peel, and the ripe smell that spoke of blue fall skies and crisp leaves. And could *apple* mean this, too? The feeling of her heart floating in her chest as she sat beside her brother, his arm around her shoulders, a piece of him come back to life.

Chapter 11

"I don't 'spect you to lay down any wagers, but you gotta be there to tend 'em and have 'em ready." Gripp was exactly where he was meant to be—in a management role rather than day laboring on someone else's schedule. He'd learned to keep an eye peeled for men who'd grown skittish of the mines, and after the last cave-in, he believed he'd found one to fit the bill.

Gripp had met Finn MacInteer by accident, run into him outside the mining office one frigid day, a couple of months after the unfortunate cave-in. The boy was skittish as a colt. Gripp had raised a hand to Finn outside in the road and invited him to share a sandwich near a trash barrel someone had kindled for warmth. He'd unraveled his whole story before Finn had taken his third bite. Folks had always pegged him a talker, catching hold of a story by the tail and following after it every which way it led.

"Name's Spider," he said by way of introduction. A name was a slippery thing, changing as need be, depending on your whereabouts or what served your purpose. He was many years past being Gripp Jessup, and he'd never liked the name anyhow. "Been in the mines for years," Gripp had told him. "In and out." He'd held up his left hand and wiggled three fingers and two nubs. "Lost two fingers down in a mine somewhere in West Virginnie. Knockers prob'ly strung 'em into a necklace. Never did find 'em. Fellers up thataway give me this name and it stuck." He shook his head. "Could be worse 'uns, I s'pose. That leg of yourn? That from the last trouble here?"

Finn had nodded, rubbing his knee. "They say I was lucky."

"What happened?"

"Ceiling fell. I was pinned, an arm and leg held under rock, stuck there with my lantern making shadows on the ceiling, listening to the knockers banging and knowing the next sound might be the last thing I heard before being squashed flat."

Gripp whistled low, his conscience not stirred a bit. The collapse had been his own doing, to settle a score with someone who'd crossed him, but he wasn't about to own up to that fact.

Finn continued. "After the dust cleared, fellers came pouring in like ants, hitching up the horses to pull the big rocks off and pounding in timbers to shore up the ceiling—what was left of it."

"Shoot. And they call that lucky?"

Finn had barked a bitter laugh. "Every time I think about it, panic bubbles up like a creek fixing to flood."

"Lucky ones weren't anywhere near the mine that day, I'd wager. Now that's what I'm thinking is a smarter move."

"I don't follow." Finn had shoved the last bite of sandwich into his mouth and chewed.

Spider had leaned in closer, looked over his shoulder, and lowered his voice. "I'm fixing to get heavy into a new venture, see? One that don't leave me black as the ace of spades at the end of the day and that don't have a chance of dropping any more fingers. Seems to me you might be the kind of feller who'd be interested in the same." He let his gaze linger on Finn's leg.

"Say as I might?" Finn had answered. "What are we talking?"

"I learned one thing from the big crash a few years ago. Diversify! In other words, it ain't no good to put all your eggs in one basket. One tumble down the hill, and them eggs is broke and running ever'where.

You ever heard of Humpty Dumpty? Well, that won't be us." Gripp nudged Finn with an elbow and winked.

Gripp had lain it all out. He'd do most of the heavy lifting since he already had the know-how and experience with running liquor. He just needed a good spot of land near a creek to operate the still, one that wouldn't be too hard for Finn to get to with his bum leg and handy walking stick. In the off-season, when they weren't brewing and getting stashes to bootleggers, he had about twenty crates full of roosters ready to fight. If Finn could tend to them while he kept the still fired up, neither one would have to work that hard, all told, and they could split the cash. Well, maybe seventy-thirty, since he had done all the planning and up-front investing. Fair was fair. No telling how big they could grow the enterprise as long as they were quiet and smart about it.

"You strike me as both quiet *and* smart. Just the kind of partner I been needing. You get squeamish about anything, just say the word and you can bow out. No hard feelings."

Gripp had Finn convinced it was a win-win, a sure ticket out of the mines, and a way to bring in some cash. "You can be careful and keep your nose clean," he'd coaxed. "Not all moonshiners are no-count outlaws. You wouldn't be doing the dirty parts anyway; I'm the one getting my hands dirty."

When he sensed hesitation, Gripp zeroed in. "Now, if you're worried about your family, this'll help them, too. You don't want to be no deadweight, under your mama's feet. You're old enough to make decisions for yourself anyhow, ain't you?" He rested a moment to let his words settle in. "Whattya say? You in?" asked Gripp, his right hand outstretched. "You ready to learn a new trade? It's decent money, and the sky floats above while you do it, a regular blue sky that won't cut loose and fall."

The boy had shaken his hand, just as he'd wagered he would. And he'd known right off at least two prime spots they could set up a still, back deep in the woods, close to water, and covered by trees and wild grapevine, where it wouldn't be easy to walk up on. As for a place for roosters, there was a space not far from Finn's own house that he could get to easy enough. They'd have to watch for coyotes and foxes, weasels and skunks, all the things that went after an easy meal.

"You ain't seen my roosters," Gripp had bragged. "They'll fight to the death and send them critters flying with their tails between their legs. It's something to see! They got spurs two inches long and sharp as a razor after a strop."

With the locations secured, he set to work assembling a still with Finn's help. Through the cold, gray months of winter, they stole blocks of time to arrange things. They hauled bags of meal, malt corn, and flour out into the woods, half dragging, half carrying their supplies. Once everything was gathered, they fashioned a stove out of stone and mud from the creek, with a hole beneath where the fire would burn and a flat top where the still would sit. Finn carved and ran a wooden trough from the creek to the site so that they could siphon cold running water throughout the process.

Making a good batch of ten or twelve gallons of moonshine took a solid eight or more days. Once Gripp had run the liquor through the still twice and it tasted to his liking, he declared the whiskey ready—around 110 proof. Many times, Gripp tasted himself into a stupor, and Finn had to take over and make sure the fire didn't burn too hot or the jugs overflow at the worm's end. This was partly why Gripp liked to have a partner—someone else could finish the work while he had a high time in the woods. Once they divvied it up into jars, gallon jugs, or barrels, whatever was on hand, Gripp sent word to his runners, and they were off to the races.

While they worked, they'd stop to warm their hands by the fire, and Gripp jawed about his past adventures and places he'd lived. One of his prime spots—his first, as it happened—was Nashville. The city had industry, the spectacle of regular pasture races with beautiful horses, and the celebrity of a new one-hour radio show that boasted fiddlers and pickers like Uncle Jimmy Thompson, Bill Monroe, and Uncle Dave Macon. Gripp hung around outside the Ryman stage and listened to the music that drifted out into the street, jealous of the attention the musicians received, their names on the marquee out front. He wanted to matter like that.

He hadn't walked Nashville's streets long before he discovered Black Bottom in the poorer Sixth Ward, named for the frequent flooding of the Cumberland that coated the roads with its silty residue. The nickname might have also had something to do with its residents—poor coloreds, many of them freed slaves, who lived and worked along the river or in service jobs in the houses of well-off whites. What drew Gripp was the colorful assortment of whorehouses, saloons, and gambling joints.

While folks elsewhere in the city were in a frenzy over some dustup about a monkey and a feller named Scopes, Gripp lost himself in the pleasures of Sadie Rue, a wide-hipped mistress who schooled him in the ways of women. Thanks to Sadie's loose lips, an amorous sheriff's deputy got wind of his midnight route. An ambush and gunfight (thank goodness for his inherited pistol) left him with a warrant out for running liquor and killing a lawman. Once more, he'd hopped the trusty L&N and lit out from Nashville, this time with a .45 caliber bullet lodged in his thigh and a smoldering lifelong grudge against Miz Sadie Rue.

"You watch," Gripp told Finn. "Won't be no time before word gets out about my—our—whiskey. This ain't the kind of fancy bourbon that needs so much time to age in a barrel for some kind of special flavor and color. No need to wait that long or pay that much when you can drink it pure and simple, the way the good Lord intended."

"I don't have a taste for neither," Finn admitted.

"Then you won't be drinking up the profit," said Gripp. "That's more for us. I gotta camp out here to keep the furnace stoked, and we don't want folks rooting out our spot. When we're cooking, you'll act as lookout. I ain't about to sit in a jail cell for nobody. Ain't been caught yet, so don't worry 'bout that none.

"Back in Corbin, I needed a lookout and had to let a feller in on my whereabouts. All he had to do was ring a cowbell in case of a raid. Ugliest feller you ever saw. Had a ring of warts that circled his neck like a collar, so I called him Toady. Toady Newsome. Nephew of one of the local lawmen, and he let on like we'd be in the clear."

Gripp continued, keeping one eye locked on Finn as he unspooled his cautionary tale. "Now Toady did keep watch, but he wasn't like you. Even though we'd worked it out fair and square, like me and you, he figured his cut should be bigger since he had to sit out in the weather, getting drained by ticks and mosquitoes."

"We're both out here working," said Finn.

"That's what I told him!" said Gripp, glad Finn could see common sense. "He didn't see eye to eye with that, so one day, he didn't ring the bell. Easy as you please, he let the sheriff and three deputies walk right by him and up the hill to the still. Lucky for me, I'd just hacked off the head of a copperhead with a spade and carried it off over the hill to chuck it into the ravine. Six black crows shot out of the treetops, cawing to wake the dead, and I dropped to my belly. Toady was at the creek, pointing the way like a tour guide."

"I wouldn't do that," Finn assured him.

Gripp left out the part about how he'd hid out behind the feed store later that evening until Toady emerged, balancing a fifty-pound sack of corn on each shoulder. Gripp was close enough to see the white wart nubs stubbling his lookout's wretched neck.

"Already setting her back up again?" he'd asked Toady, gesturing at the corn sacks with the end of his pistol. Gripp chewed a two-inch stub of a hickory stick in one corner of his mouth, and he switched the stick to the opposite corner with a quick flick of his tongue. "I only know one way to keep your big mouth shut for certain."

Gripp had fired twice, hitting Toady first in the left knee so that he'd buckle, the corn sacks falling heavy on the ground in front of him. The second shot in his gut ended him, and he fell forward onto the bags, his blood seeping through the burlap and ruining its contents.

~

Finn MacInteer was strong and plucky, even with his game leg. Gripp was happy enough to partner with him since he shouldered a good share of the work, but Gripp's trust only went so far. At the first sign of the breeze shifting, Gripp wouldn't hesitate to cut his losses. It was up to Finn whether he ended up as one of those.

It was heavy work, except for the tasting, but the money trickled in, reliable as the sunrise. Folks tended to go without a lot of things before they'd do without their corn liquor. Gripp reassured Finn that his role in the making of it had nothing to do with how people chose to spend their wages. When Finn brought up tales of families and children who missed meals, families he knew good and well had a pa who was one of their regular customers, Gripp dismissed his concerns.

"He'd get it from other fellers if he weren't getting it from us," Gripp pointed out. "You can always buy 'em a sack o' groceries to leave on their steps if you take a mind." Gripp handed Finn a handful of bills for his take, and Finn slid them into his pocket.

The roosters were another story. They weren't nearly as much trouble as brewing corn liquor. Gripp set up on a space of land just over the ridge from the MacInteer cabin in a direction they had no need to walk, where there were no patches of ginseng or deer trails. Finn had to tote water and feed to the birds.

Gripp set up individual huts for each of the birds, some fashioned from barrels, some from salvaged pieces of tin. He tethered each of them to their huts by straps on their legs, and they seemed content to scratch and peck in their small kingdoms, crowing to beat the band from sunup till sundown. Finn occasionally dragged their huts to fresh ground so that they could hunt and peck in new territory, but mostly he fed and watered them. They were as varied as folks in a city, some with plumed colored feathers on their necks and heads, some with tails that cascaded in long feathers that almost brushed the ground. Red, white, black, speckled, and one that was so black it was almost purple—they looked like pictures of fancy ladies from Hollywood.

For the most part, they were surprisingly even-tempered. Sometimes, in the interest of protecting their hens, roosters could turn mean and mount sneak attacks on a person, ambushing them and flying at their calves and ankles with wings beating and talons clawing. It was fearsome to behold.

"We had a rooster once that turned mean," Finn recounted to Gripp. "It chased my sister clear across the yard, and she ran screaming into the house in tears. My mama marched right outside and snatched that rascal up by its neck. Gave it two sharp twists, and that was that." He chuckled at the memory of his mother's ire. "Mama can turn a mean-tempered rooster into supper before you can stomp your old hat."

"Don't be wringing any necks up here," he cautioned. "I need these fellers ready to fight."

He knew how to breed them for it, honing their natural instincts to go after the color red. The fights rarely lasted long. As soon as they were placed in the ring, the birds might posture for a few moments, dropping a wing and dancing sideways, but then it was Katy, bar the door. They flew at each other, sometimes balancing impossibly on their wings while the spurs on their yellow legs pummeled furiously. Every so often, Gripp hiked up the mountain to the cock cabin, as he called it, selected seven or eight birds for the night's event, and took bets on them to win, as smug and cocksure as a rooster himself. Finn never went. He didn't have the stomach for it. Instead, he was on hand when Gripp returned, ready to doctor a gashed breast or patch a pecked eye.

Finn and Gripp got on this way for a good while, all through the winter, useful to each other in a mutual arrangement of terms. Finn was softer than Gripp might've liked, but he knew his place and kept his head down. Like any self-interested shiner, Gripp carried a stout, foot-long leather billy club and knucks in case trouble wandered his way. Once when they'd gone to meet a pair of bootleggers, the boys had been sampling a bit of the merchandise. They'd acted ill to have been kept waiting and got a little too mouthy for Gripp's taste. He'd torn into them without warning, his hair wild and spittle flying from his lips as he delivered blows. After they'd set sail off into the woods, Gripp had come back to himself, smoothed his hair with his three fingers, and slipped the knucks back into his pocket. Still breathing hard, but the dark glint had faded from his eyes, and he'd turned to Finn.

"Ain't no man alive gonna serve me disrespect," he'd said. "Or woman neither. This line of work has a pecking order, and I aim to be at the pointy end of it."

Finn shoved his hands in his pockets. "Aw, they were full o' drink is all."

"They were full o' *something* all right, and about half of it was piss and vinegar." Gripp had spat in the dirt and wiped his mouth with his sleeve. "I wager they're emptied of it now." He massaged his battered left hand.

"Reckon losing those fingers in the mine didn't hold you back much, Spider," Finn observed.

Gripp had spread the remaining digits of his left hand and stared at them for a long moment before answering.

"This wasn't from no mine," he admitted. "A Smith & Wesson .22 took those off." He shook his head. "Guy jumped me from behind and I tried to grab it outta his hands. Like to bled to death 'fore I could staunch it. Feller was mad at me over a woman, but he got over it after he drown'd his sorrows in a high-water creek." Gripp had laughed, half at the memory and half at Finn's startled expression.

Gripp had suggested Finn get him some tools of the trade and carry some ready iron, but it was one thing to run batches of liquor and tend fowl and another to beat a man or flash a gun at a cockfight. Finn still ate at his family's table every night, looking his daddy in the eye and bearing the worry and adoration of his sisters and brother he went on and on about. Families were nothing but a liability in Gripp's way of thinking. He warned Finn about other distractions, too, when not long into their arrangement, he started carrying on about some book librarian who'd begun to pay regular visits to their home, bringing things to study on. Finn claimed she was pleasant to look at for certain but smart, too, and persistent as a mosquito. Bit by bit, the words she carried up the mountain sank into his head, he said, and he was learning to read.

"That's all well and good as long as you show up where you're supposed to," Gripp told him. "In my experience, women are generally good for feeding your appetite one of two ways. Other'n that, they lay too much burden on your head."

"Maybe you just ain't known the right one," Finn ventured. "This one's different. She's like a ministering angel."

Gripp had laughed. "Remember you telling me about that feller Jacob in the Bible? Wrastled an angel, and then that angel done hexed his hip and made him limp forever. I reckon maybe since you already got the limp, maybe you just want to get straight to the wrastling part." Gripp winked and cackled again.

"It ain't like that," Finn had protested, his face a scowl.

"It's *always* like that," Gripp had said darkly, and then he let it lie.

Chapter 12

Long, cold winter months slipped by. The buffed-gray sky hung low week after week, holding in the cold and blanketing the mountains in thick blue fog each morning. Amanda longed for color other than the tenacious pine and cedar sprinkled among the barren hardwoods. A slight broken patch of blue in the sky or the flit of a redbird hunting seeds in the snow did her heart good. Now, she trotted out briskly when she made her routes, racing daylight and weather. She often had to dismount and hunt for the least frozen spots where it would be safest to cross the creeks she'd easily splashed across just a few months earlier. She was grateful for Junebug, who could navigate the creek beds and logging trails from memory. Snowdrifts blown against the banks on either side of a gulley erased the path entirely.

Many mornings Amanda set out wrapped snug in her coat and scarf, with only her nose poking out. Mooney pulled roasted potatoes from the hot ashes and handed them to Amanda to tuck in each pocket to warm her hands. She would eat them for dinner on the way once they cooled. Flurries swirled in the wind and stuck to her eyelashes as she trekked along her trails. Lots of times she spotted tracks in the snow or frozen mud by the slushy creek beds: deer, foxes, rabbits. If she'd known how, Amanda might have trapped something to make a stew, but she and Mooney had to rely on bartering with some of the families in town for such things. Occasionally she'd spy a deer's brown hide, moving against the frozen backdrop. It might raise its head and stand alert as she passed or startle with a flash of white tail and bound away, crashing through the underbrush.

Hard as the routes were with snowfall and cold, the families on the book routes looked forward more than ever to her visits. Cabin fever had set in weeks ago, and mamas were desperate for distractions for the little'uns and something to pore over by the fire as the nights stretched on. What had started as a chance to earn a wage had grown into something of a mission in Amanda's mind, almost a sacred duty as she witnessed week by week the small joys and discoveries the worn books, magazines, and scrapbooks brought to the cabins she reached.

A marvel, even Maude Harris, the granny woman who hiked out to meet her on her Friday route, still showed up to wait. Often by the time Amanda made it to the crossroads where they met, Maude would have built a fire and settled in to smoke a pipe on a stump, her cheeks rosy from the heat. It gave Amanda a chance to visit and warm herself a bit before continuing on her way. The school she visited had disbanded for the winter, which meant Amanda wouldn't see Vessel until spring. She missed their regular socializing and the faces of the children who'd run out to meet her when they spied her mule from the schoolhouse windows.

With the school off her route temporarily, between her own work at home and looking after Miles, Amanda squeezed in extra time at the MacInteer place. She had quizzed Vessel for the best way to go about teaching letters and reading. She was officially a librarian, not a teacher, as she'd never made it to the college in Berea, but the cold winter days provided the perfect opportunity for Sass and her family to study and practice what they learned. Or at least the girls and Finn.

Junebug trotted eagerly up the path to the MacInteers' place. He'd been there often enough that he knew to expect soft hands and a bit of hay to while away the time. Amanda led him around to the lean-to out back, where he would stand tied for as long as she stayed, and slid her saddlebags onto the crook of her arm. She stroked his long ears and left him with some hay before she followed the muddy path up to the porch, her breath clouds of white in the cold, still air. At the sound of her stomping boots, the door latch lifted from within, and Fern peeked out.

"Miz Rye," she gasped. "We didn't even hear you come up. Snow must've dampened your footsteps. Come in, come in." Fern ushered her through the door, taking her load and shutting the door fast behind her as the wind howled lonely through the treetops.

Inside was a bit warmer since it was out of the wind, but it wasn't close to toasty. Pages of newsprint tacked to the walls helped block the trickles of cold air that pried their way through every chink in the wood. Rai, Fern, and Sass wore layers of clothing, with fingerless gloves covering their hands. Hiccup was burrowed under the quilt on the bed, humming to herself in her private hidey-hole, and Finn sat at the table, a potato in one hand and a knife in the other. He rotated the potato as he peeled so that the brown peeling came loose in one long, unbroken curl.

Finn no longer lay abed, sweating and pale. Although he hadn't gone back to the mines, he'd apparently picked up work where he could find it and appeared stronger, less aimless.

Amanda noticed a walking stick leaning against Finn's chair. "That's a fine stick. Did you make it, Finn?" she asked, studying the scenes carved into it.

Finn was quick to lay on the praise. "That's all Cricket's doing. He carved the length of it. It being hick'ry, I'll never need worry 'bout it getting busted. It's strong as a goat's breath. Cricket here's a ready carpenter. He don't need my help in seeing what's in the wood no more."

"It's a beauty," said Amanda, running her hands along the patterns. "Why, here's a fox, trees, mountains, and birds."

Rai chimed in. "With that walking stick, Finn gets outside to sit on the porch or walks to the barn and rubs down the horses. He's getting his strength back, walking in the woods for hours at a time, despite the weather. Makes all the difference in his spirits. He's even wisecracking again, helps me snap beans or peel onions." She glanced at Amanda with a warm smile and a furtive wink. "He also studies the leavings you bring."

With Amanda there, the previously quiet room came to life. Rai stoked the stove to warm a bit of tea, and Sass and Fern drew their chairs up to the table and scattered to retrieve the books from where they'd been left in this corner or that. In no time, they sat ready for their lesson, the part of the week they looked forward to most.

Sass pulled out a wrinkled piece of paper and slid it in front of Amanda as soon as she was seated. "Looky here, Miz Rye, I finished the entire alphabet, start to end."

Amanda picked up the paper. Careful letters were written in lines over and over where Sass had practiced. Faint outlines of previous attempts were visible beneath them. Sass had traced, erased, and traced again until she'd gotten it just right. Amanda couldn't help the grin that spread across her face.

"Why, Sass, you've been working so hard, I can tell. These have come a long way since the last time I was here. This *B* is perfect, and the *W*—that's a hard one—looks just right."

Sass fairly purred under Amanda's praise, and Rai squeezed her daughter's shoulder, adding her own encouragement. "Sass is a quick study, for certain. Anytime she has a spare moment, she's a-poring over them books, writing letters with that pencil you give her." Rai glanced at her older daughter. "Fern, too. 'Cept she's got her hands full of rabbits."

Amanda turned to the older girl. "Fern? You have more?"

Fern brought a lumpy pillowcase to the table and turned it upside down. Twenty or so stuffed rabbits tumbled out, all ears and legs. Amanda clapped her hands.

"Precious as can be," she praised. "I love how they're all different. This one has flowers on its face, and this one is flop-eared because of the way you stuffed it." She laughed. "Oh, and this one"—she held up one half the size of the rest—"this little'un is the sweetest."

"That 'un came from scrap left over, but it'd be big enough for a baby to play with."

Sass flipped one over. "Finn had the idea to use cattail fluff for the tails. Ain't that something? And we rubbed black walnut stain on for eyes and nose."

Rai picked up a rabbit and held it to her nose. "We had the ideer to tuck in some smells. This 'un has some dried lavender inside. In some I put rose hips, sage, or mint."

"Daddy said we orta string 'em up in the outhouse to cut the air a bit." Finn laughed. "It ain't a half-bad notion."

"The young'uns on my route will love them to death," Amanda said. "In the spring when the school opens back up, Miz Vessel will be tickled to have some of these to give as prizes for good lessons. Thank you all so much. This is right kind and generous with all you have to do."

Rai sat in a rocker by the fire as Hiccup settled in her lap, drawn out by all the commotion. She cradled a rabbit of her own, one with a white flour-sack body and a lopsided face. One of its paws was thinner than the rest from where she'd carried it around. "The sack donations you brought from the library office were most of it. It give us a nice job to do with the days so short. Once we got Fern's pattern figgered out, they pop out pretty quick. All you need is a coupl'a rabbits, you know how they are, and it's not long 'fore you got a whole sack full."

"That's the honest truth," Amanda admitted, and they all laughed.

While the girls stacked the books, Amanda turned to Finn, who'd finished his pile of potatoes and leaned back in his chair, digging under his fingernails with the knife.

"And how are you faring?" she asked.

"Up and about. Learning letters, same as them, but I feel about as useful as tits on a bull."

"I don't know anyone else who'd a' thought up using cattails for rabbit tails," she teased, "but they're perfect. It's been nice being able to see you when I come by. If you were back in the saddle, I woulda missed out on that."

Finn grinned and nodded. "That's one good thing," he allowed. "I sure have enjoyed your stopping by more often." He fell quiet. "Don't you worry, riding around all over creation on your own?"

"Sometimes." Alice's alarming story about the three men flitted through her thoughts. "But I ain't afraid to fire a gun if it came to it." She shrugged. "'Sides, I got a boy at home to take care of, so as long as I'm able, I'll do what needs done."

Finn winked at her. "That's some gumption and spunk, I'll give you that, but I'll admit it troubles me some, thinkin' about you on that lonesome route."

A rosy bloom of color flushed Amanda's cheeks. "Is that so?" she pressed. "I'm pleased to know you're thinking of me, Finn MacInteer." She looked forward to her visits more than he knew, more than she even admitted to herself.

"To have been here right regular, you manage to stay pretty clammed up," Finn observed. "You oughta know by now I don't bite, and I done tole you prob'ly way more than you wanted to know, but by gum, you let out tidbits like a careful angler letting out a bit of line at a time. Afraid you're gonna get snagged up on a rock."

Amanda dropped her eyes. He was right, of course, but the sting of betrayal still pained her, even all these years later. She glanced around the room at the crackling fire, pile of rabbits, and the books stacked and ready. Tears brimmed and, surprised, she swiped a hand across her eyes to stop their fall. It dawned on her that keeping her guard up and distance between herself and this family—Finn in particular—was a second betrayal, one she visited upon her own self.

"There's not that much interesting to know," she told him, "but ask me later and I'll keep no secrets. Now then, Sass, let's see how far you got through the reader I left." Amanda cracked open the spine of the book, and Sass scooted closer while Fern looked over her shoulder, ready to follow along.

Sass took a deep breath, looked up at Rai, who was standing with her lips pressed together, and read: "Sunny Boy raced into the house. On the table was his supper. What do you think it was? It was a big bowl of bread and milk."

Amanda nearly came out of her chair. The whole family burst out laughing at her round eyes and mouth hanging open. "What on earth?" she exclaimed.

Rai beamed at Amanda, her eyes shining. "I told you she's been practicing. She got those letters down pretty good, and long about last week, I heard her reading to beat the band. Just took off with it."

"Sass?" Amanda marveled. "Why didn't you say so?"

Sass nodded shyly, pushing her hair out of her eyes. "I wanted to surprise you. I kept thinking about what you told me, how the letters make sounds and the sounds link together. Lots of the little words I figgered out because we looked through those picture books."

"Yes, you were quick to pick those up."

"After that, ever' chance I got I'd study over the words in the big book, matching them to what was happening in the picture. Couple days ago, lightning struck right in my head. All that puzzling and figgering, and all at once, the letters started talking to me. I could hear the sounds they made in my head, and if I just whispered 'em out, my mouth was saying the word on the page."

"Even Harley was bumfuzzled," Rai said. "He give her pages of the Bible to puzzle out, and sure enough, she could make out stories we knew was in there."

"Well, land sakes. Sass, you've opened a treasure box. You'll always have the key to that box now. Books hold all kinds of treasures waiting to be discovered. Anything you want to know, you can look up in a book somewhere."

Finn laughed. "Well, I hope you brought a bunch today, Amanda, because Sass here's been reading every darn word around here. Labels on store goods, receipts from the mine store, newspaper stories that's been glued to the wall for years now. They argue every night about turning down the lantern for bed because she's wanting one more page."

"It won't be long 'fore all the rest of you are doing the same, I'll wager. It's a wonder, isn't it, Sass? Feels like something magical?"

Sass's head bobbed up and down. "Yes, yes! It *does* feel like magic," she agreed. "Lines on a flat page get in your head and make a whole story with people and animals and everything."

Amanda tilted her head back and laughed. Sass's excitement was catching. She remembered when it had all come together for her, in her father's study, when letters made sounds and sounds made words, each one with a secret meaning that she had the power to understand. A curtain had parted, revealing a whole new way of seeing. She was a hard green buttercup bud that had finally busted out in bright yellow, open to the sunshine. All that flooded back watching Sass, proud as a peacock that just realized it has a whole tail full of feathers.

A crackle like the sizzle of onions in a skillet started outside, and Amanda jumped up from her seat and went to the window. As she'd ridden in, a misty drizzle of rain had fallen steadily, but now it had turned to sleet, and icy pellets bounced off the porch steps outside. It looked like heaven was broadcasting handfuls of salt over every surface.

"Junebug!" Amanda grabbed her coat from where it hung on the peg by the door. "You mind if I snug him in the barn? I leave him out in this and he'll be in a foul mood come time to ride home."

Finn got to his feet. "I'll help you with that." Nobody said anything as he shrugged into his coat and jammed a hat on his head. Fern raised her eyebrows and nudged Sass with an elbow. Sass paused mid-page, flipping through a new book, and Amanda felt Sass watching them as Finn held the door open and edged out with her, one hand on his walking stick and one on her lower back.

Just before they'd shut the door, Amanda heard Sass whisper to her mother, "Finn needs to be careful walking in the ice."

"Looks to me like he's making it just fine," Rai said, and Amanda glanced back to see Rai smiling at the window, her chin just above Sass's head.

Amanda untied Junebug, who'd pinned his ears back and stamped his feet at her arrival. "Sorry, Bug," she said. "Let's get you outta this mess."

Finn led the way, holding the barn door open wide so that she could lead the mule in. They worked together, Finn tidying an empty stall between the two horses while Amanda slipped off Junebug's bridle and saddle, hanging them to dry. Sleet hammered the roof above them.

"Better now?" she murmured. Junebug's ears swiveled toward her, and he shook himself like a dog, glad to be out of the weather.

Finn laughed. "He's got opinions, don't he?"

Amanda closed the stall door as she slipped out. "Most certainly. But we understand each other. He takes pretty good care of me, so it's on me to return the favor."

They lingered in the shelter of the barn, resting their arms on the stall door and watching Junebug rustle in the hay with his damp nose. Amanda thought it was the most natural thing in the world when Finn reached over and laid a hand atop her arm. In response, she tilted her head until it rested on his shoulder. She was close enough to feel his chest rise and fall with his breath. When he laid his cheek atop her hair, she closed her eyes to savor the nearness of him.

They remained that way for only a moment, but it was enough time to signal a change between them, a new tenderness that made Amanda grip the stall door a little tighter to steady herself. Her heart ached to trust him. They held hands as they walked to the barn door, letting go to wrap their coats tighter as the wind bit outside.

Chapter 13

When Harley wasn't digging like a mole underground, he would take Cricket out to hunt whenever they could. Sometimes when Amanda stopped by, she'd miss the two of them altogether as they'd be gone most of the day if the weather was clear enough. Even Digger and Tuck, who'd spent their lazy summers lolling on the porch, did their part now, trailing scents through the trees, howling and baying their deep *a-youuu, a-youuu* to signal they'd treed a squirrel or raccoon. Finn would listen for the sound echoing through the cold woods and narrate for them how the hunt unfolded.

"That'll be Digger, now. Hear that? He's got a lower voice. He's always first on the go." Finn would hold up a finger, his eyes closed. "And here comes Tuck, the copycat. He barks twice as much to make up for missing the scent in the first place. They're likely a mile off to the east, prob'ly near Flat Creek. I hope they don't go after no beavers, now." Not long after the yowls and bays reached a crescendo, a shot would echo over the roof of the cabin, and the hounds would quit yapping. "Wonder if that was Cricket or Daddy? Guess we'll hear about it when they get here."

They kept a good-natured running tally of what each of them bagged for the week. It was hardly fair since Harley spent half his time at the mines, and Cricket used those hours to set traps and snares, which counted toward his total. Harley had decreed that fish and frogs didn't figure in; they were too easy. That didn't keep Cricket away from the creeks and deeper pools of icy water, trying to snag a mess of bluegill or an occasional trout that would fry up crispy and golden.

The day of the ice storm, it wasn't long after Amanda and Finn had burst back into the cabin, red-cheeked and laughing, that they heard the familiar boots clomping on the porch steps. Finn and Amanda warmed their hands by the fire, and Digger and Tuck ducked through the open door and made themselves at home close to the orange glow of the coals.

Cricket triumphantly held up a triplet of squirrel tails, and he handed a sack of their skinned corpses to Rai. In a swirl of stomping and shaking off water, Harley and Cricket shucked off wet coats and boots and hung their hats to dry on their pegs.

"It's not fit for man nor beast this evening," Harley declared. "Started out sleet, and now it's coming down jagged icicles." He nodded to Amanda, who scooted to the side to give him room by the fire. "You might jest as well stay here for the night. It'd be miserable going any stretch in this."

Amanda hadn't considered this. She'd always been able to make it home by the end of a route.

"Mooney won't know what's kept me."

"Reckon she'll get the idea once she pokes her nose outside," he said. "It's no use. Even if your mule has pine tar on his shoes, the trails ain't safe as icy as it is, and you're liable to freeze plumb to death."

"Miles," Amanda said, looking to Rai. She would understand her need to return.

"Mooney'll look after him, and you can set out soon as you're able. It won't do him no harm."

Amanda twisted the ring on her hand, the laughter and joking with Finn fading with the worry that rose in her chest. This would be the first time she and Miles would spend a night apart. Of course she trusted Mooney; that wasn't it. Miles was her first priority, the only reason she'd gotten the book route in the first place. A thread of guilt wound itself around Amanda's heart. She should have started home earlier rather than lingering for a few extra minutes with the MacInteers. Now Miles would worry and fret because of her selfishness. She doubted she'd get a lick of sleep all night, but Harley was right.

"What can I do to help you with supper?" Amanda sighed. "Pick out a good book, Sass. You can read it while we fix these squirrels."

Harley and Cricket cleaned up from the hunt, and Rai and Amanda bustled about the small stove, feeding kindling into its glowing maw, salting the game, and chopping the potatoes Finn had peeled. Harley peeped out the window now and then, watching the light fade as the temperature dropped. Although he'd told Amanda it would be foolish to be out in the weather, the foreman wouldn't see it that way. Instead of chancing his job to the next man in line, Harley placed his boots and coat by the fire to gather extra warmth for walking the miles ahead.

"Daddy, Myrtle didn't come up to eat earlier," Fern reported. "Goats and horses look all right, but Myrtle ain't doing right, and she looks to be making bag."

Harley scratched his beard. "If that don't beat all to wait for a' ice storm. Reckon she'll be calving here 'fore too long. I'll round her up before I leave, and boys, you'll have to look after her till I get home. Chuck some logs in that woodstove out there so you won't freeze to death while you're waiting."

"Yessir," Finn said. "We'll handle it. Them chains out in the barn just in case?"

"Should be hanging on the east wall. Might orta knock the dust off, though I reckon ole Myrtle won't much care how clean they are if you's to need 'em. Iodine's sitting in the case there as you walk in."

Supper was lively. Harley and Cricket joked and teased about who was winning the hunting wager, and Fern, Amanda, and Sass talked about the folks on her route and who might like a stuffed rabbit. Poor Hiccup was in a foul mood and fussed.

"Can I do something for Hiccup?" asked Amanda.

"Oh, no, I believe she might have a tapeworm is all. She's hungry 'cause she ain't had 'ary a bite since last night, but after supper here in a minute, I'll give her some."

While Harley took his customary after-supper nap, Fern sat Hiccup on the table while Rai warmed a bit of milk on the stove and held a small jar of it up under Hiccup's nose.

"Smell that?" she coaxed, miming how to breathe deeply. "Smell it good, baby." Hiccup sniffed at the milk and stretched out her hands to drink it, but Rai held her hands down and gradually brought the jar farther and farther from the girl's nose as she sniffed. "Here it comes, good girl."

The flat white head of a worm, wanting supper just as much as Hiccup did, waved out one of Hiccup's nostrils in search of the milk. When enough of it had ventured forth, quick as a hare, Rai set down the jar and grasped the end of the worm with a rag, pulling gently until the accursed parasite was out. Hiccup barely registered anything was happening; her eyes were on the milk and bites of meat and potato that had been set aside for her as a reward. Rai deposited the hateful thing in the bucket of peelings and other chicken scraps.

Once Hiccup had her belly full and they'd cleaned up from supper, they settled on the hearth to read and visit. Amanda recounted news from town, bits and pieces from newspapers she'd seen at the WPA office, how there seemed to be more cars on the road passing through their little spot on the map. Both Rai and Amanda preferred horses or mules since a car couldn't make it up the mountain switchbacks or down a steep logging trail. Neither one had ever ridden in a car, but they didn't seem practical, and *practical* was the byword of the mountains.

"My friend Alice goes right by the rail depot on her route, and men are jumping off the boxcars like frogs in a boiling pot. They ride on top of the train, even in the cold. Guess this mine's one of the few left open, and word's out."

"I don't begrudge a man looking for work, but I hear tell it's bringing some shifty chiselers in," Rai said.

Amanda nodded. "That's a fact. Sometimes the library office opens on Saturdays. They have a radio that uses batteries, and on Saturday evenings they'll play the *Grand Ole Opry* program. Folks from all over gather up to sit for a spell and listen, and it lasts for hours. If you stay for the whole show, you might not get home till after midnight." She laughed. "We had a preacher from a nearby town come once, trying to see what all the commotion was about and why half his church was dozing during his sermon the next day." Amanda considered a moment. "I've seen a few gathered there that I'd call shifty, for certain."

"A radio?" said Sass. "Wouldn't that be fine to hear."

"Oh, yes, in the summer when it's nice out, lots of nights they'll stay open late so folks can hear some of the story shows like *Amos 'n' Andy* or *The Lone Ranger*. But I like the music best. There's some fine banjo on there; a man called Dave Macon picks like his fingers are on fire. Since I'm staying over the night here, when it warms up, maybe you girls can spend an evenin' at my house, and we can go hear the radio."

Sass's mouth hung low and her eyes grew round. "Could I, Mama?" she breathed.

"We'll have to see when it comes time, but it sounds like a fine idea. I'd fancy hearing tunes on a radio myself sometime."

When their chatter stopped, the cabin fell silent except for the *whuffles* and snuffs from Digger and Tuck, enjoying their privileged places inside. The icy rain had stopped pelting the shingles, and the only sounds outside were the wind howling and the creak of the swaying treetops as their bare branches swept the purple night sky clear of stars. Harley pulled his boots on, gave Rai's shoulder a gentle squeeze, and headed out the door with his collar turned up and his hat pulled low around his ears.

"I'll make it to the mines in no time flat," he ventured. "I'll check down the holler for Myrtle and get her up in the barn 'fore I head out.

Don't want this wind whistling down my neck any longer than it has to. Y'all keep an eye on ol' Myrtle, now."

Finn jerked his chin over at Cricket, lying sound asleep across the tick with his pocketknife open in one hand and a block of half-carved wood in the other.

"Mama, Cricket's been out hunting all day. Let him stay in here and rest awhile. Sass and I can go sit with Myrtle and come get him if we need him." He got to his feet and hobbled over to ease the open knife out of his brother's hand. "I'll lay this on the mantel for him to close in the morning. Last thing I need is more bad luck."

Sass had jumped up and pulled on her shoes and now rummaged through the coats for one she could wear. "Let's bring some tea with us. I'll put some in the old kettle."

"Mind if I join?" asked Amanda.

Finn grinned. "Sure, if you can keep the old woodstove fed."

"Rai, once you get Hiccup to sleep, you and Fern will have lots more room in the bed with just the two of you."

"Reckon so," she agreed, a smile on her lips.

The three of them tromped out to the barn in the snow, Sass leading the way and breaking a path through the layer of ice to make it easier for Finn. She carried a lantern in one hand and a steaming kettle of tea in the other. Finn followed, leaning on his walking stick and making his way with careful, measured steps and a limp, and Amanda trailed at the rear, holding another lantern and an armful of quilts. The cold was wet and heavy, dampening their hair and coats. Under the ice lay several inches of snow, and the bright moon shining through the trees cast a blue glow on the ground. In the barn, Myrtle lowed, restless.

The animals squinted against the unexpected light when they walked into the barn. As their eyes adjusted, the dirt floor and paneled pens distilled into more than dark silhouettes. The barn was orderly but chock-full of handmade wood-handled tools; lengths of rope and wire looped and hung on pegs; and piles of feed and seed sacks that

Rai would no doubt fashion into tablecloths, towels, or clothing once they were emptied. Wooden buckets hung on posts in front of the stalls, ready for the day's milking. The sweet, summery smell of hay filled the space, along with the acrid tang of manure and dirty bedding. Surprisingly, the bodies and breath of the livestock cast a little warmth into the room, and it wasn't as frigid as it would've been empty.

Myrtle, her white face bright in the dim light, rustled the hay as she circled her pen and cast anxious glances backward at her rounded sides. The brown-and-white goats in the adjacent pen seemed oblivious of her distress, some standing by their door with their tails flicking and others bedded down for the night, legs tucked up under their bellies. The two horses, Plain Jane and Lincoln, nickered a soft welcome, and Junebug pricked his ears at their entrance. Amanda found a clean corner to set the quilts and lantern down, and she and Sass filled the old woodstove with kindling and twisted bunches of hay while Finn checked the heifer.

It was easy enough to borrow flame from a lantern to light the stove, and soon a robust fire lent a little more warmth to the space. A length of pipe to vent, most likely rigged by Harley, shot out the side of the barn. Amanda imagined a steady stream of gray smoke curling upward into the trees.

Finn leaned on the side of the cow's pen and watched her awhile. "Her bag's waxing right on. Shouldn't be too awful long, Myrtle." As if in response, the heifer splayed her feet, stretched out her neck, and bawled a long, low note from her wide pink mouth.

Amanda laughed. "Easy for you to say, she says. Try being on my side of things."

"Let's tie her up and check it out." He opened the pen door and approached the heifer, talking low and soft. "Sass, I'm gonna loop the end o' this rope over the side of the pen, and you stand out there and hold t'other end of it. I don't think she will, but if she starts to throw a fit, just let 'er go. No sense anybody getting hurt in the tussle."

Sass grabbed the rope and held it tight. Now Myrtle's head was near the outside wall of the pen, and Sass reached in to pet the white curls that stuck up between her eyes. Such long eyelashes. Myrtle's thick pink tongue worked busily, licking her nose repeatedly in a nervous reflex.

"Amanda, you think you can grab hold of her tail here and pull it to the side? Nothing worse than getting whacked by a flying tail covered in cow shit. Good thing you have on gloves."

Despite the cold, Finn removed his coat and laid it on the rails of the pen. He rolled up the sleeve on his right arm as far as it would go, revealing a dark streak on his upper arm. Finn caught Amanda watching before she abruptly looked away.

"That's my coal tattoo," he said, running his hand over the mark. "If you get hit hard enough at the right angle, hard enough to break the skin, it leaves a mark like that. Lots of fellers have 'em, wear 'em like a badge of honor." He shrugged.

"Looks like a fair reminder you survived," she said. "I got this tail now."

With Amanda pulling on Myrtle's tail for all she was worth, Finn eased his bare arm into the heifer's back end. Myrtle ceased her licking and stood still, startled by the new sensation. Finn closed his eyes tight to concentrate, all the while murmuring his way through to soothe the soon-to-be mama.

"There's a nose, that's good. It's facing right. And a shoulder." He shifted positions and one eye opened. "Don't let that tail go, now." Amanda shook her head; she didn't aim to. He nudged up closer to Myrtle, his arm buried up to his shoulder. "Back to the head." He slid a finger into the calf's mouth and felt the tongue work reflexively. "Got a good suckle. He's gonna be hungry when this is all over. Hoof—is that back or front? Let's see, feels like front, but where's the other'n?"

Finn's eyes flew open, and his face contorted with a grimace. He let loose a low moan at the same time as Myrtle lowed again.

"Lord a'mercy," he grunted between clenched teeth. "Son of a gun! Come on, Myrtle, turn loose!" Myrtle stopped lowing, and with a rush of air, Finn backed a few steps away from her, drawing his arm out in one slick movement. He plunged it into a ready bucket he'd placed in the pen and used a towel to wipe it clean of blood and fluids.

"You can turn loose of that tail," he said, massaging his arm. "She clamped down on me in a big contraction keen as a needle. Like being stuck in a vise at the lumberyard. Maybe I'll get the feeling back in my fingers in a minute."

"What'd you feel?" asked Sass, still holding the rope.

"It's a big'un. Facing right, but the front feet are folded back'ards under it 'stead of sticking straight out. Means I gotta go back in and try to move things around. I'm gonna let her keep going a bit on her own first, so she's good and ready."

"Should I go wake up Cricket?"

"Naw, not yet. It'll be a while."

Amanda poured tea into the cups Rai had sent out with them, and they sat on upended buckets by the stove. For a while, the only sound was the crackle of burning wood or one of the horses snorting dust from its nose. Finn stretched his bad leg out in front of the stove and rubbed it absently.

"How's it feeling?" asked Amanda. "You're getting around a whole lot better."

Finn stopped rubbing. "I reckon." He sighed. "It don't hurt near as much as before. With Cricket's walking stick, I'm good to go, but it's not where I want to be. I'll get there by and by."

"What happened that day?" she asked, her voice soft. "In there?"

Sass stayed quiet, huddled in the old Jacob's ladder quilt her mama had given them. She leaned closer. "It's all right if you don't want to say," Amanda added.

Finn rubbed his neck and stared into the red mouth of the woodstove. "Naw, it's just a thing that happened," he said. He took a long sip of tea. "We'd worked down a new shaft on a new seam they'd dug a couple weeks earlier. Canaries tested good; horses were easy and not nervous or jiggy. I was working a twelve-hand draft we call Feather—that's on account of his feet are feathered out fancy like a Percheron or shire. The boys are shoveling and singing and whatnot in this room 'bout four feet high and six feet square. They'd shored it all up with timbers, you know, and Feather had about two and a half carts full, almost ready to pull out. I'm sitting up on the spot between the first cart and Feather's rear end, my feet braced agin his back, thinking—well, I don't know what I was thinking, maybe 'bout fishing the next day or that sweet apple pie you brought that time." He winked at her. "Casting round for ideers to make some extra money. One by one the boys drop off singing 'cause we all heard the knockers."

"Knockers?" Amanda asked. Sass bunched the quilt in her fists and held it tight in front of her, so just her eyes peeked out. Myrtle bawled and paced.

"Yeah." Finn leaned over and fed a few more sticks of kindling into the stove. "This right here's your job," he teased, "but since you're slacking, I'll pitch in. Tommy-knockers. Little miners. Mountain ghosts. Little underground people that *do things*."

Finn tore his eyes from the fire and looked at Amanda, gauging. When she said nothing, he continued.

"They can be good or bad. Lots of times before a cave-in or explosion, you hear things in the walls, a knocking and creaking, pops and moans. The mountain kinda talks to you thataway. It can jangle your nerves pretty good. Lotta fellers say that's the tommy-knockers warning you, giving you time to get out. Or could be they're the ones causing it in the first place. You never know if they mean good or bad, so you try to get on their good side, leave 'em pasties or a bit of something from your dinner pail. They say the Cherokee used to talk about the same kinda folks roaming the mountains, so likely there's something to it.

"Anyhow. The knockers started up. Didn't give much warning that day. All's we had was a creaking and cracking and then *whoom*—the timbers holding up that ceiling splintered and flew ever' which way, and the whole thing came down at once."

"How awful," Amanda breathed. Her hand flew to her mouth and shook there as she imagined the horror of it, all the dust and rock.

"Me and Feather and another feller were just outside the room itself, so we got some of it, enough to smash this leg up good and knock Feather plumb off his feet. I could hear some of the fellers calling from the other side of the fall. I told 'em I was getting help. I told 'em to hang on. Course I was just lying there under a big slab myself, not going nowhere. I told Jasper—the other feller in there with me—to unhook them cars and pull what he could off Feather so he could stand. Poor beast was shaking and trembling all over, all cut up from his ears to his tail. I told ol' Jasper to just grab onto his traces and let him go. So much dust in the air you couldn't see your hand in front o' your face even with the headlights on. Feather drug him out far enough where others could get to us. Guess Jasper told 'em what happened and where to go. Told 'em to take care of ol' Feather 'cause he sure enough took care of us, and that's all she wrote. I don't remember much after that till I woke up at home."

"Those poor men," Amanda said. Sass sat quiet as a mouse, the quilt damp from the tears that ran down her face.

"Six good souls," said Finn, his voice wavering. He swiped at his eyes with his sleeve. "Daddy was down there working to pull 'em out. That's how he came to hurt his arm. Ones that didn't die outright waited out the rescue. Two of 'em had wrote notes to their families before they smothered finally. Enough to break your heart clean in two. Willie Harmon had a pay stub in his pocket, and he wrote on it, 'Boys, trust Jesus and never work in the coal mines,' to his two young'uns at home."

"Oh, Finn, I'm so glad you got out. Selfishly, I'm glad." Amanda's eyes shone in the firelight. "Thank you for telling the story." She placed her hand on his arm and rested it there.

"That's the first time I told it," Finn admitted. "Those words been banging on my insides, wanting to be let loose, for a while. I don't know why I was spared, why the knockers let me go with just a tattoo and a busted leg. I've yet to find that out."

Outside, a piercing *crr-ack!* echoed through the night, followed by a crashing as if a great beast shook the trees. Sass and Amanda both jumped, and even the sleepy horses startled in their stalls, their ears swiveling forward. Another crack, and another, loud as a gunshot. It came from all around them in the woods, an ambush of noise. Finn shuffled to the door and opened it, and an icy blast of wind pushed against him, seeking a way in. Under the bright moon, the woods sparkled like crystal. Each branch on every tree, down to the smallest tips, was coated with several inches of ice. As he scanned the woods, it happened again, and he realized the sound was the cracking and shearing of limbs under the weight of that frozen water, crashing to the ground and breaking lower branches as they fell like glass in a shatter of ice shards.

"The trees are falling to pieces," he said.

"Finn," Sass called. "I think Myrtle's ready." Sass stood on the lowest rail of the heifer's pen and leaned over. Myrtle had gone down and lay on her side.

"Dip some more buckets o' water, Sass. Never mind Cricket. With the sky falling out there, I don't want you to get knocked on the noggin running to the house." The three of them sprang into action. Finn shut the barn door and lifted a pair of chains from the wall. Amanda slipped inside the pen, and Myrtle raised her head but didn't attempt to rise; she had more pressing matters to deal with than a stray human in her space.

Amanda knelt by Myrtle's side. Ripples of movement in the cow's belly showed the calf was alive and active. Amanda could feel the contractions come and go under her hand; Myrtle's belly would harden into rigid knots and gradually relax. Birthing was as old as time. She remembered—how could she not?—the night Miles was born and how she'd labored on and on, not in the barn on the straw, but much the same, helpless to stop the process, wanting it to end and anxious for the coming child. Frank had been gone that night—in fact, she'd sent him away—and unlike Myrtle, she hadn't had the comfort of a soothing voice or gentle hands.

Finn eased down until he sat on the ground, legs out in front of him, much like his description of how he used to sit and shovel coal. Once more he rolled up his sleeves and felt inside. He made a loop of chain and passed it into the birth canal with one hand and, two hands deep, snugged the loop around the calf's left front hoof with his eyes closed in concentration. Tree limbs cracked and crashed against the barn roof.

"Amanda, c'mere and grab ahold o' this end." She crawled beside him and held the chain, waiting. Finn repeated the process and looped a second chain over the right front hoof.

"I'm gonna push the shoulders back, and when I do, you pull on that chain. Don't worry 'bout hurting her none. She'll be a lot better off when this bugger's out." He reached inside again, half lying behind the cow now as he shifted and maneuvered the baby inside her. Beads of sweat appeared on his face. Myrtle seemed to know they were helping and she lay still, her breath heavy and wet as she bore the contractions rippling down her sides. Finn grunted with a final push and barked, "Pull!"

Amanda braced one foot against the cow's back end so that she wouldn't slide across the ground, and pulled with all her might. Finn tugged the end of the other chain with one hand and worked inside with the other, his eyes shut tight. "That's it, there it is." Amanda got some slack and stopped as a tiny pale hoof poked out. Finn kept pulling until the second hoof appeared. When it did, he loosened the looped chains and let them fall. He scooted backward, and Amanda scrambled back toward the wall of the pen. Myrtle sensed the change and struggled to stand. Once she got to her feet, she seemed to relax, curious about what was happening behind her. She planted her feet and lowed, long and low, until, with a final gush of placenta, the calf slid out in one motion onto the straw.

Sass squealed from her post on the pen rail. "He *is* a big'un! Poor Myrtle! Look at the white spot on his face, just like hers."

Amanda and Finn gathered the chains, and they slipped out of the pen to let nature take its course. Within the space of fifteen minutes, Myrtle's great pink tongue had cleaned her baby dry and encouraged him to struggle to his feet on his awkward, untested legs. Finn dropped the chains into one of Sass's water buckets and used the other one to clean up. His arms were slick with blood and birth. Amanda washed as well, and then the three of them stood back to admire the wobbly calf, bumping his nose into Myrtle's side until he found his target—her ready milk bag.

Judging by the sinking moon, it was the wee hours of the morning, and Sass threw a final split log into the stove before she curled up in the hay under her quilt. Two giant yawns later, she slept heavily. They'd decided to stay out in the barn to keep an eye on the newborn and wait out the hours till morning. Finn tossed some fresh hay to Myrtle and made a pile near the stove where he and Amanda could get some rest, or as much as they could with the racket of splintering trees echoing outside.

"Don't matter how many times you witness such, it's always a miracle," Finn said, settling back against a hay bale and stretching his legs toward the stove.

"You believe in miracles?" Amanda asked.

"See 'em ever' day," he said, surprised.

"I grew up hearing a lot about signs and wonders," she said, "but after a bit of living, maybe I'm more cautious about the like."

"Depends what you call a miracle, I s'pose. Way I see it, you can either live like nothing's a miracle or like everything is. Either way, it'll work out to be the truth. But one makes your boots step a lot lighter than t'other'n." Finn pulled his quilt up to his chin and laid his head back on the hay.

Chapter 14

Finn's crooked smile played on his lips even while he slept. Amanda let her eyes linger over his face, studying the lines of his jaw and the straight slope of his nose, his lashes so long they curled up the slightest bit at the ends. She breathed deeply, testing the safety of him as he lay there, the cautious borders around her heart giving way. She'd loved before and been fooled. It was a mistake she would not make twice.

Frank had promised independence and adventure. It wouldn't be long, he'd said, before he and Gripp had raked in enough for Frank and her to be able to make their way to the West. It might be a push getting through the middle of the country, which the papers reported were dried up like a raisin, with clouds of dust blowing in your eyes day and night, but they were young and tough. Although the gold had petered out in California long ago, Frank had met folks on his travels who told him about a rock-studded ocean, palm trees, and nothing but sunshine. Not to mention Hollywood. You never knew who you might run up against in California. They might see Greta Garbo or Clark Gable at the dry-goods store, movie stars like in the papers. Wouldn't folks back in the mountains go crazy over a postcard that carried news like that?

Pa had married them at the church on one of the last warm days of fall, with Amanda wearing Mama's lavender linen-and-lace dress and Frank all shaved and prim, with suspenders on. She'd scoured the woods early that morning before the dew had burned off, gathering a bouquet of trillium, wild violets, and devil's bit. She tucked a few in her pinned-up hair and walked to the front of the church, with one of the deacons fiddling sweet, wavering notes that made Mama cry. Frank gave her a thin gold band. It was her first and only piece of jewelry, and she felt like a queen.

When Frank showed up after working his odd jobs, they'd walk the mile path down to the creek and spread a quilt, eating supper with their fingers while the long stretches of daylight lasted and then lying passionately together under the moon. More than once, Mama pulled leaves from Amanda's hair while they sat together, piecing quilts or mending.

"There's perfectly good straw ticking up in the loft," she'd said. "I don't see how you're not eaten up with ticks and chiggers."

Amanda had only smiled. Frank loved it outside in the open air. Their entertainment was each other and a private concert of the rippling creek and the whippoorwill calls, giving way to the chorus of tree frogs as dusk disappeared into night. It wasn't long before she felt her stomach sour at breakfast and pushed away the plate of hard-boiled eggs.

"I wouldn't eat those if I were you," she'd told Mama. "They smell like they've gone off."

"Nothing in the world a bit wrong with them eggs," Mama snapped, pushing them right back. "As if I would fix a rotten egg and serve it up on the table. Get married and all of a sudden you're too big for your britches." Amanda wrinkled her nose and clamped a hand to her mouth. After a few minutes, she ran out to retch into the privet alongside the cabin, and it became clear what was truly off.

"How long's it been since you bled?"

"A few weeks, I guess," she'd said, thinking back. "Maybe more? I haven't been keeping up."

Mama's eyebrows arched so high Amanda thought they might fly right off her forehead. Like the careful latches on her father's boxes, the pieces fell into place finally, and Amanda drew in a breath, her hands settling on her abdomen. She'd fallen pregnant.

"Oh, hon." Mama had laid her hand on Amanda's arm. She was barely seventeen but older than many first-time mamas she'd known. "You'll make such a good mama."

Amanda's mind had raced. What about their plans? The ocean, Hollywood? She tried to picture herself with a belly stretched tight, breasts full of milk, going through labor. Amanda scrunched her eyes shut; that didn't sound much like the fine young wife Frank admired. Later that same week, Frank declared he'd rented a place in town, and he and Amanda moved off the mountain.

"I'll come by ever' chance I get," Mama told her, but between helping Pa with the church work and keeping their own house and garden, it turned out she couldn't spare many days away. Frank dove into what he called his and Gripp's "investments" and claimed not to have time to spare on Sundays to travel to a church meeting. For her part, Amanda didn't feel comfortable riding a horse that far back into the mountains when she started to feel flutters and kicks. Instead, mother and daughter sent word back and forth through church members who chanced through town.

～

A whuff of air startled Amanda back to the present. Myrtle blew dust out her nose and turned her big head toward the wobbly calf nursing at her side as if being a mother were nothing to fuss over. Already she'd licked his coat clean and dry until whorls of fluff stuck up here and there. Finn hadn't moved an inch, and Sass lay burrowed beneath the quilt. Amanda couldn't sleep. She remembered carrying her own child and how it had changed her, shifted the things she yearned for until they were so shuffled around, she wouldn't have recognized her old self.

While Amanda scraped together meals and kept her and Frank's square shanty tidy, the magic of the life within her grew bit by bit, enchanting her heart with its spell. If the baby had been a girl, they would have named her Lynn, in honor of Frank's musical nickname for Amanda. But she'd known it was a boy, even before the granny women touched her ripening belly in the road on her way to the mine store, studying how she carried and making their predictions. She dreamed of him at night, with Frank spooned up behind her, a little brown-eyed boy to catch frogs and lightning bugs.

She'd read out loud at night after supper, anything she could get her hands on. The days of carefree supper picnics and walks in the woods had faded with the heat of summer. Frank was too busy now, focused on the money. When Amanda read, Frank soon fell asleep, tuckered from a day spent doing whatever it was he'd been out doing with Gripp, but Amanda kept on anyway, knowing the baby heard her words.

It was a Robert Frost poem Amanda took his name from, on a night she couldn't get comfortable and her tossing and turning made Frank cranky. He'd needed to get some shut-eye, he'd said. He and Gripp had big plans the next day. So she'd slipped out of bed, lit the lantern in the small hours of the morning, and cracked the spine of Frost poems to read silently. *"The woods are lovely, dark and deep,"* she read, *"but I have promises to keep, and miles to go before I sleep."* She had no idea where Robert Frost was from, but his words reminded Amanda of the Kentucky mountains on a winter evening. She, too, had made promises—promises to the man who lay snoring like a badger in the bed he'd pushed her out of and to the lively rascal who kicked and squirmed in the waters inside her, sending ripples straight to her heart like a stone tossed into a still pond. Why, there was his name right there in the poem: *Miles*. Amanda had a feeling she and Miles had a ways to travel together. She'd turned the name over in her mind, liking the sound of it as she'd rocked in the quiet until the puny town started to wake and she'd risen to make Frank's breakfast. *"Miles to go before I sleep,"* she'd mumbled, heating a dollop of grease in the skillet for the eggs.

Months slid by, months Amanda knew Frank wasn't pulling shifts at the mine, months she grew rounder and clumsier, months Frank was gone more and more, even at night, leaving her lonely and sleepless as she barred the door to the unsavory elements of the town. She'd sit in the rocker, rubbing her belly and sipping raspberry-leaf tea to make her womb strong. Often, Amanda had jolted awake from gunshots and cursing out in the road, someone insulted or cheated or looked at wrong. It didn't matter that she wore a band on her finger or that she was swelled up like a ripe melon. Lonely men followed her with desperate eyes as she waddled to and from the store or visited with an occasional neighbor. It wasn't long before she and Frank had their first real squabble.

"Nice you could cross the doorstep, finally," Amanda had said by way of greeting Frank midmorning. He'd stumbled into the cabin, smelling like woodsmoke and yeast, his beard a scruffy tangle.

"What's that s'posed to mean?"

"I never know when to expect you anymore, Frank. Didn't sleep a wink all night because of those no-counts fighting and yelling, and you laying out all night, no telling where."

"I been working, it so happens," he groused. "To feed all the mouths 'round here."

Mad as she'd been, Amanda's eyes had welled. "Sorry to be such a burden." She held up her left hand and wiggled her fingers. "You seemed to want to take that on, so you said."

Frank had waved a dismissive hand. "I don't know what you're so tore up about. I'm here, ain't I? And I'm providing." He fished in the pocket of his overalls and tossed a rolled-up wad of bills on the table. "That right there'll go a lot further'n mine scrip. Might even get us to California." He'd grinned and sidled up to her, more than he'd done in a month of Sundays. Amanda had pushed him off.

"If you were ever serious about California, we coulda left months ago, before I got big."

Frank dropped his arms by his sides. "Why you want to be like that?" he'd asked. "You're bowed up all the time and prickly as a porcupine."

"Why can't you tell Gripp you're through? It's no good here, Frank. I'm by myself most all the time. I can handle a gun—it's not that—but this baby's gonna change things. Don't you want better? For him?"

"Shoot, I want better for *me*, puddin'. Maybe if they was just hand-ing out money easy as pie, but you wait around for that, and there's a big fat zero at the end of that line."

Two nights after they'd argued, the Kentucky wind grew tired of blowing the dust around, kicked its feet up, and settled on the town so still and hot even the jays quit scrapping with each other and sat on rooftops with their beaks open, panting like dogs. Amanda had propped the windows open and sat inside with a cup of water in her lap, dribbling trails of it down the neck of her dress and on the inside of her arms to try to keep cool. Her back had been aching something fierce all day, and all she wanted was blessed rest for a few minutes, maybe prop her feet up so that the swelling that had started up in her ankles would go down.

She'd unfastened the top buttons on her dress and flapped the thin material to stir a bit of air. Earlier, she'd carried buckets of water down the short rows of their kitchen garden, tending the parched tomatoes and beans before they withered altogether. No wonder her back hurt. She rose to start supper, a slab of ham and red-eye gravy with some sliced tomatoes, puny ones from the shrunken vines. No telling if Frank would even be there for it. Amanda wiped her sweating brow with the hem of her dress, not caring that her bare belly poked out, exposed.

A noise at the door made her turn her head, and she dropped her hem. A miracle: Frank was in time for supper for once. But it hadn't been Frank at all. Despite the heat, a cold finger of ice trailed down Amanda's spine and settled in the pit of her stomach.

"You're finer'n a frog hair split four ways," Gripp said. He leaned against the doorframe like he'd been there awhile. "Even big as you are." Gripp's mud-coated boots left a mess on the floor as he carefully shut the door and covered the distance between them.

"Frank oughta be here anytime," Amanda said, her voice bright as a knife. "I've about got supper ready." Her eyes darted to the bed in the corner and the box beneath it where her pistol lay.

Gripp leveled her with his stare. "You and me both know Frank ain't anywhere near here." He was close enough now that Amanda could smell the whiskey and the foul odor of fresh chicken shit. She swallowed hard. "All those times you two lovebirds picnicked in the woods, you never once thought to invite your good friend?" Gripp placed a meaty hand over his heart. "That was downright hurtful. After all I done for you."

"All you done?" Amanda couldn't keep the sneer from her voice.

Gripp swept an arm around the shanty. "Who you think's behind your cozy setup? Who got Frank a job? Who's the manager of this operation?" He gave a mock bow.

"You're jiggered."

"I believe you're right." Gripp pulled a metal flask from his left pocket and shook it. "A sample of Kentucky's finest." He'd barked a laugh as he pointed at her. "Or maybe that's what we should call *you*. You were something else, rolling around in the leaves with Frank." He whistled a long slow note and shut his eyes to savor the memory.

Bile rose in Amanda's throat. *Gripp had been there,* she thought, *watching.* Cold sweat dripped between her breasts, and her chest tightened. Her blue eyes welled and stung with the salt. The red-eye gravy was way past done, beginning to scorch and smoke in the skillet.

"You gonna get that?" Gripp nodded to the stove, and Amanda took hold of the skillet handle with a folded rag. She moved it off the heat and felt him behind her. He put a hand over hers and squeezed hard. "I ain't about to let you clock me with a hot skillet," he said, twisting her arm behind her and pinning her wrist there with his body. "That dog won't hunt."

Gripp nuzzled Amanda's neck where loose strands of damp hair stuck to it. She could no longer choke back her tears as he walked her across the room to the narrow bed covered with the tidily folded bear paw quilt she'd stitched with Mama, just after she and Frank had married.

"The baby," Amanda croaked. "Please."

"Way I figger, that young'un's as much mine as Frank's. I was kinda in on the making of it, y'see. Likely I was there for the blessed event, setting behind a big ol' chestnut tree with a prime view. And it wadn't no immaculate conception like your daddy preaches about, not by a long shot." He laughed again, his hands rough on her breasts now as he pushed her down onto the quilt. She lay on her side near the edge of the bed, one arm protecting her belly and the other bent at the elbow and hanging over the side.

Amanda's fingers brushed the top of the box under the ropes strung across the bed frame to hold the ticking. Outside the window, the evening sky blushed a rosy pink that quickly faded to plum and deep purple as the sun sank. Soon, the mine shift would change and the tavern would fill. If she yelled, folks would count it as just another squall between married folks if they heard it at all.

Gripp fumbled with the buttons on his overalls, his fingers whiskey-clumsy. Amanda stole a glance up at him where he knelt above her. She drew her knees up to her belly and rabbit-kicked at his legs, knocking him off-balance on the lumpy ticking and scooting her a few more inches to the bed's edge. A few seconds' pause before he righted himself would be all she needed. Amanda heaved the rest of herself off the bed and hit the floor hard with her right hip. Gripp lunged after her. He'd grasped her left ankle and jerked, sliding her closer to the bed frame and causing her dress to ride up to the top of her thighs. His eyes darkened, and he leered at her on the floor.

"You're a regular wildcat, ain't ya? That's what I heard about preachers' daughters."

Amanda flipped the wooden lid off the box and her right hand closed around the butt of the pistol. She rolled onto her back and aimed the barrel at Gripp's chest. Faced with the business end of a firearm, Gripp let go of Amanda's ankle and sat back on his knees on the bed, his hands palm-out. Amanda scrambled backward and yanked her dress down with one hand, never taking her eyes off him.

"C'mon now, Amanda," Gripp said, his voice a soft purr. "I was just fooling. Like you said, I'm a little drunk." He actually smiled at her, and something in that mirthless smile made the hair rise up on the back of her neck. It was how she imagined a swamp gator might appear; she'd heard stories of how they'd float idly in the bayou with their lids half-closed, jaws split by that crooked smile while they waited for a soft-shelled turtle. Amanda got to her feet. Her hip throbbed where she'd landed on it, and her right elbow stung where she'd skinned it on the rough floor.

"Get on outta here," she growled. An unfamiliar sound just then— thunder. The cotton curtains hanging at the window fluttered as the wind stirred, and she caught a whiff of damp in the air. Amanda's chest heaved. Her throat rasped raw.

The door banged open and Frank stumbled in, his hair damp from the first heavy drops of rain they'd seen in months. "Looks like it's gonna come a flood."

He stopped short at the scene, Gripp kneeling in his bed with his overalls half-off and Amanda on the floor, barefoot and trembling, with her hair a shambles and a gun aimed down Gripp's gullet.

Frank held his hands out like he was steadying a spooked horse. "Whoa, whoa, whoa," he said. "Gripp?" He turned his eyes on Amanda. "What's got into you, Mandy?"

Amanda stared at her husband in disbelief. Wasn't it spelled out plain? If Frank Rye had ever had any sort of a backbone, he had just traded it in for a chicken heart.

"Out!" Amanda barked the word again. "The both of you."

"It's raining," said Frank, like the weather would interest her.

"I don't care if hellfire itself is flaming down outta the sky. Get. Out." Gripp climbed slowly off the bed and edged to the door. He put a hand on Frank's shoulder and jerked his chin. Amanda wondered what kind of a story he'd feed Frank about the hysterical pregnant woman, a story Frank would no doubt swallow hook, line, and sinker because what was most important, what took highest priority, was that money kept coming in, fuel for the cockamamie adventures Frank imagined were still in his future. Amanda had had enough adventure.

That night rang in Amanda's memory like a copper dinner bell, not because of Gripp or even because that was the last time she'd seen

Frank, but because that was the night Miles chose to arrive. As soon as she'd heard them stumble off into the night, she'd lowered the door latch with trembling hands and heaved the table in front of the door for good measure. She'd sit up all night if she had to, the Colt aimed at the ready. Tomorrow, she believed, she would go back up the mountain to her parents' home, but even as she'd thought it, she'd known the long-awaited rain had come too soon. Lightning flashed blue through the window, and thunder shook the shanty walls as all the water that the sky had withheld for months came pouring forth all at once. Water ran off the dusty tin roof, cascading from the edges into the thirsty ground. The creeks would rise, and there'd be no crossing the rushing current.

She wasn't going anywhere. A spasm rippled from Amanda's lower back across the whole front of her belly, and she'd dropped to her knees. The floor was wet, from where Frank had burst in from the storm, she thought. Amanda lifted her hand from the puddle where she knelt, and what dripped from her fingers was tinged with blood. She'd moaned as a rush of fear swept through her like the lashing wind outside. That night her baby would come, and she would birth him alone.

Amanda swiped the back of her hand across her face, and it came away wet. She was always surprised that bitter, angry tears could still well up from the long-ago memories she'd tried to close away. Finn lightly snored in the sweet hay, and the easy sound of it soothed her somehow. She pondered this gentle man who grieved a fallen mine pony and taught his brother how to carve. She could no more imagine this man doing her harm than a sparrow.

Slowly, so as not to wake him, Amanda stretched out her hand and laid it across Finn's chest, watching its steady rise and fall and measuring the reassuring beat of his heart. Amanda finally fell asleep to the image of Finn's crooked smile playing in her head and the sound of Myrtle nosing and chewing mouthfuls of hay.

Chapter 15

The white sunlight reflecting off the ice-coated trees dazzled their eyes in the morning. Finn had crept out of the barn and hurried into the woods with a shotgun before first light, but although they'd heard several shots, he'd come back without a rabbit or squirrel. Harley, home from his mine shift, said he'd had to walk with a hand shading his sight or he'd have been blinded by a thousand diamonds. In a lifetime of winters, no one had ever seen an ice storm like that.

"It favors a tornado gone through," Harley reported. "Limbs down everywhere. Took me twice as long getting home because I stopped to drag some off the trail."

Amanda had already packed her saddlebags with her books and the sack of stuffed rabbits. "Reckon I'll have to do the same," she said. "Junebug can jump a tree, but I don't much like doing it." She finished up a last sip of chicory coffee and passed the cup to Ral. "Thank you again for putting me up for the night."

"You earned your keep with Myrtle," said Finn. "Don't fall asleep in the saddle on the way back. You'll fall off, and we're liable to find you thawing by the path come spring."

"I won't. I'm anxious to get home to Miles. He and Mooney will be worried sick." Amanda stuck her left toe in the stirrup and hoisted herself up in an easy motion. "I'll be back around before long," she called on her way down the path. "The rate Sass is going, she'll have everything read before I get home."

Finn hustled forward to catch her. He stood at Junebug's shoulder and fiddled with his bridle a moment. "Went out this morning and found you something to carry home in your pocket." He dipped a glove into his coat pocket and handed her a small cloth-wrapped bundle. "It can wait," he said. "You don't have to open it right now."

"Thank you," Amanda replied, her breath sending small white puffs into the air. "How thoughtful." Despite the cold, a warmth rose in her chest.

The woods were brilliant and full of the patter of dripping water as the sun climbed and its yellow rays melted the night's ice. The path was slick in spots, but Junebug minded his business and kept his feet. He wasn't overly eager to splash through the icy creek water, but he did that, too, ready as she was to be in home territory. She clapped a gloved hand on his neck, encouraging him on and smiling as his long gray ears flopped with each step.

Amanda waited until she'd rounded the first bend in the trail and could no longer see the cabin before she pulled Finn's wrapped bundle from her pocket and opened it. Despite the cold, a rosy warmth spread from inside her and blossomed color on her cheeks. In her hand lay a dainty sprig of mistletoe, a cluster of rounded green leaves and tiny white berries. He hadn't been hunting squirrels at all; he'd been shooting down clumps of this from the tops of trees. Amanda smiled to herself, imagining what might have happened had Finn presented it to her differently. But of course, he never would have. He didn't presume or grab. She'd courted only once before, and Finn was as opposite that as mistletoe from poison oak. Amanda folded the sprig back into its cloth and tucked it away, with a smile playing on her lips. When she got home, she'd press it between the pages of her Bible.

She wondered how Miles had fared the night without their customary bedtime ritual of stories, new words learned, and a kiss. Mooney was a good friend. She couldn't have asked for a more dependable person to link arms with, sister soldiers, they called one another, facing what they'd been dealt and marching on into battle. Once, she'd thought Frank was that person, but Frank had changed. More likely, she'd opened her eyes and seen him for what he'd always been. If there'd been changing, it was all her.

Sweet Miles, with his big brown eyes and sandy hair, the freckles on his upturned nose, and the little scar by the corner of his mouth from the time he'd tried to kiss a broody hen. Frank hadn't left her with many things, but Miles was her treasure. Junebug's clip-clopping hooves picked their way through the mud, and Amanda played back last night's scene in the barn—Myrtle's sweet calf taking its first breaths.

Quick as a whip, the night she first met Miles and all that came after rose into her mind. Midwives and granny women like to say that soon as a child's born, the pain and memory of its birthing disappear, washed away by the rush of love and relief a mama feels when she holds her young'un. Maybe that was true if you had a midwife handy to slide an axe under the bed to cut the pain and help ease the baby into the world with warm water and a cloth on your brow, but Amanda had none of that when Miles came. She had only a pistol in her trembling hand, a raging storm beating down her door, and a cowardly, no-count husband.

Amanda remembered every push and wail from that night, the wind outside harmonizing with her anguish. She'd prayed. Oh, how she'd prayed: for the labor to stop, for the pain to go away, for it to be over. And other, less immediate prayers when she had a minute to catch her breath: for Gripp Jessup to fall in a well and drown, for him to be poisoned by his own moonshine, for the crows to peck out his eyes. Amanda was helpless to take every thought captive in the middle of pushing out a baby, so she hoped God would forgive her these last.

A midwife would have said that for a first baby, Miles had come quickly. Amanda had nothing to compare her experience to, no mama nearby to console her, and to her it seemed anything but quick. The labor persisted and intensified for several hours, and she shifted from the bed to the chair to the floor and back again, desperate to ease the spasms in her back. She knew enough to have a clean knife at hand,

and she had the presence of mind to gather some towels and a pot of water when she had moments to breathe. Nature and the storm did the rest, and when at last Amanda lay panting on the bed, her hair slicked with sweat against her face, she cut the purple-blue cord that unraveled like a skein of yarn and held her son close, tears cooling her hot skin as his thin cries blended with her own. It was the first song they'd sung together, a keening lament that spoke of pain and fear and love.

Amanda's world had distilled into that moment in that room, and she knew with a deep certainty, with a kind of ancient knowledge that traveled from the veins of the earth to her beating heart, that despite how terrified she was of the way this child looked to her for life, she would in fact protect and save him even if it demanded her last breath. She managed to clean and feed both herself and the baby, and they slept in deep exhaustion for a few hours before he woke her again with a frantic rooting at her breast.

The storm stayed put for three solid days, soaking the mountains and sending water cascading down into waterfalls, creeks, and rivers. In all that time, no one knocked at Amanda's door, and she was so stiff and sore she could hardly move about the room, let alone venture out with a newborn into the wind and mud. She and Miles, for that is what she named him, hunkered down and got acquainted. Barely a day had passed before Amanda had already memorized the curves of his cheeks, the whorls of each ear, and the feel of his stubby baby toes against the palm of her hand.

It was another week before Amanda pieced together all that had happened in the storm. More than one family's cabin had been swept down the mountain by water or mud, the mines had been closed due to danger from flooding, and the sheriff was run ragged trying to get word of the situation beyond the overflowing riverbanks. Trees were down across the trails that hadn't been washed out. When she stepped out onto the porch with Miles, who blinked his eyes against the light, an earthy smell of upturned soil and churned silty creek water reached her nose, mixed with the dank smell of wet wood and leaves. No word from

Frank. She'd been furious when she'd sent him away, and even more so that he'd left her alone to deliver Miles, but now a current of worry pulsed through her fog of exhaustion. He was likely stranded on the far side of the river and would come slinking back with that hangdog look on his face any day now. Also, she wondered about her parents. She knew their home site was secure, not too near the water, but she was anxious to get word to them about their grandchild.

When knuckles finally rapped on Amanda's door, she swung it wide, Miles in the crook of one arm.

"High time!" The high pitch of her voice contradicted the fed-up look on her face. "Look what all you missed—" She stopped in mid-rail, for it wasn't Frank who'd appeared on the step with his hat in his hand, but the sheriff, his black boots covered in mud.

"Miz Rye." So. This was no welfare call and certainly no social visit. The man's thin-lipped grimace and the way his Adam's apple bobbed up and down told her that much. The sheriff's eyes lit on the baby waving his tiny hands in the air, and his face sagged even further.

"Rain's done quit," he said.

"You knock on my door to tell me what my own eyes can see?" Amanda raised her chin, bracing for the blow. Some bootlegger had turned snitch, and now Frank was likely sitting in a county jail cell.

"No ma'am. I come to tell you we done fished your husband outta the river this mornin'."

Confusion clouded Amanda's features, and she frowned. "The river?" She'd almost laughed.

"Edgar Mullins and his boy—they was huntin' up the banks for anything useful that might'a washed through when the creeks rose up— they seen him lodged under a gum, hung there by his overalls. Thought it was a calf got swept off at first." The sheriff stopped himself. "I'm awful sorry."

Amanda blinked at him. Miles started up a half-hearted cry, the kind that—Amanda had already learned—would work itself into a full-fledged wail soon if she didn't feed him. She looked down at her baby, turning his head by instinct to nuzzle into her chest, and she held the bundle out to the sheriff so that he would understand why this couldn't be true.

"I've just birthed him," she told the sheriff. "Not two weeks ago yet."

"Like I say, I'm awful sorry. I'll put the word out to some women down the way. Now the rain's quit, give it a week or so and the creeks'll be down." The sheriff reached into his jacket pocket and pulled out an iron-colored pistol. He held the butt of it out to Amanda. "Found this .22 under some brush close by. Looks like it'd been fired recently. Nice Smith & Wesson with his initials in the handle—F. R. Reckon it's his." Amanda took it and laid it on the shelf inside the door. She'd stow it under the bed with her own pistol later. He stepped back down the stairs and turned away, crammed his worn hat down on his head.

A thought occurred to her then. "Was he alone? Frank?" She jiggled baby Miles to get him to hush.

"Yes ma'am. It was just him. Must'a slipped and fell in, and that current's been rough with all this rain. Imagine that's how he come to be snagged up like he was."

"Yes," she'd said faintly. "I imagine so." Amanda had stepped back inside and shut the door, sinking into the rocking chair Frank had made for her. She unbuttoned her blouse and settled Miles where he could eat, his tiny mouth pulling hungrily, unaware of how his world had just changed.

"Hush, little baby, don't say a word," Amanda sang to him in a whisper, too stunned to cry. *"Papa's gonna buy you a mockin' bird."* She'd sucked in a breath when the truth of that line sank in. Papa wouldn't be buying this baby a thing. It was all on her now, their childish plans for adventure washed away in the rising river.

∽

Amanda and Junebug passed the naked berry thicket along the trail. Each thin branch that had held plump blackberries in the summer was now etched in ice like a glass sculpture. Along with Finn's mistletoe, Amanda had taken with her a paper-wrapped parcel of wild berry preserves that Rai had given her. She pictured Mooney spreading a thick helping atop a hoecake and was thankful she had something to give her for watching Miles, not that she ever would have expected such a token. More than anyone, Mooney had shown her what she'd missed by not growing up with a sister. Amanda probably owed her life to Mooney. Far more than berry preserves could pay.

Amanda's eyes stung a bit as she remembered it. True to his word, the sheriff had told his wife about the newly widowed young mother he'd met, and before the sun slid past the treetops that day, another tap echoed on Amanda's door. This time, a trio of women stood on her porch, their arms full of food and their sleeves rolled up. Amanda stood in her bare feet, her hair hanging in a limp braid down her back, and felt her exhaustion settle into her bones so completely, she nearly collapsed.

They stepped across the threshold and went to work. One of them gently lifted Miles from her arms and settled her into the chair while another put the last sticks of kindling in the stove and drew pail after pail of water to heat for a bath. The last, strong-armed, with a friendly face, headed around the back to chop a stack of wood to have on hand. They scurried like mice around the kitchen, tidying and scrubbing where Amanda had neglected since Miles had come. In between filling the tub with warm water, they fed her bites of ham and poke greens to make her blood strong and made her sip lady's slipper tea for extra strength.

Amanda didn't know them; she hardly knew anyone in town, Frank preferring they keep to themselves. The bathwater drawn, one of the women helped her undress and step into the water. She sank down and hugged her knees to her chest. How long had it been since she'd looked in a mirror? She could only imagine what she must look like. When she'd settled there, the water surrounding her like a wool cloak, warm and comforting, she rested her forehead on her knees and let her tears flow freely into the tub, the first she'd shed since the sheriff had brought the news. A warm bath, a good cry, and a cup of tea: her mother used to say that was close as you could get to the Holy Trinity here on Earth.

The ministering hands of the women never stopped. They wasted no breath on words that would've meant little in her state. Instead, they sang or hummed, their harmonies as natural as the wind skipping through the treetops. Without realizing she was doing it, Amanda swayed in the water as they dipped and poured, scrubbing and washing her clean. She wished Mama were there—a common tug when the torch of motherhood was passed. But these women, strangers, no less, mothered her and Miles just right. An hour later, Amanda was dry and warm, wearing fresh clothes with her hair pinned up, and she lay in her clean bed sipping hot tea with Miles bathed and nestled in beside her, grunting and cooing. Her larder was stocked, at least enough for the next week, and she had enough kindling to keep a fire going.

Two of the women gathered their things to make their way home, but the third, the one with the friendly face, stayed. She'd sat on the edge of Amanda's bed, her round face flushed. Amanda noticed for the first time that she was far along pregnant. With her short black hair and dark dress topped with her white apron, she looked like one of the cheerful chickadees that sometimes landed at her window when she spread crumbs to lure them.

"Now then," the woman began. "My name's Mooney, and we're all of us in the same bit of a fix, trying to get by with just our own selves and our young'uns. Many hands make light work, so we do what we can when someone's in need. I'm sure there'll be a time when you can return the favor." She rubbed her round belly and smiled. "We were sorry enough to hear about your husband."

"I need to get word to my family," she said. "They don't even know about Miles yet."

"Sheriff sent one of his deputies up the mountain to tell your folks. Somebody figured who they were—the preacher up in Pickins, they said. Dependin' on how passable it is, they should be here 'fore too long, and y'all can decide about a funeral and such. No need to worry none till then."

"I'm grateful, Mooney. Truly. I never felt so cared for in all my days." Amanda clung to Mooney's hand. She thought a minute. "Where's your husband?" she asked.

"Aw, last I heard he'd made it down south to the Gulf, aiming to throw nets for shrimp. That man never swallered a shrimp in his whole life, less you count its crawdad cousin." She rolled her eyes. "He's full of ideas but empty on brains. Reckon the day he lit out for the railroad was the last I seen of his skinny backside." Mooney rubbed her belly again. Amanda remembered having a constant hand on her belly herself not that many days ago.

"Well, bless you, Mooney. Maybe our young'uns will be friends, seein' how they'll be close in age."

Mooney had smiled and squeezed Amanda's hand. "No two ways about that. I'm countin' on it."

Never in a hundred years would Amanda have featured herself shy of turning eighteen, bouncing a baby in her arms beside her husband's fresh grave. Daddy presided over the funeralizing, which included his daughter's husband and four others who'd died in the waters, including a boy who'd foolishly tried to snag a catfish for supper right when the river crested. It had taken a full month for the ruins of the mountain to be passable. Debris had to be cleared from trails, and mud on the steepest parts had to harden into ruts before it was safe for horses to pick through.

A yellow autumn sun shone through the newly budded trees of the graveyard, warming the faces of the stone markers. The birds chirruped and twittered so loudly that Daddy had to raise his voice to be heard at the back of the gathering. After so many days of rain and mud, the dry sun made the occasion seem almost festive, and more than one mama pinched a boy's ear or snatched up a collar to keep their restlessness in check. Mama and Amanda stood looking not at Daddy or at the clods of dirt piled beside the grave, but hypnotized by the baby in Amanda's arms, blinking his unfocused eyes against the light like a sleepy cat. Had there ever been anything so tiny and perfect, so easy-tempered and quick to smile, despite his hard beginning? Mama apologized over and over, eaten up with sorry that she hadn't made it for his arrival, even more so because Amanda had been alone for so long afterward.

"How could you have known?" Amanda reasoned. "Unless you'd sprouted wings and flown down the mountain, you couldn't have made it down in that flooding without ending up in the ground today yourself."

They'd arrived only that morning, with the coffins already laid out in the graveyard. Amanda had begged the diggers to wait until her daddy got there. They'd tried to explain that the moon was too old and they'd have to cart in extra dirt to fill the graves back in. Graves were meant to be dug on the new moon, so there'd be dirt enough left to throw away after, packing it tight. Dig on the old moon, and the filled hole would stay loose and not settle. The grieving widow's wishes won out. Her parents had ridden up to Amanda's cabin, laden with jars of past-summer goodness put up from Mama's garden and a quilt she had pieced for the baby. Daddy had even fashioned a jangly ring of tiny keys from scraps of iron as a play pretty.

They'd found Amanda not only having settled into her new role but also tending to a housemate, another woman who'd just given birth the day before. She sat propped up in the bed under the quilt, her dark hair tucked behind her ears and her eyes heavy.

"This is Mooney," she'd told them, "and little Maisie. I couldn't have managed without her these past days. We're in the same boat, so I'm takin' a turn at the oars now."

"I hate like everything I can't go to the graveside with you," Mooney said.

Amanda waved her off. "Don't be silly. What's the sense in you being on your feet all that time? I'll bring you a plate from the gathering after."

"See if you can stick in a' extra piece of jam cake," Mooney said with a wink.

"*Two* babies!" Beady had fussed over them both.

Daddy had stood by the door, casting anxiously about for a place to settle his eyes. Amanda could tell he was having trouble imagining his daughter being someone's mother; the whole situation had him rattled. He would be much more comfortable out in the graveyard, speaking words over the departed.

Baby Maisie had arrived, if not easier than Miles, then at least much less lonely, with a houseful of eager-handed women. When it came time, the midwife had quickened the birth by blowing red pepper into Mooney's nose through a quill to induce sneezing. They'd been there to flip Maisie and dose her with catnip and turpentine and had buried the afterbirth behind the cabin. Amanda watched all the activity with apprehension, counting all the things she'd not done, and prayed her love and fumbling care for Miles in the days after he was born were enough to protect him.

After the graves had been covered over—and sure enough, the diggers made a show of needing more carts of dirt to finish the job—they'd stayed long enough to share the picnic meal. Several families had made it into a day to clean up and decorate the graveyard (two birds with one stone), but Amanda felt no gaiety. Neither did she cry at the sight of Frank's fresh, mounded grave. She'd loved him, seduced by his otherness, his bouts of attention and tenderness, but like a first taste of whiskey, it hadn't taken more than a good sip to leave her dizzy. She'd loved him without knowing him, not really. While she stood by the rectangle dug in the earth, hearing but not listening to the words her father spoke, the memory of Frank that repeated in Amanda's mind was of him leaving that night with Gripp, the way he'd looked at her and found her somehow weak but not worth protecting, the scale tipping in favor of money and the next grand thing. Nestling Miles close to her body, she gave him her little finger to grasp. To Frank, even before he'd seen his own likeness in his son's face, the baby was another load to carry. At least Miles wouldn't have to feel that like the sting of a willow switch across his legs his whole life.

"Can we get on back home?" she'd asked Mama. "I'm wore out, and Miles needs to eat."

"Let me just tell your daddy," Mama had answered. "He'll likely be here the rest of the afternoon."

"Here, you take Miles, and I'll fix a pail to take to Mooney." Amanda made sure to add an extra slice of jam cake for her friend and was wrapping a few pork ribs in paper when a woman approached her. She wore a plain gray cotton dress that she'd tried to spruce up with an added collar, and her brown hair was twisted into a low knot at the back of her neck. She was some years older, lines around her gray eyes that were the same color as her dress. Amanda didn't recognize her, likely a miner's wife.

"Sorry 'bout your loss," she said, nodding toward the grave sites. The woman's voice was odd, but Amanda had heard so many sorries that day, her ears were worn out.

Amanda nodded at the woman and topped the pail with some deviled eggs, which wouldn't keep long. She wondered if the vinegar in them would sour Mooney's milk.

"I guess it's a blessing your folks were able to get here and straighten things out," the woman persisted.

Amanda turned to her, the dinner pail hanging in her hand. The question in her expression must have issued a license for the woman to continue.

"I see you got a young'un now," the woman continued. If her words had had teeth, they would've drawn blood. "Maybe that'll slow you down some."

"I don't take your meaning," said Amanda.

The woman laughed, though her eyes showed no mirth. "No, I think I got you pegged. You're—you *were*," she corrected, "Frank Rye's wife. That makes two of us." She held up her left hand and waggled the ring on her finger. "Seems he was plowing more than one field."

Amanda froze, the blood drained from her face. "That's not so," she said. "Frank may've been a lotta things but he wasn't two-timin'." Even as she said it, her confidence wavered.

"That's what I figgered you'd say," the woman told her, fishing in her dress pocket. She pulled out a creased sepia photograph—a wedding photo, something Frank had told her was an extra they could do without—and in it, a trim couple, she seated with a slight smile playing on her lips, and he standing behind her in a dark suit with a stiff, short collar, his hands lying possessively on each shoulder. Amanda would know him anywhere: it was Miles's father, her late husband. The day felt suddenly too warm, and her knees threatened to buckle.

"Here you are"—the woman pointed her long finger at Amanda's chest—"carryin' on not two counties over, gettin' with child, and pushin' him to who knows what ends so you can live the life of Riley while he's supposed to be sendin' money back to his wife—to *me*."

Amanda glanced around the graveyard. The woman had grown shrill, and several folks were looking. Mama walked toward her, holding Miles over one shoulder, her free hand patting his back. Her father stood with his arms folded under a stand of white oaks, his Bible tucked under one arm. He looked to be having a serious talk with a group of men, their faces grim. Even from that distance, she thought she could see veins bulging in his neck, and she figured they must have asked him to mediate some cockamamie dispute; that usually got his dander up. The limestone grave markers winked in the light as the sun passed in and out of the clouds overhead.

Amanda's shoes were still muddy from stepping in the dirt of her husband's grave. Her belly still showed a small bulge from having carried his child inside her.

"Well, Frank ain't sending money to anyone no more. He never said a word to me about having a wife. Never." A thought struck her then. "You have children?"

The woman shook her head. "No, he weren't around long enough to get that far. Mines closed and he lit out—to find work, he said. I never did hear from him after that." She looked at the mounded dirt a few yards away. "Till now."

"I s'pose that means we were never truly married," Amanda said.

"Way I heard it, you made your own money and don't need what my husband give you." The woman's eyes scrolled up and down Amanda's body. "Why he'd want to take up with such as that, I can't say."

Mama joined them then, and Amanda traded the dinner pail for her son. Her mother looked between her daughter and the woman, who stood with her lips tight and jaw clenched. Amanda held Miles close and turned to the woman, whose name, she realized, she still didn't know. It was too much.

"I just buried a man today. He wasn't who I thought he was in a number of ways, that's for certain. But he's nothing to me now." She flung her hand toward the grave. "Help yourself to what's left, but weren't nobody to blame for any of this except him. I don't aim to lay down beside him and let you stomp all over me, so you best go back to your two counties over."

Amanda turned on her heel and stalked off toward home as Miles started to fuss. She imagined Mama was as full of questions as she was herself, but it would have to wait. Her breasts tingled with the familiar sting of her milk letting down and she hurried on, knowing if she didn't, her blouse would be soaked by the time she reached the cabin, and Miles's wails might be loud enough to wake the dead.

～

"Your fretting like that is just gonna make the baby fuss more." Mama sat at the table, watching Amanda nurse and rock at a furious pace. "You're gonna wear ruts in the floor with that rocker and topple over!"

Mooney was up and dressed, little Maisie lying in a wooden vegetable crate draped with a quilt, and she stepped behind Amanda's chair with her hands out. "Whoa, there, Nelly. What's put a hive in your bonnet?"

"A woman at the graveyard." Amanda kept her eyes on Miles, trying to steady his flailing fists. "She claimed to be Frank's wife."

Mama hooted with such dismissive astonishment that Miles startled, started up fussing again. "That's plainly not so. I was right there when you tied the knot."

"She showed me a picture of them, a *wedding* picture. It was him. She had a ring, Mama."

"Anybody can put a ring on their finger," Mama tutted.

"Well, no wonder you're fit to be tied," said Mooney. "Did you knock her into next Tuesday?" She mimed a well-aimed uppercut.

"I didn't knock her anywhere, Mooney, although the more I sit here, the madder I get." Amanda paused. "But not at her. I believe her. What does it help her to tell a tale like that? There's nothing from Frank to inherit and only shame to carry. It's me that's a fool. I never was married for true, and now I have Miles to bear that."

"Why would you believe her?" asked Mama, rising to her feet. "Any stranger can say anything, desperate for money or gain." She stopped, realizing what she'd just said. "But we *knew* Frank."

"No, Mama," Amanda said, "I don't believe we did."

She would have continued, would have told the story about the night Miles was born—the storm, what Gripp Jessup had done and the things he'd told her, how Frank had folded and scattered her honor like ashes, leaving her there bruised, with her pregnant belly already contracting—but her father opened the door. His face was red and his breath loud, like he'd run the whole way from the graveyard. His eyes cast around to settle on the silhouette of Amanda's mother. Amanda hastily threw a blanket over Miles as he nursed.

"Get your things, Beady. We're heading back up home."

"Jack?"

Mooney sat near the hearth beside Amanda's chair. She placed a hand on the arm of the rocker. Amanda's feet had quit pumping, and the rocker stilled.

"Never in my days have I been so cut," he said, the familiar melody in his voice gone quiet as he tried to control the quaver. "We raised you in the Lord, Amanda. You witnessed nothing but love and kindness in our home, and we put the seeds of God's Word in your heart. I come here fast as the water went down to see our grandbaby and make sure you was safe."

"I know, Daddy. I know," Amanda said. That woman at the graveyard must have spoken to him, she figured. She'd never seen her father so riled.

"I preach your husband's funeral—your *husband*," he said, "and not ten minutes after, I stand there getting a' earful. What a shame Frank had to make his living in such a way, whiskey, bootlegging, who knows what all else, and all the while his wife was—" He choked out the words, no longer able to keep the anguish from his voice. "His wife—my *daughter*—was hiring herself out for money at the train station like a . . ." He stopped, a shaky finger pointing midair at Amanda as she sat still as a stone.

"Money?" she whispered, confused. The woman—Frank's wife—had said something like that, that she'd made her own money and hadn't needed Frank's earnings.

"They thought the preacher should know." Daddy drew himself up straight. "Given I'd just done the funeralizing for several of their friends and neighbors straight outta the Good Book. Thought I should know it was anybody's guess who my grandson's daddy might be. What a fool they thought me," he croaked. "All these years of labor and calling likely gone to seed."

Tears brimmed and ran down Amanda's cheeks. She wasn't sure which upset her father more, the disgraceful thing she'd been accused of or the black mark on his good name and reputation. Mama stood white-faced, gripping the table's edge, while Amanda said nothing, too stunned to speak, and clutched the baby in her thin arms. Mechanically, Mama put her few things in the sack they'd carried with them and stood by her husband in the doorway. Daddy had not stopped shaking.

"You look as if you're having a fit. Can't we talk about all this?" Mama cast a sorrowful look at her daughter, sitting with Miles in her arms, the blanket askew.

Amanda blinked slowly, trying to take in the situation. Apparently, there was nothing to talk about. If her father could so quickly believe the tale—however convincing it must have seemed—then she had lost them already. It would be one more thing she could add to the list of what Frank had taken from her. She watched as Mama's eyes memorized the baby's tiny head, covered in a cap of downy hair, his lips slack and sated with milk. Amanda bent her head to him as well. He was her focus now. There sat Mooney beside her—probably they assumed she was a partner in this, her baby the child of an unholy union as well. Mama pressed her knuckles against her quivering lips as Daddy guided her out the door to their wagon. Sometimes still, Amanda would startle awake in the night, imagining the slamming of that door.

Amanda shrugged, shaking off the bad memory. There was nothing for it now. Although when she was with a family like the MacInteers, cutting up with each other over supper and each one doing their share, Amanda had to admit that a kind of homesickness for her own parents settled in her heart. She still taught Miles bits of scripture, as her daddy had long ago taught her, and she sang to him the same songs she'd learned as a child. She wouldn't throw out the baby with the bathwater. Where was the common sense in that?

Chapter 16

Beady Wick must have combed over her conversation with Rai MacInteer a hundred times since the woman and her children had come to the assembly. She'd been chatting along easy as you please when Rai had mentioned meeting Amanda by way of that librarian job. Sounded like she'd been up to their place at least a handful of times, which was more than Beady could say. She couldn't stand it. She wanted like everything to ask after her daughter, but it was outright shame that stopped her tongue. What kind of mother wouldn't already know the answers to the questions she wanted to ask?

During the service, she'd almost worked herself up to ask anyway—just a small inquiry, so she wouldn't seem eager—but then Jack had started up with the snakes and the MacInteers had slipped out right quick. Beady had been snappish with him for the rest of the week until he'd finally demanded, "Out with it, woman! What's got you riled?" And of course, she couldn't say.

Oh, why had Jack chosen that exact moment for his faith testing? Beady could see by Rai's hasty exit that the woman didn't fancy having her children cooped up in the same room with rattlers. Some folks just didn't take to the serpent handling, and Beady had to admit she didn't come to it natural herself. Jack had journeyed back to the church at Blackstrap time and again to witness the services and understand their methods right about the time their daughter Amanda had been courting

Frank, the man she'd eventually married. The mountains were chock-full of snakes, and most folks killed them on sight, given the opportunity. Jack explained their use in parsing out a person's trust and measure of faith, a quick and definitive means to sift the wheat from the chaff.

Jack had assured her he wouldn't be putting himself in harm's way because it was part of his calling. Why would God call him to such if he couldn't stand up to the rigors of being tested? In Blackstrap, he said, he'd run across two boys—twins, in fact—who agreed to help him rustle up some snakes.

Jack had been so stirred up by the process that he'd come home briar-scratched and sweaty, eager to tell Beady the tale. "The three of us set off through the broom sedge, and 'bout thirty minutes later, a buzz come out of the grass."

Beady's hand had paused midbite as she'd sopped up the red-eye gravy on her plate. She pictured the barbed fangs sinking into her husband's leg and shuddered.

"Now Pete—that's one of the twins—raised a finger, and we all froze like stones where we stood."

"What if you'd been bit, Jack?"

"Well, I wasn't," he said, continuing without a pause, "so Pete and Repete fanned out on either side while I stood still, holding the open mouth of that sack.

"A fat timber rattler drew itself into a coil, with its head raised up. One of them boys eased that hook to press down near the end of its tail, you see, anchoring it to the ground, while the other'n stretched his arm toward the snake's head." His dinner forgotten, Jack wielded the fork and mimed the motions with his arms while he spoke.

Beady had lost her appetite. She held the edge of her apron in her hands, worrying and twisting it as Jack talked.

"Repete pinned the snake's head to the ground between the forked ends of the stick, and now, with both ends held down, it couldn't thrash or strike. Right about then, up come a cloud of this foul, musky smell.

"'He's mad he's been snookered,' Pete said. That ol' snake, he bobbed and twisted but couldn't move free without use of his tail.

"Then they gimme a sack and told me what to do. Everything them boys did was cautious and slow, not like I'd imagined it would be. Well, Repete pushed the head down inside the sack and backed off. Pete tickled its underbelly so it would shy away, farther into the sack, as he dropped the tail. Once it was bagged, I clamped the top shut quick as a hare and gave it a twirl.

"Them boys said we prob'ly done passed by three or four without knowing about it. Nice warm day like that, they li'ble to be stretched out anywhere."

"Lord a'mercy," said Beady, letting out a long breath. "That sure won't make me sleep good at night."

Jack laughed. "Just need to put 'em in a wood box with the lid shut, but holes for air. They don't need a lot of vittles, or water neither. A fed snake is livelier. You want 'em a little peckish if you plan to grab one up. They'll still bite—that's always a possibility, make no mistake. Toss in a mouse 'bout once a month and then leave 'em be after that for a week or so."

"There's a steady supply of mice in the corncrib," Beady allowed.

"Slow and steady is the name of the game," Jack explained. "You move real easy like. Hum if you have to, to calm the jangles in your nerves."

Beady was all set to be Jack's helpmeet like the Bible said, and she reckoned since she'd faithfully supported her husband in all their days together this far down the road, she could keep on traveling. She'd just have to watch where she let her feet fall on that road now.

"Now, Beady, if he bites you, don't necessarily mean nothing." Jack spoke as if Beady intended to take up the vipers herself, which she most certainly did not. "It's not the biting that's the problem; it's the poison what harms you. It's up to the snake and the good Lord whether they give you a dose of that."

Beady considered this. She knew of folks who'd been snake-bit. There were heaps of remedies for such a thing, provided it wasn't in the throat or face. She'd seen dogs and horses with faces so blown up with poison they couldn't draw a breath.

Jack had returned to Pickins late that day with three timber rattlers jumbled up in a weathered gray box. He'd assured Beady that he'd secured the latch and lashed it to the back of his saddle good and tight. For weeks, Jack watched the serpents in their box in the barn, getting used to their sounds and smell. He'd seen his share of them, like anyone else living off the land, but never in such close quarters and never with the insight of the Spirit. He took to toting his square of a shaving mirror in his shirt pocket so that he could use it to reflect the sun into the dark corners of the box through the air holes without opening it, warming them with its light and studying their movements and moods.

In the heat of the summer, at the end of a sparsely attended Sunday meeting, Jack nudged Beady, and she knew immediately he'd felt a tug from the Spirit. Today was the day. He'd fed the assembly that day from Genesis and the story of the Fall, the serpent in the garden being the perfect introduction to the signs and wonders possible for the redeemed. Without fanfare, he slid the weathered box from its place behind his pulpit and rested it on a bench he'd tugged up front. From that day forward, Pickins's Nose was baptized in the spirit of the Holiness movement.

A vision of Amanda nursing her new baby sprang into Beady's head. Had it really been four years ago? Like any good mother, her main concern would be to do for her young'un. Once you felt the weight of that baby in your arms, was there anything you'd not do for it? It had taken her and Jack so long to have a child. There was nothing Amanda could do that would make her stop loving her, and it tore her heart out that she couldn't see her and her grandson.

Beady had to stand by her husband, though. It was her highest duty. And to Jack, his reputation was everything. They had to live to a higher standard, he'd told her, even if it meant sacrifice. Amanda would know that, wouldn't she? All she'd need to do was repent of her ways, and they'd welcome the prodigal back. With each passing day of those four years, that possibility seemed less and less likely. Beady had almost—almost—convinced herself life absent of Amanda could be bearable. Young'uns left home and moved off all the time, and you hardly saw them after that. She rarely got over to Paducah to see her own family herself. But then Rai MacInteer had chanced along with her passel of children and news about Amanda to boot, and it was almost more than Beady could stand.

How many times had she wished away the past? If she could turn back the clock, she'd erase that Frank Rye and Gripp Jessup clean away. She never had cottoned to the pair, and somehow, she figured, this whole business was pinned on them.

Chapter 17

Every now and then, Gripp got an itch to see some sights. He'd tell Finn to mind the birds and he'd take off for a week or more, usually after they'd cooked and sold a fair batch and he had a few dollars burning a hole in his pocket. He'd ride the train to a suitable town and spend his money on whatever pleasures he could find for a day or two. He deserved some kick-back time after all the work he put in.

Plus, there was something about riding the rails that curbed his restlessness. It made him feel better, somehow, to scout around for confirmation that he was doing pretty well for himself. Judging by the sorry towns that slid by the moving train, there were plenty of folks doing far worse. Perversely, such a fact bolstered his spirits.

It was on one of these jaunts that Gripp stopped in a town where a tent meeting was going on. He'd mistaken it for some sort of carnival or he would've kept on riding. Unfortunately, the tent and its late-night praise and altar calls tended to put a damper on the carousing he meant to do in town. The tent, hung with lanterns and buzzing with activity, served as a momentary reminder to folks in town of how they ought to behave.

Gripp was in no mood for chastising or confessing, as he told the young lady whose bed he shared. "I've had enough preaching to last me a lifetime," he said, stroking the curve of her hip. Had she told him her name? He couldn't remember.

"It don't seem to have done you no good," she teased, biting the tip of his finger. "Now, what cause did you have to go to church?"

"I'm a' upstanding gentleman, as you can plainly see," Gripp said. He gestured downward with a proud flourish.

"Indeed." She arched an eyebrow and smiled.

"I had a partner one time who was courting a preacher's daughter," he recounted. "I had to play nice with the family to make some connections in the area. Unfortunately, that meant going to Sunday meetings. At least we got a home-cooked meal on the tail end of the sermons."

Gripp leaned on one elbow and became animated. "The preacher feller, now he was something. I seen him—more'n once—recite some passage from Ezekiel that could staunch blood. Just make a bleeding place on man or beast dry right up, no joke. Beat everything I ever saw.

"This one time I rode with the preacher to another church, trying to get the lay of the land. The feller goes on and on until I thought I might lose my mind with boredom. Can't even tell you what the subject was."

"Sounds about right," she purred.

"I got what I came for in the end. Hooked up with twin brothers with access to a stock car, perfect for making deliveries further off."

"You were making deals with the devil under God's own roof," she observed, shaking her head at his naughtiness. "You got some guts, I'll say that."

"That ain't all I got," he growled, pulling her close.

~

After one of these jaunts, when Gripp got back into town, having sown some oats, he happened to pass by an office where he caught sight of a dark-haired woman leading a mule with bulging saddlebags. Beside her walked a small boy, laughing and tossing rocks into the dust. Gripp swore he recognized her, though she had a few years on her since he'd seen her last. She reminded him of Frank Rye's wife—or rather, his widow—that preacher's daughter, and he felt a stirring in his trousers.

Could *she* be the ministering angel Finn had been going on about? The librarian woman? Now, wouldn't that be a small world? For now, Gripp let it go. He didn't aim to ruin two good partnerships over the same woman anyhow, not when business was so fine. All the same, he tucked the image of the woman away in his head and noted the direction she rode, in case there was call to get reacquainted somewhere in the future. He figured she probably owed him something for his two lost fingers.

Chapter 18

A ravenous pileated woodpecker was going to town on a nest of carpenter ants embedded in the hickory outside the MacInteer cabin. The huge bird was persistent, Sass granted him that; he was liable to cut the tree right in half with all that hammering. She peered at him from the front door, his plumed red head bobbing quick as a whip. She wished he'd hush his constant *ratt-a-tatt-a-tatt* so she could concentrate. Now that the weather had broken, spring chores were plentiful, and fitting in time to read of a morning wasn't easy. Miz Rye had worked some kind of magic: the book woman was friends with the schoolteacher and—imagine!—the teacher had loaned out a particular book Sass had mentioned. Sass finally held in her hands *Nancy Drew and the Secret of the Old Clock*, the book she remembered from her brush with school, but unless the ants gave out in that tree, she wouldn't be finishing it soon.

Mama had granted Sass an extra few minutes that morning before she had to join her and Fern in the garden. Since Sass had surely shown a knack for picking up words, and since school was so far off and likely out of the question, Mama had appointed Sass to teach the rest of the family. Each morning, Sass copied out a handful of words on small slips of paper and affixed them to objects around the cabin—*chair, table, bed, kettle*. By the end of each week, without even studying on them extra much, those words settled in their heads by seeing them over and over, just like feet learning the path through the woods to the ginseng patch.

Mama told Sass that in the middle of ordinary tasks while her hands were busy kneading dough, mending, or sweeping out the cabin, the letters tossed 'round and 'round in her head like turning over garden soil, and they stuck in her memory. Sass knew the same was true for Finn, Fern, and Cricket because when she quizzed them at supper, they raced to see who could spell or read the word quickest. Even her daddy chimed in, always game for a contest.

Sass finally gave up and shut her book. That Nancy Drew was something else. She lived in a place Sass could hardly imagine, rode in cars, and traveled like it was nothing. She was so smart she could figure out what other regular people couldn't. Reading her story filled up Sass's chest with air and a curious lightness. As different as their lives were, she and Nancy were also the same. Nancy cracked open a door inside Sass, one that beckoned her to wonder and stretch.

There was a spot she and Finn used to hike to—they called it Far Knob—that looked from below like little more than a pile of boulders as they climbed to it from the bottom of the slope. It had been too steep even for Finn to carry Sass on his back. They'd each had to grab saplings and brace their feet against stones on their way up to keep from sliding back down the steep ascent. At the top, breathless and their clothes snagged with brambles, they'd clambered onto the knobbed rock face and marveled. The sky opened up in a broad sweep, and as far as they could see, to where the blue sky faded to a haze of gray in the treetops, rounded mountaintops rose and dipped in blues and greens, constantly shifting between sunlight and shade from clouds sailing by overhead. Birds soared up here, big birds that opened their great wings and rode the twisting currents in wide circles in search of prey beneath the trees.

"Look out there, Sassy." Finn pointed. "Tucked away up here, sometimes I get to thinking we're all there is, our fishing hole, the weeds in the garden, the coal mine, and Digger and Tuck barking at raccoons all night." Sass had felt that, too. Their nook of the world was like the small end of a telescope, but turn it around and peek out the big end, and look what all was revealed. Since the book woman had come, the times she and Finn had spent up on Far Knob often nudged at her insides. The books Sass read took her back to standing on the top of those rocks. She started to see her mountain home and her place there as a page in a far bigger story, one that stretched out farther than even the eagles could fly.

On her last visit, Amanda had worked things out with Mama so that Sass and Fern could ride along with her on her way home and spend the night at her place. Mama sent them off, riding double bareback on Plain Jane with a packed lunch pail and bedroll and strict instructions to mind their manners and help out however they could. They'd walked down to the WPA office with Amanda, Mooney, and the little ones, Miles and Maisie, to hear the radio shows Amanda had told them about. How strange to think a voice spoke to them from a whole other place far away. Amanda had told them the president of the United States sometimes talked through the radio, too, to give updates on what was happening in the country. He called the sessions Fireside Chats, so it would seem like he was right there visiting with you, like a neighbor in your own house.

Besides hearing the radio show, Sass and Fern had helped make supper, take care of the horses, haul wood, and play with the children. Miles and Maisie were easy and so smart. It was no wonder when they lived with a librarian in their very own house, with access to books and such just down the road. When she and Fern added their voices to the singing and playing after supper, Mooney declared that angels must've paid a visit, it sounded so pretty. Mooney was made of kindness and couldn't get over finally getting to meet some of the family Amanda ran on and on about.

"That one time she came back here in the morning so worn out she slid right off Junebug and straight into bed, covered in icicles and smelling like a barn. Thought for certain she'd be coming down with the ague soon after."

"That was when we had to pull Myrtle's calf," Sass said with a laugh.

"I was so worried, I had half a mind to tie a young'un on each side of my saddle and ride up into the hills to fetch her." Mooney ruffled Miles's fine sandy hair. "I sang so many songs to a certain little beetle to get him to fall asleep that night, I couldn't talk for a week. She was lucky, 'cause she woulda gotten a' earful if I'd of had my full voice."

"I told Miles I'd been out collecting rabbits," Amanda said, "and it took me all night to get a sackful. I let him pick the one he liked best. Mooney, Fern here's the one who thought up the rabbit idea."

"Mercy." Mooney clapped her hands together. "Best thing since pockets on a dress. Them rabbits pop up all over the place. I see kids toting 'em through town all the time, don't want to let go of 'em." Fern flushed and stared at the floor. Sass had never known her to be so shy at home. "I wouldn't be surprised if you could turn that sort of thinking into a business of some sort down the road."

Sass and Fern had hardly slept, their first time off the mountain for an entire night. They'd been disappointed when Finn showed up early the next morning, riding their plow horse, Lincoln, ready to escort them back up the mountain. Mooney had risen even earlier, rattling skillets and stoking the stove for a big breakfast of ham, eggs, and hoecakes. She'd invited Finn in for a bite when he arrived and peppered him with questions like Nancy Drew would've done, Sass thought. Did Mooney figure Finn as a suspect? For what? When they'd set off for home, Amanda had handed up a sack of apples to Finn for a meal on the way, and Sass noticed she no longer wore the ring she was so accustomed to seeing on the book woman's left hand. A pang of sympathy struck her. It would be a shame if she'd lost something so fine.

Casting dark looks up at the woodpecker, Sass sighed and ventured out to the garden to join Mama and Fern. Bright sprigs of wild buttercups danced here and there in the breeze, and fat bumblebees flitted between the quince and forsythia. Sass breathed deep. The damp, earthy smell of everything come alive in the spring made her want to go exploring. She wished she'd risen early enough to go fishing with the boys, but she knew Finn would go back to the mines soon, now that his leg was mostly all mended, and that he wanted to spend some time with Cricket in particular. Cricket was a couple of years away from thirteen, and it wasn't so long ago that Finn had been in his place, counting the days before he'd have to go below ground like a mole. Still, she wished she could trade the hoe in her hands for an afternoon of baiting hooks and skipping rocks. She loved to sit in silence, listening to the music of the stream as it flowed around rocks and fallen branches, the only interruption the regular plink of their lines as they cast out near the banks to reach the run-ins where roots of trees growing near the water held fish close against the land.

"Judging by that waning moon last night, it's nigh on time to start planting taters," Mama said. "Provided Finn and Cricket come back with a nice string o' fish, we can throw some fish heads in the furrows."

"Fish head, fish head," Hiccup sang, absently parroting Mama's words. She sat in the dirt and sorted seed potatoes by color. "Fishy fishy fish head."

"I can make markers for the rows this time," Sass offered, "like we seen—saw—in the scrapbook pictures."

"I don't doubt it, but if we can't tell the difference between beans and taters just by looking, I reckon we might need more help than a signpost. Markers might be more for other folks." Folks who aren't counting on their next meal coming from their own hands' work, she meant.

They hoed down the rows for the better part of an hour, the sun warm on their backs as they chatted and sang. It would be an easy matter to drop the seed potatoes in once the moon rose and finish the job. Hiccup had them sorted into piles of Irish, red, and sweet potatoes, and except for her muddy hands, she had managed to stay fairly clean in the process. Mama was dusting her off when they spotted Daddy stalking toward the cabin, his hat gripped tight in his hand. Something had put a burr under his saddle.

Mama left the girls tidying up the garden tools and went to meet him. On their way to throw the weeds over into the chicken pen, the sisters dawdled long enough to hear bits of Daddy's tirade. Mama's calm answers were so soft they couldn't make them out.

For months now, while Finn shuffled back and forth into the woods, Sass took notice of Mama standing with her hands on her hips or wringing them in concern as she watched him from the window or doorway, but she'd held her tongue. She knew he was working things out in his mind and healing how he thought best. Truthfully, she preferred him up and active, even if he came home plumb exhausted at the end of a day, than propped up in bed, staring at nothing out the window. He was mighty intent on something, she knew, enough to brush her off. Once or twice, he even spoke sharply to her and Cricket, which they'd chalked up to the pain in his leg.

". . . what the devil he's thinking?" Daddy yelled. "This ain't the way to do it!" Boots stomped and dishes rattled on the shelves. ". . . was almost *proud* to report it to me, like I'd be all for the idea. Bad as it is in the mines, I don't see how serving jail time makes you any freer."

Sass and Fern looked at each other, eyes wide. Jail? Who was going to jail? The scuff of wood against wood and a final slam—that would be Daddy shoving a chair against the table, unable to sit still. He wasn't often angry, but when he was, it was best not to be a piece of furniture.

"Fishing, are they? Well, he'll be squirming like a worm on a hook by the time he's heard me out! Tell him to come find me in the barn. Shift is canceled tonight anyhow." The door slammed with a *thunk* Sass thought might loosen a shingle or two. Good thing Digger and Tuck had gone with the boys, or they'd be hunkered under the porch, their tails flat against their bellies. Sass and her sisters hastened their steps to the chicken pen and tossed the armfuls of weeds over the wire. The hens fell upon the greenery like it was manna from heaven. They weren't choosy, squabbling with each other over the right to scratch and peck to fill their gizzards.

Daddy stayed in the barn the rest of the afternoon, and Sass spied him now and then as she passed by, doing chores around the yard. He curried the horses until they shone and oiled their tack until it handled soft as melted wax. He scoured water buckets and mucked out the stalls, tossing manure into the compost pile behind the barn. When working out a temper, it helped to do horse chores, smell the sweet hay and leather tack. Sass sensed a change in Mama, too, since Daddy had come home. She seemed aggrieved, her mouth set in a line, not to be crossed. Sass was grateful Mama wasn't prone to outbursts, too, or they might not have a place left to eat supper.

Digger and Tuck reached the cabin first, toenails clicking on the porch steps. Finn and Cricket carried a string of fish, already cleaned and gutted, that would make a delicious supper, and Mama busied herself with the cast-iron stove. Fern rose to help, but Sass stayed at the table with Hiccup, a book spread between them.

"We left that sack of fish heads hanging on the garden post for the taters later like you said, Ma," said Cricket. "I'm gonna go clean my knife."

When he'd disappeared around the side of the cabin, Finn set their dinner pail down on the table. "All right," he said. "Reckon someone needs to speak up."

Mama turned from the stove, her lips pressed tight. "Your daddy's in the barn wanting to have a word."

Finn's mouth worked a bit as he considered this; then he nodded. "Best be heading out there, then." He leaned his walking stick inside the door. He didn't rely on it so much anymore, unless he planned on traveling a long distance. When he'd been gone a minute, Sass started to close the book, but without even turning around, Mama heaved a sigh.

"In case you're thinking of sidling out there, Miss Nosy, you can just sit your tail back down and stay put. Your daddy wanted you to have a ringside seat, he'd a' sent you an invitation."

Caught, Sass minded, but she couldn't let go of all that had unfolded that afternoon. What had Daddy so tore up? What did he and Finn need to talk about? And the worst: Why would Finn be going to jail? It wouldn't go over well to ask her father outright, and she had a feeling this wasn't going to come up in conversation with her brother. She'd been wrong about how alike she and Nancy Drew were. Sass had no clue how to figure out this mystery.

Supper was mighty quiet. If it weren't for Hiccup being wound up and full of sunshine, no one would have spoken two words. Daddy speared his battered fish like he was trying to land it a second time and nearly choked on a bone, he ate so fast. Finn, who'd spent all day catching the mess of bluegill and trout, had lost his appetite and rearranged bites on his plate four or five times before leaning back with his arms crossed over his chest.

"Moon's in tonight, so we're planting taters," Mama announced as she stood to clear the dishes. "Sass, you can scout for some morels if you've a mind before then. Don't stray far before it gets too dark to see. Take Hiccup with you. She's full o' pep yet."

Sass grabbed up her sack and headed outside to catch up with Hiccup, who'd gotten a head start. It was easier to breathe out here in the warm spring evening air; it was too close inside the cabin.

"C'mon, Hic, I know where there's a stand of ash not too far thisaway. You can carry the sack."

They set off through the woods on no particular path, Sass worrying over Finn, and Hiccup skipping behind, dragging the sack. Sass headed in the general direction, figuring she'd recognize the spot when they neared. A lambent light bathed the budding hardwoods as they walked, and apparently, every bird for a hundred miles had the same idea and flitted from tree to tree, calling to each other. Hiccup walked the entire way with her lips in a pucker, trying to imitate the whistles and tweets. They'd gone quite a ways when the normal bird chatter was broken by an unmistakable sound that made Sass stand still.

"Did you hear a rooster crow?" As soon as she'd asked, another trumpet came. *Err-er-ERR-errrrr.* "Must be one running loose. No cabins over on this land. Too steep." Sass spotted the grove of ash trees she'd hunted and picked up her pace. "Over there, Hiccup. Get your sack ready." They picked their way through the underbrush, and Sass knelt down to let her eyes adjust. "Aha!"

A natural teacher, Sass pointed out the small rectangular-looking mushroom. "See here how the cap has these pits and ridges? That's what you want. They're brownish and curly-like, and the cap's stuck on the stem like a man wearing a tall hat." Hiccup squatted beside her sister and examined the mushroom, her expression serious. Young as she was, Hiccup knew the importance of being able to spot and collect edible and medicinal plants. Sass plucked a morel from the soft ground and split it lengthwise using Cricket's Barlow knife. "See how it's hollow all the way down? That's how you know a real morel. If it ain't hollow, it ain't fit to eat. If you try one, it's liable to make you sick as a dog."

Once they'd spied the first one, a whole passel of others popped up like magic all around them. The persistent rooster kept up his bugling all the while Hiccup hopped between bunches, holding the sack open for Sass to toss them in. Hiccup tallied until they reached forty, give or take. She wasn't certain about her numbers after that, and Sass judged they'd collected what they could use up fresh anyway.

Something white darted through the brush in a zigzag, and soon after came a commotion of something bigger crashing through the underbrush and swearing. Sass and Hiccup stood silent and watched as a man clad in worn overalls clambered and stumbled through the woods. His prey ducked under a thicket of mountain laurel and crowed. The loose rooster was still on the run, apparently, and its owner, judging by his red face and cursing, was nigh done giving chase. He might have run past the sisters if Hiccup hadn't laughed, but how could she not? It wasn't every day you were gifted such a spectacle. At the sound of her giggle, the man stopped short, breathing hard, and held up a stick he brandished.

"Who's that?" he called. "C'mon, now, where you at?"

Sass held Hiccup's arm to shush her, and they stood still as frozen rabbits. Sass hadn't seen this feller before; he certainly didn't live near, as far as she knew. Why he came to be chasing after a rooster in the middle of nowhere was a mystery (second one today) but one Sass wasn't sure she wanted to solve. It was decided for her when the man lowered his stick and turned to face them where they crouched by the ash grove. When his eyes met Sass's, a slow grin spread above his beard.

"Hunting mushrooms, are you? Don't care for 'em myself. You wouldn't want to give me a hand catching this no-count rooster, would you?"

"Why you after him if he's so no-count?" Sass countered. She didn't know why she'd asked instead of just declining and heading back the way they'd come. The trees closed in a bit more now that the day had worn on some, almost like they leaned in to listen.

The man chuckled and scratched his beard. "Fair point." He aimed a finger at the thicket. "That particular rooster happens to be one of my best, despite his being so ornery. I'd hate to lose him to a fox out here. Need to get him home before the sun sinks." As if to taunt him, the rooster stepped out just enough to be seen and crowed again, his neck stretched as far as it would reach.

"He's a pretty one." Sass squeezed her sister's arm. Hiccup had an eye for chickens, had loved to feed and care for their small flock at home since she was small. Theirs were run-of-the-mill layers, though, mostly black, red, and mottled. This one had white feathers all the way down his yellow legs and fluffed black-and-white plumage around his neck. His tail stuck up in several directions at once, shiny black feathers that looked purple when the light caught them just right.

The man dropped his stick and walked toward them. Sass didn't let go of Hiccup's arm. "We need to get back home," Sass said. "S'posed to plant taters this evening and can't spare time to catch a chicken." Why had she volunteered that, about the potatoes, like she needed an excuse to leave? She snugged up the neck of their morel sack and hung it across her shoulder by a loop of twine. In the time it took her to knot and swing the bag, Hiccup stepped away and made a beeline for the thicket.

"With y'all to help me, it won't take long." The man had already turned on his heel and headed after Hiccup, heading to the left while she headed right. "If we can just get him cornered, I can grab him."

Sass huffed impatiently after her sister. She'd give Hiccup an earful on the way home. Already, she knelt down in front of the thicket in her cotton dress, reaching in toward the rooster with her palm out. She wore a loose wool sweater against the chill of the spring evening, and she'd no doubt snag it on the branches. Whose fault would that be? Sass could picture her mama handing *her* the sweater for mending— *"You're older and should've made her take care."*

"Don't reach in after him like that. He's liable to take your finger off," the strange man warned. Hiccup drew back, her eyes wide.

"Is he mean?" Sass asked. Mean roosters didn't stay around long at their house. Their daddy said they weren't worth the trouble and they kept after the hens so much they'd quit laying.

"Just you run him out this direction and I'll grab him when he comes out." Sass and Hiccup closed in on either side of the bramble of vines and branches. The rooster fluttered and flapped his wings as he danced from side to side, hemmed in. He had only one exit, and it was in the man's direction. Hiccup rustled the branches on the right, and Sass thrust her sack as far into the left side of the thicket as she could and flapped it at the bird like a flag. He darted out the back, squawking, his cocky bravado gone, and the man lunged at him, scooping him up and pinning his wings under an arm in a single motion.

"Got him." The rooster struggled, kicking his clawed feet, but the man held him snug.

He was even prettier up close. Hiccup clapped her hands, delighted.

"Well, there y'are, then," Sass said, brushing the dirt off her knees.

"I sure do thank you, ladies. He woulda been a fox dinner for certain if you hadn't come along. I'm strapped right now, but I'd be happy to pay you with a sack of goose feathers or a passel of black walnuts back at the house."

"No need." Now that Sass had Hiccup in hand again, she intended to march her home directly.

"You didn't even get to pet him," the man said. He squatted and turned so that the fancy tail feathers drooped over his elbow. Hiccup couldn't resist. She reached out a hand. "He can't hurt you none from this direction." The rooster's tail feathers slid through her fingers, slick as oil, and she let her hand creep up to the plumage on his neck.

"I do believe he likes it," the man said. Sass huddled down in her sweater. The light was dappled here, and the air started to dampen as the evening dew settled. "What about you, little miss?" he asked Sass. "You want to touch him, now he's caught?"

Sass shook her head. "Naw. Like I said, we need to get back. They'll be waiting for us at home."

"This 'un ain't the only rooster I got. There's a whole bunch lives back at my place, anytime you want to come see 'em. Just over the ridge back thataway. Not all of 'em are ornery as this 'un is. He's my favorite, though. That's why I's so eager to catch him when he run loose. Look at that beak on him. I named him Pecker." His fat tongue poked out between his lips and wet the corners of his mouth. He lifted his free hand and stroked the bird's neck and down the length of his body. "Nice Pecker," he purred. "Good boy."

The bird's clawed toes hanging in the air like old crippled hands gave Sass the willies. She raised her eyes to the man and swallowed hard. The hand that was in her pocket, the one that didn't have a hold of her sister, closed on Cricket's pocketknife, the one she'd used to slice the morels. Sass turned her slight frame to face Hiccup and block the man's gaze. Her heart pounded in her throat like she imagined the rooster's had when it beat its wings, tangled in the thicket.

"C'mon, Hic." She tugged. "Let's go." Something hard in Sass's voice made Hiccup finally pay attention. She stepped to Sass's side and they started off back the way they'd come, their feet quick. Sass usually had to pull and drag Hiccup along as she dawdled and skipped, but now her short legs kept up with Sass's longer ones as they hurried toward home.

Sass turned back once to see him standing, the captured rooster cowed in the crook of his arm. The man pretended to tip his hat at them, and then he cackled a barking laugh, like the wild dogs she sometimes heard yip and carry on in the dark. He made no move to follow but called after them, "I got *lots* of roosters. You can come back and pet mine anytime now."

They made it home before dark. Mama hadn't even lit the lanterns for planting yet. They had to wait until the moon was high above the roof anyhow. Most of the way home, Sass scolded Hiccup for worrying about the lost rooster in the first place instead of coming on home like she'd wanted. Sass had promised her an extra story before bed if she'd keep quiet about what had happened. With the bad feelings between Finn and her daddy, she didn't want to add to the mix, and nothing had really happened anyway. They'd just stayed a little too long, and Sass had known better. She already knew that and didn't much covet a talking-to about it on top of the way her stomach churned. Daddy didn't need one more thing to be vexed about.

"You got my knife?" Cricket held out his hand, and Sass dug in her pocket.

"Came in handy," she said. "Glad we had it."

"Nothing more useful than a good pocketknife," Cricket said. "That there's my best one. Remember that time I used it to fashion a little mouse outta ash wood? Gave him fishing-line whiskers and a slip of leather for a tail. Put him up on the mantel with his nose hanging off, and Mama took a broom and like to beat the chimney down when she saw it. I think it was my best likeness yet." His shoulders shook with laughter.

"Girls," Mama called. "Lay that sack of morels on the table and come on out to the garden. Cricket, you do that again and the chimney won't be the only thing gets a beating."

Sass was suddenly bone-tired, and taters were the last thing she wanted to worry about, but if they didn't worry about them now, she knew, they'd for certain worry about *not* having them later. She laid the sack on the table, and a flash of white caught her eye. A feather hung in the burlap weave. Sass's throat burned, and she bit her lip to stay the tears that welled there. She plucked the feather from the threads where it was snagged and opened the door of the cast-iron stove, where the fire from supper still smoldered. Unhooking the iron poker from the side of the stove where it hung, she pushed the feather deep into the glowing coals until it was nothing but ash.

Chapter 19

Sass stuck close to home after her run-in with the rooster man, as she thought of him. The familiar woods that surrounded her cabin no longer beckoned as a welcome retreat for her to explore and admire. She was no child. She'd heard low-voiced stories at shuckings and on occasions when the women would gather to string beans or piece a wedding quilt. *"The Mitchell girl showed up on her front porch with her dress torn and bruises on her face. Her uncles and pa aimed to settle it. Sheriff found a stranger's body floating down Flat Creek a few days later, full of lead."* Mountain justice tended to be swift and unmerciful, meted out for trespasses of honor, thievery, or more heinous acts, and even the official lawmen, who more often than not were kin to the parties involved, looked the other way in sympathy and accord.

Sass didn't want to stir up trouble, and she sure didn't want to be gossiped about the way the women talked about the Mitchell girl. Sass didn't even know her, but she pitied her because her name always carried knowing looks and whispers, her story remembered and repeated forever and ever, amen. The mountains were full of stories, pitiful and otherwise. That's how folks here came out of the womb, finding their voices with that first breath, a wail of complaint, their speech of a rhythm and pattern unlike anyplace else. When Sass had heard the radio show and President FDR chatting with the country, her ears had picked up the difference right off. The voices from *elsewhere* were less colorful, less musical.

Every chance they got, folks had a story ready to go. The other night after supper, they'd taken turns reading from the Bible, and Fern had read that God made the world just by speaking it so. Maybe when God shared His breath with folks in the first place and made them alive, that same breath mixed with ours to speak and sing and spin tales, tales of remembering and made-up fancies, too, for the sheer joy of it. That preacher, Amanda's daddy, had said the Word became flesh and lived alongside of us. He'd meant Jesus, though Sass couldn't figure exactly what sort of word Jesus might have been to begin with before God put skin on Him. *Mercy*, perhaps? Or maybe *Forgive*?

What about the stories you didn't care to remember? If they weren't spoken out loud or set down on a page, would they disappear as if they didn't ever happen? Sass remembered the night Myrtle birthed her calf, when Finn told his story about the cave-in. He'd done tamped the whole thing down, keeping it from the air, and felt freer for its telling. Sass rolled that over in her head, considering. She didn't think she wanted to let the rooster man loose quite yet.

Mama had let up on the planting for a blessed day because the horns of the moon weren't facing right, and she piled everyone in the wagon for a rare trip six miles down the far side of the mountain into the free town, where goods were a fair price better than at the closer mine stores. It had been dry enough that the wagon could get down the creek bed without hanging in a rut, and Cricket, for one, could use some shoes. Mama had several small bags of seeds she wanted to trade, if she could, for different ones so that they could eat something other than pole beans and tomatoes all summer. Finn handed Mama several dollars to use if she needed it.

"I don't believe we're needing anything bad enough for that," she said, fixing him with one of her hard looks.

"It's either that or back to the coal, and I intend to keep on top of the ground 'less I'm laid out in a pine box. I'd 'preciate you picking up a bit o' cloth for a new shirt. This 'un's done worn through." He poked two fingers through a hole that flapped down the side. "I'd go along with you myself, but I've got work to do."

Mama shook her head slowly but said nothing, her lips pressed tight together. She clucked to Plain Jane, who perked her ears forward and set off down the trail, the wagon creaking and swaying behind her muscled bay hindquarters. In about a half mile, the trail opened up enough that they could quit ducking and pushing at the branches as they brushed by, and Mama sang softly to Hiccup to pass the time, pausing at the end of a line to let Hiccup chime in.

"Twinkle, twinkle, little—"

"Star!"

"How I wonder what you—"

"Are!"

The sun shone warm on their legs as Fern, Cricket, and Sass sat opposite one another in the wagon bed, braced against the sides. Sass was tired, and she'd woken up with her head aching. Her eyes roved over the trees and underbrush as the wagon rolled past. Blushes of pink and white colored the sides of the trail, the palette of redbuds and dogwoods opening their petals to the bees that hovered, intent on the sticky pollen. They passed familiar thickets of wild blackberries already in bloom, and Sass spotted one or two pawpaws with budding fruit starting on the branch tips.

"Stop, Mama! Stop the wagon," Sass yelled. Before Mama had pulled up the horse all the way, Sass had clambered over the side and jumped to the ground, her headache forgotten.

"Land sakes, Sass." Mama twisted around in the seat to see what in the world had put a bee in her second daughter's bonnet. Cricket leaned over the side, scouting the woods.

"Look at it, the poor thing," Sass cried. She stood between two dogwoods, their branches full of buds and a handful of opened blossoms. An enormous spiderweb had caught the light as they'd passed by, the filaments spun in concentric circles and reaching from tree to tree. The web's owner, a large black-and-yellow orb weaver, waited on one edge. Sass picked up a stick and poked at the center of the web, where a two-inch bundle wrapped in sticky threads still showed signs of movement. When Cricket saw what Sass was after, he was over the edge of the wagon and fast on her heels.

"Oh, mercy. It's a *spider*," Fern complained. "That's what it *does*."

"When we passed, I thought I saw . . ." Sass nudged the web again, and it bounced and swayed, anchored firmly. "Look, there's its beak," she said, pointing. Cricket stood at her elbow now, his neck craning up into the branches. "We have to free it."

"It's not moving, Sass." Mama sighed.

"It is," Cricket yelled. "I can see its head twisting."

Sass aimed her stick where the web was anchored closest to her and swung, dislodging it from its tree and causing the web's circles to deflate as it flapped in the breeze like a sheet hanging on the wash line. The heavy bundle in its center caused the web to spin in on itself and stick together.

"Get it! Get it," Sass cried as Cricket jumped repeatedly, reaching for the flying threads. The spider abandoned its home and hightailed it into the tree onto solid footing. Sass's fingers gingerly touched the wrapped bundle. It seemed to sense its miraculous second chance, and it struggled against its bindings.

"Cricket, your knife." He dug in his pocket and flipped open the blade. Now that the spider was no longer front and center, Fern and Hiccup were more interested.

"Bring it over here," Fern commanded.

"Let me see," Hiccup called.

Sass held the bundle in her hand, and for certain, a thin beak poked out of the fibers, no bigger around than the stem of a flower. As Cricket cut away the web bit by bit, he revealed the hummingbird's emerald-green feathers, and its tiny black eyes opened.

"Fern! Fetch me one of Plain Jane's sugar cubes, quick. And the water pail." Sass pulled the web off the bird's feet, the tiniest feet she'd ever seen, wiping it off her fingers and onto her dress. The bird was free now, but it didn't fly away. It couldn't have been caught for long. Maybe it had a chance. It lay twitching and testing its wings, its feathers a stuck mess from its struggles in the web. Sass dipped her fingers in the water pail and let drops of water moisten the feathers, rubbing gently with the hem of her dress.

"Make a handful of water, Mama, with the sugar," Sass said. Mama caught on, all of them involved in the operation now. She wrapped the reins around a post by the wagon seat. Plain Jane's ears swiveled back and forth as she stood still; this was not an ordinary trip to town. Once Mama filled her cupped hand with water, Fern dropped the cube in, and Sass held the bird's beak up to the small pool they'd made.

"Come on, birdy." Hiccup beckoned to it. "Don't you want to fly, birdy?"

"There it goes." Cricket pointed. They stood around Sass's and Mama's cupped hands, all their heads bowed closely in a circle that blocked out the sun. The bird's threadlike tongue darted once, twice. In a matter of a few minutes, it had sipped from their pool of life enough to right itself and flit its tiny perfect feathers. Its throat, the red of a jewel, bobbed as it sipped. When the little creature had had enough, Sass stepped back from their circle and held her hands out toward the woods, the sun reflecting on its brilliant green feathers. Its wings buzzed only twice before it lifted from Sass's hand and zipped up to a nearby branch, where it seemed to take stock of itself and its surroundings.

"Bye, birdy." Hiccup waved.

"I hope it'll be all right." Sass watched it until it zipped again, chittering and buzzing so fast she lost sight of it.

"That was somethin'," Cricket marveled. "I never seen one up close like that."

"Now that the day's good deed is done, can we get on the way again?" asked Mama. They climbed back into the wagon, and the mare shook out her traces and resettled the harness.

"Finn will be sorry he missed that," said Sass. "He's the one showed me how hummingbirds drink sweet water. He made a little eating spot like that from the sugar he had for the mine ponies once."

The rest of the way to town, they were in fine spirits. Once they pulled up in front of the general store, they climbed out of the wagon and scattered through the store, except for Hiccup, who stayed by Mama's side as she greeted and chatted with folks. A visit to town was a chance to catch up on news and see fresh faces. This time, Fern lingered at the back, near where a tall, muscled, light-haired boy stood on a ladder and stocked the highest shelves. She kept asking him to reach things for her so that they could keep talking without him getting scolded by the store's owner. Cricket and Sass stared into a glass case that held fishing tackle—rows of line, jigs, lures, weights, and sinkers.

"Think of the strings of fish I could bring home with one or two of these, Sass." He studied on them intently, and Sass knew he was imagining how he could rig something similar from scraps in the barn.

For a while, Sass followed Mama around as she fingered bolts of fabric and asked about the prices. Except for the candy, which she knew Mama would not purchase, nothing in the store much interested her, and Sass wandered outside to stroke Plain Jane's soft nose as the mare dozed in the sunshine, hip cocked to rest a rear hoof. Other horses stood tied farther down the dusty lane, some by the feed store, some outside the saloon (even this early) at the edge of what passed for town. Sass toed the dust and squinted down the road, glancing briefly back inside the dim store at Mama, who had planted herself on a stool at the counter to debate the best stitch to use for a side seam. No telling how long they'd be. They still had to look at shoes for Cricket if he'd ever quit drooling over the tackle.

Sass wandered idly past the storefronts full of things beyond her reach, nodding occasionally to women she passed and stopping to speak to a girl her age she'd seen once before. Her red hair hung in a thick braid down her back, and she wore a blue cotton dress and shoes. The girl swung a book in her hand, and Sass recognized it as one she had actually read.

"How'd you like your book?" she asked.

The girl stopped and regarded Sass in her plain dress and bare feet. "This 'un?"

Sass nodded. "I liked it fair enough, but my favorite is the one about the clock."

"Oh," the girl said. Alma Reed. That was her name. She was one of the girls in the schoolroom that day long ago. "You read this one?"

"Reckon so. I like all the Nancy Drew ones," Sass said. Alma seemed surprised, but she agreed that she liked them, too. When Alma's mother called to her from the front of the general store, she turned to go but waved at Sass.

"Nice to see you again," Alma said with a smile.

A warmth spread beneath Sass's ribs. It was an unfamiliar sensation, but Sass recognized it—pride. Knowing how to read had sparked a new confidence inside her. The feeling lasted until Sass reached the Feed & Seed. The earthy smell of growing things and acrid tang of fertilizer drew her inside. In the back of the store, she stood in front of the square wooden cubbies filled with all manner of grains and seeds. A metal scoop hung from a nail on the wall near a scale that dangled from the ceiling on a pulley chain. Sass had no intention or means of buying such bounty, but she loved the slick feel of sticking her hands in the bins and running the seeds through her fingers like water. There was corn, buckwheat, barley, and sorghum for grains, and in the smaller bins, muskmelon, radishes, turnips, and several types of beans. Buying seed for a vegetable garden was wasteful when you could save and dry your own or trade with neighbors. All the colors and sizes laid out together was dizzying. Imagine the tangle of garden if all those seeds sprouted and grew. Come summer, you could eat all you wanted.

Dreaming about the impossible bounty, Sass paid no mind to the voices at first, but like a clap of thunder wakes you from a sleep of a night, the sound of one particular voice froze her to the spot. She clenched her fists so tight the grain could've been milled into flour right inside her sweaty palms.

"I got me a feller to help run the operation, don't worry 'bout that. You just need to haul it cross the line into Perry and Knott."

"I might need a' advance to get the car up to snuff."

The two men stood just outside the back door. Though she wasn't all alone in the store—folks shuffled by down the aisles on either side of her—Sass held her breath as the Feed & Seed fell away around her.

"You get any ideers 'bout crossing me, give a thought to that last cave-in. It ain't nothing to lay a charge if a score needs settled—I done it before. A whole army of knockers can't save you from that slate ceiling when I set the blast." He laughed, and the cruel sound of it set Sass's teeth on edge.

"That how you lost them fingers?" The second man tried to joke through the bluster, but Sass heard the nervous warble in his response. Cave-in? Sass swallowed down the sick that rose in her throat. She pushed away the memory of her and Fern coming back to the house to find Finn lying blackened and battered in the bed. That hadn't been an accident?

"My fingers ain't your concern, less they're pulling the trigger of a barrel aimed your way. We have us a' understanding?"

Sass clung to the side of the seed bins to keep her knees from buckling straight to the floor. She turned her head toward the front of the Feed & Seed, searched for her mother, remembered she'd come here alone. The back door opened, and a man she didn't know pushed through, barely glancing at Sass as his boots clomped up the aisle of the wood-planked floor toward the front. Before she could tell her feet to move, the voice's owner pushed through into the back room. Sass knew in that moment how a small brown rabbit felt, held frozen in a field under a hawk's gaze. Although her eyes studied the floor and all she saw was the tips of his dirty boots poking out from the edge of his overalls, she knew when the boots didn't move past the seed bins that he'd seen her.

"Well, if it ain't my handy-dandy rooster catcher," he drawled. When Sass didn't answer, he latched onto her upper arm with his rough hand and dragged her easily out the back door. He pushed Sass up against the wall of the building and stuck his left hand in her face. Shiny red nubs poked out where his first two fingers should've been, and Sass's gaze traced the long red scar that ran down his arm and disappeared into his shirtsleeve.

"Seems you got a knack for showing up in odd places," he said, his breath a sour mix of tobacco and whiskey. "I'm gonna be straight with you, little miss. I don't know what you might or might not of heard just now, but the other day when you met my rooster, I follered you and your pretty little sister home." Sass raised her eyes then. She'd checked behind them that day. He hadn't really followed them, had he? She was grateful Hiccup had stayed with Mama at the store today. "Maybe you didn't see me, but that's 'cause I can walk quiet as a Cherokee in them woods."

The man stuck his spoilt hand in his pocket, still holding on to Sass's arm with the other. He regarded her, decided to take another tack.

"You look like a good Christian girl," he said. "I'm sure you don't want to go spreading gossip and tales 'round town 'bout the likes of me. Things that don't concern nobody else. You prob'ly got family in the mines, too. Be a shame if something were to happen to 'em down in the dark there, where no one would see it coming." He regarded her, his eyes traveling the length of her body slowly. "I know who you are. You go telling tales, girl, and I'll take your big brother right down the mountain with me. Sheriff'd be *real* interested in the location of that still he's been running. Bet he'd like to slam the cell door on him real tight. No telling when you might see his face again."

Sass moved her head side to side, and his lip curled into a sneer. "'Sides, it ain't like anybody'd pay you no mind. You're just a hillbilly from the boonies, and not even half-growed." He pulled his claw hand from his pocket and hesitated a half second before running a finger across Sass's chest. He gave one of her nipples a hard twist, and her eyes brimmed hot with tears. That cackle of a laugh again. "Not even a handful, even for half a hand! More like chigger bites." He leaned his left elbow against the building, pinning her on one side, while with his right hand he reached around behind her and grabbed between her legs. She felt the scrape of his dirty fingernails through the thin cotton of her dress. Sass did her best to twist away, pushing upward with her toes to escape, throwing her elbows out against his arms. She didn't think to holler. She was using all her strength to push him away, to free his hold on her. He watched her squirm, no flicker of pity or shame in his features. He was strong and she was weak; he did it because he could.

He let her go then and backed away, satisfied he'd made his point. He looked back once and pointed at her again before he rounded the corner of the Feed & Seed. He raised a finger to his lips and disappeared down the alley between buildings. Sass stood there still, her back and palms pressed flat against the wood of the building, bracing against it and remembering to breathe as her heart thrummed in her chest. She squatted down and hugged her knees tight, trying to keep from being sick. She had to tell, didn't she? But that's the one thing she couldn't do. What about her daddy, in the mines every night? Or Hiccup, the next time they picked blackberries or hunted sang?

Images of Finn's smashed leg flitted across her memory like pictures in a book, his pale face as he lay there in the bed for weeks.

What he'd suffered. How Mama had worried so, more than Sass had witnessed before—and she'd seen her share of worry—more even than when Hiccup had caught the ague and had a fever for days. Sass knew it could've been so much worse, and the tears started. Not tears of sadness or fear, but tears of pure anger that burned as they fell into the dust at her feet. Pain shot through Sass's jaw, and she realized she'd been clenching her teeth so hard she might've cracked a tooth. What good were tears in the dust? Salt water never grew no seeds.

A scrap of paper rustled against her ankle, and she plucked it off the ground. It had become habit now to read everything that crossed her vision, so she unfolded the page. It fell open in soft creases—some kind of list, a name on each line. As she studied it, she remembered the man taking his hand in and out of his pocket. He must have dropped it while he was busy tormenting her. Sass had pockets, too.

She wiped her eyes with a sleeve of her dress and folded the page back. Casting a quick glance down the back side of the building, she tugged open the back door and darted inside, brushed down the center aisle past the burlap sacks and lengths of twine, and headed out the front. Her eyes swept up and down the road. No sign of the rooster man. Sass backtracked to the general store, folks passing by in a blur. There, Mama and Cricket stood out front by their wagon, placing packages in the bed. Hiccup sat on the bench seat, swinging her bare feet.

"There you are, Sass. I didn't know where you'd got off to. You three stay put and I'll go round up your sister," said Mama.

Sass climbed up into the back of the wagon and hugged her knees to her chest, ignoring Hiccup's questions and Cricket's chatter about the new lures he'd examined. She couldn't wait to point the wagon back up the mountain. She needed to talk to Finn something fierce.

Chapter 20

The path from town to home always passed quicker because Plain Jane counted on corn and a rubdown at the end when she went that direction. Fern hummed as she sat on the front seat beside her mother, and Cricket and Hiccup swung their legs over the back edge of the wagon, watching as the road beneath their feet changed from packed-down dirt to rutted grass to the thicker leaves and underbrush of the old logging trail that led north.

Sass sat in the front corner of the wagon bed, hugging her knees tight and gazing out at the trees along the way, though she wasn't really paying attention to the woods. She chewed her thumbnail down to the quick and then sucked on the salty trace of blood that seeped out. When Mama glanced backward, she scolded her.

"Take your hands from your mouth, Sass, or you'll get worms."

Sass kept her hands folded in her lap for a minute, but her fingers soon crept to her hair, where she wound and twisted a lock around and around until she'd knotted the end into a fine mess without even noticing.

"I saw a newspaper in the store today," Cricket called from the back. "There was a picture on the front of a great big contraption, looked like a flying cloud, caught a'fire. All the old-timers out front were talking about it."

Fern sat up importantly. "I heard that, too. My—friend—in the store told me about it. It was something they called a zeppelin—a flying machine with folks inside it—that caught fire and crashed. Hindybur, I think was its name?"

"*Hindenburg* is what folks were sayin'," reported Cricket, his shoulders back. "Some kinda airship way up north in New Jersey."

"How awful," said Mama. "Why folks'd want to dangle up in the air like that in the first place seems like a foolish notion to me."

"They're not dangling, Mama," replied Cricket, now an expert on the subject. "They're flyin'! Seems grand. Reckon it'd be like being on top of the mountain all the time, looking down on everything below like a' eagle." His arm dipped and dove in the air as he squinted up at it. "I'd try it!"

"What goes up must come down, Cricket MacInteer. You're a boy, not a bird. Best to keep your feet on solid earth where they's planted."

They rode on, winding in dappled sunlight beneath the newly leafing hardwood canopy. The white and pink sprays of dogwoods in bloom brightened in the occasional clearing.

"Y'all watch for green ramps or dandelions along the way," Mama directed. "They'll add some taste to our meat. Once the garden comes in, we can count on some better eating." She pulled Plain Jane up short and sent Cricket springing out to the edge of the path after a tender sassafras sapling.

"Mind the snakes, now," she called. "It's getting warm enough to see 'em sunning. Adaire Miller just told me, while I was looking at cloth for Finn's shirt, that her nephew went to bring in kindling and wasn't paying a bit of attention in the world. Got bit by *two* rattlers at once't. One in the foot and one in the hand. Lucky they was near enough to call on the mine doctor or he might'a been no more for this world." Mama shook her head with the pity of it. "Adaire says his arm swelled up so big, his skin like to split right open."

Hiccup pointed past where Cricket dug, farther out into the woods. "Mama!" she cried. "Morels!"

Sass's head swiveled to look, her heart quickening in her chest. "I believe you're right, Hiccup," Mama said. She tossed a burlap sack to Hiccup and sent her scampering to where she'd seen the telltale mushroom caps. Cricket joined her, and the two of them gathered several handfuls into their sack in a few minutes.

"Those'll go just right with the ramps and taters for supper tonight," Mama said.

"Sass showed me how to find 'em and cut 'em just right." Sass tried to catch Hiccup's eye, to remind her to leave it at that.

"Did she now? That's right, you two collected a nice poke of morels not long ago."

Hiccup nodded. Sass threw a loose clod of dirt at her to get her attention. "When we saw that rooster."

Stop talking, Hiccup, hush, hush, hush!

"A rooster? Back in them woods?" Mama laughed. "Hiccup, are you telling another one of your flying-bear stories?"

Hiccup had had quite an imagination when she was a toddler and once burst in breathless and excited after playing in the yard, babbling she'd seen a flying bear go right by the chicken pen. Even after he'd asked questions every which way, Daddy never could get out of her what she'd actually seen or whether it had been anything at all. Ever since then, they'd dubbed fishy tales "flying-bear stories."

"No. Sass and me caught a white rooster with the rooster man."

Sass stayed quiet, knowing she was taking a chance that Mama would diagnose her with some illness and dose her with something when they got home.

"Is that so?" Mama said to Hiccup. "Extra roosters running loose might end up in a pot if they're not careful."

"Oh, no, this un's not for eating," she replied, her explanation serious. "This 'un's a pet."

Mama mussed Hiccup's hair and swatted her on the fanny as she and Cricket climbed up into the wagon. "Go on with you now." She signaled Plain Jane to start up once they'd all settled in.

At home, Sass endured a double dose of horsemint and boneset tea and swore to her mama she did not have a cough or stomachache. Mama threatened to make her eat an onion roasted in the ashes of the stove, but Sass perked up enough after the tea that she convinced her to relent. No sign of Finn since they'd arrived home. Cricket and Daddy had stabled Plain Jane and fed the livestock while Fern and Sass unloaded the wagon and helped Mama start supper. The sky faded into shades of purple and orange as the sun dipped, and a damp, thick fog rose from the creeks and rivers to blanket the mountains like a shroud. The lantern lights within the cabin shone out into the haze of fog like a yellow-eyed panther. Sass sat on the front porch, absently stroking Digger's soft ears while she stared off into the trees. Tuck curled up beside her. They always seemed to ferret out her troubles.

Talk at the supper table was about the ride to town, the hummingbird they'd rescued, and the things they'd purchased. Daddy had spent the day a few miles away at a neighbor's house, trading his labor for a share of their honey stores come summer. The man had set up several hollow stumps he'd made into beehives, and Daddy wanted to learn the skill so that they could have a reliable source for something sweet instead of chancing on a tree in the woods. Cricket told Daddy about the airship that had caught fire, and he allowed that it might be a wonder to fly like that somehow. Daddy said the world was changing fast, no telling what Cricket might do. It would be a blessing if it were something other than mining. He'd been casting around for options and was chewing on some ideas. As usual, when he finished supper, Daddy hit the bed for a quick nap before he had to head to the mines, but even by the time he gathered his dinner pail and water, Finn still hadn't come home.

Sass tried to read by the fire, but her mind kept jumping around like a Jesus bug on creek water. She turned page after page, but all the while her hand kept reaching into her pocket to feel the folded scrap of paper she'd picked up outside the Feed & Seed. Where had Finn got off to? She gave Daddy a kiss when he left for his shift and promised to be good. She started the same page over again for the third time, remembering nothing of what she'd just read. The doses of tea sloshed in Sass's stomach, making her feel queasy, but darned if she'd let her mama know. The last thing she wanted was another remedy. Her head ached from all the thoughts that raced there—the rooster man, what she'd heard him say about the mines, how he'd touched her and made her sad and angry all at once, the list she'd found. Finally, she curled up in the bed with a lantern nearby, trying to concentrate on her book. Tomorrow the book woman was due to come, and Sass wanted to finish so that she could trade for another, but try as she might, her eyes grew too heavy to read any more or wait for her brother.

In the middle of the night, Sass woke with a start, feeling like she'd wet the bed. She sat up and let her eyes adjust to the light from the dying coals in the hearth. Cricket, Fern, and Hiccup lay sound asleep, head to toe in the bed beside her, and Mama's light snores carried from her bed behind the curtain on the opposite side of the room. Sass reached a hand to her underwear and, sure enough, felt a sticky wetness, but she still felt a pressing urge to go to the outhouse. Confused, she slid out of bed and turned up the lantern light. She slipped into a pair of brogans by the door and stumbled, groggy, behind the cabin as the dogs whined after her and trotted behind.

Half a moon hung low in the sky, and tree frogs and crickets sang all around her as Sass opened the outhouse door. She hung the lantern on its hook and squatted, yawning big enough for her eyes to water. A horned owl's hoot questioned outside—*who, who, who, who-oooo?*

"Just me, silly," Sass whispered. She looked down at her underwear as she pulled them up and gasped. She'd have to wash them. A red stain of blood soaked them through. Panicked, she pulled up her dress and examined herself in the dim lantern light. It was all over her thighs and hands where she'd smeared it, all down the back of her dress. It didn't hurt, but Sass stifled a cry. Had she cut herself? When? How? Then a sudden horrible thought: *the rooster man*. Had he somehow caused it? Sass lived on a farm and knew how babies were made, but there was more to it, she knew. You had to like boys first, like her sister Fern, or be married to one like her mama, and then somehow, blood came. Was that right? Somehow, *it* knew about how he'd come close and touched her. That must have been the signal for her body to start. Sass groaned, this crimson stain evidence of her shame. How could she hide this from Mama? It wasn't like she had a drawer full of extra underwear, let alone a drawer itself.

She crept out of the outhouse, careful not to let the door squeak, and let the lantern and moon light the path to the barn. Once inside, she hung the lantern once more—Daddy had taught them young never to leave a lit lantern near bedding or hay—and spoke softly to the horses rustling the hay, their dozing interrupted.

"Sorry, Janie girl, I need to borry some water," she said. Sass cast around for a bucket, and she tipped Jane's water bucket into her own. That oughta be enough to wash with, she thought. Sass stripped off her underwear and squatted over the bucket to wash and rinse the blood out. She crumbled a bit of salt off the horses' salt block to help ease the stain and ground it in with her fingers. Then, she pulled her dress over her head and used a ratty blanket that had been tossed over top of a saddle to cover herself while she scrubbed and rinsed the dress, trying to wet only the soiled spot. The horses hung their noses over the stall doors and *whuffled* puffs of breath at her. On the ground where she squatted, blood dripped into the hay. She couldn't wash her things over and over all through the night. Sass bit her lip and pulled the blanket closer around her shoulders, shivering in the chilly damp of the night. She fingered the edge of the old quilt and pulled a scythe from its peg on the barn wall. It didn't take long to cut and tear several strips of the quilt. She wrapped one inside her underwear and pulled her wet garments back on, wincing as the cold fabric stuck to her skin, and retrieved the lantern to return to the house.

"Sass?" The voice came out of the dark, from the back corner of the barn, where bales of hay were stacked in neat rows. Sass nearly dropped the lantern when she jumped. "What're you doing out here in the middle of the night?"

Finn stood in the half-lit barn in a spot where the white moon cast a thin light through cracks in the planked walls. He rubbed a hand across his jaw, scratching his patchy, half-grown beard.

"What—what're *you* doing out here?" she shot back. Had he seen her?

"Got back late and didn't want to wake the whole house up, so I bedded down out here." He jerked a thumb toward the hay, where she now saw he'd made a kind of nest with a holey old quilt, like the one she still wore around her shoulders.

Sass's face flushed hot. She was glad for the darkness. "I—I just came out to check on the horses. Owl woke me up and I went to the outhouse." It was partly true. "Jane needed some water," she said, pushing the bucket aside with her foot. It was hollow, flimsy. Finn would see right through her. But Finn didn't notice.

"All right. Well, watch your step on the way back," he said, yawning.

Sass held the lantern with one hand and tried to hold the back of her wet dress away from her legs with the other. "Finn?"

"Yeah, Sassy?"

"I got something to tell you."

He smiled at her, with that lopsided grin she loved so well, and leaned against the rough center beam in the barn. "Let's hear it."

"Who you been working with since you quit the mine?" she asked.

Her brother's eyes darkened, and his face grew serious. "What's Daddy been saying?"

She shook her head. "Nothing. Not a word. I don't know what y'all are in such a tiff over if that's what you mean."

"Then what's it matter? I bring in enough to make up for what I made in the mine—more than enough. I guess Cricket got shoes yesterday, didn't he? I guess Mama got her some sugar and coffee?"

Sass nodded. This hadn't started right. "Yes, yes, for certain. I ain't saying nothing about that. I know why you don't favor going back to the mine." Her eyes fell to his leg. Where he leaned against the beam, he still cocked his hip, all his weight borne by its opposite. "You told it straight out the night you pulled Myrtle's calf. I don't blame you a bit and wish Daddy didn't have to neither. Or Cricket soon enough."

"Out with it, then, Sass."

"In town today," she began, "I heard a man talking at the Feed & Seed." Sass sifted through the facts in her head. What should she tell, and how much could she leave out? A low, dull ache pained her stomach. "He claimed to have had something to do with the accident—the one you were in at the mine. He said he'd done it, set a charge to settle a score. On purpose, Finn." She had his attention and let her words settle.

She could see his mouth working in the dim light, the muscles in his jaw tensing and releasing. "Nobody'd be low as that," he said, finally. "All those fellers in there that day."

"That's prob'ly how he walked away from it. Who would even think anyone was to blame?"

"Who said it?" Finn asked. "Who was the feller?"

Sass bit her lip; her heart thumped wild under her dress. "I don't know his name," she whispered. "But when he saw I'd heard, he—" She broke off, swallowed down the lump that had risen in her throat.

Finn stood solid on both feet now, peering at his sister's face in the moonlight. "What? Did he do something to you?" Even in the dim barn, Sass knew color had started rising from Finn's collar to his cheeks. He clenched his hands, his hackles up like a fenced-in coyote.

"Did he?" he demanded. The horses moved uneasily at the sound of his raised voice.

Sass stared at the hard-packed dirt floor of the barn. "He said he could do it again. Said he knew Daddy worked there and could make something happen." Hot tears slid down her cheeks and landed in the dust by her shoes.

"We'll go to the mining office and you can tell. The sheriff'll be after a feller like that quick as a spring hare."

But she was already shaking her head. "No, Finn. I can't tell. If I do—" Sass wiped her nose on the quilt. "He said he'd tell about what you—what kinda work you been doing. That you'd be in jail for running moonshine."

The air whooshed out of Finn like he'd been gut-punched. Sass knew what he'd been up to—of course she did. He hardly looked at her as she stood there shedding tears for him. What was it their granny used to say? *"Wicked chickens lay deviled eggs."* Finn's shoulders sagged as he thrust his hands into his pockets.

"Aw, Sassy," he said. "I'm awful sorry you come to know about that."

Sass was crying full out now. It actually felt good to release the tears, like a breath she'd been holding in for too long. Finn crossed the distance between them in a few steps and hugged her tight before she knew what was happening. She was aware once more of her wet clothes, the reason she'd come out to the barn in the first place, and she twisted free despite wanting to be comforted more than anything.

"I've seen him before," she blurted. "In the woods way back off the path behind the cabin where the grapevine gets too tangled to walk through. Me and Hiccup were hunting morels and seen him back there with a rooster. He was on the mountain, Finn, not just in town. *Our* mountain. He knows where we live."

"This man." Finn doled his words out slowly, an odd expression on his face. "What does he look like?"

Sass wrinkled her nose like she'd just caught a whiff of polecat. "Just a regular person." She wiped her tears and wiggled the fingers on her hand. "But on his left hand, two of his fingers is missing, and a long scar runs up his arm."

"Saints preserve," Finn spat. The color drained from his face, and he ran an anxious hand across his brow. "I let the devil himself through the back door."

"What can we do?" she asked.

Finn laid a hand on top of Sass's head. "*We* ain't gonna do nothing tonight. It's late, and you should get back inside before Mama wakes up and has a fit, seeing you're gone. Better to figger things out when the sun's up."

"Promise you won't go flying off like buckshot. Promise you'll be here tomorrow."

"I promise, Sass. I give you that."

"He dropped somethin' at the store yesterday." She reached into her pocket, pulled out the creased scrap of paper, and handed it to him. "Maybe it can help?"

Sass's brows arched, and her brown eyes looked up at Finn as he unfolded the page. He scanned the list scrawled there. It was a list of names, and judging by the soft creases in the paper, it was something that had been looked at over and over again.

He read it out loud: "Dep. Ed Hunter, Frank Turnbull, Toady Newsome, Cotton & Fluff McCarty, James McKenzie, Elmer Russell, Warren Sylvis, Tate Monroe, F. M.?" Each name tolled like a bell in the darkness of the barn. Even the horses stilled at the sound of Finn's voice. "What's this?" He looked up at Sass. "The last ones on here are the fellers killed in the cave-in. And this one." He paused. "Toady Newsome. I know that name. But these other'ns?"

Sass stared at Finn, her eyes round and her lips working. "I don't know, Finn, but I got a cold chill up my back the first time I read it, like someone done walked over my grave." She paused. "That last 'un. Just the letters *F. M.* I was worried that was *you.* Finn MacInteer."

Finn scanned the list again. "Those letters got a question next to them, maybe because I's only hurt and not killed? But come to think, I can name other fellers on the wrong end of Spider's temper and fists, and their names ain't here." He swallowed hard and held Sass's gaze.

"Spider?"

"That's what he goes by, at least." Finn ran his fingers down the names again. "He didn't *say* Toady was dead, but this here looks like a list of folks that may've ended up that way." Finn shivered and spat in the hay like he'd tasted something sour. "What sort of person keeps a list of something like that and, from the looks of things, studies it over and over? I don't know what them last letters are for, but it ain't good."

He whistled long and low. "I'm glad you showed me this, Sass. Thank goodness for Miz Amanda showing up so we could read it and know it was important." He folded it back and tucked it into his shirt pocket. "You don't need to worry 'bout me, list or no. This may be his ticket far south of here, where the fires don't die." Finn tweaked Sass's nose and smiled at her. "Get on back to bed now, and we'll see about all this in the morning."

Sass scuffed in the borrowed shoes back to the cabin, still wrapped in the dusty barn quilt, the hounds dancing curious around her. She turned down the lantern and closed the door as silently as she could. Her eyes adjusted to the darkness, and she stood in the quiet for a moment. Cricket, Fern, and Hiccup lay under the quilt, sleeping side by side like opossums on a branch. The dying fire glowed orange in the stone hearth, filling the room with the comforting smell of woodsmoke, and white moonlight filtered through the muslin at the window in a filmy haze. Her mama stirred briefly behind the curtain that hid her bed. Plain or poor didn't matter; this was the only home she'd ever known, filled with them she loved best. The thought of something weaseling in to ruin this filled Sass's eyes with tears once more. She hadn't cried this much in a month of Sundays and was plumb wore out with it. Sass walked to the bed and nudged Hiccup over so that she could lie back down.

Her heart was buoyed some by talking to Finn—confession was good for the soul—but her soul still carried its second burden. She hadn't told him how the man had touched her, hadn't told the shameful truth about why she'd gone to the barn. She hadn't done it in a while, but as she drifted off to sleep, Sass prayed for God to keep her family safe and to find a way to strike down the hateful man who plagued them. She hadn't meant to allow him to do what he did, so if God could take away the bleeding, she told Him she'd much appreciate that in the meantime.

Chapter 21

Morning broke in a sky of uniform white, a solid mass of clouds that promised rain. Amanda had shown up early at the MacInteers' cabin, trying to get a head start on the weather. She'd brought Miles with her, finally giving in to his begging to ride along. He was growing so fast, and Mooney would probably welcome a break from his whirlwind of boyish energy. By the time they arrived back home, she hoped he'd be worn out enough to go straight to sleep. The whole MacInteer family was bent on their knees in the garden, putting seeds in the dirt before the sky let loose. Sass saw her first and stopped to wave. Even before Cricket had tied up Junebug with the other horses, Amanda felt the change in the air around the place, saw the way Finn and Sass traded glances, the way the two of them seemed bowed under some unseen weight.

Rai stood and brushed the dirt from her dress where she'd been kneeling. "Reckon that's about the end of it," she said. "Got the last of the peas put in the ground just in time." She craned her neck up at the sky. "That breeze is picking up. Come on inside for some tea, Amanda, and show us what you brought. This little feller stow away in your knapsack?"

Amanda laughed. "This is my Miles. He finally wore me down enough to bring him along."

"Mighty pleased to meet you, Miles," said Rai. "You got a fine mama there." Miles nodded and flashed her a shy smile.

They washed on the porch. Harley and Finn went to the barn while the others disappeared indoors, eager for Amanda to reveal what she carried in her saddlebags this time. Sass stacked up their previous picks on the table so that they could trade them out for new ones. Rai sprinkled a handful of flour onto the table and dumped a bowl of dough into the middle of it. She rubbed some flour into her hands and then plunged her fists into the dough, beating and folding it back and forth to work the yeast through. Her strong forearms were a blur as she thumped and punched.

"Before I forget, Rai, Maybelle Lincoln says to tell you that goulash recipe you put in the scrapbook was the best thing she's had in a coon's age."

"'Tween you and me, Maybelle Lincoln ain't exactly what you'd call handy in the kitchen," Rai replied, but as she turned to the stove to heat the kettle, she couldn't hide the smile spreading across her face. "I'll add another 'un that's better if you got space for it."

"Of course. We can always add pages. But it's not just Maybelle says that. Mooney said to tell you the same, and *she's* about as good as they come."

"Miz Rye, do you have any books on airplanes?" asked Cricket. "Or aviation?" He pronounced the last word carefully, proud to show he knew it.

"Hmm." Amanda dug in her pack. "It must be your lucky day, Cricket. I just picked up these two from the school last week. *Jingleman Jack, Aviator* and *The Boys' Book of Aeroplanes*. We don't usually find two on the same subject like that, but we just sorted through a box of new donations that came in from Boston."

Cricket's eyes grew round as moonflowers, and his feet danced excitedly on the floor. "Golly! Could I borry them both, do you think? I'll read every word."

Amanda laughed and laid them both on the table. "I'd be happy for you to read them. I don't know of anyone else who'd be that excited about planes."

"Thank you! Thank you!" Cricket stammered. He grabbed the two slim volumes and dashed out the door.

"He's heading for his favorite spot up the crook of that hemlock by the side of the barn," Rai told Amanda. "First drop of rain and you hightail it back in here with those!" she called after him. She finally quit working the dough and wiped her brow with her sleeve, leaving a smudge of flour on her face. "He's gone on and on about flying since he read about that airship in the paper. Prob'ly would never have taken a notice if it weren't for him reading everything in sight. Guess we have you to thank for that. Maybe when times get a bit better, that reading will help him do all right for himself." Her hands formed the dough into a smooth ball, and she plunked it back into its wooden bowl, covering it with a damp scrap of flour sack before washing and rinsing her hands in a bucket perched by the stove.

"They picked it up fast; that means they already had some smarts," Amanda said. "Fern, I found a sewing magazine with patterns in it. Maybe you want to add to your rabbits? You know, you're so fine with a needle, if you had enough different kinds, you could ask at the stores 'round the free town. Maybe they'd be willing to sell some for you?"

"Really?"

"I can ask around for you when I do my route if you like," Amanda offered.

"Would you? Wouldn't that beat all? Putting wares in a' actual store?" Fern was already flipping through the magazine. "I could do that one easy," she whispered. "Or that. I'm heading out by the corncrib where it's lighter and look this over right quick. Thank you, Miz Rye!"

"Sass? How about you? Interested in some more stories?"

Sass slumped in the rocker, her hand on her belly. She shrugged. "Whatever you have is fine," she said. Amanda and Rai exchanged a look.

"I've given her a dose of ratsbane and some Sweet Annie tea. She ain't been right since yesterday." Rai dried her hands on her apron.

"I'm just tired is all, Mama."

Rai laid the back of her hand on Sass's forehead. "No fever." She shook her head. "I don't like to see you so puny. It ain't like you." She walked over to the rumpled bed in the corner. "'Scuse the mess, Amanda. We were so keen on getting in the garden before the rain hit that I ain't had time to tidy up much. Sass, come lie down while I visit with Miz Rye if you feel so poorly."

When she flapped the quilt to straighten the bedding, she revealed a dark spot on the sheet and her mouth fell open. "Oh, Sassy."

Sass's face crumpled. "I'm sorry. I'm sorry. I didn't mean to."

Rai crossed the room and knelt on the planked floor in front of the rocker, holding on to Sass's knees. "Of course not. It's not your fault. It's nothing to be ashamed of, for certain. Or sorry for, silly. I should've known. My goodness, I've been so absentminded lately with Finn . . ." Rai trailed off.

Sass's brow furrowed. "But how could you have known?"

"How long?" Rai asked. "How long have you been bleeding? How were you taking care of it?"

Amanda smiled gently and stayed quiet, giving mother and daughter a private moment. She sat at the table while Hiccup sat on the floor beside her with Miles, their heads bent together as they flipped through a book of baby animals and chatted to each other.

"Piglet," Hiccup pointed, whispering. "Puppy, kitty, colt," Miles added. He was further along in reading, and the words came faster.

Sass looked down at her lap. "It started last night," she admitted. "I tore up a quilt from the barn." Tears choked her voice. "I'm sorry, Mama. I didn't *want* him to touch me." She clapped a hand to her mouth.

"What? Who?" She grabbed Sass's knees tighter. "Who touched you, Sass?"

"The man with the rooster," she whispered.

Rai shook her head. "What? You mean what Hiccup was spinning tales about?" At the sound of her name, Sass's sister looked up from her book. "You didn't say anything then. I thought that was a story."

Sass shook her head. "No, he's real. We saw him when we were hunting morels."

Hiccup nodded. "The rooster man. Yes, I told you, Mama!"

Rai swallowed hard. "Sass. Hiccup, too? Did he . . . Hiccup, too?" Sass shook her head no, and Rai let out a big breath. "Hiccup, why don't you and Miles go outside and find Fern? I bet she'll read that book to y'all. Tell her Mama said so."

Hiccup and Miles hopped up and skittered outside with the book, although Amanda knew they wouldn't sit still outside for long. Too many trees to climb and bugs to catch. Rai pulled a low footstool over to the foot of the cane-bottomed rocker where Sass sat, her face pale and blotchy from crying.

"Shall I go?" Amanda asked.

"No, it's all right. You might be a help to me," said Rai. "Sass, I meant it before when I said this ain't your fault. You ain't done a thing in the world wrong, you hear? You need to tell me what's got you so worked up now."

"You know what you say about gossip? How it's like emptying a goose-feather pillow in a whirlwind? Try as you might, you can't never collect back all those feathers into the pillow again." Sass wailed. "I didn't want to let loose those feathers. Now everyone will know the shame of it."

"No, no, Sass. This is different. This kind of secret just grows bigger 'n' bigger the more it keeps hidden. Lettin' it out in the daylight's what shrinks it, takes away its hold on you."

Amanda pictured a tumble of goose feathers swirling down the road, out of reach. She knew all too well how gossip worked. She knew it had cost Sass to tell, poking at a wound she'd rather let alone. Amanda realized what Rai said was right, though. Shame like that needed fresh air and daylight to put out its fire.

Sass nodded. "There's more to it, Mama," she squeaked. "I told Finn last night. Not the part about this." Sass gestured to the bed and waved a hand in front of her abdomen. "I saw the rooster man again yesterday in town. I overheard him with another feller at the Feed & Seed."

"I was right down the road," said Rai, her hands balled into fists now. "I was runnin' my mouth, talkin' about shirt cloth and barterin' for coffee."

Sass's story spilled out of her, the words tumbling like a rain-swollen creek down the mountain. She told what the man had admitted doing at the mine, how he'd threatened her and their family, how there was no way to tell without Finn getting in a heap of trouble or, worse, causing harm to Harley. She choked out in halting words how he'd come close to her, said and done ugly things, and explained that that was what had caused her bleeding to start.

"Baby girl, that was gonna happen anyhow. It don't mean nothin' bad. You're just grown enough for it to start up on its own. Only the moon and God causes a young woman to mense, not some no-count feller takin' liberties." Rai smiled. "I shoulda told you to expect it 'fore now, sweet pea, and you wouldn't a' got all upset. I'm all kinds of sorry 'bout that."

Rai pulled Sass onto her lap, big as she was, and the two of them clung to each other there in a mingling of relief, release, sorrow, and anger while Amanda watched, touched by their closeness. When Sass's tears stopped, she looked up into her mother's face.

"Mama?"

"Yes, honeybun?"

"You don't have to dose me with any more of that tea now."

Rai laughed. "It wasn't all *that* bad, was it?"

"I'd rather lick a chicken's foot." Sass's face twisted in a sour grimace.

Amanda sat with her hands folded tightly in her lap, and Rai laughed and turned to her. "Amanda? You all right?"

Amanda came to herself and nodded, clearing her throat.

"I just—can't get over how brave you are, Sass," she stammered.

Harley and Finn entered, letting in the promise of rain with a breeze that lifted the curtains and loose tendrils of Amanda's hair.

"Hi-dee." Harley nodded to Amanda but clearly had no intention of staying to chat. "Finn and me need to strike off to the county seat, Rai. Reckon you can fix up a dinner pail or two for us to carry? We'll likely be gone three or four days."

Sass stood up to let her mother rise, and Amanda searched Finn's eyes for an explanation. His firm-set mouth and squared shoulders told her all she needed to know. They were going to the sheriff to report what Sass had overheard. Which meant Finn would have to take his chances and give his own testimony about the bootlegging when he told them where to find the still and what routes they ran their whiskey. Which also meant when he turned himself in, there was a good chance he might not come back for a time.

"I'll help you," Amanda said, blinking briskly. She bit her lip and nodded once to him. Amanda meant it as a salute to him, a signal that he was doing a good thing, even if—especially if—his own stakes in it might be a high price. Amanda and Rai got busy pulling supplies from the larder, the last of the dried apples from the past autumn, jerky, potatoes, and a few salted slices of ham with corn pone.

Harley headed back out. "I'll get Cricket to help me get up the horses. That's gonna leave you without for a few days." Rai nodded.

Sass swallowed hard and wrapped her arms around Finn, burying her face in his side. He laughed, but it rang hollow. "What's all this? It's a trip down the mountain is all."

"I know it." Her voice was muffled.

Rai gave him a satchel. "There's extra socks in there and that new shirt Fern stayed up stitching last night."

Amanda and Sass peeped out the window as Harley and Finn packed their things on the horses and filled jugs with water from the well. They watched as Rai handed them the dinner pails and lingered a moment, her hands and lips moving. Rai's cheeks colored, and her hands fluttered like birds in a cage, startling the horses. Finn's hands twisted the reins into knots as he listened and blamed, Amanda knew, himself.

Rai collected the books they'd left on the porch and brought them inside with her. Her mouth was set firm. "Sass," she said, "Finn told me about the list you'd found."

Sass shrugged. "Reckon the sheriff can use it?"

"I imagine so." Rai sighed. "That feller seems to have found more than his share of trouble. Finn says the cur told him he had his fingers shot off by a Smith & Wesson .22. Wish whoever done it had aimed a bit different."

The hairs rose on the back of Amanda's neck. "What'd he say this feller's name is?"

"Goes by Spider, Finn says, on account of him having only eight fingers."

"What's he look like?"

Sass shrugged and screwed up her face. "Not near as tall as Finn. Got a dark beard and a chipped tooth in front. Mean, dark eyes and a long scar up one arm. When he smiles, it ain't nice. No warmth in it. Makes you feel kinda cold and nervous."

"And what's on this list?" Amanda pressed.

Rai glanced at Sass. "Finn says it looks to be names. Lot of 'em are fellers who died in the cave-in Finn was in. He didn't recognize all of 'em. Like he was keeping a tally," she spat. "If the sheriff gets a'holt of him, hanging will be too easy."

"Sass, do you remember any of the other names on the list?" Amanda's voice was unnaturally high.

"Reckon I read it enough times. Deputy Ed Hunter, Frank Turnbull, Toady Newsome, and the six miners. There might have been some initials at the end."

"Turnbull," Amanda muttered, turning the name over in her mouth. "It can't be the same."

"You know something?" asked Rai. "Guess we don't hold no secrets between us no more." That was true enough, and although Sass had feared releasing her secret, it turned out knowing other women on her side were bearing it with her had replaced that fear with a kind of grateful kinship.

Amanda looked out to lay eyes on Miles, who was laughing and using their pile of sticks to build a lean-to hideaway. Harley and Finn were checking the horses' feet and finishing up the last of the heavier chores. She lowered herself into a chair, placed her hands flat on the table in front of her, and began. She told them about Gripp Jessup and the night Miles was born, the changes she'd seen in her husband, and running into the woman at the graveyard after his funeral. She remembered the sheriff coming to her door with Frank's gun, how Frank had been found drowned in the creek, and how the barbs of gossip worked their way into her parents and caused the rift between them that had never been mended.

"He must have come back," Amanda said, finally. "Counting on a different sheriff and using a different name."

When she had finished, she drew in a deep, wavering breath and raised her eyes to Rai. Sass sat on the bed with her knees tucked up to her chin and her eyes wet.

"That woman at the graveyard asked after Frank Rye," Amanda said. "Not Turnbull. But when I heard that name, I remembered something Frank said once. He told me about his granddaddy Turnbull, who came from way away near Memphis, Tennessee. Frank admired him, said he was a river man, working boats on the Mississippi. Maybe Rye was never his name at all. Maybe it was Turnbull all along and Gripp knew that, encouraged him to change it so it'd be easier to cut loose of the law. There was so much I didn't know about Frank, it wouldn't be a surprise to know his name was just one more thing."

"Lord a'mercy, girl," breathed Rai. "What you done been through."

"Nothing to be done for it now," Amanda said. "Guess that's long in the past, although sometimes the memory of it all is clear as creek water. Hearing Sass here bravely tell her bit got me to thinking about my own. If Gripp killed my Frank and put it on a list, I'd wager Spider's name is just another lie he's telling."

"So you're saying Gripp Jessup and that Spider Finn's in with are the same feller? Y'all sit tight a minute while I see the boys off."

Rai scooted outside as Harley and Finn mounted the horses. Amanda watched from the window as Finn's face turned an angry shade of red. Amanda imagined Rai had connected the dots for them. Father and son turned the horses and headed down the trail, Harley first and Finn following, with Plain Jane's nose practically on top of Lincoln's tail. She could hear the dogs baying and barking as they ran ahead.

Rai came back in, bringing with her the scent of honeysuckle and rain on the way.

"It's a good thing Harley's with him, or Finn woulda took off loaded for bear, come what may." She breathed out a long breath. "Ain't much riles a man more than the thought of trouble coming to someone they're sweet on." Amanda's mouth dropped open at this revelation. "The two of them are fit to be tied. It's best they're leaving for a spell to let the sheriff sort this mess out. Reckon things would get a far sight worse with the law if they was to set things right their own selves."

Rai pulled out the risen dough and then dusted her hands off on her apron, leaving smeared handprints of flour. She stood with her hands on her hips for a long moment, her chest rising and falling with measured breaths. Outside, the first rumbles of thunder echoed across the top of the mountain.

"I'll tell you what we're gonna do," she said, pointing at the dough in the bowl. "First we're gonna rest. Then, just like this here bread, we're gonna rise. Gather up that flock of young'uns out there and get 'em in 'fore the rain hits. After, we're gonna sit here and fill our bellies. Then, we're gonna hitch up your mule to our wagon and head back to your place. Will he pull?"

Amanda nodded. Junebug would do anything she asked.

"All of 'em can stay there for a couple days 'cause there ain't no way I'm leaving any of 'em here while that son of a cuss is loose on this mountain. I'll make Mooney a pie for her trouble. Then, you"—she pointed a finger at Amanda—"and me are gonna hightail it up to Pickins's Nose and have a come-to-Jesus meeting with the preacher." Rai paused to take a breath. "After that, well, I ain't thought that far, but I'm sure it'll come to me. I'll be on the lookout for signs and wonders."

"I have a couple stops left on my book route."

"We can get to 'em on the way." Rai took one breath before setting them to task. "Sass, set a table and help me get these beans a'going. Amanda, call those young'uns in 'fore they get soaked. They're like a bunch o' turkeys looking skyward. Liable to stand out there with their mouths open till they drown. It's a wonder the world turns, with the foolishness of children and men the world over."

Chapter 22

The few families who remained on the rest of Amanda's route raised their brows a notch or two when instead of a lone woman on a gray mule, here come that mule toting a wagon full of young'uns and Rai MacInteer, to boot. These families weren't set to host a crowd, so Amanda kept her stops shorter that day. Several children peeped 'round their mamas' legs at the door, clutching Fern's stuffed rabbits to their chests, and Amanda pointed them out to her. Fern told Amanda she'd studied over the patterns Amanda had given her, and although one or two looked simple enough to make, she might like to try her hand at making some out of ideas in her own head. Amanda suggested she talk it over with Mooney when they got into town, for Mooney was handy with a needle and could help her with some tricky stitches.

Rai mostly stayed in the wagon, trying to keep Cricket and Miles from scooting over the side and running willy-nilly all over creation each time they stopped. She'd call out to folks on the porch, asking after this or that one, passing along notions about how the tomatoes might do further on, or tsk-tsking when they told of earaches or risings. She'd offer advice on what they might try as remedies—steeping rue leaves in oil and squeezing some into the ear, lard and sulfur with some mashed yellow root to draw out swellings. It was plain to Amanda that although Rai was only just shy of fifty, folks saw her as a granny woman.

Mooney had stopped being surprised long ago at what Amanda collected from folks along her route. She'd come home with everything from jars of pigs' feet and pickled okra to threadbare scraps of fabric meant for quilt pieces—and once, a live catfish that had slapped against Junebug's flank for a solid mile and had him in a fine mood, with his long ears flattened back against his neck by the time they'd arrived. Although a wagonful of MacInteers was a load, to be sure, it wasn't the worst thing, especially when Rai gave Mooney a loaf of fresh sourdough and a blackberry pie made from the last of what she'd put up last summer. When Amanda and Rai told her what had happened and that they were headed up the far side of the mountain to Pickins, Mooney's lips pursed tight and her eyes grew round as hoecakes.

"Well, I'll allow that's the last thing I thought this day would bring," Mooney finally said. "You aim to take Miles with you?"

Amanda shook her head. "Why would I?"

"Might ease things, having a grandbaby underfoot, is all."

Amanda shrugged. "I don't know, Mooney, it ain't like they been clamoring at the door to see him so far."

"No, but I reckon if God had called Abraham to sacrifice his *grandbaby* instead of his stubborn half-grown son, it might'a been a whole 'nother story."

"We'll see how it goes this once first," Amanda said.

Rai and Amanda set off at the first pink shades of morning. They threw an old saddle blanket over Junebug's back and doubled up behind his withers, Amanda in front. Amanda wore the brown trousers she usually wore when she rode her circuit, and Rai bunched up her skirt and let her legs hang bare from her knees to the tops of her shoes. Each wore a straw hat to shade their eyes from the rising sun. They packed a satchel of apples and bread, and for the first time since she'd left with Frank, Amanda pointed her mule's nose in the direction of her parents' home.

Strangely, she wasn't thinking of Gripp Jessup or the gossip her father had swallowed. Or even what would happen when she rode up to her parents' home as if it were as ordinary a thing as a sunrise. Instead, she pictured Sass gathering sang in the woods as she'd met her that first rainy afternoon. Sass's face as she'd stood there in the path with her hands on her hips, full of spunk, her secret delight and pride when she'd read without stumbling straight through the book Amanda had brought. She marveled at Sass's bravery, her instinct to protect her little sister and the whole rest of her family, even if holding that secret made her drop down dead. Of course, Amanda drifted back to what had happened with Gripp the night Miles was born, and as Sass held out in her palm the slivers of her broken heart, the piercing splinters in Amanda's heart worked back and forth, her old scars opening once more. Anger boiled up in her, remembering Sass's story about the rooster man. Her father used to preach against anger from his pulpit, lauding self-control, having witnessed one too many men fond of moonshine taking out their frustrations on their wives. There was another kind of anger, though, one born to right wrongs. Amanda could spit from the injustice of it all, takers who lived just for the grabbing, casually ruining those who trusted. Beneath her, she felt Junebug quicken his stride as her emotions raced. Even the mule sensed a change in the woman atop his back.

The day broke warm and fine, the loveliest of spring mornings before the mosquitoes grew thick and a hot, wet heat cloaked the mountain valley. The sky was the kind of cloudless blue that made it seem deep as a well or a clear, cold lake, and the tree branches held the eager birdcalls of nuthatches, woodpeckers, and all manner of finches and wrens, busy courting, nesting, and foraging before the day grew too hot. Amanda and Rai laughed at a pair of jays, actually in a tug-of-war over a fresh-plucked earthworm. Each attempted to fly away with the prize but found they were tethered to each other by their meal, until at last the poor worm stretched too far and the surprised jays broke apart. Amanda wondered which had won the lucky end of that wishbone.

Junebug's easy gait and the sweet spring air filled with the scent of honeysuckle and the hum of fat, lazy bumblebees were balms to jangled nerves. Rai pointed out plants along the path. She couldn't help telling

Amanda what this or that one was good for and when and how best to use each one. They talked about children, of course, as mothers do, the heartache of seeing them come to trouble and the pride that blossomed when they proved themselves.

"You're a good mama," Rai said. "I can see that clear as a drop of rain when you're with Miles. I'm sure it's been a time raisin' him alone."

Amanda shrugged. "Sometimes, for certain. Mooney's been a godsend." She paused. "I think she might have her eye on a feller in town. I notice he's been havin' an unusual hard time keeping his shirts mended for a few months now. She won't say it out loud, but she's sweet on him, sure as sugar."

"Well, that can happen. She's young yet. You both are." They let that settle.

After traveling a ways in silence, Amanda said, "Can't say what to expect when we get up home. You don't know of any leaves to crush into a mending tea for harsh words, do you?"

"Reckon folk'd be beating down my door for the likes of that." Rai laughed. "Onliest way to the other side of that is straight through." She patted Amanda's shoulder. "We'll get there when we get there."

Rai asked Amanda to tell her what it was like growing up a preacher's daughter, so Amanda jawed about their place always being busy, folks in and out, coming to ask for advice or blessings or forgiveness. An only child, she never wanted for attention. Jack Wick was a born teacher and saw to it that Amanda learned more than just letters. He'd gotten through school but no further than that, no fancy universities or degrees—who could afford it? And he had a gift in that voice that drew folks to hear him despite—or maybe even because of—not having extra schooling. Amanda recalled that even Jack's lullabies and bedtime stories seemed enchanted, the way he told them. Her mama had been strict but kind. You'd think in the middle of all that busy, all the people, she'd have had scores of friends, but she had been sort of set apart by girls her age. Amanda admitted that she'd been lonely after a while, even though she had learned long ago to keep her own company, and maybe that's what had made it easier for her to fall for Frank and the buckets of attention he paid her.

They laughed over Amanda's tales of having a pet duck and carrying it around by its neck everywhere. Amanda recalled fishing in the stream, catching crawdads, and learning to ride horses, piece a quilt, and fix a meal, all the regular things a girl from the mountains would do. It was a fine growing up, she allowed. Having Miles had shown her that young'uns weren't always a Sunday picnic. It wasn't her parents' fault she had itched to look beyond the next holler and imagined something extraordinary for her life. Like her Miles, she had a will of her own and was determined to use it.

As the path grew steeper, they had to lean forward to help Junebug muscle up the slopes. Rai spotted a black bear in a thicket a ways off the path. It was the time of year when they foraged, growing fat off berries and insects. Soon after noon, they caught glimpses of the whitewashed church through the oaks and hickories.

A pair of juvenile black-and-tan beagles howled as they approached the house. Junebug's ears swiveled forward, but he was used to dogs at most every house they visited, so he paid these no mind. Rai slid off first and Amanda followed. She held the mule's reins and surveyed the place that was at once so familiar and so foreign. Red and black chickens scratched in the dirt around the tidy garden to the side of the house, and the same white curtains fluttered in the front windows. Tall green sunflower stalks surrounded the garden fence, their heavy heads about to bloom and open to the sun. Beady always said sunflowers made her happy to look on them, their round black centers like faces lifted up to heaven. She must have saved a whole sack of seeds to have planted enough to now circle the whole garden. On the porch sat the two cane-bottomed chairs with a tin bucket between them and a sack of early peas ready to be shelled. A skinny orange tabby cat wound itself around Amanda's ankles, and she bent to pet it.

"Remember me, Jo-Jo? You're looking kinda puny. Getting old, I guess."

No one came to meet them. Amanda tied Junebug to a porch post and gave him a pat. She drew herself up tall and tried to calm her hammering heart by breathing slow and deep as she walked up the front two steps and knocked. It seemed so odd knocking on the door she must have gone in and out of thousands of times without a thought.

"Hello?" she called.

"It'd be a shame to have come all this way to miss them," said Rai.

"They wouldn't both be gone. Not usually. Let's check the church building."

Amanda led the way down the path between the house and the church, shooing the now-friendly beagles out from under her feet. No clanging sounds rang from her father's forge out back, so he wasn't busy smithing. The door to the church creaked when she opened it, a screeching echo in the stillness. It looked the same as when she'd last seen it. The rough wooden pulpit up front flanked by a short bookshelf, the simple wooden benches on either side, and few other embellishments, with the exception of a lantern or two hung in the back and a plain cross standing in one corner at the front.

There, toward the front, a woman knelt on the plank floor with her head bowed low onto the bench in front of her. She looked thin beneath the cotton dress she wore, and her graying hair was pinned up in a neat bun by the nape of her neck. Her hands were clasped together, and Amanda and Rai could hear her murmuring in a steady chant, although her words weren't plain. Tears sprang to Amanda's eyes.

"Mama?" she said, and the murmuring cut off. The woman raised her head and gripped the bench she'd been leaning on.

"Lord a'mercy, if that don't sound just like my Amanda," she said.

Amanda cleared her throat. "Mama," she said again. "It's me. I've come for a visit with Miz MacInteer."

Beady seemed to come to herself then and turned toward the door. When she saw the two of them, her hand flew to her mouth and she rose to her feet.

"Well, I never," she breathed. "Thanks be." Beady closed the distance between them and wrapped Amanda in a tight embrace.

"Let me look at you." She took Amanda's face between her palms and drank her in. "A sight for sore eyes, ain't you?" She wiped at her eyes with the back of her hand. "Oh, my land. My stars. My word." When she ran out of exclamations, she turned to Rai. "And Rai MacInteer, do I have you to thank for this visit?" Without waiting for an answer, she waved her hands. "No matter, I'm just thankful you're standing before me. Let's go on up to the house and have some tea, then."

Beady made her way down the aisle and back over to the house, turning her head as if to reassure herself she wasn't imagining them. Amanda compared this woman to the one she'd last seen half a decade since, the one she'd held in her mind as "Mama," and tallied up the differences. This one was a bit grayer and seemed thinner. Amanda was sorry, then. Sorry she'd stayed away, nursing her wounds, sorry she'd held on to her stubborn like a favorite prize she didn't want to give up.

Inside, Rai helped light the stove while Beady got the water going. Amanda looked around the place, fingering a quilt she'd never seen draped over the back of a chair, where she imagined Beady sat of an evening, reading or sewing. She ran a finger over her father's shelf of books, spotting one or two new volumes. She wondered if he knew she brought books to the hills—likely so; folks brought them news from town fairly regular. In this corner, the curtained bed, in that one, a coat rack, broom, and gun. On the mantel sat the familiar round-faced clock and its copper key for winding it twice a week on Tuesdays and Saturdays.

"Where's Daddy?" Amanda asked.

Beady shook her head. "He's had to go over to Cutout for some smithing, and I'm sure a bit of preaching while he's at it. If he'd a' known you were visiting . . ." She trailed off and turned away, likely not wanting to speak a falsehood. "But I'm glad you're here."

That's where it stood, then; they were a house divided. No wonder her mama looked worn. As long as she'd been alive, they had functioned as a unit. She'd never questioned their affection for each other, watching the way her mama gazed at her daddy and hung on his every word, and the way he bent to her and was quick to share her load. The curtain hanging by their bed was thin, and Amanda had been lulled to sleep by their whispers and giggles many nights. This was different. Of course they'd disagreed over matters, but they didn't stew. "Never go to bed angry" was their oft-repeated rule. Amanda wondered how many nights they'd broken that rule in the past five years. She'd never seen Beady's mouth bite back words about her husband, dithering between fealty and feelings. Such a struggle had cost her.

Steaming cups of tea in hand, Beady led the way to the front porch, where the fresh air and sunlight were plentiful and the sack of peas waited for eager hands. It was as natural as the sunrise for them to dig into the sack and start shelling as they talked, the musical plink of peas hitting the tin-bottomed bucket keeping a steady rhythm.

Once Beady had asked after Miles and Amanda told her how smart and kind and strong he was, how he'd learned to read early and his favorite thing right now was finding animal tracks, Rai began. She reminded Beady of when they'd visited the church and asked for prayers for Finn, and yes, he was doing much better, thank you. Then, she unraveled the rest: the man called Spider and how Finn had gotten mixed up with him, her daughter Sass and what had happened, what they knew about his role in the cave-in.

"Amanda?" she said when she was through. Rai threw a handful of peas in the bucket and put a hand on top of Amanda's where they rested in her lap atop her peas. "Amanda can tell the rest."

Amanda looked her mama in the face and told her all the things she'd been too ashamed or tired or sad to say years ago when she'd been a young widow holding her new baby. The words she'd kept in for so long tumbled out like water, filling in dry cracks and soaking into the thirsty ground, seeping into dark places where seeds waited to receive them—seeds of forgiveness and healing. They stirred down deep in

Amanda, and she felt the tender sprouts break out of their casings and reach out a tentative, searching tendril of green. She held her memory of Sass in her mama's lap before her, the girl's brave example a banner she waved for courage to continue. She spoke the words aloud so that they no longer held power over her with their demand to hold it close, keep it secret. The name Gripp Jessup was like any name. It rolled off her tongue and into the light of day, where it lay exposed and blinking, forced out of the shadows like a swamp rat.

Beady had left off from the peas in her lap long ago, growing still and pale as her daughter's words rained on her like a storm. More than once, her eyes filled with tears. How the path between Amanda and her had grown over all that first year of her marriage to Frank. Beady could tell herself it had been to give the newlyweds room, but truth be told, there had been a spark of gladness and relief that Frank (and with him, Gripp) had gone down the mountain, even if he'd had their daughter on his arm. He'd seemed taken with her, willing to provide. Not everyone could share the bond she did with Jack, and as husband and wife, Frank and Amanda had to work out their own terms with each other.

Beady had never imagined—Lord, Amanda had never said—things had changed so mightily. The day the waters had dropped enough for her and Jack to make it down the mountain, the day they'd arrived to greet their grandson and newly widowed daughter, Beady had been full up. Such a mix of joy and sadness, like oil and water, stirred inside her. She hadn't known what to think at first when Jack had burst into the cabin, full of stories and blame, the look on his face more pained and dark than she'd ever seen before. She remembered pressing her hand to her mouth to keep the pieces of her heart from flying right out. She'd thought she might drown in the grief that welled up in her like a sea, greater than the cresting rivers that had taken animals and people.

Beady had held on tight to the seat of the wagon like an anchor all the miles home, afraid she might be swept away by the flood of it.

Jack had parsed it out to her over the next days, repeating things he'd been told, the words that had stung him to his core, and she'd begged him to consider other sides—she was their *daughter*. But Beady was Jack's *wife*, and that put an end to the matter; the two had become one long ago, and that was not to be forsaken, especially if it cost him his life's work in the bargain. Should they wager that, too? How would it seem if they overlooked such behavior? Sin was sin, no matter who did the doing. So Beady had stopped protesting, quit asking to go for a visit, and ceased talking about it, although her heart was sorely bruised. She never stopped praying for Amanda and her small son, never stopped picturing her grandson's tiny features and the feel of the ovals of his soft, wrinkly heels in her hands.

Now, Beady, who'd been empty so long, her union with Jack a stagnant stalemate, was full up again. Hearing her daughter's tale, picturing her on the hard ground, giving birth alone to that sweet boy, filled her up with nine shades of angry. She was madder than a nest full of hornets at the wasted time, wrongheaded stubbornness, and most of all, the evil doings of that feller Gripp Jessup who, in her humble opinion, had just opted for a heavy dose of hellfire and brimstone. In the back of her mind, Jack's melodious voice whispered, *"Vengeance is mine, saith the Lord."* But Beady also remembered reading something about being the hands and feet of Jesus, and *that* was a task she felt called to do.

"I'm sorry as I can be, baby girl," Beady said, wiping her tears. "I can't say as I believed all the things your daddy heard that day, but I can't say as I didn't believe 'em neither, and that right there I'm shamed to tell."

"I know what Daddy can be like, and I know you're bound to him."

"Ain't I bound to you, too? Even if you left to make your own way." She shook her head. "I thought when he wasn't at the funeral that y'all had rid yourselves of that other devil. I knew from the get-go that he was a no-count."

"I wish we had. Things might've ended differently, but Frank was no angel either." Amanda shrugged. "All that's past, Mama. Right now, Rai here is bound and determined to knit us Wicks back together." Amanda smiled. "I'm glad of it."

"It's a shame to carry on a whole life based on misunderstandings and hurt feelings," Rai said. "With boys working in the mines, you reckon right quick that life is too short for such."

"Where is this Jessup feller now?" Beady asked.

"He's laying in a spot back of our cabin a ways, near his still and twenty or so roosters. Finn says he's set up a shed there where he holes up."

Beady thought for a good while and shucked another handful of peas. Busy hands made her think clearer, and an idea had begun percolating. Sometimes, in the name of what folks considered fairness, county lawmen missed the mark. Beady didn't aim for that to happen in this case. If you didn't dig out the root of the weed permanent-like, come spring, it'd sprout right back twice as determined.

"You know, I remember when ol' Gripp Jessup was hanging 'round here pretending to be a ready disciple of the Gospel, getting in Jack's good graces and sidling up to him. Jack was bound and determined he'd dunk that boy in the creek and wash him clean, but Gripp never did feel the Lord's pull. He was too caught up in his own schemes," Beady fumed. The last time she'd gotten her dander up like this, a family of raccoons had ransacked the church building, shredding songbooks and leaving their filth behind. Beady had trapped and skinned every last one. "I declare, if he had'a been baptized, so much filth woulda run off him, it might'a poisoned the creek water from here clear downstream to the Mississippi. Way I see it, he done had his chance."

Amanda looked up from the peas. They'd almost emptied the sack.

"I was counting on you seeing it that way," Rai said, her voice steady and even. "My boy was fool enough to get mixed up with him, and he's aiming to make it right by going to the law. Knowing Finn, he might not allow it was made right *enough*, and the last thing he needs is more worry on his shoulders. If they can land the slippery cuss, the sheriff might come down on Gripp for some of what he done, but he won't know the whole of it. I got daughters, too." Rai tossed the last of her peas into the bucket.

"Well, then, looks like we got some work to do." Beady stood and brushed bits of green shell and pea strings off her lap. "Jack'll be home directly. Amanda, you and I are gonna have a sit-down with your daddy and set him straight. He shall know the truth, and the truth shall set him free."

"Do you think he'll listen, Mama?"

"Oh, he'll listen all right, if he fancies having a wife to warm his bed at night. I'm like you, Rai—I done lost a child once and don't aim to go back for a second round of the same. Your daddy's set to preach another church a couple days from here. Once he's off in the morning, we're gonna head back to the MacInteers' place and settle some accounts." She held up a finger. "Don't even say it," she cautioned her daughter. "I'm leaving Jesus at the house to look after things while I'm gone."

They spent the rest of the afternoon sharing the day's work—bringing in wood for the stove, butchering a chicken for supper, boiling a pot of greens, and tending the chickens and goats. Rai kneaded another batch of dough and set it to rise, and Amanda helped Beady gather the few items she needed to bring with her on the journey. They fed and curried Maxine, the draft mare Beady would ride the next day, and by the time the sun dipped almost to the horizon, Jack Wick trotted up the path and headed to the barn on his horse. There was no hiding Junebug, grazing on a tethered pasture line just behind the garden.

"Beady?" he called as his boots clomped up the front steps. She heard him knock the mud off, and he carried them inside in one hand. He stopped at the threshold at the sight of Amanda setting plates at the table.

"What's this?" he asked. Jack's voice still held its music, although it held a touch more of a rasp to it in the past few years.

"Hi, Daddy," said Amanda. "This here's Rai MacInteer. She visited the church to ask for prayers, if you remember." Polite to a fault, Jack nodded and gave his attention to Rai. "How do, Miz MacInteer? I do remember your visit. And I believe we may have come to call on your son while he was laid up."

"That's a fact," she replied. "And he's doing much better now, up and about and healing just fine. If you'll excuse me, I think I left my wrap in the barn earlier. I'll just go fetch it before supper." Rai scooted past Jack and out the door, leaving the little family alone with each other for the first time since before any of them could remember.

"Before you come loose, just hear me," announced Beady. Jack had once told her he'd married a woman tough as jerky and sweet as scuppernong wine. A thousand times over the years, they'd compromised and bent to one another; she knew Jack felt her worth. Jack had tried to tell her what had caused him to react as he had after Frank's funeral. He'd done a fair bit of searching and came up with the usual things—pride, hurt, embarrassment, but it went deeper, she knew.

Her whole life, he'd forged Amanda like a piece of iron in his smith, shaping and bending her by teaching and example. How many times he'd repeated the phrase *"You're a Wick."* Anybody in these parts had to grapple with their name. It announced where you were from and, more importantly, *who* you came from. Being a Wick, he'd told her, was like a wick in a beeswax candle, drawing up virtue and knowledge from your wax to keep your flame a'going. Being a Wick meant reaching back before Jack and Jack's daddy and even his granddaddy before him. It meant standing firm for the meat of what made you, and in Jack's particular case, his one and only child was his solitary chance at legacy and him being called as a man of God. He'd surely felt like the martyrs in the early church must have when folks cast stones unto death. When that passel of locals from town had surrounded him and pelted him with their accusations, assailed him with their tales of how Amanda, his one chance at leaving anything to carry on past him in the world, had turned her back on her upbringing and had left him as a fool to be mocked, something had broken in Jack. Something he couldn't abide. "Beady," he'd said, "my name is dust."

"Our daughter's come up the mountain, and she has a tale you need to hear 'bout as much as a body needs the Gospel. I've done sat here for five years waiting and hoping, and I declare this ain't going on one minute more." Beady pointed, and Jack sank into a chair at the table. "Just hold your tongue now. It's *her* turn."

Amanda again unwound the spool of telling. Knotted in the thread of it was foolishness, no doubt, mistakes made and regrets that she'd revisited time and again like a tongue searching the empty place where a tooth used to stand. But there was no more sin than for anyone who walked the earth. Amanda testified like it was a Sunday service, plain and true, a mix of ugly and grace all in one. She left out Sass's bit—Beady thought because that wasn't hers to share. She told how Frank's death hadn't been by accident, but the rest of Gripp's long list of transgressions could wait. By the end of her telling, tears fell unchecked from Jack's eyes, and he unexpectedly knelt before her on the hard plank floor, her hands in his.

"I ask your forgiveness, surely and truly," he croaked. "The prodigal wasn't who I imagined. I'm ashamed, for certain, of my temper and pride, for casting you aside in favor of folks' false words. I had no cause and only stirred up more trouble for you." He glanced up at Beady. "For all of us. I've had a rod of iron rammed down my spine over this, and it's time to melt it in fire."

Amanda, her face streaked with tears, leaned down and hugged her daddy 'round the neck. Beady's heart swelled when she watched Amanda breathe deep and close her eyes against the prickle of Jack's gray whiskers.

"When you get back from your trip," said Amanda, "I know a little boy who'd be over the moon to see you."

Beady clapped her hands together once and breathed deep. "That's done," she announced. No sense lingering over sentiment when there was work to get on with. "Now then, Amanda, call Rai back in here or supper's gonna get cold."

Chapter 23

Gripp was already three sheets to the wind as he stumbled up the slope to the lean-to that served as his home for now. No thanks to Finn, who'd been scarce as hen's teeth for the past couple of days, he'd spent two days hustling in the adjoining county, off-loading his latest batch of corn likker. His usual patsies, Pete and Repete, were nowhere to be found, so he'd had to grind it and do it all himself. If any of them three lazy parasites thought they'd see a share of this haul, they could think again. In fact, he might just have to teach them a lesson in dependability next time he ran across their sorry asses. He'd been helping himself to generous sips of the last of his jars all the way back up the mountain. Every now and then he belted stray bits of songs: *"Mosquito he fly high. Mosquito he fly low. If old man 'skeeta light on me, he ain't gonna fly no mo'."*

One of the roosters set up crowing as Gripp tripped over himself. He needed to get Finn out here to clear some of these brambles. A feller couldn't hardly walk two steps without getting tangled. He guessed he'd have to feed and water the birds on top of everything else. Gripp made it to the top of the slope and spied his lean-to, nestled under the overhang of an ancient rocky outcropping. It wasn't fancy, but it did the job. He cooked over an open fire and did his business in the woods. It was fine for warm weather. Come winter, he'd need to find something snugger. He threw his pack down toward the back of the shack, careful to set down his jars on the stump he used for a table, and headed out to feed the cocks.

He cast corn around their separate barrels and carried a bucket of water from the creek. They drank eagerly. Some of their pans had dried out, and without Finn around to tend to them, they'd gone without. Like as not, he was somewhere taking up with that book woman he was sweet on. If he couldn't rouse that boy, he'd have to rustle up some other help. He needed the birds in good shape if they meant to win their fights. He pulled one or two shelters to fresh ground before he gave up and decided he would get to it tomorrow.

"That'll have to do you for now, chickadees," he slurred. Gripp rubbed a hand across his eyes. He must have had a bit more 'shine than he reckoned because his vision didn't normally wobble like that. He wouldn't puke; if a 'shiner couldn't hold his likker, he might as well hang it up as a crying shame. All the same, Gripp shuffled inside his shack and lowered himself to his pallet in the corner. He heaved a heavy sigh, took another bracing sip from his jar, and dug into his satchel. It was full of rolled-up bills, which he intended to stuff in an empty lard can and bury near the wall of stacked rocks he'd run across nearby, something he could come back for in case he needed to sail out quick. For now, though, he reckoned it wouldn't hurt to lie down for a spell, just until the ground stopped tipping.

Gripp pulled off his boots with a grunt and fell back onto the ticking. He'd have to get to work firing up the still come morning. He had to admit, he made some of the best moonshine east of the Mississippi. He'd lay his against any man in Kentucky, and maybe throw in Tennessee for good measure. "A fine, fine libation," he mumbled to himself.

While he waited for the room to stop spinning, Gripp remembered the woman he'd seen coming out of the WPA office in town. She would make a nice handful, he thought, if he could get the young'un out of the way. Gripp rubbed his eyes, trying to ease the blur. That boy, now, he brought to mind something, stirred up from his befuddled memory. The way he walked and swung those arms, the way he cocked his head almost called to mind—*oh, come now, what was that feller's name, blast it.*

He'd almost dozed off when the name hit him like a thunderclap. The boy danced in his mind like a puppet, blinking those dark eyes, just like Frankie used to do. That was it! Ol' Frankie Turnbull. Gripp laughed to himself, thinking of the good times the two of them had had before he'd been forced to end their partnership.

His eyes flew open when the thought struck him. What if that was Frankie's boy? By gum, the timeline would be about right. If the boy was around, maybe Frank's ol' girl had stuck around, too. Gripp grinned at the memory of her, and his hand crept mechanically to his crotch. He reckoned they could get reacquainted. His wheels spun. If she was one of them book women, it wouldn't be that hard to figure out her route and arrange a little meeting. His pulse quickened. Wouldn't that be a sweet opportunity? Just thinking of it made him thirsty.

Gripp took another long swig from the jar and smacked his lips. A quick nap to clear his head would be just the thing. He was snoring loud enough to shake the timbers in no time.

Chapter 24

Beady and Rai had made no bones about it. When they hit town, Amanda would stay with Miles and the others while they went on up the mountain. She'd had more than her share of Gripp Jessup, and they stood firm on leaving her out of the last bit of it. They'd left less than twenty minutes after Jack Wick had set off for his preaching arrangement. Odds were, when he showed up for the Gospel meeting, there'd be one or two wanting to get married or buried while he was at it. It always took longer than he figured on. Beady scrawled a note for him and left it on the kitchen table next to a slab of pie he'd be sure to notice. She'd gone down the mountain, it read, and he should collect her from the MacInteers' by suppertime the next day.

They had Junebug and Maxine ready to go in two shakes of a lamb's tail. Rai and Amanda were already seated astride the mule while Beady secured the door.

"I gotta run in the church a minute," she said, leading Maxine down the path and tying her up outside. She dashed into the dim-lit building and emerged carrying a solid box draped with one of her old flour-sack tablecloths. She stooped by the church steps and yanked up a handful of mint, which she stuffed beneath the cloth. She positioned Maxine near the church steps so that she could reach up behind the saddle and lash the box securely on top of the horse's broad rump.

"Mama?" Amanda said. The question hung in the air.

"Needed some supplies," she replied. "Never you mind. Best get on the way."

They made good time down the mountain, singing and chatting in the way of mountain women, sharing tales and tidbits about family and friends. Amanda and Beady filled in the gaps of the past years—Amanda telling about Mooney, the WPA job as a packhorse librarian, and the folks she'd met, Beady going on about the garden, the church, and folks Amanda might know who'd passed on or fallen ill.

"How about fellers, Amanda?" ventured Beady. "Anybody you might be sweet on?"

"There might be one," she allowed. "But it's tangled right now. We'll have to see."

"There ain't a knot in this world the good Lord can't pick apart." Rai smiled at Amanda as she spoke. "Just needs a bit of time. Now then, I been thinking 'bout Gripp. Sass says he's short two fingers."

"Way I figure," said Amanda, "that was Frank's last good act on earth before Gripp drowned him in the rising creek. I 'spect he went down fighting. The sheriff found Frank's gun near the shore."

"Finn said Gripp told him he lost them fingers in the mines at first, but then changed his story to allow a feller shot him in the hand," said Rai.

"You can't believe a word that leaves that feller's lips," spat Beady. "That list he kept? Names of folks he killed this way or that over the years? There's a well inside that boy that bubbles up nothing but blackness."

Amanda nodded. "You know, I remember Alice, one of the WPA girls, said she'd met a group of no-counts on her route. I declare, the way she described one in particular made me turn cold. I reckon I suspected even then it coulda been him come back to this area. I wish I'd have said something. Maybe Sass—"

Rai stopped her. "Only thing that might'a done is sink Finn in deeper. If he'd a' known who Gripp was to you, what he'd done, he might be tied up in more than bootlegging. I know my boy, and kingdom come couldn't stop him from keeping you from harm."

Amanda blushed to the roots of her hair.

Rai continued, "Finn and Sass told me where the shack's at, back of our place. Him being that close, it was prob'ly a matter of time before he set his sights on the girls. No way in the world Finn woulda led him there if he'd seen Gripp's true colors. It's no excuse, but Finn was keen to keep out of the mines after that cave-in. He wasn't thinking right."

"Nobody blames Finn," said Amanda. "Plenty of folks would've done the same."

"That shack's where Finn says Gripp keeps his birds and supplies. Sounded to me like he had Finn doing most of the actual work while he drank all day and came back in the evenings drunk, sleeping it off until midmorning."

Beady started humming the chorus of a hymn. "I've about had all the talk I can stomach of Gripp Jessup," she said. "I reckon we all know what he's made of by now."

They stopped only once, just to rest and eat. Amanda gave Beady a leg up on her tall mare before she mounted Junebug, and they set off again, eager to be on their way. The temperature climbed as they rode, the late-spring sky a piercing blue studded with high white clouds. Birds called to each other in the trees, and a pair of cawing crows followed them for miles, curious or hoping for a dropped morsel or something shiny to collect.

At Amanda's, Beady fussed over Miles and gave him two books she'd stashed in her satchel. She told him his grandpa would visit soon and promised to be back in a day or so, and they'd make a special cherry pie. Mooney had had a high time with her crowd of visitors and clapped her hands when she heard they'd be staying an extra day.

"Why can't we come with you now, Mama?" asked Hiccup.

"I've got something to do up on the mountain just now, but soon as I can, I'll send for you." She planted a kiss on top of Hiccup's head.

"We're catching crawdads in the creek later on," Miles told her, and Hiccup brightened.

"Will there be dragonflies?" she asked. "Butterflies, too?"

"Tons."

Hiccup nodded and skipped off to make a net with Cricket out of an old screen door and a stick he said he could carve for the purpose.

Rai lingered over Sass and tipped her chin up with a finger. "If Finn and your daddy get done with their business, they'll come through town in a day or so. I wager they'll stop for some goods at the store while they're here. Mooney'll leave word, and y'all can come on back with them. Plain Jane can pull the wagon back up."

"You really think Finn will come back?" asked Sass.

"I'm hoping and praying. The rest isn't up to us."

"What do you have to go do?" she asked.

"Miz Wick and I need to take care of something important," she said. "It's one of those loads mamas carry. Be sweet while we're gone."

Amanda put a hand on Sass's shoulder. "How about you go with me to the WPA office, Sass? I've got a lot to catch up on, and you could be a big help."

With that, Rai and Beady nudged Maxine onward. The mare was plenty docile but wasn't used to logging so many miles in a day. She pinned her ears back to show she expected extra corn at the end of this. Once more, they picked their way over trails, through creeks, and up and down narrow sloping hills to get to the MacInteers' home. This late in the day, clouds of gnats started to form and caused Maxine to toss her head and swish her tail in aggravation. Crickets and tree frogs had already begun their dusky trills when, finally, Beady pulled Maxine to a halt outside the MacInteer barn.

She pulled off her box of supplies, along with the saddle and the bag she'd brought with her. Maxine got a rubdown, an extra helping of corn, and a clear bucket of water before Beady jumped to help Rai finish up the chores that had been left undone for the two days she'd been away. Farms weren't meant to be left for long. The hens had already gone to roost by the time Rai scattered their feed and filled their water. They sat on eggs long overdue for collecting. They could hear the goats' bleating across the yard; they needed milking straightaway.

Once all the immediate chores had been done, they took a moment to wash and rest with some tea and warmed corn pone by the stove inside.

"All's I could think there and back was a ready pistol," said Rai. "It would be a fitting end to him, but an obvious one. Someone's gotta pull the trigger."

"I got a better idea," said Beady.

Rai waited. The cabin had grown warm with the stove going. She fanned herself with an old newspaper, the front page full of news about war fronts overseas. At least her boys weren't mixed up in that, she thought. One less thing.

"That box of supplies I brought from the church," said Beady, "happens to be full of timber rattlers."

Rai's jaw fell open. She recalled the service they'd attended and the snake wrapped around Jack's arm at the front as a display of his faith. "Beady Wick"—she smiled slowly—"that may just be the best idea for mountain justice I ever heard."

"I was hoping you couldn't smell 'em along the way or hear 'em moving around in there. I put some mint on top to cover the musk. I remembered when Gripp was attending years ago, he never could abide no snakes. Gave him the willies through and through. He could hardly stand being in the building with 'em. Guess he saw one or two folks get bit by and by, and you know that's never real pretty. Fortunately, we had remedies and could get to the mine doctor if it came to that, but way up here on the backside of the mountain in the dead of night, it's plumb impossible to find a doctor."

"How can we make sure?"

"Nothing sure but death and taxes, but way I see it, the Lord's on our side here. It's not like we're pulling a trigger. We're just enlisting the Lord's own creatures to do His work if He wants it so."

Rai nodded, following the logic.

"Most of the ones Jack keeps he don't feed regular to make 'em sleepy. These 'uns are newer, and he fed 'em 'fore he left, so they're apt to jump at anything. Plus, they ain't been used to handling. I threw in some lemon balm and valerian root 'fore we left to take the edge off 'em, but that's long gone."

"Finn told me where the still is so we'd be sure to avoid it. He also told me Spider—I mean, Gripp—was due back from a run today. I expect if we leave right now, we can make it back 'fore midnight."

Beady and Rai took with them a lantern; the box, which they held between them by its handles; and a pistol to have as a backup, both against Gripp and in case they ran across a bear or panther. They wasted no words, concentrating on where to plant their feet on the ground as they walked, neither keen to upset the box they carried, despite its hefty latch. When they got within a quarter mile of the site, Rai turned down the lantern and hung it from a belt she'd tied round her waist. They let their eyes adjust to the dark. A white waning moon hung low in the sky, casting a pale, thin light on the trees. Somewhere up to their left, an owl called, and they froze.

Rai motioned forward and they walked softly, straining their ears for any sound that didn't belong. They picked up the trickle of a nearby creek and knew they must be close. Rai spotted the tangle of grapevine that Finn had described, the reason they didn't venture much past this spot, but she also thought she knew how to go around it. A rustling to their right made them stop in their tracks, but Beady shook her head. It was only a mother possum creeping along the ground in search of food, three babies clinging with their pink feet to the wiry fur on its back.

The roosters would have long since gone to roost, but sometimes if they were disturbed, a rooster would crow at night, and Rai didn't want to chance sounding that alarm. Silhouettes of the rooster shelters appeared here and there through a clearing in the trees. Then, she spotted a patch of green. It was foxfire, the glowing substance well known to mountain dwellers, and it lit a path around the grapevine like a divine map. Beady and Rai followed the glowing foxfire until they spotted the shed. Again, they stood still, barely daring to breathe. Any moonshiner, let alone one such as this, might shoot first and ask questions later if they were surprised by strangers.

Beady touched her ear and pointed to the shed, nodding. She could hear him in there. Rai closed her eyes, and sure enough, she heard it, too: the long, loud snores of a man who was laid out on drink. The time was right. Finn hadn't said anything about dogs, but if he'd had one, any hound worth its salt would've barked by now. The pair crept forward, their skirts brushing their shins. Inch by inch, Beady eased the door open, and they both wrinkled their noses from the sour, unwashed smell of a place that hadn't known a scrubbing in its life. There, in the corner, lay the source of their ills, the man of different names who preyed on mothers' daughters. Moonlight shone weakly through the doorway, and in the dark, the white of his bare feet and outflung arms glowed.

Beady gestured to Rai to set the box down by the end of the pallet. She leaned down and, with a flick of her wrist, unfastened the iron latch, one that Jack Wick had no doubt fashioned in his forge. No need to open the lid. With the latch undone, the snakes would escape. They'd learned that lesson the hard way. Beady had told Rai that afternoon: the first time Jack had brought home rattlers and accidentally left the box unlatched, the lid was flipped and the box empty the next day. They were one long muscle, after all, and could push open surprisingly heavy lids by pressing against the top. More than one would be out in no time. To make sure, Beady riled them up a bit. She'd picked up a length of grapevine and thrust it into the holes on the side of the box, blindly poking at them until she heard the telltale rattles that meant they were coiled and ready. After so long in the cool darkness of the box and all that jostling, they would be drawn to the warmth and movement of a body.

Beady and Rai crept back out the door and waited just 'round the side of the shed. Sooner or later, he would wake to pee. Likker ran through a body faster than coffee.

It wasn't long before they heard the *thunk* of the wooden lid as it hit the floor. The snakes were free. Gripp had heard it, too. His snoring stopped, and there was a rustling of the straw ticking as he shifted on his pallet, smacking his lips in a groggy haze. Rai gripped Beady's hand as they crouched in the shadows beside the shack. He fumbled in the dark, thumping around and knocking over the jar that had been beside his bed. He cursed. Sooner than they'd expected, the first yelp. Had he stepped on one? Lain down on top of one that had curled up in the bed?

With a jerk of her head, Beady squeezed Rai's hand and whispered, "For Sass."

There was more fumbling. Rai and Beady detected the rattles, but then they were listening for them. Gripp was probably still not aware of what he faced in the dark shack, and the more he fumbled and shuffled around in the dark, the likelier he'd come too close to another. The metal clank of a lantern sounded, and another yelp, another curse.

Rai squeezed back. "For Amanda."

A faint yellow light now glowed from beneath the door of the shack. Something heavy toppled over, perhaps stumps he used as a table and chair? Gripp's yelps of pain turned guttural. He hollered in earnest now, with a fear and a dread that must have crept up from the pit of his pickled gut. There had been five snakes in the box. Rai thought surely the moment the lid had come off, all five had wasted no time escaping their prison. Another yelp and a holler. Gripp sobered up in record time. Rai counted at least three times he'd been bitten.

Rai, her eyes shut tight, whispered, "That 'un's for Finn."

"Wake up! Wake up!" Gripp yelled, his words still slurred.

Beady whispered in Rai's ear, almost, but not quite, laughing. "Fool thinks he's dreaming." Rai held tight to Beady's hand, trembling and sweating.

The mattress ticking rustled.

"He's prob'ly crawling up onto the bed to get his bare feet off the floor," whispered Beady.

Gripp began to moan, whether in fear or because of the poison that now flowed through his body, it was hard to tell. A fine ruckus ensued, with Gripp yelping a strangled cry. He must have met with fangs again—he likely put a hand on one in the bed. His lantern clattered as it fell to the floor and its light was doused, and there was a beat or two of stillness where Beady and Rai heard the buzzing rattles clearly. If he had only stayed still, he might've avoided the fangs, but likely his every nerve pulsed with fear and surprise. The shack fell quiet. They waited an eternity, listening, but heard only raspy breathing from inside.

It was enough. Beady and Rai lit their lantern and made their way back down the way they'd come, following the foxfire and moonlight, no longer caring if the roosters crowed. When they reached Rai's home, they washed their faces and hands and drank long, cool swallows of water from a bucket drawn from the well. They'd made it back before midnight, and they fell into bed, exhausted from the past two days. When the sun shining through the windows in the morning woke them, they lay in the same positions they'd been in when they'd fallen asleep, having slept deep and dreamless from moon till morning.

"We have to go back for the box," Beady said over coffee the next morning, and Rai nodded.

"I know," she said. "Eggs?" She stood at the stove and cracked four brown eggs straight into the cast-iron skillet.

"Thank you." Beady pushed her plate across the table and wrinkled her nose. "It'll smell like a snake den in there. No worse'n it was. And we'll need to wear good boots. Don't want to wind up bit ourselves."

"Cricket and Finn have some old ones by the door there. We can prob'ly fit 'em. Let's go after breakfast and chores, get it done," Rai agreed, flipping two fried eggs onto Beady's ready plate. Beady forked the runny yolks onto a hunk of cornbread and took a bite.

"Salt?" asked Rai.

"Nah, they're good as is."

~

Now, on their way up to the shack, the roosters tried to outdo one another with their crowing. They perched on top of their shelters and beat their wings with their necks outstretched. Some strutted back and forth as far as their tethers would reach, making throaty squawks and warning them away.

"Maybe we should release them all," Rai said. "They'll be up here with no one to tend to 'em."

"If we do, they'll just be at each other's throats. Sheriff and his boys'll be here soon enough if Finn talks to the right folks, and *they* can deal with a passel of fightin' roosters wantin' to come at 'em with spurs a'flyin'. Personally, I don't much fancy that."

The whole way up the slope, they'd kept their eyes peeled for snakes. Given the night they'd spent, every stick and length of thick vine had them sidestepping. Not a soul came out to greet them or warn them off with a shot. In the light of day, the liquor still sat in plain sight behind the grape-vine, its fires unlit. Rai knocked twice before she opened the door, just a visitor happening by, curious about the squatter on her land. She stood well back and let daylight fall across the floorboards. A foul, musky scent met them, mixing with the cool and earthy smell of wet leaves in the morning air. Straight off, she counted one, two, three vipers coiled in one corner away from the bed and tangled with each other. A rustle from the opposite side of the shack gave away a fourth taking refuge in the woodpile stacked there.

Beady stepped beside her and held a lantern aloft to better light the room. Rai pointed to the box on the floor where they'd left it. Anyone finding Gripp here would surely question its presence and might rec-ognize it for what it was. Beady took a couple of tentative steps into the shack. Her shadow fell over Gripp where he lay, and they couldn't help but stare. Whether because he'd been drunk or how many times he'd been bitten, he hadn't tried to leave the cabin for help. Both his feet were swollen to twice their size, the skin so tight his ankles had dis-appeared. His damaged hand, the one with three fingers, was streaked with red and swollen as well. But it was his face that held their gaze.

Rai came to stand beside her. "There's the last 'un," she whispered, pointing.

In the crook between Gripp's neck and shoulder, the brownish-gray body of the snake lay curled like a kitten snuggled for warmth. Its tongue darted in and out, testing the air currents that had changed since they'd entered. It had bitten Gripp twice—once in the neck and once in the face, apparently as he lay. If they didn't already know who he was, it wasn't certain they could have recognized him, as grotesque as he looked. As they stared, the slit of one eye cracked open. When it registered their presence, it opened wider, as wide as it could, though Gripp didn't move. His throat and lips were so swollen he couldn't speak. But Beady could.

"Listen to me, you sorry devil," she spat. "I reckon you done played your last ace. You remember me?" The slit narrowed. "Reckon you do. These snakes come from the church, so they know to do the Lord's work. They offer a test of faith, but it appears you put your faith in the wrong things."

"You shouldn't never have laid a hand on my daughter," added Rai. "And you almost cost the life of my boy. Reckon that score's done settled."

Beady lifted the lid back onto the box and latched it there. While she stooped down, Rai's eye caught sight of Gripp's satchel, lying where he'd dropped it when he'd come in. She picked that up, too, and showed Beady its contents.

"You prob'ly won't be needing that no more," Beady said. "And the law would just take it if they found it. It's the least you can do for the woman you left a widow."

They backed out the way they'd come in. When Gripp saw they intended to leave him there, the slit opened again. The snake nestled by his neck might strike again if he moved. Not that he could move. Likely, he could hardly draw breath. The women closed the shack door and sealed him in shadow once more. When Gripp's heart gave out, as it surely would soon enough, his body temperature would drop, and the viper next to him would go in search of a meal and a place to bask in the sun.

Chapter 25

The knot between Sass's shoulders, the one that had climbed up her neck and made her head ache on and off for the past months, finally unwound. She was so relieved to see Finn's face at Amanda's door that she almost cried, and might have, too, but for how surprised and happy she was when Amanda had leaped up and hugged on him right in front of God and everybody.

When Daddy and Finn had arrived at Amanda and Mooney's, worn-out and dusty from their long trek to the sheriff, the situation couldn't have turned out better if they'd scripted it themselves. Finn would not have jail time. Daddy had heard it from some men in town that the sheriff had raided the still site, tipped off, he knew, by Finn, who'd drawn a map of the location. The sheriff and his deputies approached with caution, of course, since renegade moonshiners fiercely protected their investment and craft. As it turned out, all the fight had gone out of the feller who went by Spider. One eager deputy burst into the shed and found him lying in a pitiful state, snake-bit all to pieces and long dead. One rattler crawled right out of one of the man's boots on the floor, which goes to show why you should always knock your boots out before sinking a foot in.

Although Finn had implied he might have had firsthand knowledge of the operation, the sheriff had allowed him to walk with a warning on account of his father vouching for him and being willing to give up the locations of the operation. The law was able to bust up the equipment handily and put an end to this particular bootlegging. The other information the two of them had presented—about Gripp being responsible for a cave-in at the mine and several past killings—had less evidence behind it, but things had a way of working themselves out, the sheriff said, and in this case, that had been true for certain by the looks of the way the feller had met his end.

"I never woulda believed it," Finn told Sass. "I can't recall ever seeing so many rattlers in one spot in all my days in the mountains. I spent many a night myself out in that very shed and never thought of it as especially snaky. Must'a been the knockers," he said, "roaming the woods like the Cherokee say. Maybe they wanted to settle up for what he done in the mines and lured 'em in there."

Amanda confirmed she'd come upon a right plenty this year. "They must be thicker'n we knew. Best to keep a sharp eye out near the woodpiles."

As for the orphaned roosters, one of the women from the WPA office in town suggested they distribute the carcasses to deserving families on the routes ridden by the packhorse librarians, many of whom had been hard-pressed to feed their children since the stock-market crash. That way, they wouldn't go to waste, and folks in the region might benefit to boot. The sheriff allowed that was a fine idea, mostly since it saved him from figuring how to haul a whole flock of fighting birds back to the county seat.

They all piled on the wagon back up to the MacInteer place, where Mama and Beady Wick had prepared a full meal. There, Amanda introduced Finn to her folks, forgetting he'd already met them, and the look in Amanda's eyes and the way Finn stood near her in such a close and familiar way set Sass grinning from ear to ear. Amanda promised to visit soon, on her next library circuit. Daddy and Jack Wick shook hands, for it turned out Jack had already spoken to Daddy about wanting an apprentice or two for blacksmithing. It took a toll on a body, all that bending and lifting, he'd said, and he couldn't keep at it like he once had. They agreed Finn and Cricket would be quick hands at forging and were keen to learn a trade that would keep them aboveground.

Knowing Finn wouldn't have to spend time in jail, locked away from the trees and fresh air, was a miracle. More miracle still was what had happened to the hateful rooster man. Jail would've been too good for him, had the law been able to tie him down for all he'd done. The way Sass saw it, justice had come with a swift and clever hand. It wasn't for her to question, so she let it be.

Up on the other side of the mountain some days later, in the little white church in Pickins, preacher Jack Wick told his wife he was flummoxed that he'd neglected to latch his serpent box and had lost all five of the newly caught vipers. Beady hummed to herself as she hoed the garden rows and watched as Jack turned the box over to empty it of the dry grass and few leaves inside. She paused her work on the melon patch when she saw Jack pick something from the bottom of the box. It was a clump of hair snagged under a splinter in the wood. She held her breath as he examined it, turning it this way and that in the sunlight before he stashed it in his pocket.

Since they'd been spending time with their grandson, Beady couldn't remember ever being so happy. On their way to and from visiting Amanda and Miles, she and Jack had had a chance to talk.

"Isn't this a sweet time?" she'd asked. "Watching our girl be such a good mama?"

"I'm just ashamed we missed so much of it because of my stubbornness," said Jack.

"My hands ain't clean, neither," said Beady. "If my faith and heart had been stronger, if I'd refused to let resentment build walls . . ."

"We've each clutched our grudges with both hands," said Jack. "I'm sorry as can be about that. With my hands full of that mess, I had no room to hold the gifts that were waiting for us."

"We're both imperfect and impulsive, Jack," said Beady. "Reckon that's being human. I forgave you a long time ago."

He'd kissed her soundly on the cheek. "I declare it's good to have things restored. I've missed the affection of my good wife."

These past years, their faith had surely been tested. Jack stacked the wooden boxes that had rested in the front of the church and carried them out to the barn. He'd confessed to Beady that he'd felt a distinct calling to lay aside this particular element of faith testing. Beady set her hoe against the gate and followed Jack on his way to the barn. There, he leaned over Maxine's stall and gave her a pat. The mare's winter coat had almost shed all the way out. Beady watched from behind the doorway as Jack picked up the curry comb and knocked it against a post. Clumps of strawberry-roan horsehair fell out onto the ground in a cloud of dust. Jack bent over and picked up a clump, then dug in his pocket. He held the bit of hair that he'd found snagged in the wood of the viper box between his thumb and forefinger and compared the two. Beady knew he hadn't ridden Maxine when he'd picked up the reptile box from the feller who'd caught them.

She stepped out from behind the barn doorway, the afternoon sunlight streaming in around her as specks of dust floated and sparkled in the sunbeam. Jack drew in a breath. "You look a vision with your hair come loose round your shoulders and lit from behind like that."

"Supper'll be ready soon." She smoothed her apron. "Maybe we can make a picnic out of it since the day's so nice? Jack? Why're you staring at me so?"

Jack smiled at her and closed the space between them. "Picnic sounds fine." He put his arm around her waist and led her out into the sunshine, pulling her close. "I'll draw some water from the well and carry a quilt to sit on."

As they walked to the house, she looked up into his eyes with a contented smile, and he loosened his fingers, letting the strawberry-roan horsehair fly on the breeze like dandelion seed.

Chapter 26

Late one June afternoon, when the day had not finished wringing its last pleasures from the sun, Daddy came in from helping a neighbor get up a small field of hay and announced it was time to visit the lightning bugs that evening. Sass looked up from her book, and a smile spread across her face. She'd nearly forgotten. She'd been little the last time they'd gone, and Hiccup had never seen them.

"I'll get the wagon ready," Cricket yelled as he dashed out the door.

"Mama, I'll fetch the ham from the smokehouse. We can take sandwiches on the way," Fern offered.

Hiccup came inside, flushed and sweaty. She'd been catching june bugs all afternoon and flying them in circles with a string tied around their bodies. "Where's Cricket goin'?" she asked. "He wouldn't say. Said it was a surprise."

"Just wait and see," Sass breathed. "It's magic!"

Sass was disappointed Finn wouldn't be with them. He'd been called out with Jack Wick on a blacksmith job down at the mine. Finn's way with horses and him being familiar with all the mine ponies and mules made the foreman hire them on as the regular farriers. Cricket had been learning smithwork, too, but he preferred the forging part. So far, he'd made an ash shovel and poker for the fireplace and an iron meat fork with a long, twisted handle so fine that he'd already had requests for others. All his skills at carving and whittling gave him ideas for how to fashion things that Jack, in all his years of practicality, had never thought of.

They rushed to pile into the wagon and headed down the path, laughing and talking. Hiccup tried to guess what sort of magic they would see.

"Is it faeries?" she asked. "Mushroom circles? A rainbow? Foxfire?"

"Nope, nope, and nope," Cricket teased. "You'll just have to wait and see."

After a good trek deeper into the woods, the light dimmed as the trees closed in around them. A deer in velvet crashed up the slope beside them, and startled crows cawed in protest. Soon, they could hear other families like theirs and see the twinkling of their lanterns through the trees on several sides. Daddy pulled up the horse and jumped down to tie her to a tree while everyone piled out. They'd have to walk a ways from here deeper into the thicket.

"A singing?" Hiccup asked, skipping along to keep up. "Music?" Fern took her by the hand and pulled her along with a mysterious smile.

Finally, they emerged into a natural clearing ringed by ledges of limestone rock, maybe an ancient sinkhole or a site the Cherokee used for meetings. Folks set up their blankets and lanterns all around and in the middle on the grass, wherever they found room. The MacInteers found a spot big enough for all of them, and Rai passed around their picnic supper. Talk was friendly as always when folks who usually lived far apart got to visit. The only way they knew to come was by reading the moon or word of mouth.

"Psst, room to squeeze in?"

Sass whirled around on the blanket to see Finn grinning at her. He must have taken off smithing early to get to come. And a double surprise:

"Amanda!" Sass squealed. "And Miles!" She patted the quilt next to her, and Miles squeezed in between her and Hiccup.

"Do *you* know what's happening?" Hiccup asked him, but he just shrugged and shook his head. Clueless.

Mooney came soon after. They heard her twinkling laugh in the dusky woods before she appeared with Maisie in tow. A tall, ropy feller with a bushy mustache followed behind her, carrying their supper in a basket draped with a scrap of flour sack. Fern elbowed Sass, and her mouth twisted into a smile. "Looks like Mooney's sparking," Fern whispered. "She's got her work cut out for her, trying to fatten that feller up."

"Mind if we join?" Mooney asked. "Y'all, this here's Dale McNeal." They spread out a blanket and arranged their basket as Maisie scampered and ran with her friends.

"McNeal? You kin to the McNeals over in Far Gap?" asked Daddy, and for the next half hour, Daddy and Dale chased the McNeal rabbit near and far, until they'd nailed down who was who, which uncle or cousin lived where, and what each of them did for a living. Satisfied all the connections had been made, Daddy took a long swig of well water and leaned back on his elbows.

Finn and Amanda settled on their quilt, his back against a sweet gum tree and Amanda leaning in beside him. On the way to the spot, she'd spoken to several families she had become friends with on her packhorse route. They never failed to be excited to see her and ask her for things to bring next time. They called her their visiting angel, their ray of sunshine. She was right where she wanted to be. So many times she remembered yearning for something else, something important or glamorous. She'd been certain whatever that was lay beyond these mountains. She watched her son giggle as he played with Sass and Hiccup. Was anything more important than that laugh? Finn's chest rose and fell as she leaned on him, and with one hand, he absently stroked her arm just to feel her nearness. He smelled of woodsmoke and lye soap, and his warm breath tickled her ear. She yearned for nothing else; everything she could possibly want was here, on a worn quilt on a summer's night.

A hush fell over the folks in the crowd, and one by one, their lanterns winked out so that they all sat in the dark woods, the moon the only source of light but for some patches of foxfire glowing on the surrounding slopes. They sat quietly as their eyes adjusted. Finn reached over and took Amanda's hand. Somewhere, a baby cried and a toddler snuggled closer to his mama's skirts. A murmur rippled through them as it began. First, a single lightning bug blinked its yellow-green signal.

"There." Someone pointed at the beacon.

"There's one."

"Another." Here and there, others appeared, almost tentative. On–off, on–off. Like shy raindrops as a storm blows in, the fireflies gathered in speed and numbers as they swept into the clearing and joined in. With each spark of light, a chorus of delight rang out, followed by a shushing when folks grew too loud.

All at once, cued by some invisible signal, the woods burst with the yellow-green glow of the fireflies. They twinkled and blinked their silent calls to each other—*here I am, here I am*. Hiccup held on to Miles's arm and gasped. "Oh!"

"Wait, Hiccup, wait," Sass whispered. In the light of the fireflies, Hiccup's and Miles's upturned faces glowed with wonder.

Something shifted in the air, and the fireflies cascaded as one, dipping and turning through the trees in swoops and swirls, this way and that. It reminded Amanda of a school of minnows or the massive flocks of starlings that migrated in the fall, but with a *halo*. Not only did they move as one, but they *signaled* as one, so the woods fell dark as a cave one minute—*lost*—and lit up like daylight in the split second they all glowed—*here I am*. They danced and circled, their mesmerizing lights holding their audience spellbound.

"Magic." Hiccup nudged Sass and nodded, her eyes round as saucers.

Finn leaned over in the dark to kiss Amanda's cheek, and his lips came away wet with her tears. "It's beautiful," she whispered. "Like a secret . . ."

"Miracle?" he offered. "I told you there were some of those still around." Finn opened Amanda's hand and placed something small and round in her palm. It was too dark to see, so she held it up to her eyes, and when the next firefly signal lit up the clearing, she gasped.

"I made it in your daddy's forge," he said. "Ain't no diamond in it, but I figured maybe God give us enough sparkle tonight."

Amanda turned her face up to his. For once, the book woman was at a loss for words.

Her eyes spilled over as she kissed him on his warm mouth, the light of the fireflies mimicking the rhythm of their heartbeats.

Epilogue

In the years that followed, Amanda continued to ride her packhorse librarian circuit, faithfully making stops on her route until the program finally ended in 1943. Outside her official job, she visited with the families she'd encountered in the rugged and isolated hills whenever she could. It was harder with a couple of young'uns underfoot, but Miles was sweet to mind his siblings when she had need. Jack and Beady were just a stone's throw away, close enough for Miles to ride his donkey for a visit. When he could, Finn took Miles along to the forge for the day, where he dreamed up things for Cricket to fashion and delighted his grandparents with his smarts. Finn was the father Miles never had, as steady and grounded as they come, the opposite of Frank Rye in almost every way.

Sass made it through the eighth grade, the highest she could go in Vessel's mountain school. After that, Rai and Beady saw to it that she applied to and attended the school and college in Berea. She couldn't imagine where they'd found the money for such an extravagance. All they said was that the Lord had provided. And He might provide for Miles and Hiccup, too, if they studied as hard as she had. Fern had set her sights on a fellow from the next hollow, and sure enough, the two of them declared their intentions to marry and make a homeplace.

In Berea, Sass saw her first real library, one so big it couldn't be toted on the back of a mule, with so many volumes of books she thought she might faint from the wonder of it. She learned of other mountains, mightier and taller than hers and much farther away, but none that called to her like the string of Appalachian hills she knew so well. After a time, she became a teacher and set out to teach her students the power of words. One day, she thought, she might write her own story and tell about the people and the mountains that had formed her.

News of Pearl Harbor lit a fire under Cricket, and he enlisted before Harley—and certainly Rai—could have a say-so. He traveled farther from the mountains than any of them had ever gone, shipping out to places with names they couldn't pronounce, let alone find on a map. He trained as a pilot, the fascination that had begun with the Hindenburg zeppelin blossoming into a lifelong vocation. Before every mission he flew, Cricket hung from his instrument panel a small hound dog he'd carved from a hunk of coal so that if his plane went down, he might, in his last moments, remember the blue-green hilltops of eastern Kentucky and the mountains he would always call home.

AUTHOR'S NOTE

Anyone familiar with the region knows that Appalachia is a paradox of past and present, areas of stunning beauty and a rich and storied people surrounded by crushing poverty and the scars of strip mining. Roadside signs proclaiming "Jesus Saves" rise a stone's throw from the crowded opioid clinic where, it seems, too many modern-day residents have planted their mustard seed of faith. Yet, it's still possible to witness creek baptisms, foot washings, and here and there, congregations brave enough to handle the region's indigenous vipers. Folks still hold fiercely tight to family and land, and defending the honor of such is as much of a reflex as breathing the mountain air.

Talk to the old-timers, who still gather on porches and at Sunday picnics after church or at the cemetery, and they'll spin hilarious, winding yarns about any given subject. They swear by the signs of the moon and dowsing for water and, though they listen patiently to more scientific explanations, will continue doing it the way they've seen it work with their own eyes. Listen to them pick and sing, their rhythms spot-on and their hands leathered and scarred from years of hard labor, and something about it is transportive—the melodies, lyrics, and voices a mix of shared experience and kinship with this land and its people, their struggles and simple pleasures.

And the food! If someone asks you to pull up a chair 'cause Granny's nigh 'bout got supper on the table, I suggest you do so, and tuck that napkin 'round your neck. Appalachian victuals are drawn straight from the ground, hoed and tended all summer and put up in glass jars that reflect their bounty on windowsills dappled with sunlight. Historically, meals could be plentiful or lean, depending on the season and the Good Lord's providence. Old-time Appalachians were well acquainted with gratitude and were strangers to laziness. They ate what they grew; made furniture, tools, and fences by the skill of their hands; and worked hard, above and below ground.

The southern Appalachian region was hardest hit during the Depression, when coal mines closed and left many not only jobless but homeless, as the mining towns often supplied room and board (such as it was). As part of FDR's initiatives for the nation's recovery, along with Eleanor Roosevelt's encouragement, the Works Progress Administration (WPA) Packhorse Library Project was launched to help ease the region's isolation and poverty through literacy. Compared with other parts of the United States, Appalachia was much more remote and increasingly detached from literacy and access to reading material in schools, libraries, and certainly individual homes. The Packhorse Library Project operated from 1936 to 1943, employing mostly women to ride routes through the least accessible areas of the region. Resourceful and hardy, these women brought light to the hills, by way of words, reading, and news of a world outside of the region. The companionship and friendships formed along their routes must have been extraordinary.

ACKNOWLEDGMENTS

It feels like I've held my breath for an untold number of years and, with the release of *Light to the Hills* and Sass and Amanda's story, can finally exhale. I'm grateful—ironically—beyond words.

Thank you to Cate Hart at Harvey Klinger, my intrepid agent who loved this mountain story from the get-go and was determined to find it a home. She resonated perfectly with the place of the novel and its unique inhabitants. Her patient exchanges with me shaped the book into something wholly right, its best version. Gratitude, also, to Alicia Clancy, Tegan Tigani, and the extensive cast at Lake Union, who, much like in *The Velveteen Rabbit*, made Amanda Rye and Finn MacInteer finally become real. #TeamGoBigOrange.

When I first saw a tweet about the packhorse librarians several years ago, I was drawn to the subject. Horses! Books! The South! Three of my favorite things woven into one. Delving into the research that went into this story did not disappoint.

I am indebted to the folks at the Museum of Appalachia in Norris, Tennessee, for the outstanding displays and history reflected there, in particular on musical instruments and herbal remedies. I spent a night in a charming old schoolhouse inn in Benham, Kentucky, where the Kentucky Coal Mining Museum is located. The museum's extensive display of photos, gear, and memorabilia is a heartbreaking testament to the hardworking miners who spent their lives underground. There's a makeshift "cave" in the museum, meant to give visitors a small taste of what it might be like to stoop and crawl through tunnels in the darkness. That experience flavored Finn's tales of his days in the mine.

Jason M. Vance, at Middle Tennessee State University, provided a wealth of helpful information and samples from his research into the packhorse librarians. The scrapbook photos he shared spawned the idea for the community scrapbook Amanda passed among the mountain families.

Finally, undying friendship and love to those who read early drafts and cheered on Amanda, Sass, and their families and to those whose encouragement bolstered this journey—you know who you are, but for posterity: Jan, Karen, Tracy, Kristin, Sara, Renee, and Dawn, and chief of all champions, Bob, Savannah, and Ben.

RESOURCES

Alvey, R. Gerald. *Kentucky Folklore*. Lexington: University Press of Kentucky, 1989.

Appelt, Kathi, and Jeanne Cannella Schmitzer. *Down Cut Shin Creek: The Pack Horse Librarians of Kentucky*. New York: HarperCollins, 2001.

Boyd, Donald C. "The Book Women of Kentucky: The WPA Pack Horse Library Project, 1936–1943." *Libraries & the Cultural Record* 42, no. 2 (2007): 111–128.

Golway, Terry. *Together We Cannot Fail: FDR and the American Presidency in Years of Crisis*. Naperville, IL: Sourcebooks, 2009.

Henson, Heather. *That Book Woman*. New York: Atheneum Books, 2008.

Kentucky Coal Mining Museum, 231 Main Street, Benham, Kentucky 40807.

Kitchen Sisters. "The Pack Horse Librarians of Eastern Kentucky: The Director's Cut." Podcast. http://www.kitchensisters.org/2018/09/24/the-pack-horse-librarians-of-eastern-kentucky-the-directors-cut/.

Mulvey, Deb, ed. *"We Had Everything but Money": Priceless Memories of the Great Depression*. Greendale, WI: Reiman Publications.

Museum of Appalachia, 2819 Andersonville Highway, Clinton, TN 37716.

Price, Sadie F. "Kentucky Folklore." *Journal of American Folklore* 14, no. 52 (1901): 30–38.

Roberts, Leonard W. *Up Cutshin and Down Greasy: Folkways of a Kentucky Mountain Family*. Lexington: University Press of Kentucky, 1988.

Vance, Jason. "Librarians as Authors, Editors, and Self-Publishers: The Information Culture of the Kentucky Pack Horse Library Scrapbooks (1936–1943)." *Library and Information History* 28, no. 4 (2012): 289–308.

Vance, Jason. "A Taste of History: Recipes from Pack Horse Librarian Scrapbooks." *Kentucky Libraries* 73, no. 4 (2009): 4–7.

Vance, Jason. "KY Packhorse Scrapbooks." Online photo album from the FDR Presidential Library. https://www.flickr.com/photos/jasonvance/sets/72157683436797831/.

Veneble, Sam. *Mountain Hands: A Portrait of Southern Appalachia*. Knoxville: University of Tennessee Press, 2000.

Wigginton, Eliot, ed. *The Foxfire Book*. New York: Doubleday & Company, 1972.

BOOK GROUP QUESTIONS

1. Ultimately, whose story is *Light to the Hills*? Who is the main character, or are there many?

2. Images of light and darkness (good and evil) are prominent throughout the book, from the darkening stormy woods at the beginning to the fireflies near the end. Were some more effective than others? What sorts of light and darkness in the human heart are portrayed? What "light" is evident in the hills by the story's end?

3. Appalachia is full of strong women. Compare the mother-daughter relationship between Rai and Sass MacInteer and Beady Wick and Amanda Rye.

4. Family is everything in the hills of Kentucky. What does family mean to the MacInteers? Who stands out in the cast of MacInteer siblings?

5. In the first chapter, we already see there are dangers in the hills—storms, strangers, snakes. What other dangers appear? How do the characters face them, or how do they not?

6. Gripp Jessup is the only male point of view we see first-hand. Do we need to hear from him? Does his story matter?

7. There are lots of animals populating the story. What is their role in the lives of the families we meet?

8. Names and nicknames are important in the Appalachian hills. How does the importance of "who you are" come up? *Cricket*, *Hiccup*, *Spider*, and *Sass* are all nicknames. What can we learn about the characters from their monikers?

9. Are there other "characters" in the story that aren't flesh-and-blood people? Poverty? Religion? Words? Appalachia itself? How do these "characters" interact with the main cast?

10. Did you think what Beady and Rai did was believable? Did they cross a line?

11. Although *Light to the Hills* is primarily a story about strong female characters, the men have pivotal roles to play as well. How would you characterize Harley MacInteer, Jack Wick, Frank Rye, and Finn MacInteer? What are their strengths and weaknesses?

12. Appalachia is often stereotyped. Before reading the story, did you have any notions about the region? Did those change? Did you learn anything surprising?

ABOUT THE AUTHOR

Photo © 2019 Dawn Harrison

After changing locations frequently in a military family, Bonnie Blaylock finally put down roots in Tennessee, where she co-owned a veterinary practice with her husband for twenty years. They live on a small-acre farm where they raise chickens, donkeys, and bees, and they achieved a family goal to travel to all fifty states before their children graduated. Bonnie writes about the South, family, growth, and more on her personal blog and is a contributing writer for various online publications. A graduate of the University of Tennessee, she lives near Nashville. Learn more at www.bonnieblaylock.com.